W9-AJP-068

GRISELDA TAKES FLIGHT

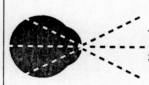

This Large Print Book carries the
Seal of Approval of N.A.V.H.

GRISELDA TAKES FLIGHT

A NOVEL OF BRIGHT'S POND

JOYCE MAGNIN

THORNDIKE PRESS
A part of Gale, Cengage Learning

GALE
CENGAGE Learning™

Detroit • New York • San Francisco • New Haven, Conn • Waterville, Maine • London

GALE
CENGAGE Learning

Thorndike Press, a part of Gale, Cengage Learning.

LIBRARY OF CONGRESS CATALOGING-IN-PUBLICATION DATA

Moccero, Joyce Magnin.
  Griselda takes flight : a novel of Bright's Pond / by Joyce Magnin.
    p. cm. — (Thorndike Press large print Christian fiction)
  ISBN-13: 978-1-4104-3852-2 (hardcover)
  ISBN-10: 1-4104-3852-X (hardcover)
  1. Sisters—Fiction. 2. City and town life—Fiction. 3. Large type books. I. Title.
  PS3601.L447G75 2011b
  813'.6—dc22   2011020841

Published in 2011 by arrangement with Abingdon Press.

Printed in Mexico
1 2 3 4 5 6 7 15 14 13 12 11

For Nancy Rue
Who brought wings to my words

ACKNOWLEDGMENTS

It's hard to believe that this is the third Bright's Pond book. Writing is a solitary venture, but it's never done alone. I want to once again thank my dear friend Pammy for reading every single word — the good and the bad. The CRUE for praying and supporting me from the very beginning, the women of my Wednesday morning Bible study for prayer and support. My friends Terri Gillespie, Priscilla Strapp, Jon and Reni Clemmer, and Kay Schaul who cheered me on to the finish line. Along the way I needed technical assistance and would like to thank Peter Yesner and David Horvath for teaching me about flying small airplanes, Dr. Nancy Rist for teaching me about comas and, of course, my editor, Barbara Scott, who teaches me to be a better writer.

And I would like to say thank you to my family.

1

"Time does have a way of making hurts
smaller. It's the distance. It's like being in
the airplane and looking down at Bright's
Pond with all that space between me and
the town. Everything looks so small, even
my troubles. From up there I had a sense
that any problem could be solved.
It's about perspective, I think."
— Griselda Sparrow

If you've seen one pumpkin, you've seen
them all. Unless the pumpkin is named
Bertha Ann. The gourd offspring of Nate
and Stella Kincaid created quite a stir in
Bright's Pond a few months back. Well, it
wasn't all Bertha Ann's fault. As it turned
out, Stella had some explaining to do. And
Nate? Let's just say Nate had his own battle
brewing to save Bertha Ann and not only
control the mildew, a feared and dreaded
malady to gourd growers everywhere, but

9

his temper as well.

Nate and Stella Kincaid had been growing prize-winning pumpkins for going on ten years, ever since my sister Agnes Sparrow prayed, and Nate's pumpkin took first place in the 1967 Tri-County Pumpkin Festival in Shoops Borough with a whopper of a squash weighing an astounding one hundred and fifty-seven pounds.

That was back in the days when Agnes, who weighed just over seven hundred pounds, settled her massive girth onto our red velvet sofa and dedicated herself to a life of prayer. It had become nearly impossible for Agnes to venture outside any longer.

I will confess that when Agnes prayed, things happened: several healings that we know of, a few incidents of lost objects being located miles from where they were last seen, and several other more minor miracles such as car engines starting when there was no earthly reason.

Agnes lives over at the Greenbrier Nursing Home now, where she continues to pray, but no one has reported an actual bona fide miracle in at least eight months.

Some folks claim it's because the nursing home doctors put her on a strict diet to make her lose weight and this has somehow

10

weakened her powers. Agnes told me she's decided to welcome the diet and follow her doctors' orders, but I still find Baby Ruth wrappers and crusts from lemon squares in her trashcan.

Folks can't help but feed her. I keep my eye out for ill-gotten food booty and confiscate what I can. Just a few days ago I found an entire rotisserie chicken in her closet.

But even I've let Agnes eat some sweets and brought her a meatloaf special from The Full Moon Café a couple of times. For those of you who don't know, that's a big hunk of meatloaf with a side of mashed potatoes swimming in a pint of brown gravy with a small dish of green peas alongside for color. It's not about the veggies. It's about the gravy.

"Does my heart good, Griselda," Agnes had said as she poured extra gravy on her potatoes. "A body can only eat so much lettuce without worrying she's going to sprout a cottontail and long rabbit ears."

I remember I smiled that day because it made me see that it's the occasional sweet or savory indulgence that puts the curlicue on an otherwise plain existence.

Harvest Dance time — the town's annual celebration of cooler days and good friends

— waited for us just around the corner of next month. I sat in a booth at The Full Moon along with the rest of the dance committee as we wracked our brains for this year's theme. That's when Stella rushed inside. She looked like she had seen a ghost. In a way she had.

Stella interrupted Ruth Knickerbocker as Ruth tried to convince Mildred Blessing that Bright's Pond was not ready for a murder mystery theme. Yes, I was on the committee *that* year. Studebaker Kowalski talked me into serving after Ruth begged him to snooker me into service. I hated committee work. I much preferred my life as a loner. But with Agnes safely tucked in at the nursing home I thought it might be kind of nice to stretch my social skills. Working on the Harvest Dance seemed a safe goal to reach.

"Griselda," Stella said. "I need to speak with Agnes."

All the ears in the diner perked up.

I grabbed Stella's hand that shook so much you'd think she was conducting the "Stars and Stripes Forever." "What's going on? Come on now, sit down here and tell us. You look terrible."

Stella squeezed into the booth next to Stu and Hazel. "I — I just can't come right out

12

and say it in front of all these people. It's a personal matter, and Agnes is the only one who can help me sort it all out."

Zeb stopped by our booth with a pot of coffee. He refilled our cups and asked Stella if she'd like a drop. Zeb owned The Full Moon Café and prided himself on excellent customer service and good food.

"No, thanks. My stomach's churning something fierce."

"Something wrong with Bertha Ann?" Zeb asked.

Stu tried to contain a chuckle but was unsuccessful.

"No, she's coming along nicely," Stella said. "Nate managed to get the mildew under control, and we built a tent for her. Poor Nate. He's been camped out with her day and night, spraying for bugs, wiping her down with milk, and checking her vine positions. He says she'll grow to be more than five-hundred pounds."

"That amazes me right down to my knee-caps," Ruth said. "I hope Bertha Ann takes first place. Imagine that — a five-hundred-pound pumpkin. Why, Bertha Ann will weigh nearly as much as Agnes. We sure can grow 'em big in Bright's —"

She plopped her hand over her mouth like she had uttered the worst insult in the

13

world. I touched her hand to let her know that I didn't take offense. Everybody knew my sister was big. At last weigh-in she was a quarter pound over 625, having lost thirty pounds since checking into the nursing home.

I sipped my coffee, and Zeb set a Full Moon pie — a luscious lemon meringue in an aluminum pie tin — on the table. "You all might as well split this," he said. "I plan on making quite a few for the dance. Think I'll add some orange food coloring to the meringue this year."

"Ooooo," Ruth said, "that'll give your pies a harvesty look."

Zeb smiled even though I could tell he was upset that his punch line had been hijacked. He would have said he was making Harvest Moon Pies.

I smiled and let my fingertips brush his arm. "That's a good idea, Zeb. Full Moon Harvest Pie sounds like a great idea."

He smiled back at me, and for a moment my heart sped and I felt my toes curl in my white Keds. Zebulon Sewickey was a handsome man, even if he was wearing a greasy white apron and paper hat.

"Anyhoo," Stella said, "I just have to talk to Agnes. Do you think it would be all right if I went over there this afternoon some-time?"

I sipped coffee and then let a breath escape through my nose. "I — I suppose so. Nate can drive you over around two o'clock — after lunchtime."

Stella leaned into me and whispered. "I can't do that. Nate doesn't know anything about my predicament, and I'm afraid to tell him what with all his stress over Bertha Ann and the contest and the rain and all."

I patted her hand. "Okay, okay, don't fret. I'll drive you over myself. I planned on going later anyway."

"Thanks, Griselda." She gave me a kiss on the cheek, hugged me, and then scampered out the door like a mouse. Stella was a little thing, only about five feet tall, with long brown hair she always kept in a ponytail that hung straight down her back. She had a preference for blue jeans and flannel shirts — usually green and red and gray.

Stella never learned to drive. She said it was too hard — too many things to be aware of all at the same time — so she often relied on me or her husband and sometimes Studebaker to get her where she needed to go. But Stella never seemed to want or need to go anywhere. She could walk to the Piggly Wiggly and to see Doc Flaherty, who

15

treated her for a rash that erupted on the same day Nate switched to a new herbicide. Marlabeth Pilky at the Paradise Trailer Park had specially mixed it for him. She was known in these parts as an herbalist — a folk-healer — and Nate relied on her expertise for various pumpkin afflictions.

The committee table grew quiet for a few moments after Stella left. I figured everyone was debating whether to comment on Stella's interruption. But leave it to Ruth to get the ball rolling.

"What do you suppose that was all about? My goodness but she seemed all in a swivet. You don't suppose she's got the cancer now. Lot of that going around these days what with my Hubby Bubby and all."

Ruth's husband died from a malignant brain tumor nearly six years ago, but the event still resonated like a raw, freshly pumiced callous in her thoughts.

"Nah." Stu waved away Ruth's theory. "She doesn't look sick, and believe me I know."

He sipped coffee and pulled a piece of crust from the pie. Studebaker had been one of the first cancer healings in Bright's Pond. The doctors wrote him off as pretty much a goner until Agnes prayed for him. He said he felt as though a million fire ants

16

were crawling all over his body. Claims he tingled for three days. It still gives me the willies when they give Agnes the credit. But that morning, Studebaker stopped short of singing Agnes's praises, and I was proud of him. After all, as Agnes always says, any miracles come express from God.

I sliced a piece of pie and licked lemon off my finger. "I can't imagine what the trouble is. Stella is usually so quiet, you know. Just sticks to her pumpkins and such."

"And for her not to tell Nate," Ruth said, "it must be something mighty troublesome."

"I suppose we'll find out sooner or later," Studebaker said. "Right now we have bigger fish to fry. We need to decide on a theme for the dance or it's going to be nothing short of a sock hop."

That was when Mildred, who had been silent through the whole Stella visit, finally added her two cents. Mildred Blessing was our Chief of Police and an odd combination of feminine brawn and schoolgirl curiosity.

"I can tell," she said. "I can always tell."

"Tell what?" Boris Lender asked. Boris was the Bright's Pond First Selectmen — kind of like a mayor, but a clause in the town charter prohibited the election of a mayor per se. And to tell the truth, the First Selectman had just the right amount of power — kind of like salt in a stew — with just enough to make all the components work together.

"That there is criminal activity afoot," Mildred said. "Stella Kincaid is acting suspicious. Her body language and facial expressions have all the earmarks of someone hiding a crime."

Ruth laughed and said, "You're crazier than a bedbug. Stella is not a criminal, Mildred, so just stuff that talk in your sack. My goodness. I can't imagine Stella Kincaid ever engaging in anything illegal or criminal, and you should be ashamed for even thinking such a thing."

I tapped Ruth's foot under the table. "Let's get back to committee business please, and let Stella worry about her own problems."

"Fine," Mildred said, "but mark my words. Something foul is afoot in Bright's Pond."

2

The committee meeting broke up about forty minutes later. We never did settle on a theme. Mildred had to go on duty, I needed to get to the library where I worked, and Stu had business up at the Paradise Trailer Park where his cousins Asa and Ed lived. Ruth just looked tired and perhaps a bit downcast because Mildred poo-poohed her suggestion to have an "Under the Sea" theme.

I'll admit that I sided with Mildred and inadvertently added to Ruth's dismay after laughing at the thought of mermaids in Bright's Pond. We gave her what was left of the Full Moon pie as consolation. The committee planned to meet at the library the next day, then we went our separate ways.

Before I left the café, though, I made sure to spend a minute with Zeb. He and I were an item — had been since high school. We had our share of break-ups over the years, but that summer we had found our way back together. I think it had a lot to do with Agnes moving to Greenbrier. Before then it seemed I never had time for him; Agnes had a way of coming between us.

"I like your harvest pie idea," I said.

He came out from the kitchen and leaned across the counter — spatula in hand. "And I like you. Will I see you later?"

I smiled. "I imagine so."

I wanted him to steal a quick kiss, but when Zeb looked around the café and saw all the people, he ducked his head. Zeb wasn't big on public displays of affection.

One-thirty rolled around pretty fast, so I headed over to the Kincaids to pick up Stella. It was the first sunny day in the last four, but a few gray clouds lurked in the distance. The Kincaids lived in one of the smaller houses in Bright's Pond, but they owned the most land — twenty or thirty acres.

I parked Old Bessie, my red pickup, on the street and climbed out. The air felt cool and crisp and definitely smelled of autumn, that musky brown smell that tasted like the first sip of apple cider with cinnamon. From the Kincaids' street I had a good view of the mountains. They stretched on forever that day, the blue-grey sky a dome that helped me see what Agnes saw when she said living in Bright's Pond was like living inside a snow globe. I lingered a moment and took it all in. For as long as I have lived in Bright's Pond, I've never tired of the view, although I will confess to a growing desire to take a little vacation, perhaps to see what was on the other side of those hills, outside of the glass confines of the snow globe.

I was about to knock on their front door when I heard voices coming from the back of the house. Sure enough, Nate and Stella were out in the pumpkin patch tending to Bertha Ann. A carpet of huge green leaves and vines covered the plot of land they affectionately called The Nursery. I saw two other large pumpkins, but Bertha Ann rested under a purple tent held up with thick poles. She was their princess.

"I said I already sprayed all around." I heard Stella say with a tinge of annoyance in her voice.

"Then how come she got so many dang blame beetles jumping around on her leaves, Stella? Huh? Tell me that."

"Maybe you got the wrong spray, Mr. Bug Buster. Ever think of that? Maybe you need to take a sample of them bugs over to the county agent and get an opinion."

"So now you're telling me how to raise Bertha Ann?"

"Well, she's my pumpkin too, you big goof. There ain't no crime in identifying the proper bug for the proper spray."

"I know what kind of bugs they are, Stella. Them dang rotten cucumber bugs."

"Then you better get the Diazinon, Nate."

I coughed, not that I really needed to. I wanted their attention and figured their pumpkin problems were none of my beeswax.

"Oh, Griselda," Stella called. She had turned with a start. "Is it one-thirty already?" She brushed dirt from her blue jeans.

"Why's she here?" asked Nate. "We got work to do. Need to fertilize before the rain comes back."

Stella turned back to Nate, who picked a bug from one of Bertha Ann's leaves and crushed it between his thumb and index finger. "I thought I'd go with Griselda and pay a little visit to Agnes, if that's okay with you."

Nate screwed up his mouth and tossed a rock over the pumpkin patch fence into the cornfield on the other side. He was a big man, must have stood six feet four inches with shoulders as wide as a door. "Go on," he said. "Don't know why you need to see her though. She stopped praying for us and now look what's happening to our patch."

It wasn't Agnes's fault, but I could see there was no point in pressing the issue.

"I just thought it would be nice to visit," Stella lied. Then she tried to reach up and kiss him but he turned away — much to Stella's embarrassment, I'm sure. "Be that way," she said.

We had driven about a mile before Stella spoke. "Honestly, that man is impossible anymore. All we do is bicker, bicker, bicker."

"He's just worried about the weigh-off," I said.

"I know, I am too, but he doesn't have to treat me so mean. I'm not treating him that way. And sometimes I hear him . . . I hear him out there talking to Bertha Ann about me. Now that ain't right, Griselda. A husband discussing his wife with a pumpkin — she is a pumpkin."

"I'm with you. That doesn't even sound right." I turned left onto Route 113. Now it was only a straight haul to Greenbrier for about four miles. I was just about to ask Stella what was going on when I heard the buzz of a low-flying airplane overhead.

"Look at that," I said. "I can see the pilot. Why is he flying so low?"

Stella grabbed onto the dashboard and ducked. "Holy cow, that's nuts! Are they allowed to fly that low?"

The sight nearly took my breath away. But in a surprisingly good way. "Wow. It must be exciting to fly a plane like that."

"And dangerous," Stella said.

I kept the plane in sight as long as I could.

We drove another mile or so before I turned the subject back to the matter at hand.

"Are you going to tell me what the real problem is, Stella, or should I wait until you tell Agnes?"

Stella gazed out the window. The farms with mostly mowed over cornfields whizzed by. I could hear a flock of migrating red-winged blackbirds overhead, no doubt making their way to a cornfield to rest and forage.

"Look at them," I said. A black cloud of birds soared in the sky, dipping and swirling on the currents like spilled ink. "They are magnificent."

Stella didn't respond for a long second or two. "I'm sorry, hon. Did you say something?" Her southern accent dripped through. Stella had come to Bright's Pond from Tennessee about ten years ago. She was twenty-three when she arrived with one suitcase and very little to say.

"I was noticing the blackbirds, Stella. They're amazing."

"Blackbirds, right." She strained to look at the sky. But I knew she couldn't see anything but blue. "They're beautiful."

She couldn't have cared less. Whatever was preying on her mind must have been mighty heavy. I decided I would have to wait until we were with Agnes to learn about it.

The Greenbrier Nursing Home was a series of four long, one-floor, red brick buildings arranged in a square. A steel flagpole stood in the center and flew three flags. The Stars and Stripes, The Commonwealth of Pennsylvania's blue flag with two horses reared up on hind legs with a golden crest in the middle, and The Greenbrier Nursing home's green and white banner lowest but not least.

"Here we are."

"My stomach is upset now," Stella said.

I pushed the gearshift into park. "Why so nervous, Stella?"

"You'll learn soon enough." She pushed open the truck door and hopped out. "Guess the whole town will find out sooner

25

or later once my troubles make their way into the rumor mill."

Agnes admitted herself into Greenbrier about nine months ago. It was time. Her weight had reached nearly 750 pounds from what we could estimate. Her asthma attacks became more frequent, and after keeping herself imprisoned at our house for nearly ten years, she was ready for a change.

Fortunately, and probably because of her size, Agnes had a single room at the nursing home. They gave her a specially reinforced bed able to hold about a thousand pounds. It was much wider than regular hospital beds so finding sheets to fit was difficult and expensive until the Society of Angelic Philanthropy, which did secret charitable acts in Bright's Pond, got together and started sewing two sets of full size sheets end to end to make them fit. At last count they had completed six sets of sheets — all white except for one set with daisies all over, like a meadow.

"She's in room 116," I told Stella, who was moving a little slow, maybe even cautiously, kind of slinking down the hall like she didn't want to be seen. "All the way at the end of the hall."

"How can they stand the smell in here?"

Stella asked pinching her nose. "It's worse than the cow barn."

"Guess they get used to it."

"Can you die from swallowing bad odors?" Stella asked.

I smiled. "Don't know for sure. But I never heard of anyone inhaling too much stink and keeling over."

A man in a wheelchair came whooping around the corner. He made vroom vroom noises as he blazed passed us. It took a second before it registered that he had no legs.

"I hate it here," Stella said.

Agnes's door was open, which meant we could walk right in. Sometimes I would arrive and the door would be closed, which meant the aides and nurses or doctors were in with her doing whatever it is they needed to do.

"Hey, Agnes," I called. "Brought you a visitor today."

Agnes made a noise and managed to pull herself up with the aid of a triangular trapeze bar that dangled over her chest. She sat mostly propped up in a tangle of blankets and sheets. Two thin pillows supported her head and one them had fallen to the side so much it was about to fall on the floor. Other than the bed and a hospital tray table,

Agnes's room was decorated with homey touches like her mahogany highboy dresser brought from home, the matching nightstand, and a pretty little lamp with a pinstriped shade. The objects from home made it appear less medicinal.

"Stella?" Agnes said. "Is that Stella Kincaid? Praise Jesus! I haven't seen you in a dog's age. How's the prize-winning pumpkin business treating you?"

"Hi, Agnes. This year we named our entry Bertha Ann. She's doing fine, real fine, getting bigger every day. Nate's been busy with mildew control and taking care of the pests."

"Kind of like me," Agnes said with a chuckle. "They keep telling me they're gonna haul me down to the truck stop scales out on the turnpike to get an accurate number. They think I might have dropped a few pounds. But I am not letting them hoist me onto a forklift ever again." She slapped her knee. "If that wasn't the most humiliating experience of my life I don't know what is."

I patted her hand and kissed her cheek. "Don't worry. I won't let anyone haul you around on a forklift again. But right now, Stella has something personal she needs to discuss. I didn't think you'd mind."

Stella moved closer to the bed. Agnes

28

readjusted herself and that was when the precarious pillow fell, causing several Baby Ruth wrappers to float to the floor like autumn leaves. I snatched them. "Where'd you get these?"

"Oh, Griselda, you're such a worrywart," Agnes said. "It's only two or three candy bars. Stu brought them by. Ain't gonna hurt me none. The so-called food they give me here isn't fit for a dog most of the time. I'd do just about anything for a tuna salad on white bread, like you used to make me. You always made the best tuna salad with the tiny shaved carrots mixed in and sweet onion."

"I count five wrappers," I said.

"Five wrappers? You better toss them out before nurse Sally finds them."

"Agnes, you promise to tell Stu not to bring anymore, and I'll see about the tuna salad, maybe without the bread."

Agnes smiled. Her tiny eyes grew as wide as they could in their sockets.

I crumpled the wrappers and was about to toss them in the trash.

"Hold on," Agnes said, "mind shoving them in your pocket and getting rid of 'em at home? Don't need the evidence lying around. I think she looks through my trash."

Agnes grabbed onto the trapeze bar and

pulled herself up even more. It seemed to take a full thirty seconds from start to finish. "So, Stella, what's on your mind?" I watched Agnes take a breath. It always pained me to see her struggle for air.

Stella opened her mouth to speak, but no words came out. She walked toward the windows. "You got a right pretty view, Agnes. I can see so far, and that grass is still so nice and green, and look at those trees all around. The fall colors are a little off this year, don't you think? Probably on account of all that rain. Not enough sun —"

Agnes clicked her tongue. "Stella. Now I know you did not come to talk about leaves."

Stella turned around. Her eyes glistened with tears. "Okay, here goes. I got a phone call yesterday. It would appear that my —" she paused and took a shaky breath — "brother has been in an accident, and he is right this minute lying in a coma right here at Greenbrier, in this very building." She tossed the words out fast and hard. And then she started to blubber.

My heart leapt into my throat. Agnes coughed so hard I worried she might have an asthma attack. "Brother?" she said. "We never knew you had a brother."

"And he's here? At Greenbrier?" I added.

"In a coma?"

Stella wiped her eyes and nodded. "For going on two weeks now. The people here just found me yesterday."

Agnes patted her bed. "Sit, Stella. Tell us the story."

For the next little while, Agnes and I listened, listened and nodded and stroked Stella's arm as she told us a sad, sad family story about betrayal and lies, backbiting and blackmail.

"So you see, we haven't spoken for going on ten years."

"I had no idea you were carrying all that hurt," I said.

"Do you know anything about the accident?" Agnes asked. "About what put him in a coma?"

Stella shook her head. "All I know is what they told me. A few weeks ago Walter was up near the coal mines. They're not sure what he was doing, but he took a spill down one of those — what do you call them? — slag heaps up there near the quarry and knocked himself unconscious — or so they think. They brought him here two weeks ago."

"How did they find you?" Agnes asked. "I mean if he can't talk or —"

"They used his driver's license to track

down his home in Tennessee. When they called the number a woman answered."

"A woman?" I said. "Is your brother married?"

"Not that I know of," Stella said. "The nurse said her name is Gilda."

"But how did they find you?" Agnes repeated.

"I'm getting to that, but I'm not a hundred percent sure. The nurse said she found my name, my maiden name, in Walter's wallet and when she mentioned it to the woman in Tennessee she told her I was his sister — does that make sense?"

"Yes," Agnes said. "It makes sense, but it sure is a lot to take in."

"I know," Stella said. "It's more complicated than pumpkin growing. My mind has been reeling since I got the phone call."

"Just take it easy," Agnes said. "You'll start to feel better now that Griselda and me know."

Stella swiped at more tears. "I just don't know what to do. Should I go to his room? And if he has a girlfriend or a wife then maybe he doesn't need me, maybe he doesn't even want me."

"How can I help?" Agnes asked.

"I can't decide if I should go see Walter or not. I mean what if he wakes up, sees me, and has some kind of stroke or something. I don't want to kill him by surprise, and he's probably happy with things the way they are seeing how he ain't bothered to look me up or —"

"Now, Stella," Agnes said. "Did you ever go looking for him in all this time? Ten years?"

Stella looked ashamed and then piped up. "Weren't you listening to that tale of woe I just told you? Calling me those most awful names and cheating me out of my half of the inheritance? I mean, Lord, Agnes. He's a scoundrel."

"Maybe he's changed," I said.

That was when a nurse came in carrying a little white paper cup. "Time for your pill, Agnes."

Agnes looked at the small orange clock on the wall. "My goodness. We all been yakking for nearly two hours. It's after four o'clock."

"I am sorry," Stella said. "I didn't mean to take up so much time, but I thought you needed to hear the whole story about what happened to my family and Walter and all."

Agnes patted Stella's hand. "Perfectly all right, dear."

"So are you gonna go see him?" I asked.

Stella pursed her lips and stood. "I just

can't say, yet. We got so much trouble in our family. Maybe it's best to let it go. He's got what's-her-name . . . Gilda, and I'm sure scads of other friends who will rally around."

"But only one sister," Agnes said. She looked at me and smiled.

"I did come here for another reason," Stella said. "To ask a miracle."

Agnes screwed up her face. "I'm not in the miracle business too much anymore, Stella."

"You can still pray — and I know, I know, it's up to God and all — but I was hoping you might ask the Almighty to keep Walter in that coma for a bit longer — until I get it sorted out."

Agnes chuckled. "Now that's a new one. Most folks would ask God to bring a loved one OUT of a coma not to remain locked inside."

"Just for a short while longer," Stella said.

Agnes closed her eyes. We waited, expecting to hear her pray when her eyes popped back open. "I need to think on this one, Stella. But rest assured. It's all under God's control."

Stella nodded and then opened her purse. A brown leather bag held closed with some kind of hemp string knot. She sneaked something under Agnes's pillow. "For later."

I leaned down and kissed Agnes on the cheek. "I'll be back tomorrow."

"That's fine," Agnes said. "And see about the tuna salad?"

I shook my head. "I'll try, Agnes, but it might go against your doctor's rules. Bad enough the folks from town are sneaking you candy bars and M&Ms. Don't think I don't know it's not just Studebaker." I looked at Stella. She looked away.

Agnes harrumphed. "Worry wart."

"Stella," I said when we got to the hallway, "now you know sneaking Agnes candy is against the rules."

"Ah, it's just a Three Musketeers."

When we got to the truck, it occurred to me to ask, "Stella. Just one thing. If Walter wasn't looking for you, why was he up here in the mountains? I mean why isn't he down south? Isn't that where your people are?"

Stella took a long moment before speaking. "That's a good question, Griselda. I'm sure I don't know why he was up here."

3

Stella barely looked at me or spoke the whole way back to town. She sat in her seat and picked at her fingernails. It was almost as if she regretted spilling the beans to Agnes and me, and I ached to tell her that I wasn't standing in judgment about her. I could understand her struggle. But I didn't say anything.

It wasn't until I pulled up in front of her house that she finally spoke. "I'm glad it's out in the open, Griselda. But would you please keep it to yourself?"

I assured her I would.

She reached over and kissed my cheek. "Thank you, Griselda. You are a good friend."

"Think Nate got the bugs under control back there?" I said as she pushed the truck door open.

"Oh, he's a pain in my rear end," she said. "He fusses more over that pumpkin than he does the mortgage that is always late."

"Are you gonna tell him about Walter?"

Stella shrugged. "I'm afraid to. He's so tense right now what with the weigh-off coming around. One more problem might send him over —"

"I think you should tell him."

Stella paused a moment. "Heck, I haven't even made up my own mind about Walter, let alone whether to tell Nate all this. He doesn't know much about my life before we got married."

"I guess you can wait to tell Nate, but Walter? He could die."

I pulled away from the curb with an uneasy feeling setting in my stomach. I had known Stella for several years and in all that time she never seemed vulnerable in any way. She always went about her business without a care. I guess it goes to show that everybody has their troubles. Some are better at hiding them.

It was Thursday, meat loaf night at The Full Moon. It used to be on Mondays, but Zeb decided to change it on account of more people came out on Thursdays. And I will admit to having a weakness for Zeb's meat-loaf, so I headed to the café.

Mildred Blessing's police cruiser was

parked in her usual spot. Zeb gave her a reserved parking spot because she was a guardian of the community, and he felt it was a good idea to honor her that way. She also gets free coffee while she's on duty.

Dot Handy waited the counter while Babette Sturgis took care of the booths. Babette had blossomed into a pretty young woman, having just this year graduated from high school. She attended the Shoops Community College, studying to become a kindergarten teacher.

"Evening, Griselda," called Dot. "Will you be sitting at the counter tonight? Might be a bit of a wait for a booth."

I looked around. The café was crowded with families, so I sat on one of the red vinyl counter stools.

Dot wiped the space in front of me. "Meatloaf?"

"Yep. And coffee."

I could hear Zeb whistling in the back.

"You hear the big news?" Dot asked.

My thoughts jumped immediately to Stella and her brother. How in the world could Dot have found out anything? Agnes would not have gotten on the telephone and blabbed to everyone, and Stella, I was certain, had told no one but me. Impossible. I played it dumb. "What news?"

"About Cora's house. They finally rented it out."

I took a breath. "Oh, is that all? Well, that's good news for Cora's family. I know they were eager to get a family in there." Cora Nebbish was a dear friend, an older woman who waitressed for Zeb right up to the day she died of heart failure.

Dot poured my coffee and slid the silver creamer my way. "It's not a family that moved in, Griselda, that's why everybody is talking. Word is that Stanley Nebbish went and rented it to some hussy, a fast and loose type woman. Goes by the name of Glinda or something."

Zeb came out of the kitchen with my special — a plate filled to the brim with a hearty slice of meatloaf, mashed potatoes drowning in brown gravy with tiny bits of onions swimming around, and a side dish of peas and carrots with a pat of butter melting on top. It smelled scrumptious. If I closed my eyes, I could easily imagine sitting around a family dinner table.

"Her name isn't Glinda," he said. "She's not the Good Witch of the North, Dot. It's an even stranger name than that."

Studebaker Kowalski took the seat next to me. He carried his plate and coffee with him. "I was sitting over by the window all

39

by my lonesome, Griselda. Don't mind if I join you, do you?"

"Course not, Stu."

"I know it starts with G," Dot said. "Gracie? Gwendolyn?"

"Her name is Gilda," called Mildred. She was just coming out of the ladies room, adjusting her gun belt. "Gilda Saucer."

"Now, see there," Dot said. "If that ain't a hussy name, then I never heard one."

I swallowed. *Gilda? Walter's Gilda? Here from Tennessee?*

"I don't know for certain if she's a bona fide hussy, but she does look the part," Mildred said. "I wandered over while she moved some things inside. She didn't have much. Just a couple of suitcases and a trunk."

"Probably to hold all her stripper clothes," Dot said. "If strippers got clothes. I mean —"

"We know what you mean, Dot," I said.

"She's a bombshell," Mildred said. "Tall, bleached blond, tight skirt. Lots of red lipstick and nail polish."

"See that," Dot said. "I don't know why we got to have a hussy move into our town. Cora is probably rolling over in her grave, madder than jumpin' blue heck at Stanley."

"I heard," Mildred continued, "that she is

40

only renting the place on a month-to-month lease. Not even a full year like respectable folk."

"Well, that's all the proof I need," Dot said. "She's a hussy."

I ate some of my mashed potatoes. "So what do you want to do, Dot, run her out of town?"

Dot filled Stu's coffee cup. "Now I ain't saying that, I'm just saying we should keep an eye peeled, you know. For Cora's sake."

"Might not be a bad idea," Mildred said. "Single woman moving to town with just a couple of suitcases. Does seem suspicious."

I swallowed some peas and figured maybe I should get on over to Stella's as quick as possible and tell her about Gilda before word spread.

It was pitch dark by the time I got to the Kincaid's house. They had one dim bulb burning on the porch. I parked Bessie and made my way to the back, figuring they were still fighting off cucumber bugs. I got about halfway there when all of a sudden the place lit like an invasion, like Martians had that minute landed in the Kincaids' pumpkin patch.

"Stella," I called. "It's me, Griselda. Everything all —"

Just then I heard a loud pop. And then another and then three more. Pop. Pop. Pop.

"Stella," I called. I knew Nate was upset over the bugs but not enough to shoot her.

"Stella," I called again and made my way to the back porch.

The lights went off, and I was able to see Nate by the light of another dim bulb, sitting on the back porch with a shotgun resting on his knees.

"Jumpin' blue heck," he said. "That miserable rodent got away again."

"Nate," I said, "what are you doing?"

"Groundhog. Super large thing. About the size of one them Volkswagen Beetles, been tearing up my patch. I've been trying to kill him for a week."

Stella appeared at the back and pushed open the screen door. "Did you get 'im?"

"Nah, he got away again."

"I am not sleeping with those ridiculous floodlights blaring on and off all night long."

"Well, I ain't turning them off," Nate said. He sat back down with his gun. "I got to wait for that monster to come back and then . . . BLAM!" He pointed his gun at the pumpkin patch.

"Stella," I called, "it's me, Griselda."

"Oh, Griselda," she said. She pushed the door open farther. "Come on inside. It's chilly and . . . and crazy out there."

"I ain't crazy," Nate said, "but I'm gonna get that woodchuck. Right between the eyes."

I slipped past Nate. "Good luck, Sheriff."

Nate grunted something and then said, "And bring me a cup of coffee."

Stella plugged the percolator into the wall.

"Has he been doing this every night?" I asked.

"Yep. Groundhogs are bad for pumpkins. Just one can destroy the whole patch."

"Can't he just use poison or something?"

Stella shook her head and pulled a red Thermos from a cabinet. "Nah, not good for Bertha Ann. Poison could kill her too."

I sighed and sat at the kitchen table.

"So what brings you here?" Stella asked. "I got some peach pie left over from supper. Do you want a piece?"

I rubbed my stomach. "No, thanks. I just came from Zeb's."

The coffee pot made gurgling noises. "Okay, suit yourself, but I know you didn't come out here to sit in my kitchen and drink coffee."

"No, there's something I think you should know." I lowered my voice to a near whisper.

"Is it about Walter?"

"In a way. I found out that a woman

43

named Gilda Saucer has rented Cora Nebbish's house."

Stella's eyes grew so wide her forehead disappeared.

"What? When? You mean she's in town. Right now?"

"Dot Handy told me that she just moved in. Didn't bring much with her, according to Mildred Blessing. They're calling her a hussy. Dot said she looks like a stripper."

Stella rinsed the Thermos in the sink and then dried it with a soft towel trimmed with red and gold roosters. "Just like him to take up with a woman like that."

"That's just Dot Handy's opinion. You can't take her word."

"Sure I can. I know my brother and now that she's moved to town, I won't have to go racing over to Greenbrier. Gilda can do all that."

"I don't see any reason you still shouldn't go. It might be a good idea to meet her. Aren't you the least bit curious about why Walter was up here and what he was doing at the quarry?"

"Maybe a little but —"

"Well, you'll never know until you get over the past and go to Greenbrier and see what's going on."

"Stella!" Nate called, "got that cof—" But

before he finished the floodlights burst on, and we heard three more pops of the gun.

"Dang! He's a smart one."

Stella filled the Thermos. "I better run this out to Nate."

"Will you at least think about it? Pray about it? Ask God to help you decide."

"All right. For you, I'll pray about it. But not for Walter or his . . . girlfriend."

4

The next morning on the way to the library I drove past Cora's house with one eye looking for Gilda Saucer. Curiosity, I suppose. Not that I knew what she looked like. But seeing Cora's house gave me reason to pause. I missed my friend, Cora. I flirted with a passing thought about stopping and knocking on the door, but it wasn't like I had a batch of lemon squares to offer Gilda Saucer if she was inside, and what would I say to her anyway? Maybe I just wanted to look inside Cora's house once again. Anyway, I decided there was no hurry in getting the library opened and headed on down to the café for a cup of coffee since it was barely ten o'clock, and I rarely had library patrons before noon, especially when the air had a bite to it like it did that morning — a crisp autumn snap with the smell of wood smoke in the air.

A woman fitting Gilda's description sat at

the counter again. She had been there earlier, around breakfast time. She ran her finger around the rim of a cup half-filled with black coffee. She stared straight ahead like she had something awful on her mind. Must have been Walter. I watched her dump three spoons of sugar into her cup and stir the coffee with slow methodical strokes. Then she licked her spoon in that upside down way children did.

I sat next to her.

"Hi, my name is Griselda Sparrow." I offered her my hand. She had one of those limp handshakes that always made me feel weird.

"Pleased to meet you," she said. "My name's Gilda, just like Hilda only with a G." Then she sipped her coffee. The explanation I was certain came standard with her name.

"I hear you moved into the house on Hector Street."

Zeb poured my coffee. "Morning, Grizzy."

I nodded at him. "Hey, Zeb."

Gilda shot me a glare. I noticed her bloodshot eyes and thought she might have been crying. "Guess what they say about small towns is true," she said.

"Excuse me?" I averted my eyes.

"You know, gossip."

"Oh, well," I said. "I don't know if it's gossip as much as it's that change is very noticeable around here."

"There is no reason to go noticing me."

"We don't mean any harm. We're just a little curious when new folks move into town."

"You know what they said about curiosity, don't you?" She wiped her lips on a paper napkin. She stood and moved toward the cash register. I watched her saunter out the door.

Zeb returned carrying two breakfast specials. "She's an odd one," he said. "But she sure is prettier than a —" he looked at me. "Sorry, Griz. I didn't mean to say —"

"Does she come in everyday?"

"Sure does — hold on, let me get those guys their breakfast."

I watched him drop the plates at a booth.

"Yeah," Zeb said when he returned. "I get the feeling she hasn't done any grocery shopping yet. She comes in for coffee and sandwiches — likes baloney."

Zeb went back into the kitchen, and I finished my coffee with my thoughts on Gilda. Why in heaven's name would she have rented Cora's house and not even bought groceries? Unless she's spending all her time at Greenbrier sitting with Walter.

48

Well, if that isn't dedication, I don't know what is.

The library would have to wait. I made my way to Stella's. I found her out back nursing Bertha Ann.

"How's it going, Stella?" I called to her across the pumpkin patch.

She poked her head out from around Bertha Ann. "Hey, Griselda. What brings you here?"

I tiptoed my way through the vines toward Stella and tripped over one that seemed to deliberately snag me. "I was wondering if you decided to go see Walter."

Stella looked away and then turned back, locking her eyes on mine. "I thought about it and — and I can't find the power to go. I know you and Agnes think I should, but how can I?"

"Just go, Stella. I'll be with you."

"But Griselda, he's in a coma. What if he wakes up and sees me and gets all upset or something?"

"Is that what you're really afraid of, Stella? Upsetting him?"

She brushed hair out of her eyes and wiped her forehead with the back of her grubby hand. "What else?"

"I think you're afraid you might have to

stand up for yourself and tell him how you feel about what he did to you and your mother."

She pulled another weed. "Be that as it may, there is no law that says I have to go."

I heaved a slight sigh. "I spoke with Gilda this morning."

She stopped yanking. "You what? Walter's Gilda?"

"She was at The Full Moon. I sat next to her and introduced myself. That's all. She seems a little . . . off, strange. If I were to hazard an opinion, I'd say she might be in love with Walter and very concerned for him."

"Then let her take care of him. Keeps me from needing to go there at all if she's so dang blame in love."

"She seems tired is all I'm saying," I said. "And she is eating all her meals at the café. She could be spending day and night with him."

"Her business, not mine."

"Yes, but . . . but Stella. You need to see him, too."

Stella yanked harder. "I can't, Griselda. Leastways, not yet."

I made a couple more attempts to convince her but to no avail.

"We'll keep praying," I said finally. "I better get to the library before folks think I went out of business or something."

"Okay, I hope you have a nice day." Stella went back to her weeds.

I turned to leave.

"Griselda," Stella called. "Why do you care so much about my brother?"

"I care about both of you and — and I just have this feeling that —"

"What?" she said, sounding irritated. "That what?"

"That he needs you, Stella."

She made a noise and hurled a clump of scraggly vines into a pile of pumpkin patch debris.

Mildred Blessing was waiting at the library when I arrived. She had come for a fresh supply of crime novels. She read them like Agnes ate M&Ms.

"I was beginning to think you were closed for the day, Griselda. I was just about to split."

"No, no. I was over at Stella Kincaid's."

I watched her eyebrows lift. "Really. I just know something is going on with her. Feel like telling me or will it wait until after I arrest her."

I laughed and turned the key in the library door. "You are not going to arrest Stella and

51

you know it. She's done nothing criminal."

"Well, somebody has."

I pushed open the door and a whiff of cold air shot out. "Just let me get the heat up."

"Sure . . . sure, Griselda. I can wait. I'm not really on duty today."

I reached into the basement stairway and flipped on the furnace switch. "I thought you were always on duty."

"Nah, not really. But it's a boatload of responsibility being the only cop in town. Hard to take a real day off. I feel I need to be at the ready, you know, but the commonwealth requires me to take time."

"Makes sense, Mildred. I got a new Rex Stout in and a couple more Raymond Chandlers if you want them."

"Sounds good."

"I'll go get them."

I checked out Mildred's books while she waited, still with a kind of pensive look about her, like she was expecting some major crime to break out at any second. To be honest, other than an occasional fracas down at Personal's Pub or a problem up at the Paradise Trailer Park, nothing much happens of an illegal or police emergency nature in Bright's Pond.

I pushed the books toward her. "Here you go. Enjoy."

Mildred picked up the books and clutched them to her chest. "I'll just sit over there and read until the rest of the committee gets here."

I glanced at the clock. Close to eleven. The Harvest Dance Committee was on their way to the library. We thought a meeting at the library might help, less distractions here than at the café. And sure enough right on time the door opened and in walked Studebaker, along with Ruth and Boris Lender. Zeb had to tend to customers, but he said he would be fine with whatever we decided. It had become imperative to settle on a theme. Time was a wasting.

"Come on in," I said as though the library was my home. In a way, I suppose it was. The library had always been a place of sanctuary for me; even as a child I found comfort among the stacks of books. "I thought we'd sit at the periodicals table. I'll put coffee on."

"I brought lemon squares," Ruth said. "Still a little warm from the oven."

Studebaker tried to reach under the tin foil and snag one, but Ruth slapped his hand away. "You just wait until the coffee is served."

Boris, being a lawyer, had a yellow legal

pad in front of him and three very sharp Dixon Ticonderoga pencils. He was a quiet sort of man but had no trouble speaking his mind when it was appropriate. He could, of course, invoke his authority if there was ever the need. And frankly, I can't remember a time when he did.

"I've been giving it some thought," Studebaker said. "And . . . and well, I think you're all going to like this idea."

"Just spill it, Stu," Ruth said. "Somebody has to come up with an idea or we just won't have a dance."

"Oh, simmer down, Ruth," I said. "We'll have the dance. We always do. We're just having a little trouble coming up with a theme is all. But we will. Now let's hear Studebaker's idea."

He straightened his back and smiled and then said, "The old west, John Wayne, Dodge City, The OK Corral."

No one moved a muscle until Ruth's jaw dropped open like Howdy Doody's.

I wasn't about to say anything, although I liked the idea immediately, and excused myself to get coffee. Boris lifted the foil off of the lemon squares.

"Well, how 'bout it?" Studebaker asked. "Cowboys, an old western saloon. We could even put down some wooden sidewalks and do some square dancing and —"

"I love it," Ruth said. "I do declare Studebaker Kowalski, this time you got something special. Even better than my mermaids."

I heaved a small sigh as I poured coffee. I was happy that Ruth finally broke the silence. I figured no one wanted to be first to jump on board. Even Boris had something positive to say.

"Hot dog, Studebaker. That is a capital idea. I can see it now, cowboy hats and —"

"Oh, oh." Ruth waved her hand. "You can wear one of them ten-gallon-size hats and wear a sheriff's badge, Boris."

"Hold on a second," Mildred said. "I'm the only sheriff in town."

I brought the tray of full coffee cups, cream, and sugar to the table. "This is beginning to sound like a great idea."

"I like it," Boris said. "I'll play the part of a circuit judge passing through town to try cattle rustlers and chicken poachers."

The ideas flowed like the Susquehanna River that day. We had more plans for the dance than ever. I knew Mildred would be pleased, and Zeb would have a blast making pies and cowboy-inspired treats. This was shaping up to be one of the best Harvest Dances in Bright's Pond history.

Mildred, Studebaker, and Boris left, but

Ruth stayed around for a little bit. She was my good friend, and I enjoyed having her company. Sometimes I think she could sense when I felt lonely, especially since Agnes moved to Greenbrier.

"How long are you working?" Ruth asked. She placed the coffee cups in the sink.

"I should probably keep the library open for a little while after school lets out. The kids might have research projects or need a book for a book report."

"Okay, I'll stay with you. I got nothing better to do, except scrub my tub. I hate scrubbing the tub, Griselda. Hate it more than scrubbing the toilet. It gives me a crick in my back and pain in my neck."

By three-thirty there were six kids in the library looking for information on everything from the Renaissance to hot air balloons. I enjoyed helping them and in a short while they were all on their way home with books and copies of magazine articles.

By four o'clock Ruth and I were ready to go home.

"Going to The Full Moon?" Ruth asked as I locked the door.

"Nah, Zeb is picking me up around six. We're going to the movie."

"Ooh, la la. You two been seeing a lot of each other, haven't you?"

"We've been out a couple of times." I felt my neck go warm and the blush travel to my ears. I hated that my feelings were always so visible. I pretty much turn into a pomegranate whenever I'm nervous or surprised or . . . when someone reacts to the simple fact that Zeb Sewickey and I have been dating. It's not like we're engaged or anything. Just two friends spending some time together.

Ruth grabbed my hand. "I can't wait to dance at your wedding."

I let a nervous giggle escape my throat. "Oh, Ruth. Please don't get ahead of things and whatever you do, don't go blabbing this around town. We're just friends — that's all."

"Uh, huh. Could you drop me at my house?"

Dot Handy always took over the kitchen when Zeb was not there, which was not very often. And she did a pretty good job keeping up with orders. But I knew, I just knew that about an hour into the movie, Zeb would say he needed to check on the café. I suppose it was his right, but it also made me a little frustrated. And that evening was no different.

"I'll be right back," he whispered in my ear, just as Shelley Winters dove under the water for the third time. "Just want to check on the café."

I said nothing. How he could walk out on *The Poseidon Adventure* was beyond me. Just beyond me. So there I sat, all alone, with a tub of popcorn watching a disaster movie. Maybe the only disaster was not on the screen that night. I decided to tell Zeb that if he wanted to keep on dating me he would need to get his priorities straight.

He slipped back next to me about twenty minutes later and slid his arm around my shoulders. "What did I miss?"

My stomach tightened. "All the good parts."

The September air was still warm that evening so Zeb and I decided to walk the few short blocks back to my house. We stood on the porch a minute before I pushed the door open. I took one step inside when he grabbed my hand.

"Hold on a second, Griselda . . . I . . ."

I searched his eyes, convinced that the man was about to kiss me.

He tilted his head and moved close, pulled me into his arms and planted a kiss, just a small one that nearly missed my lips. Then he looked into my eyes and I felt them close as he pulled me even tighter and kissed me long and thoroughly. My left leg spontaneously lifted as I leaned in closer, just the way my Mama used to when Daddy would steal a kiss when he thought Agnes and I weren't looking. My heart beat like hummingbird wings even after Zeb said, "Goodnight, Grizzy."

5

I closed the door behind me and stood with my back pressed against it, feeling Zeb's presence still outside. I knew that if I opened the door he would be standing there, on the porch, waiting, I thought, for another kiss. And I toyed with the notion but let it go, thinking that maybe I wasn't quite ready for a second kiss.

Arthur twisted his lithe body around and between my ankles, purring and growling for food. He was always and forever hungry, and I will admit that I often indulged his appetite with tuna and liverwurst — two of his favorite tidbits. But that night I told him, "No, you'll get fat."

There were days since Agnes left when my big old house seemed to grow larger, the rooms wider, the ceilings higher. It was sometimes hard living alone, and I often wished Agnes was still in her bed in the viewing room. That evening was one of those times. I missed her in a way I believed people with amputations missed a limb. And yet I knew it was better for her to be at Greenbrier, better for her and for me.

I had settled down in front of the TV with a cup of tea and two slices of toast with raspberry jam when the telephone rang. It was Stella all in a huff. She and Nate had another one of their brawls.

"He is just so worried about that dang blame pumpkin that he forgets all about me."

"Maybe you need to be a little more patient, Stella. You have your own problems and maybe that's making it harder to cope with Nate this time around. You know he gets like this every year. But if you don't tell him about Walter, he'll keep thinking you're all right and keep on bickering with you."

She paused and I heard her breathing into the phone. I also heard Nate hollering. I couldn't make out what he was saying, but he sounded awful angry. I didn't like the fact that he had that shotgun.

"Are you okay, Stella?" I asked. "Do you need me to come get you?"

"No, no. He'll get it out of his system. You might be right, Griselda. Maybe I should let this whole Walter mishmash go."

"Now, I didn't say that, Stella. I only

61

meant that if you're already upset, then it'll be harder to handle Nate when he gets like this."

"It's the drinking."

"Drinking? Nate doesn't drink."

"That's what I mean," Stella said. "Ever since he stopped, he's been just the dickens to live with. Like living with a grizzly bear."

"Tell him you're sorry and just go to bed. Meet me at the café in the morning for breakfast."

"Oh, Griselda, I wanted to tell him about Walter, but I . . . I just can't. And I can't keep sneaking out of the house." She paused. "Oh, good he went out back to hunt that groundhog again."

"You might feel better if you tell him."

BLAM!

"Stella?"

Nothing, not a sound.

"Stella? Are you there?" I had to fight an image of Stella lying on the kitchen linoleum having taken the blast intended for a groundhog. "Stella?"

I heard the phone drop. And then all of a sudden I heard Nate whooping and hollering. "I got him, Stella, I got that miserable varmint! I got him!"

Stella picked up the receiver. "Thank the good Lord, Griselda, if this ain't a sight.

Nate is standing in my kitchen holding the biggest darn groundhog I have ever seen by the tail. It's about as wide as my oven door. Look at that thing. It's got orange eyes."

"Probably from gnawing on pumpkins," I said.

"I got him, Stella! I got him!" I could hear Nate in the background. He sounded like a little boy with his first fish — or groundhog in this case.

"That's nice, sweetie pie. You did. You got him."

Stella hung up on her end, and I took a deep breath. "Now maybe those two will start getting along again," I told Arthur. It was nice to think for a minute that Stella and Nate had reason to celebrate. Now she just had to tell him about Walter. I hoped she would but didn't count on it.

I had just slipped into bed when I heard a terrible banging on my front door. Even Arthur, who usually didn't give a hoot about noise, perked up. "Oh, my goodness, Arthur," I said, "you don't suppose Nate finally went off the deep end and —"

The banging increased and I heard hollering. I thought I heard someone calling my name. I pulled on my bathrobe and practically stumbled the entire way down the steps — ignoring my need to pee.

"I'm coming, I'm coming," I said.

I pulled open the front door and there stood Ivy Slocum, sopping wet in the rain, and crying so hard she rivaled the downpour. She was drenched inside and out.

"Griselda," she cried. "This is terrible. Just terrible."

I took her arm and gently pulled her into the house. "What is it, Ivy? What happened?"

I led her to the living room and helped her sit on the red velvet sofa. "Can I get you something first — tea? coffee?"

She shook her head. "No, no, I couldn't. Not now."

"Well, at least let me get you a towel."

When I got back with two yellow towels, Ivy was sobbing into her hands. I couldn't begin to imagine what had happened. I hadn't seen or heard tears like that since our friend Vidalia passed away.

"Did someone die?" I asked. I sat next to her and patted her knee.

"Yes, yes. Al . . . Al . . . Capone." She emphasized the last syllable with a sob that nearly shook the floorboards. I had never known Ivy could be so emotional.

"Your doggie, Al Capone?"

Ivy looked at me through glistening eyes

as if to say, *No, Griselda, the actual gangster.*

I felt like an idiot for a second until Ivy nodded her head and her long white hair, a tangled mess, bounced on her shoulders.

"How, how did this happen?" I pushed tissues into her hands and waited until she blew. She wiped her red nose and swallowed.

"I . . . I found him on my porch. He had come home. I heard a noise — scratching on the door — and went to see, and there he was. Oh, Griselda, he just lay down at my feet and . . . and . . ." I patted her hand as tears rolled down my cheeks.

She blew a second time and looked at me. "He had a chicken bone stuck to his cheek and smelled like barbecue sauce. You know how he liked to raid Personal's trashcans."

"I do." Al Capone spent many hours down at Personal's Pub begging for scraps and emptying the cans. He often brought barbecue chicken back to Ivy.

"Where is he now?"

"Still on the porch. I don't know what to do. He's too heavy for me to lift. I covered him with my rain slicker and put my rain hat on his head so he wouldn't get any more soaked than he already is."

"That's good, Ivy." I glanced at the mantel clock. It was nearly eleven o'clock. "I think it's too late to call Doc Flaherty or the vet so you just sleep here —"

"If I can."

"If you can. And we'll take care of this in the morning."

"You mean we should just leave Al Capone out in the rain?"

"I could call Zeb and maybe have his body moved to your garage, but I think he'll be OK. He's protected under the porch roof."

"That old porch leaks but okay, if you say so, and if you're sure no night critters will gnaw at him."

I wasn't sure about that, but I chose not to dwell on it.

By ten o'clock the next morning, we had Al Capone at the vet in Shoops. Bill Tompkins helped us get him into my truck. Dr. Fish was a lovely young woman. She treated Al Capone and Ivy with kindness. After examining him for a few moments, she said, "If I were to hazard a guess and without a necropsy —"

Ivy winced and cringed and snuffed back a sob.

Dr. Fish put her arm around Ivy's shoulders. "Sorry, but I would say Al Capone died from an infection. Most likely, given his love for tramping around town and raiding trash bins, I'd say a chicken bone got caught in his bowel, perforated the lining and, well, infection set in. He was probably sick for a few days."

"He had been out a lot," Ivy said. "I was so happy to see him last night." Then she sobbed and fell into my arms.

Dr. Fish helped Ivy to a chair and then pulled me aside. "I could just take him and cremate the remains."

"Cremate?" Ivy said. "No. Al Capone deserves a proper burial."

"That's fine," the doctor said. "But do it quickly before . . ."

Ivy thanked Dr. Fish, and we headed back to Bright's Pond with the now stiff-as-an-ironing-board Al Capone in a large green plastic bag.

That afternoon practically the whole town turned out for Al Capone's funeral, even though the rain still poured. Ivy asked Studebaker to say a few words. We gathered in her backyard near a hole big enough for the dog but maybe a little too shallow in my opinion. Ivy asked Stu to dig it, and let's just say digging is not one of Studebaker's favorite activities.

But still he managed to make us laugh and cry as he recounted Al Capone's many exploits throughout the town and his ongoing feud with Eugene Shrapnel. Eugene surprised us all when he arrived for the service.

"I . . . I hate to admit it but . . . but . . ."

Ivy put her hand on his shoulder. "But you're gonna miss the old pooch."

Eugene shrugged her hand off with a harrumph. "No. I'm glad that scoundrel is gone. Now maybe my roses will grow proper."

But Ivy didn't relent. She grabbed Eugene's arm. "You big faker. I can see it in your eyes. You're gonna miss Al Capone. You liked having him to chase."

Eugene looked over the crowd. "All right, I admit it. Where else do you think the mutt would get steak to eat, real steak, not that gristle they serve at Personal's?"

That was when Ivy leaned down and pulled Eugene's head into her bosom. He nearly suffocated, but when she finally let him go, everyone saw a smile for the first time ever on Eugene Shrapnel's face.

"Ah, phooey," he said. "I gotta get home and into some dry clothes. This dang blame weather ain't fit for man nor beast."

That was when I noticed Stella making her way into Ivy's backyard. "Griselda. Griselda. I need to talk to you."

She stopped at Ivy. "I am so sorry for your loss. It's a terrible thing."

We all paused a moment as Studebaker threw dirt on top of Al Capone. A few minutes later he was finished and patted the mound down with the back of his shovel.

"What's the trouble, Stella?" I asked.

"It's Nate. First it was the rain, then it was the groundhog and the bugs, now it's the rain again. I swear that man is going to worry himself into an early grave — oops, sorry, Ivy."

Ivy chuckled. "All God's children gonna die sooner or later."

A crack of lightning and roll of thunder dispersed the crowd.

"At least God controlled his temper long enough for us to get him in the ground," Ivy said.

"Wish I could say the same for Nate," Stella said. "I just don't even want to be near him. Do you know that fool got so angry at the mildew that he knocked down the cow fence and is right this minute out looking for Lulabell?"

"Oh, this is getting ridiculous." I linked arms with Ivy and Stella, and we headed back to Ivy's kitchen. I saw a deep-dish cherry pie on the counter. "Is that one of Charlotte Figg's pies?" I asked. Charlotte was new to Bright's Pond. She had bought a trailer up in the Paradise Trailer Park several months ago. Charlotte Figg made better pies than anyone in town — and that included Zeb Sewickey. I'd never tell him that, but it was the truth. Ivy, Stella, and I ate pie and drank coffee and tried to come up with ways for Stella to keep Nate from going nuts every other day.

"I wish he had a brother or a friend. Another man who could help out with things," Stella said.

"I could ask Zeb, but —"

"No offense, Griselda," Stella said, "but Zeb's better off frying baloney and crimping crust. You know what I mean?"

I did. And I wasn't offended. I was only acting polite.

Ivy peered out the window toward Al Capone's grave. "I'm gonna miss him. Miss him a lot."

"I know you are," I said. I thought about suggesting she get another dog but thought better of it. Maybe too soon, yet.

"I'll just get another dog," Ivy said all of a sudden, like a cloudburst. "I know folks might think it's too soon, but he was a dog after all, not a husband."

"That's a good idea," I said.

Stella clinked her spoon on her coffee cup. "Hold on," she said. "You mean we have to wait a respectable time to replace husbands but not dogs."

"Stella Kincaid," Ivy said, "what are you planning?"

We all laughed.

"Nothing," she said. "I just like being with my girlfriends. It's . . . safe."

I pulled Stella close for a hug. "Sometimes I feel God's presence more when I'm with good friends, more than when I'm sitting in the pew. He's here, with you, with Ivy, with me, and He will lead us all through our valleys of shadow together."

That was when we all started to cry — each for a different reason, but with a common thread.

"Oh, my goodness, will you look at that!" Ivy said. "Maybe Jesus is here for a much more serious reason."

"What are you talking about?" I said.

"It's Al Capone. He's rising up from that grave."

Stella and I darted to the window. "What in jumpin' blue heck are you talking —"

She was right. Al Capone's body had risen up from his grave and was floating in a puddle.

I didn't know whether I should laugh or not, but I certainly wanted to.

"It ain't really a resurrection." Stella said. "Is it? Because I haven't ever —"

That was when Ivy punched her on the shoulder. "No, Stella, it is not a resurrection. At least I don't think so. You hear any trumpets, Griselda?"

"Nah, I didn't hear the trumpet."

"Now what?" Ivy said as she plopped herself on a kitchen chair.

"Well, we learned one thing. Grave digging should be left to the professionals."

"I shoulda known that Studebaker would screw it up," said Ivy.

"Ah, don't blame him," I said. "He doesn't know anything about how to bury a body. Can you really expect him to?"

"Nah, I guess not," Ivy said. "I better get out there and try to pin Al Capone down so he doesn't float away." Ivy buckled on her rain slicker and hat and then pulled on her matching rain boots. "I'll be right back."

Stella looked a bit pensive.

"Thinking about your brother?" I asked.

She nodded. "Yeah, I am. What if he dies, Griselda? What if he dies before he ever sees me again?"

I held her close. "That won't happen. He'll wake up. I just know it."

"But what about that woman, Gilda? Do you think I should talk to her? Let her know who I am?"

"I do, Stella. I think you need to talk to

Gilda. Meet me at the café in the morning. We'll start there."

6

The next morning I woke with a renewed vigor to get to the bottom of what was going on with Walter and Gilda Saucer — if that was her name. The more I thought about it, the more things didn't stack up.

Gilda sat at the counter, on the first stool as usual, working on a cup of coffee. She wore a tight blue skirt and white sweater and pretty much looked like she had once again just rolled in from a hard night of dancing and cavorting. It still didn't make much sense to me that if she was at the nursing home all night holding Walter's hand why she dressed so sexy. Unless, of course, she wanted him to have something nice to see when he opened his eyes.

I didn't see Stella and worried that maybe she had gotten cold feet. Most likely Nate had put her to work. She was right, that man needed another man on the farm.

"Good morning, Gilda," I said on my way

past her. I took a seat at the counter leaving two spaces between us. Zeb was in the kitchen frying eggs and scrapple. It smelled good, warm and inviting. He looked at me through the pick-up window.

"Morning, Griselda, I had a nice time the other night."

I could feel Gilda look my way. "That a girl," she said. She outlined the rim of her coffee cup with her index finger. "Glad to see someone in this town is getting some action."

I prayed I wouldn't blush. "Morning, Zeb. Yeah, the movie was good. Thank you."

Babette wiped the spot in front of me "Coffee?"

"Sure, Babs. And maybe some eggs and scrapple. It smells good this morning."

"Okie dokie, Griselda. Coming right up." I watched her write my order on a small slip of paper, then she drew a tiny heart in the corner. That had become Zeb's way of knowing it was my order. He stopped charging me for meals.

"So what did you see?" Gilda asked.

"Excuse me?" I said.

"Movie. What did you see?"

"Oh. *The Poseidon Adventure*."

"The shipwreck movie?"

I nodded.

75

"I prefer something more romantic," she said. "You know Doris Day, Cary Grant."

"Uhm, yeah, I know what you mean." Babette pushed a cup of coffee toward me and then the cream pitcher. "Thanks. But this movie was romantic in its own way. Disaster can bring people closer sometimes."

Gilda put her empty coffee cup on her saucer and watched Babette fill it. "Thanks, honey."

The café was quiet, almost too quiet. After Babette set my breakfast in front of me, Zeb made his way out of the kitchen. "What you got planned for today, Grizzy?"

"I don't know." I dipped the corner of a triangle of toast into a yolk. "I have some shopping to do, the library, and then I'll probably head on over to the nursing home, you know, check on Agnes."

"Want some company?"

"Nah, that's OK. I think I want to go alone this time. Have some stuff to discuss with her."

"I understand," Zeb said. "You want to talk about me." He winked.

That was when Studebaker and Boris came in. "Morning, all," called Stu. "Coffee, Babette, soon as you can get it."

"OK, Mr. Kowalski, I just put on a fresh pot."

I watched them take a booth. "Morning, Stu," I said. "Morning, Boris."

"Morning, Griselda," they said together.

I turned back to my meal, thinking that I did not want to get into an unscheduled Harvest Dance discussion.

"Did I hear you say nursing home?" Gilda asked, practically in a whisper. "You mean Greenbrier?"

"Yes. My sister lives there."

"Oh, that's funny," Gilda said. "I got a . . . a friend, guess you can call him that over there. In a coma."

Now, of course, I knew all of this, but she didn't know I knew. "I'm sorry to hear that."

"Ah, nothing." She waved her hand. "It's his own stupid fault. The moron got himself hurt looking for a buried treasure. Can you believe it?"

I shook my head. "Buried treasure? Around here?" It sounded ridiculous.

"I know, I know. But apparently there's some money locked in a safe buried around these parts and Walter, that's his name, Walter went exploring."

Walter. Yep. It was the same guy. "Treasure? Really?"

"Yeah." Gilda stood up and then moved closer to me. She sat down right next to me with a thud. "He said it was the loot from a robbery a few years ago. Loot from one of the coal companies up here and a bank robbery."

With that Studebaker spoke up. "Coal company?"

Gilda spun around. "This is private conversation, I beg your pardon."

"I'm sorry," Stu said. "But I used to be a miner. Worked for the Lehigh Coal Company."

"That's the one. But you didn't rob them now, didja?"

"No, but —"

"But nothin'. Now I gotta go, sister. Go visit Walter and see if he's waking up. Don't think he's ever gonna wake up, and we have to get married and all."

I shook my head. "I'm sorry, Gilda. Maybe I'll see you over there."

I watched through the window as she climbed into a yellow Pontiac convertible.

"Well, ain't she something," Studebaker said. "Ain't she all up on a high horse."

"Ah, she's upset about her fiancé," Boris said. "Poor man is in a coma. You can only hope a pretty young thing like that would care that much if it happened to you."

"Care?" Babette said. She refilled my cup. "There's something suspicious about that woman. Mom says she's a tramp. I just think she's got something up her sleeve. Maybe she just wants the treasure for herself."

"She's a good customer," Zeb said. "That's all I care about."

"But didn't you hear what she said?" It was Hazel Flatbush speaking. I didn't even know Hazel was there, but apparently she had been sitting in a back booth taking in the whole discussion. "She said they had to get married. Only one reason folks have to get married."

"Pregnant?" I said. "She doesn't look pregnant, Hazel."

"Still early," Hazel said, "and she's such a skinny-minny."

Well, if this didn't put another fly in the already too sticky ointment.

"I'm more interested in that treasure myself," Stu said. "It could be true. There were lots of robberies a while back. Coal mines and quarries used to lose their entire payroll to bandits in these parts."

"But how would a guy like Walter learn about it?" I said.

"Oh, it's easy enough," Studebaker said. "Newspaper accounts and such. Treasure hunting is kind of a sport to some people. Finders keepers and all that."

"Huh," I said, just mildly fascinated. After

79

what Stella told me about Walter being such a greedy Gus, it made sense that a man like him would go treasure hunting.

I finished my scrapple. Zeb knew how to make it crispy enough on the outside with exactly the right amount of mushiness on the inside. Then I made my way to the nursing home. Weatherwise, it had turned out to be a postcard-perfect day. I smelled oak and maple wood smoke as I made the short trip to Greenbrier — folks were already out burning leaves. The sun glinted through the many trees on the Greenbrier property, and I stood a moment and watched as a breeze stirred up fallen leaves on the parking lot like a big spoon in a pot of soup.

I found Agnes in her room sitting in her specially made wheelchair. It was good to see her out of bed. Her back was to me as she seemed to be lost, peering out the window — or so I thought.

"Griselda," she said, without turning around. "I was beginning to think you weren't coming."

"I'm here, Agnes. It's still kind of early."

"It is?" I watched her turn toward me.

"Sure. It's not even ten o'clock."

"Easy to lose track of time in here, Griselda. My routine is all different and the nurses and aides keep coming in and out giving me this pill and that pill."

I sat on the visitor chair. "How are you doing, Agnes?"

"I'm fine, just fine. Hungry though. They stopped feeding me, you know. Starving me to death."

"They didn't stop feeding you. You get what you need, according to the doctor, which is still quite a lot. It seems to be working. I think you look a little thinner."

"I am. I am. Leastways that's what my nurse said. They think I might have lost about thirty pounds already."

"Must feel good."

"I suppose. But I do miss my lemon squares."

"Well, maybe I can talk to the doctor and get him to let you have just one."

Agnes managed to wheel closer to me but with great effort. "Griselda," she said, "hand me that notebook over there and get me a pen, a blue one, and then pour my water. At least they let me have all the water I want. And then go get me a fresh straw. For heaven's sake, they expect me to use the same straw for days and days, and that one has a split going right down it and —"

"Agnes," I said. My heart pounded like a trip hammer. "Slow down. My goodness, you'd think you been sitting here all morn-

81

ing just waiting for me to get here so you could start ordering me around, get this, get that. It's like you aren't happy to see me, just my two hands and two feet, so I can be at your beck and call."

Oh, my goodness gracious, I couldn't believe I said all that. It came out like sewer water from a cracked pipe, spewing all over the place and smelling so bad.

"Beck and call," Agnes said. I watched her face turn red, like a large beefeater tomato. "Beck and call? Is that what you said?"

"That's right." My heart still pounded. "Beck and call. Just like at home."

"Well, I am so sorry, Griselda, so sorry that I am such a problem for you. It's hard for me to do things, you know. Hard for me to move around." She labored a couple of breaths. "Why . . . why you never complained before. I thought you understood. And now, now all of sudden, you're all high and mighty and too good to help your sister, your only sister." Her breathing became ragged as she needed to gasp for air.

"Agnes! Stop this. You can ring the buzzer for the nurse and ask for a new straw. You can pour your own water. What if I wasn't here for you?"

Tears ran down her cheeks.

"Ah, Agnes. Don't cry. I'm . . . I'm sorry.

Maybe I'm just in a bad mood."

"Bad mood nothing, Griselda. You meant everything you said. I am just a big, fat, really fat, bother for you."

I needed to find a way to slow my heart. I thought it might just beat right out of my chest. "It's not that. I . . . I want you to do things for yourself. Maybe if I hadn't been so easy, so darn easy all these years you'd . . . you wouldn't be here."

"Never said it was your fault."

"But I let it be. I always felt so sorry for you, so I just did what you said all the time without question."

Agnes turned away from me, which I have to say was a little anticlimactic given the fact that it took her a good couple of minutes to do what it would have taken another person a second or two. But it was Agnes's version of turning her back on me and so I let her do it.

"I never told you, Agnes, but —" I went to the window so I could see her face. "I think I might resent you. I gave up a lot to take care of you when all along you knew, you knew why you got this way and did nothing about it."

"Oh, so that's it. Go ahead, rub it in. What I did was terrible and all, but — but —"

A nurse poked her head in the door.

"Everything all right? Why, Agnes, you're just as red as a candy apple."

"It's my fault," I said. "I'm sorry."

"Maybe you should go," Agnes said. "My blood pressure is probably through the roof. And besides I don't want you to do anything you don't want to do — not anymore, not for me."

I sighed. This was not what I wanted. But I will confess that a part of me felt relieved that I had finally spoken up. Now if I could only do the same thing with Zeb and make him listen to reason and try to understand that I was enjoying my freedom just now, and it had nothing to do with him — at least I didn't think it did.

With a new courage burbling inside, I decided to speak with Zeb. I had a thing or two to tell him. For one thing, he needed to agree not to leave the movie theater unless it was a real emergency. For another thing, he needed to be willing to kiss me in front of people, well, at least hold my hand — otherwise a woman had to wonder if she was an embarrassment.

I pulled into the café lot and stepped out of the truck. But I never made it inside. Ivy Slocum caught up with me first.

"Griselda," she called from half a block

away. "I've been looking all over town for you." She picked up her pace.

"I made up my mind," she said. She wore a Penn State sweatshirt, blue jeans, and a pair of taupe Hush Puppies on her feet, I supposed in honor of Al Capone.

"About what?" I said. "Want to get a slice of pie?"

"No, no. I am just too excited."

"So spill it. You look like a kid in candy store."

"I feel like one. I want to go into Shoops, to the SPCA, and pick me out a new pooch."

"Right now? Today?"

"Yep. I'm ready."

"Why not?" I said. "Let's go." My talk with Zeb would have to wait. Except as I got back into the truck, I saw him in the café window. He shot me a look that spoke disappointment in volumes.

"Should we go by and get Ruth?" Ivy asked once she settled down in the truck cab.

"Probably. Ruth enjoys visiting the SPCA."

I pulled away from The Full Moon. "Sooooo, where's Al Capone, now? Did he ever stay buried?"

"Nope." Ivy shook her head. "He resurrected himself three times. Twice last night and once this morning in that big downpour. Floated halfway down Filbert Street. I snagged him just before he went into the sewer drain."

I started to laugh but pushed it back inside.

"Go on, laugh," Ivy said. "It's funny. God never intended us not to laugh at the funny stuff. If you coulda seen me running down Hector Street in my robe and galoshes. These ample breasts of mine flopping up and down like ducks in water. Nearly knocked myself out rounding Filbert."

"So what did you do? You couldn't have carried him back."

"No, that nice Bill Tompkins came out and carried him home. He's on the porch — Al Capone, not Bill. I made up my mind to bring him to the vet and let her — you know — do what they do."

"So we need to pick up Al Capone first?"

"Yep. If you don't mind. But I think we should get Ruth before Al Capone. It's gonna take all three of us to lift that waterlogged dog into the truck."

Ivy went to Ruth's door. "I won't be a minute."

"I am just so tickled to be going along," Ruth said as she squeezed in next to Ivy. "I can't remember the last time I went to the SPCA. It's a weird sort of place, don't you think? All them puppies and dogs and kitties that ordinarily make a person happy to see but at the same time you know they're all about to meet their maker. Now ain't that a crying shame? Just a crying shame. I want to bring them all home."

"It is a crying shame," Ivy said, "but we can't bring all the waifs home, Ruth."

Ruth pulled the door shut. "I know that, Ivy, I'm just saying I would like to bring them all home. I know I can't really do such a thing."

"Come on, you two," I said with a bit of a chuckle. "Let's get going before all the good dogs are taken."

"Let's not forget about Al Capone," Ivy said.

Ruth patted Ivy's knee. "Oh, don't you worry. Al Capone might be gone, but he'll never be forgotten."

"No, no," Ivy said. "I mean we have to go get him."

"What?" Ruth said. "But we buried him in your backyard yesterday."

"He didn't stay buried," I said. "We need to get him and take him to the vet in Shoops."

"What's she gonna do?" Ruth said. "Bring

him back to life?"

"No. She's going to cremate him," Ivy said.

Al Capone's body lay on the porch. Ivy had wrapped him as best she could in her yellow rain slicker and rain bonnet, which she had pulled down over his eyes. His tongue lolled out to one side. My heart ached when I saw him. Al Capone had been my friend also.

"You two get on his back end," Ivy said. "I'll be up front."

Ruth and I looked at each other, but we were not about to say anything to Ivy. We leaned down together to lift. A smell wafted from Al Capone's body that rivaled any of the basements in Bright's Pond. As a matter of fact, it rivaled any smell at Greenbrier.

"On my count," Ivy said. "One — two — three."

We lifted the pooch about nine inches off the ground and proceeded to carry him to the truck. I had let the tailgate down. "Now, lift," I said. And we did with a collective grunt that is probably still echoing over the mountains.

Ivy straightened the bonnet on Al Capone's head and off we rode to Shoops.

As we pulled onto the main street, I heard that same airplane from before overhead.

Leastways I thought it was the same. The pilot flew low, as if he was going to land, even though the nearest airport was in Wilkes-Barre.

"Ever been in a plane?" I asked.

"Only once," Ivy said. "Didn't care for it."

Ruth shook her head. "Too scary."

"Not to me. I think I'd really like to fly some day, you know. Go somewhere far away."

Dr. Fish greeted us and instructed a couple of her helpers to get Al Capone.

"Can I have his ashes?" Ivy asked.

"Sure," Dr. Fish said. "You come back later or tomorrow or whenever you can and we'll have them here." Dr. Fish smiled. "And again, Ivy, I am so sorry."

The SPCA was located on Sandy Hill Road, even though there was neither sand nor a hill anywhere in sight. The building sat at the end of a short driveway. We could hear the dogs barking and howling the instant we turned onto the cement drive.

"Just listen to them poor pooches," Ivy said. "I just want to take them all home."

"Do they keep birds here?" Ruth asked. "I always thought that maybe one day I'd get me one of the talking birds, you know."

"Birds?" Ivy said. "Birds? This is the

SPCA, Ruth, why would they have birds here? Ever see a *BIRD* catcher driving through town?"

"I was just asking," Ruth said. "I mean folks turn in their unwanted pets now, don't they? And birds are pets just the same as dogs."

"But you already have Russell," I said.

"Ah, he's just a little silly parakeet that doesn't talk. I was thinking about one of those mynah birds that can say real words and —"

"You can ask," I said.

I pulled into a parking spot, and we piled out of my truck. The main building was small with a high cyclone fence to one side that looked like it might have gone the complete length of the long building.

"That's the kennel," Ivy said. "All the dogs have their own cages with a door in the back so they can get let out to run and . . ."

I pulled the door open, and the barking grew louder.

"Oh, dear me," Ruth said, "they do sound so pitiful and sad."

A skinny, stringy sort of woman sat on a stool behind a short counter. Her hair was mostly gray but looked as if it had been dyed red at one time. She wore pointy glasses and a gray work shirt with two pens and a pencil poking out of the breast pocket. Her face was pinched and reminded me of a Pekingese and rightly so.

"Can I help you?' she asked, barely taking her eyes from a paper on a clipboard she was studying.

"I came for a dog," Ivy said.

"What kind of dog?" the woman asked.

"Don't know."

The woman hung the clipboard on a pegboard behind her. "Well, if you don't know what kind of dog you lost, then I can't rightly help you now, can I?"

"No," Ivy said, "you don't understand. I didn't lose a dog . . . well, I did, I mean, I lost Al Capone but not in the way you mean. He's getting cremated today."

Ruth started to chuckle. "That's right. We don't have to worry about Al Capone floating down the street anymore."

The worker blinked her eyes a couple of times. "Al Capone? Al Capone is getting cremated?"

"Not *the* Al Capone," Ivy said. "My former and now sadly deceased doggie, Al Capone. Peritonitis. Imagine that, dying from a chicken bone stuck in your works."

I watched the woman shake her head as if she had just that instant awakened from a strange dream. "Okay, so you want a new dog."

"That's right," Ivy said. "May we just take a look at them doggies in the back?"

The worker nodded. "Just come and tell me if you see one you like."

I pulled open a heavy door with a window in it, and the barking grew even louder and the smell even stronger. A row of cages went on for a very long time. The pooches barked and whimpered and whined.

"It is kind of like walking down doggie death row," I said.

"Heavens to Betsy," Ruth said. "I . . . I just can't stand the sound of all these poor animals. Do you think they know they're in line to be . . . to be . . . well, I just can't say the words."

"Euthanized," came a voice behind us. A tall teenager wearing hip-high rubber boots and carrying a dripping hose squeezed past us. "Excuse me, but I got to spray down the cages."

There were big dogs, little dogs, some in between. A few jumped and bounced as we passed by and others cowered as if they were afraid of us.

"Poor thing," Ivy said, stopping in front of a cage with a medium-sized dog that looked to be part German shepherd and part something else. "Look at him. He looks so gall darn sad."

It was true. He was the saddest dog I had ever seen. He sat hunched on his rump, looking up at us with wide, glazed-over eyes. He seemed to be imploring us to set him free.

"He's the one," Ivy said. Then she got real silent, and I saw a tear drip from her eye.

"What's wrong, Ivy?" I put my hand on her shoulder.

"I was just this second imagining what could have been if that Mildred Blessing had ever arrested Al Capone. She woulda brought him here to be . . . to be."

"Now, now, Ivy. We all know Mildred never really wanted to arrest Al Capone. She enjoyed the hunt too much."

Ivy nodded her head. "I guess so, but first thing I'm doing is getting him some dog tags, you know?"

"Good idea, Ivy. I'd do it today. And teach him to stay out of Eugene's rose garden," I said.

Ruth had wandered off down the row and was talking to the boy with the hose. I couldn't hear what she was saying to him over the din of the dogs. But she all of a sudden came running back to us. "Did you hear that? Did you hear that? That young fella just told me they did get a bird in last week, but nobody claimed it and . . . and, well, they had to put it down." She sniffed. "When I think of someone putting down my dear sweet Russell, I . . . I . . ."

Ivy tapped Ruth's shoulder. "Not now, Ruth. This ain't about you getting a bird. It's about this poor, sad animal that sits here before us begging for a home. Just look at him."

Ruth crouched down and put her hand through the cage. The doggie licked her palm. "He is a sweet thing, Ivy. I think you should claim him."

"He is a cutie," I said, "and seems to have a good disposition." The dog's eyes grew wider as though he understood what I said. His tongue lolled out to the left.

"See them spots on his tongue?" Ivy said. "That's a sign of a good dog."

"You sure?" Ruth said. "There was that dog down the street. He had spots and was the meanest beast alive."

"That don't mean he was a bad dog. Just maybe his training was wrong."

Ivy removed the pink index card from the cage. It was stuffed in a plastic sleeve hanging on a chain. "Says here he's nine months old, a male, part Shepherd with some coonhound in him. And according to this he was given to the SPCA on account of a child developed allergies. Oh, and his name is Mickey Mantle."

The dog perked up the instant he heard his name.

"He musta been named after the ball player," I said. "That's funny, Ivy. First you had Al Capone and now you have Mickey Mantle."

Ivy patted the dog's head. "Mickey Mantle it is. Great name. Number Seven was the best baseball player ever."

Ruth and I followed Ivy to the front desk where the worker sat munching on a doughnut. "Find one you like?" she asked as a drop of red jelly dripped onto the counter.

"Yes, I did," Ivy said. "This here, Mickey Mantle."

The woman took the card and after Ivy signed some papers saying she would take good care of him and have him neutered, we were on our way back to Bright's Pond. Ivy sat in the truck bed with Mickey Mantle.

It gave Ruth and me a chance to talk, and we weren't so squeezed in the truck cab with Ivy in the back. Every so often I glanced in the rear view and saw Ivy sitting there with her arm draped around Mickey Mantle.

"Anyway," Ruth said, "I am glad Ivy got

herself a doggie and all. I knew she was lonesome."

"I am, too, Ruth."

We were silent a few blocks. Both of us kind of sizing the other up like we both wanted to say something but didn't know how to start. Finally, Ruth spoke. "Now, I know something is going on around here, Griselda," she said. "And not just with Ivy. Are you gonna tell me?"

I rolled the window down a little. It was starting to get warm in the truck even though I didn't think the temperature had gotten above sixty yet. "Ruth, I know a little secret, but you got to promise me you won't tell another soul."

"Oh, of course," Ruth said. "Cross my heart." And she did. Her eyes gleamed like a woman about to learn the secret recipe for Twinkies.

"I promised Stella I wouldn't tell anyone until she was ready, but . . . well, that woman who rented Cora's house —"

"The hussy everyone is talking about?"

"She's not a hussy."

Ruth straightened her back against the truck seat. "Really, Griselda? What do you know?"

I told her all about Walter in Greenbrier and how Stella is all upset and not sure what to do.

Ruth barely breathed through the whole story. It wasn't until we reached Ivy's street that she spoke. "I just knew it. I just knew something was up and to tell the truth, Griselda, I always thought Stella was hiding things about where she came from and why she even moved to Bright's Pond. I think Mildred is right about her."

I pulled up to Ivy's house. Ivy came around to the side of the truck. "Thank you, Griselda. I'm going to take Mickey Mantle inside now and show him around. Think I'll buy him a nice doggie bowl, maybe one of them cute ceramic ones with the word *Dog* on it, you know."

"That's fine, Ivy. I'll talk to you later."

Ruth said good-bye and we watched Ivy and Mickey Mantle saunter up to her porch. They both turned. Ivy waved and for a second I thought I saw a mighty mischievous glint in Mickey Mantle's eye.

I heard Ruth's stomach growl, and it reminded me about that talk I wanted to have with Zeb. It was getting close to early supper hour.

"You hungry, Ruth?"

"I sure am."

"Let's head to the café. I need a bite myself."

She laughed. "That's funny, after just coming from the pound and all."

The Full Moon was crowded as usual for supper. We took a booth toward the middle of the cafe.

"This is nice," I said. "Been a while since you and I had dinner together without there being some reason for it."

"Sure is," Ruth said. "First time I've been in here in a long time when I wasn't discussing the Harvest Dance or some other church business."

I tried to spy Zeb and caught the top of his paper hat moving around behind the kitchen pick-up window. Dot Handy had just slapped two more orders on the turnstile and I heard her holler at him. "I got a couple of mighty hungry truckers out here, Zeb. Better put the throttle down."

"Yeah, yeah, tell them to go honk their horns. I'm cooking as fast as I can."

"Uh oh," I said. "Sounds like Zeb is off to a rough start this evening."

Dot came over and filled our coffee cups. "How are you girls doing?"

"Good," Ruth said. "We just got back from Shoops."

"Uh-huh, that's nice. You girls catch a glimpse of that hussy over at the counter. She blew in about ten minutes ago. Funny how she came back after just being here for meatloaf."

I looked around Dot's wide hips and saw Gilda at the counter. Bleached hair piled a mile on top of her head. She sat cross-legged at the counter, which hiked her tight skirt nearly to her waist. Her gold sweater made her breasts pop out like small torpedoes.

"She's got on one of them pointy bras," Ruth said. "Now why would any woman want her breasts to look like they been ground to a point in a pencil sharpener?"

I snorted coffee I laughed so hard. "Stop it, Ruth. We don't even know her."

"She's that hussy," Dot said. "The one that —"

"Dot, pickup," hollered Zeb.

"Be right back."

I watched Dot deal out three plates full of breakfast foods onto the truckers' table and pour coffee. She hurried back to us before I had time to explain anything to Ruth. "Anyway, she's the hussy that moved into Cora's house."

"Oh, dear," Ruth said. "Poor dead Cora."

I swallowed. It was all I could do to keep from spilling the beans about Stella to Dot.

"Gilda?" Ruth said, looking at me.

"Yep," Dot said. "She's a hussy. Hussies

always got them kind of odd-ball names."

I shook my head. "Maybe we should just order our supper and let the woman alone."

"Good idea, Griselda," Dot said. "She looks like she frequents one of them . . . swanky bars down in Shoops though, don't she?"

We ordered our meals, and Dot went behind the counter.

"So that's her? The woman that's mixed up with Stella's long-lost brother who's in a coma. Sounds like a soap opera."

The woman, Gilda, finished her coffee and got up to leave. She paid her bill to Dot and left without once looking our way or any way except where she was going. Of course, her breasts made it out the door two minutes before she did.

I took a breath. I hoped she was in love with Walter and not what everyone else thought. "She could have been up all night with Walter," I said.

"Dressed like that," Ruth said. "I doubt it, Griselda. I doubt that a lot."

7

Sundays in Bright's Pond pretty much revolved around church and dinner. Dinners that could somehow make the whole previous week worth the while. Of course, when Agnes was still at home, I needed to cook for her quite often, but there were many a Sabbath when Ruth and our friend Vidalia, God rest her soul, and even Ivy Slocum would happen by with beef roasts the size of Agnes's forearm. They would place yellow bowls of steamy mashed potatoes and vegetables on the table alongside hot biscuits yearning for butter and gravy.

And there were the pies, fresh from Ruth's oven or Zeb's café. Blueberry in spring, apple in winter, pumpkin in the fall. Summer was the domain of Full Moon pie.

That Sunday started out no differently, except for one big difference. Zeb met me at the church door. He wasn't what you would call a churchgoing kind of man, although it never occurred to me to question his faith.

"Zeb." I smiled. "You coming to the service?"

"Thought I'd give it a try."

Ruth interrupted us. "Griselda. I've been looking for you. I need to get started on those bandanas we talked about for the dance — oh, excuse me, Zeb, fancy meeting you here."

"Morning, Ruth," Zeb said.

She turned her attention back to me. "I was wondering if you got any books up at the library that would give me a nice western scene to look at. I thought it would help set the mood and maybe give me some ideas about cowboy costumes — you know, vests and chaps and all. I thought I might whip together some western duds for folks. Maybe a few vests or bananas."

"Ban-DAN-as, not bananas,"

"I know that," Ruth said. "It just slipped off my tongue like that."

Zeb laughed. "This is gonna be one swinging hoedown."

"Yes, it should be fun," Ruth said. "Hope you can square dance."

"Oh, don't you worry about me. I got some dosey in my dosey doe. What about you, Griselda?"

The thought of square dancing made me cringe, so I turned my attention back to Ruth. "Sure, Ruth, come up to the library later, and I'll see if I can find you some pictures."

Her eyes darted between me and Zeb. "Two's company, three's a crowd. I'll let you two alone."

Zeb and I greeted a few more people and made our way through the crowd into the sanctuary. I spotted Ruth sitting right smack dab in the middle of one of the back rows. Her little blue handbag rested on the place next to her like she was saving it for someone. "Let's sit with Ruth. I don't want her to think we don't want to be with her."

"Sure," Zeb said.

Studebaker and Boris made a point of saying hello, as did Hazel Flatbush and Dot Handy. Edie Tompkins came by. "Well, hello, Griselda. Why, Zeb Sewickey, fancy seeing you here. And, Griselda, so nice to see you out with . . . with a friend."

"We're at church, Edie," I said. "We're not on a date or anything."

She pursed her lips. "Uh-huh, it is nice to see you out, like I said. Not having Agnes to take care of all day must be quite . . . refreshing. Guess you feel like you lost a ton of weight." I watched her nostrils flare.

103

That was when Sheila Spiney, who played the piano, began the Introit, and the music filled the small auditorium like smoke fills a pub. Folks gathered themselves together and took seats. I watched the people from the Paradise Trailer Park file in like inmates from the state hospital. The one woman who always wears that heavy brown sweater always did intrigue me.

Edie and her husband, Bill, sat in front of me. As much as I hated to admit it, and would certainly never admit to Edie Tompkins, the biggest gossip in Bright's Pond, I was relieved not to have Agnes to take care of anymore. Yet that morning as the hymn music, sweet and subtle, swooned around the room, I felt a tug in my heart, a tug that made me regret I told Agnes I resented her. I wished I could have taken it all back. Agnes never set out to hurt me. Events of the past were exactly that — the past, and I needed to let it go.

It was difficult to listen to Pastor Speedwell's sermon. I reckoned I heard it all before anyway, but between my falling out with Agnes stuck in my head and Zeb's body so close to mine, I gave up on the preaching.

"So Grizzy, how about if we head out for lunch?" Zeb asked about two seconds after

Pastor Speedwell said the benediction. "We can head over to the café and —"

"No, I . . . I need to go see Agnes."

"Agnes? For heaven's sake, Griselda, you are still tied to that woman. It's like she never moved to Greenbrier."

Fortunately, Ruth intervened. "Maybe you can help me find those western pictures, Griselda, when you get back from visiting Agnes. I think it's nice that you go on over there when you can. She needs you. And it's nice to be needed."

Zeb took my hand and gave me a little pull. "Come on, let's go shake Speedwell's hand, and if you want I'll go to Greenbrier with you."

"OK, I just want to stop at home and freshen up and maybe find a treat for Agnes."

That was when Zeb stopped short in his tracks, forcing Hazel Flatbush to ram into me. She apologized and scooted around.

"You don't mean food now, do you? Didn't Doc Flaherty say Agnes's diet was everyone's concern, that we needed to stop bringing her sweets and treats and pie?"

I looked at my shoes. "I know. It . . . it's just that I had a few words with her so I wanted to make it up, I suppose."

"Best thing you can do is let it go and not

bring her any food."

"OK, OK, I still need to stop home and visit the bathroom, maybe get a drink of something before we head over there."

We never made it to Greenbrier that day. Stella was sitting on my porch steps waiting for me. I barely set a foot on the property when she started talking.

"I did what you said, Griselda, I told Nate about Walter, and he went off the deep end. Said he didn't have time to take care of no brother-in-law he never met and one that cheated me out of my inheritance to boot."

"Why did you tell him that, Stella?" I pushed open the front door.

"It all just came out."

"Come on inside."

Zeb didn't follow us.

"Are you coming in?" I asked.

"No, Griselda. I can see you have other people to take care of now."

I swallowed. "But, Zeb, this is important."

Zeb kissed my cheek. "So am I. So are we."

I waited until Zeb was out of sight. "That man infuriates me. It's like I'm supposed to be alive for him and him only."

"Men," Stella said. "They're all big babies."

"Yep. When he needs to run over to the café at the drop of a hat, even leave me alone at the movie, well, that's all OK, but if I need to do something, then it's a big fat problem."

I headed into the kitchen and started coffee percolating.

"Now, what do I do, Griselda? Nate is so awful mad at me right now, and I still haven't seen Walter, and I have yet to convince myself that I even want to so maybe telling Nate was a little premature anyway."

But I was too preoccupied thinking about Zeb to answer. I heard her all right. I heard every word she said. I just didn't really care all that much just then.

"Griselda, are you listening to me?"

I sat at the kitchen table. "Of course, Stella. I think you should be glad the cat's out of the bag. Now maybe Nate will help you figure things out."

"Nah, he's too angry at me. Claims I lied to him even though I don't get the big deal."

"Men don't need a big deal to get them in a swivet, you know. Just about anything can change their world, and they don't like it, I suppose. In a way I see Zeb's point, but what am I supposed to do? Totally ignore Agnes and my friends?"

"We were talking about me," Stella said.

I stood and grabbed two cups with saucers and carried a half of a pumpkin pie to the table. "I think I have whipped cream in the fridge. So what are you gonna do?"

"Oh, I reckon I'll ride it out like I do practically everything else. A person can ride out just about anything if she sets her mind to it."

Stella and I sat for a while talking about everything but our most obvious problems until the doorbell rang. It was Ruth Knickerbocker, carrying a beef stew in a blue and white Wedgewood casserole dish.

"I can't eat it all by myself," she said. "So I figured I would take a chance that you were home and I see that I'm right."

"Come on in, Ruth, Stella's in the kitchen."

"Stella Kincaid. Well, that's fine, Griselda, just fine."

The afternoon didn't slow down until six o'clock that evening, after Ruth and I returned from the library with three Xerox copies of scenes of Dodge City showing a saloon and wooden walkways, which gave me an idea to see if Nate and Studebaker might build a wooden walkway leading to the town hall. I just came in the house when I heard the phone ring.

I answered. It was Agnes.

"How come you never came today, I was waiting for you, or are you still mad at me?"

"I'm not mad, Agnes, I got sidetracked. I'll come out tomorrow, OK?"

"Bring me pie, Griselda. I haven't had a taste of pumpkin all season long."

"It's only been fall for less than two weeks. And the doctor said you can't have sweets."

She hung up on me for the first time in my life.

8

Monday morning came all too quickly. Awakened by the sound of rain splattering against the windows and the wind howling around outside like a pack of wolves, I pulled the covers tighter. "Great day to go to Greenbrier."

I might have stayed in bed another half an hour, I'm not certain, I only know that I couldn't listen to Arthur's incessant mewling anymore and made my way to the kitchen. I plopped wet food, Seafood Banquet, into his bowl and then flipped on the radio in time to hear that a riot had broken out in Chile and that a new movie called *The Exorcist* was playing at the Wilkes-Barre Drive-In.

Seven o'clock was way too early to go to Greenbrier. One thing I learned was that visiting in the morning left me open to seeing and smelling things I would rather not. It was always best to wait until closer to lunch time, after the nurses and aides got the residents settled and secure for the morning in fresh gowns or clothes, medicines had been doled out, and most of the folks were sitting upright in wheelchairs or at tables in the common areas.

Hoping she hadn't already had breakfast and was out and about on her wanderings, I called Ruth and invited her over for eggs and toast.

"Of course, Griselda, I'll be right over. I was feeling a little . . . all by myself this morning also. You know how much I miss my Bubba."

"I know, Ruth, so why don't you come on over. I'll get eggs scrambled."

Ruth was always good for company, and I will admit that I was feeling lonelier than ever. It might have had something to do with the growing tension between Agnes and me or maybe it had something to do with Zeb. Land o' Goshen, only God knew where that was leading! I liked Zeb well enough, and I guess you could say we had been dating on and off for several years. But Agnes always seemed to get in the way. Now that she was pretty much out of the picture, you would think it would get easier. Still, I seemed to find other things to distract me or pull me away from him.

I scrambled four large brown eggs in a red bowl, placed four slices of toast in the toaster, and got the pan heated. It wouldn't take Ruth long to get to the house — even walking she could be here in five minutes. But I wanted to wait before I started the eggs.

Sure enough, a couple of minutes later, I heard the doorbell.

"Hey, Griselda, thank you for asking me over."

"Sure thing, Ruth, come on inside. I just have to cook the eggs."

I poured the beaten eggs into the hot pan. They sizzled a second, and I worked them around with a fork until they were fluffy and sunshiny yellow.

"What's the real reason you called me over here, Griselda?" Ruth shook salt and pepper onto her eggs.

I smiled and sipped coffee. "Just for company, Ruth. I have a sort of busy day between the library, visiting Agnes, and then the Committee meeting tonight. Are we meeting at the café or the town hall?"

"It's at the town hall tonight. Boris said the library is too cold, and he thought we'd get more done away from the distractions of the café — if you know what I mean."

"If you are referring to me and Zeb —"

"No, no, well, not altogether, I mean. I think that hussy woman, Gilda Syrup —"

"Saucer. Gilda Saucer."

"Gilda Saucer is creating a ruckus, and she seems to be there so much. Why she won't eat at her own house is beyond me."

I stared down at my uneaten eggs. "It's hard to eat alone in an empty house, especially when the person you love is gone."

Ruth stood and grabbed the coffee pot. She filled our cups. "Are you talking about Agnes now?"

"I suppose. She and I had some words."

"Words? The dickens you say. Why you and Agnes never argue, leastways not since that unfortunate turn of events last year, but that was understandable considering everything but —"

"I can't explain it, Ruth. I just all of a sudden resent her or something. It's like my eyes have been opened to how much she took advantage of me, and I needed to tell her."

"But she couldn't help it, Griselda. She being so . . . so fat and all. She needed you."

I took a breath and finished my eggs. Ruth probably couldn't understand what I was really saying and that was OK. Just having her there to listen was good enough. I knew Agnes and I would figure things out —

eventually.

"So how're things at the library?" Ruth looked pensive a second or two. "I just realized something while I was sitting here."

"What's that?"

"You do a lot of things alone, don't you — living, working."

I patted Ruth's hand. "Thank Jesus I have good friends."

"I got started on making bandanas," Ruth said. "I hope no one minds but I found this pretty red and blue paisley print. Course the art society at the high school will paint the background scenery like they always do, and they always do such a nice job. But I thought I'd make a batch of bandanas for folks. Hand them out as they turn in their tickets."

"Sounds good by me, Ruth. I can't wait to see what you come up with."

"I hope to get one finished before the meeting tonight. There's really nothing to making them. Pretty much hemming a square."

We yakked a little while longer until I decided it was time to get over to the library and Ruth needed to get back to making bandanas and cowboy vests. I dropped her off in front of her house. "See you tonight."

"OK, Griselda, thanks for breakfast."

■ ■ ■ ■

I drove up to the top of Filbert Street and parked near Hector's Hill — a place where I had a clean view of the large, empty field that seemed to go on forever, the place where Ruth and I flew kites in memory of friends who have passed. It was still only ten o'clock and I remembered I wanted to listen to Vera Krug's *Good Neighbor Show.* She always reported the happenings in Bright's Pond, even though she lives in Shoops. She does it as a service because Ruth is her sister-in-law — although they don't much act like family. I wanted to see if she mentioned the Harvest Dance.

I tuned in WQRT. For some reason the reception was always better in my truck if I parked on top of the hill and kept the wipers flapping — which I didn't really need anymore. The rain had stopped and the sun peeked out from the clouds.

But then, in a sudden flash I saw something out the passenger side window I had never seen in Bright's Pond. An airplane, a small airplane, making absolutely no sound, like a glider was flying slow and frighteningly low. It was the same plane I had seen twice before.

"It's gonna land on Hector's Hill," I said out loud. "Oh, my goodness gracious!"

And sure enough, I watched as the small white plane with blue stripes landed. First the back two wheels touched ground and spit up dust into a swirly cloud and then it seemed to hop and skip a few seconds until the front wheel made contact and the plane jostled to a complete stop. All without making much of a sound at all.

I dropped the truck into drive and moved as close as I could to the plane, thinking that maybe the pilot was hurt or sick or worse. I jumped out of the truck and headed toward the plane. At first I didn't see any movement. Nobody climbed out of the plane, and I started to think maybe I should proceed with more caution. So I continued to creep up on it and then stood still as the door opened up and the pilot hopped out.

He stood there like a mannequin at first. Then he shook his head and rubbed the back of his neck.

"Hello," I waved to get his attention. "Are you all right?"

He waved back. "I'm fine. It's my plane that's broken."

I moved closer, the whole time thinking that Zeb would be telling me I was nuts for getting so close to a strange man — no telling what kind of maniac he is. But seriously, I couldn't imagine any self-respecting axe murderer to be landing on Hector's Hill at twenty past ten on Monday morning. Just didn't make any sense.

"Is everything all right?" I asked when I was standing about five feet away from him.

"Not sure. My oil light flashed on, and I thought I'd better cut my engine and ease her down in case it was leaking, and from the smell I'd say I'm right."

The pilot was tall, I'd say over six feet, with sandy blond hair that waved in the slight breeze, a leftover from the brief rain. His chin was square and strong. He needed a shave, but I kind of liked the dirty face look.

"My name is Cliff Cardwell." He extended his hand. His rough palm felt good against my smooth hand.

"I'm Griselda Sparrow," I said.

"Pleased to meet you, Mrs. Sparrow."

"Miss." I took my hand back.

He smiled into my eyes and my heart skipped a beat. "Is there anything I can do to help?" I asked, feeling suddenly nervous even though I wasn't sure why. "Do you need to make a call or anything?"

"I need to look under the hood first, so to

117

speak, and see if I can figure out what happened."

I watched as he unhooked the engine cover and pushed it open. He looked inside like he was any old mechanic checking under the hood of car.

"Creepin' red lizards," he said. "Cracked a hose. It's leaking all over."

He stood straight and wiped his forehead with the back of his hand. "I need to replace it."

"Not sure where you get airplane parts around here. Nearest airport is in Wilkes-Barre."

"That's where I was headed. Wilkes-Barre." He looked around. "So where am I, exactly?"

"You are exactly on top of Hector's Hill, but the name of our town is Bright's Pond."

"Bright's Pond. I never heard of it."

"Most haven't."

"So, Miss Sparrow, can you point me in the direction of a telephone booth?"

"I can drive you into town. The Full Moon Café. You can make a call there."

"And get a cup of coffee?" He smiled again in a way that made the gold flecks in his brown irises dance.

I parked out front of the café next to Studebaker's baby blue Caddy.

"There's a phone right inside the door."

"Thanks, you coming in?" he asked.

"I was planning on opening the library — that's me, the librarian. But maybe I should introduce you to everyone first."

"I'd like that. Maybe somebody inside would know where I can find what I need."

"OK, but I don't know where you'd begin to find airplane parts around here."

"Oh, any farm would have what I need most likely."

"Really? Then you might want to talk to Nate Kincaid."

He opened the door and hopped out.

"Nate?"

"Yep. He's a farmer. Raises corn and pumpkins. Has a few cows."

"Sounds like a start."

"I doubt he's in the café, but you can make your call at least and then maybe one of the fellas will get you out to the farm."

The café was not very crowded and there was no sign of Gilda. I saw Stu and Boris in their usual booth, probably talking about the dance or some silly political issue.

"Zeb," I called. "Come on out here."

Dot Handy was taking orders. Babette was mostly likely at school.

"Where you sitting, Griselda?" she asked.

"I'm not staying. I just brought this man,

Cliff —"

"Cardwell," he said.

"He had to land his plane up on the Hector's Hill. It was an emergency. He needs to make a phone call."

That was when I watched Boris jump to his feet. "See, I told you. I told you a plane just landed up there. But no one believed me. I saw you pass over the town hall not a half hour ago."

Cliff laughed. "That's right. I cracked an oil line. I thought it would be safer to land than to chance making it all the way to Wilkes-Barre. When I saw that beautiful field, I took a chance it would be OK and landed Matilda, quick and sweet."

Boris moved out from the booth. "Told you, Studebaker." He walked close to us and extended his hand. "I'm Boris Lender, First Selectman of Bright's Pond. Welcome to our town."

"Thank you," Cliff said. "Hope you don't mind me landing on your field. I really had no choice."

Boris put his hand on Cliff's shoulder like he was a returning war hero and about to receive the key to the city. "No problem. No problem at all. I'm just glad we had a field big enough."

Zeb came out from the bathroom adjusting his apron.

"Zeb," I said, "come meet Cliff Cardwell. He's a pilot who made an emergency landing up on Hector's."

"Really? Holy cow! A real emergency landing? I didn't hear anything."

Cliff shook Zeb's hand. "Nothing too exciting. Just a hose. So I cut the engine and let her drift in real peaceful and smooth."

Well, I got to say that the men swooned over Cliff the pilot like women swooned over Cary Grant. Dot and I exchanged glances and snickers.

I whispered into Dot's ear. "He isn't Charles Lindbergh."

Dot laughed. "No, he's cuter than Lindbergh."

She was right about that, but I was not about to admit that to Dot.

"Maybe I'll have a cup of coffee," I said. "It's a lot more interesting here than at the library."

"Sure," Dot said. "How often does a pilot land in Bright's Pond?"

I sat at the counter and only overheard snippets of conversation until Nate Kincaid's name was brought up. Studebaker offered to take Cliff to the Kincaid's farm.

"I'm sure Nate will have what you need,"

Stu said.

"But what's your hurry?" Boris said. "Can you sit awhile, get something to eat? Zeb makes a heck of a baloney sandwich."

"Sure thing," Cliff said. "I'm a bit hungry, but I will need to make a call first. I was expected at a . . . a meeting in Wilkes-Barre."

Studebaker and Boris watched Cliff make his way to the telephone like they were watching a celebrity. He smiled at me on his way past. "Thank you, Griselda, for helping me out."

"I'm just glad I was there, Cliff." This time I smiled into his eyes.

He reached into his pants pocket and pulled out loose change. He counted through it and then turned to Dot. "I don't suppose I could get change for a dollar."

"Oh, sure thing," Dot said. "I can give you all dimes and nickels."

"Thank you," Cliff said as he handed her what looked like a freshly minted dollar bill.

Zeb came out from the kitchen and leaned on the counter near me while Cliff made his phone call.

"Can you believe it, Grizzy, the way Stu and Boris are acting toward that fella?"

"Uhm, they are a mite smitten now, aren't they?"

I glanced at Cliff in time to see him remove his leather jacket.

"Smitten," I repeated. "They sure are."

9

I excused myself and was heading for my truck when I saw Ruth running down the street. "Griselda!" she called. "Griselda! Did you see it? Did you see that . . . that thing, whatever it was flying so close to us? It zoomed right over my house and then it disappeared. Disappeared like a rabbit down a hole. Poof." She huffed and puffed.

"I did, Ruth, I did. It was an airplane. The pilot landed on Hector's Hill."

She stopped close to me. "I need to catch my breath. I sure got a fright, especially when it disappeared like that, and it was flying so quiet. Not making a sound. Then it disappeared right out of the sky. Are you sure it's not a UFO?"

"It's an airplane, a small airplane. He turned off the engine and let the plane glide in for a landing. I was there. Saw the whole thing."

"Really, Griselda. You saw it? But . . . but

what happened? Is the pilot OK? Did it catch fire? Airplanes do that you know. They explode."

"He's fine. He's inside the café talking to Boris and Stu. His name is Cliff Cardwell."

"Imagine that," Ruth said. "A plane landing on Hector's Hill. This is just so exciting. And you say he's inside?"

"Yep. Go on in and meet him. I need to get to the library."

"Are you planning to make up with Agnes?" Ruth pulled her sweater around her as the breeze kicked up again. "I was so excited when I saw the plane land I didn't think of how cold it is."

"I can give you a ride home if you like?"

She glanced at my truck and then at the café door. "Nah, maybe I'll just go inside. You know, get a slice of pie. Stu will drive me back."

I smiled. "Sure, Ruth. I'll see you at the meeting tonight."

"Seven o'clock," she said.

The library was cold. I cranked up the heat, sat at my desk, and opened the morning's mail. There was nothing too exciting as usual, bills that I would give to Boris, a couple of publishers catalogs I would bring home and read later, and the usual junk mail.

The door opened and in walked Tohilda Best, the president of the Society of Angelic Philanthropy.

"Griselda," she called, "I was beginning to think you weren't gonna open today."

"I'm sorry, Tohilda. There was a little excitement. Seems a pilot made an emergency landing on Hector's Hill."

"I heard all about it. Everyone is talking about it. I heard he was a government agent forced to make an emergency landing after he learned that his plan had been sabotaged."

I laughed so hard I snorted. "No, no. Where in the world did you hear that? He's just a regular guy from what I can tell. His oil hose broke. That's all."

"That's a good thing because I didn't really believe all that about him being a secret agent and all. What in tarnation would an agent be doing in Bright's Pond, Griselda?"

"Nothing that I can think of. Now how can I help you?"

"Well, I was just wondering if we could have a meeting here in a little while. There's been three more births out in the backwoods, and we need to decide on what to bring them — if we can find them."

"Sure, do you know what time you want to meet?"

Tohilda looked at the clock on the wall behind me. "I told the girls to be here at eleven o'clock. Is that all right?"

"Sure is. I just need to get on over to Greenbrier later."

"Oh, I understand, Griselda. Such a service you do for your sister. How is she anyway? Losing weight, I hear."

"You heard that right. She's doing OK. A little cantankerous from time to time."

"I can well imagine after eating anything she wanted all those years and now being so . . . so what's the word?"

"Restricted?"

"That's it."

I nodded. "You can set up over at the periodicals table. Should I put the pot on?"

"Would you mind, Griselda? I know the girls will enjoy coffee, and I have brownies in my bag. Made them fresh this morning. Might even still be a little warm."

Tohilda made her way to the long, heavy table. She set out a tablet of paper and a couple of pencils, which were sharpened to a deadly point. Then she removed a sack of brownies from her bag, which she placed on the table.

I brought a paper plate to her for the brownies. "Maybe they'll look more appetizing on a plate," I said. "They smell so good."

"Take one."

I did and it was delicious, and I had to fight the urge to bring one for Agnes.

At eleven o'clock on the button, the library door opened and in walked the entire SOAP committee, Ruth Knickerbocker among them. She enjoyed doing charitable things for folks, but I never knew if it was the charity or the secretiveness of it that she liked — the sneaking around. I read an old adage somewhere that said, "Do good and forget it." That was Ruth. She never talked about the SOAP's doings.

I greeted the ladies and left them alone to do their planning.

By twelve-thirty I was on my way to Greenbrier — the perfect time. Just after lunch when Agnes would be settled and happiest.

"Didn't think you would come," she said. She was in her wheelchair. She wore a flowered housedress with snap buttons and wide pockets she had stuffed with tissues. Her feet had been squeezed into yellow slippers, and her hair was a little greasy and shorter than I remembered it.

"Did they cut your hair, Agnes?"

"Yes. The nurses said it would be easier to keep clean."

"How often do they wash it?"

She touched the bangs and then rubbed her fingertips together. "Not often enough."

"Maybe I can wash it while I'm here."

"Oh, could you, Griselda? They have that big, wide shower down the hall. Big enough to accommodate the chair. You can come right inside and wash it. Could you, please?"

I remembered Jesus' words. "Whatever you did for the least of these, you did for me." Although you couldn't tell by looking, Agnes was indeed one of the least in my mind now.

"I will," I said.

Agnes looked out the window. "The trees are really turning. Look at the colors out there, Griselda. I so enjoy the view."

"It is pretty, Agnes. It's like they all of a sudden burst into flame. I was worried there wouldn't be much color this year."

"But God came through again — especially with the sugar maples."

"There was some excitement in town today."

"Really. Tell me. Tell me slow."

I told Agnes about the plane landing and about Cliff Cardwell and how Ruth thought it was a UFO.

"I left him at the café. I think they were getting ready to take him over to the Kincaids' farm. He said any good farmer would have what he needs to get his plane flying again."

"That's good. I like to hear that the people are rallying together."

"Sure are. I think the guys — Stu and Boris and even Zeb — are pretty impressed with him."

She laughed. "They are such boys. Bet they all want a chance to go for a ride with him. You know, soar over Bright's Pond."

For a second I let myself think about that. It would be nice, to be up in the sky, soaring through clouds, looking down on the earth like a bird. "You'd see things in such a different way, wouldn't you, Agnes? I mean from up there. Up in the sky."

"Seems to me you wouldn't mind a turn either."

I smiled. "How 'bout if we see about that shampoo?"

"OK, OK. But first I got to hear about Stella. Did she see her brother yet?"

I shook my head and sat on Agnes's bed. "Not yet. She did tell Nate though, and he's madder than a hatter over it."

"Why?"

"Oh, I think he's more angry that Stella

lost out on that inheritance money."

"Makes sense. How they getting along otherwise?"

"Not great. But there was a glimmer of bliss the other day. Nate finally killed that groundhog that was threatening Bertha Ann."

Agnes laughed. It was the first time in a couple of weeks that I've seen her laugh so hard.

"It's nice," I said.

"What is?"

"Seeing you laugh."

"I reckon I've been a mite surly, Griselda. This isn't easy, you know. And . . . and well, I've been thinking. I need to say I'm sorry. I'm sorry I took advantage, if that's what you call it. Believe it or not, it wasn't easy to let you do everything for me."

"I understand. I guess I should have stood my ground more."

"But I do so love your tuna sandwiches, Griselda, and your iced tea. And I think I miss lemon squares more than anything."

I made a mental note that I would sneak one lemon square the next time.

"Now about that shampoo, Griselda? My scalp is so blessed itchy."

I nodded my head. Change would not be easy.

10

The phone started to ring the second I set foot in the library. I made it a point to be there around three o'clock for the school kids. There were always three or four regulars who came by to study, and then there were the ones who came in because they didn't want to incur the wrath of a parent for not getting their homework done — usually a research project or a book report. And truth be known, I enjoyed helping the children,

Zeb was on the phone. "How about coming over to the café for dinner before the committee meeting?"

"I don't know. I have a lot to catch up on around here," I said.

"Ah, come on, Grizzy."

"OK, if the kids clear out in time, I'll meet you at the cafe. Are you coming to the meeting or —"

"Yep. Gonna close the café early. Mondays

are my slowest evening. Probably make a habit out of closing early on Monday."

"How did Cliff make out?" I asked.

"Cliff?"

"Yeah, silly, the pilot? Cliff Cardwell."

"Oh, Grizzy, why you so interested in him?"

I felt my dander get up slightly. "I am not interested, just concerned."

"He's fine as far as I know. Studebaker took him over to Nate Kincaid's farm. That's the last I heard, except I do know that plane of his is still up on the hill."

"OK." I was distracted by a group of students coming in. "I gotta go. I'll see you around five."

I closed up the library as soon as the last student, Mercy Lincoln, checked out her book-report book, *Something Wicked This Way Comes* by Ray Bradbury.

"This is a great book," I told her.

"Oh, I know that, Miz Griselda. Teacher said this here Ray Bradbury is top dog."

"She's right."

She smiled and we walked out of the library together. We stood on the steps together each of us taking a deep, long breath of fresh air. "Miz Griselda," she said. "Do you think a girl like me could grow up

133

to be a writer like him?"

"I have no doubt."

"You mean it? Cause that is exactly what I am fixin' to do."

She ran off toward the woods. Mercy was one of the backwoods kids who came into Bright's Pond for school. She was a sweet little thing who always returned her books on time. She checked them out one at a time. Devoured every word and came back for more, whether or not it was a school assignment.

After a quick stop at home, I walked down to the café. It had turned into a crisp fall evening. Not so cold you couldn't stand it but cool enough for my heavy sweater. I enjoyed the smell of wood smoke and molasses in the air that evening. Hazel Flatbush must have been making a batch of gingerbread, one of the first of the season. I stopped as I passed her house, another big old Victorian with miles of gingerbread trim on the outside. I smiled. "Lots of gingerbread inside and out."

That was when I spied Mickey Mantle rooting around in Hazel's azaleas.

"Come on, boy," I called. "Get out of those bushes."

He looked up at me, smirked, and took off in the opposite direction. I wondered how long it would be before Mildred got the call to chase the pesky mutt down.

Zeb waited inside the café. Gilda was there also — the only customer left. Even Babette had gone home.

"Hey, Griselda," Zeb called. "I was just getting to know our newest neighbor here a little better. Did you know she rented Cora's house?"

"I did," I said, hanging my sweater on the coat rack.

"Good to know someone so nice is living there, you know?"

Gilda beamed at Zeb with wide eyes, long lashes, and pudgy pink cheeks.

"We can wait until Gilda finishes her sandwich, can't we, Griz?"

I took the stool next to her. "Sure thing." I glanced at the clock above the waitress station. "We still have twenty minutes or so. The meeting starts at seven o'clock."

Gilda took a bite of her baloney sandwich. "Oh, gee whiz," she said with her mouth full. "Am I keeping you folks from something?"

Zeb shook his head. "No, well, not really. We just have a dance committee meeting down at the town hall."

I watched Gilda swallow. "Dance committee, huh. I can't remember the last time I went dancing."

"You are certainly invited to ours," Zeb said. "It probably ain't nothing like what you're used to. It's just folks, you know. But we would love to have you."

Gilda pushed the last corner of her sandwich into her mouth, chewed, and then dabbed her lips with a paper napkin. "Well, ain't you just the sweetest little thing? I just might take you up on that."

I had never seen Zeb make such a fuss over anyone in all the years I had known him.

She pushed her plate toward the edge of the counter. "I better be going."

"Now, hold on a second," Zeb said. "Can't send you home without dessert."

He snagged a Full Moon pie from the carousel and cut a large slice, which he placed in a small plastic container. "Here you go, Gilda, on the house, too. Consider it a welcome-to-town gift."

"Gee whiz. Thank you, Zeb. I will enjoy this later."

She paid for her sandwich and sashayed out of the café with Zeb's eyes glued fast to her caboose before turning his attention to me. "Guess we should be getting on down to the town hall." He grabbed the money that was in the cash register, turned off the lights, and locked the door.

"Gilda Saucer is real sweet," he said as we headed toward the town hall. "Wonder why she's here though, you know? Seems a little strange."

"She didn't tell you?"

"Tell me what?"

"Her fiancé is a patient in the medical building over at Greenbrier, same building as Agnes as a matter of fact. He's been in a coma. That's why she rented Cora's house, so she could be close to him. There's no telling how long he'll be like that."

"Wow, that's awful, Griselda."

He didn't know the half of it, and I had neither the time nor the inclination to tell him about the Stella Kincaid connection.

"It looks like it's going to be a clear night," Zeb said. "We might as well walk. Then we can take our time on the way back to my house. Maybe go by way of Hector's Hill and sit a while or maybe even stroll down to the pond."

"I would like that."

Zeb pulled open the town hall door. Everyone but Nate was already there. Boris sat at the head of the meeting table with Dot Handy at his right hand to take notes. Mildred and Ruth sat next to each other. Ruth was wearing one of the bandanas she had planned to make for anyone who wanted one. She looked kind of cute with it tied around her neck with a loose knot near her left shoulder.

Instead of getting right into dance business, Cliff Cardwell became the main topic of conversation. Seemed that his plane had captured everyone's imagination. Ruth finally spoke up.

"I finished nine bandanas and six vests," she said. "Aren't they darling?" She made certain everyone saw her bandana.

"What do you plan on doing with them?" Boris asked.

"Hand them out at the door for folks to wear. It'll be just like a western scene," she said. "Don't you watch western movies? They all wear bandanas and vests. Well the men mostly but still —"

"Speaking of which," Studebaker said. "I spoke with Miss Lacy down at the high school, and she has the students working on scenery and signs."

"Wasn't Nate building a bar for the saloon?" Boris asked. "Where is he anyway?"

No one knew, but I figured he was home either arguing with Stella or tending to Bertha Ann.

"Oh, don't worry about Nate," I said. "If

he said he'll build a saloon, he'll get it done."

"Good," Boris said. "How's the tickets coming, Mildred?"

Still in her uniform and looking a bit pensive, Mildred obviously had something besides the dance on her mind.

"I haven't gotten around to actually ordering them yet, Boris. I plan on driving into Shoops tomorrow though, and I'll visit the printer then."

"Just so we have them in time," Boris said. "I forget what happened exactly last year, but I know it was a big rush at the end and the printer had to work extra to get them to us."

Ruth looked instantly guilty because the tickets were her responsibility last year, and she had left off some vital information. "I did my best. It was just so hard to coordinate everything and then that printer fella gave me such a hard time that —"

"It's OK, Ruth," Boris said. "No one is blaming you for anything. The dance is still three weeks away but I think we got everything pretty much under control." He looked at a checklist he had scrawled on a yellow legal pad. "What about food and beverages?"

"Oh, that's my department," I said. "I got

139

some of the church women making food and treats, and I heard about a woman who lives up at Paradise who is supposed to make the best pies in the world."

"Oh, my goodness," Studebaker said. "You must be talking about Charlotte Figg. Yep, I've tasted her pies. Now no offense to you, Zeb, but she makes the best pie, blueberry, apple crumb, peach, you name it."

"Well, I thought I'd ask her to bake some pies in exchange for two free tickets. We'll pay for ingredients as always."

"Sounds good," Boris said. "Be nice to have some different pie for a change."

"Hey, hey," Zeb protested. "My Full Moon pie is still a hit, and I am planning on making it extra special this year. You remember that, don't you, Ruth? Harvest Moon pies."

"Of course, Zeb, no one is saying your pies aren't tasty," Boris said. "It will just be nice to have something different."

"I for one would love a cherry crumb," Stu said. "I don't know what that woman does with the cherries to give them the right amount of tartness and sweetness, but —"

"Criminy, Stu," Boris said, "can we please discuss the dance. That is why we're here."

It took close to ninety minutes to get all

the other dance details worked out from the number of folding chairs we would need to who was going to collect the tickets at the door — even which basket to use. The one they used last year was much too large according to Ruth. Dot Handy had all her notes organized in a small blue binder with tabs for each area of discussion. She sometimes wrote feverishly and other times merely made doodles. Dot liked to draw turtles. But she never missed an important point and was often called upon to read back what someone had just said — like a court reporter.

It was a little after nine o'clock when Boris adjourned the meeting. Mildred bolted out the door like she had just gotten word of a bank robbery while the rest of us lingered at the table.

Zeb and Ruth discussed pies while Boris and Stu finished off cups of coffee.

"I'm not saying your pies won't be the hit they always are," Ruth said. "I'm only saying that variety might be nice."

I waited quietly until Zeb had his fill of pie talk. "Fine, fine. Extra pie never hurt anyone." Zeb looked at me. "Are you ready? Griselda and I are planning to take a walk up to Hector's Hill."

"It's a bit chilly," Ruth said.

"Oh, I'm sure Zeb will keep Griselda warm," Stu said. He winked at me.

Stu took Dot and Ruth home. Ruth loved to ride in his big, blue Caddy. Dot didn't much care as long as she arrived home safe and sound. Boris lived just a block away from the town hall so he walked the short distance.

"Good meeting, everyone," he said as he plunked his black hat on his head. "This is shaping up to be our best dance yet."

He said that every year.

Zeb and I held hands as we headed toward Hector's Hill. His was warm and rough and strong and made me feel instantly safe — even though in Bright's Pond there was not much anyone needed to be kept safe from — except maybe a stray skunk on the prowl or a family of possums making their way across the street from one forage place to another.

Hector's Hill was dark except for the stars — millions of them — overhead and the twinkling house lights below. The hill had always been a favorite place to take a date in Bright's Pond. It was quiet and serene — a good place to be alone but not so far from home.

The night made Cliff's plane look out of place. Perhaps it was the mood. Maybe it was the fact that it seemed an intrusion in a place that was natural and untouched except when the grass was mowed or the weeds that had a tendency to overgrow were yanked by the roots and burned. Yet, I couldn't help smiling and feeling quickened when I saw it.

"Isn't she pretty?" I asked.

Zeb and I had sat on Star Rock — a giant boulder so named because just about everyone in town had at one time or another sat there gazing up at the Milky Way. My father told Agnes and me that this had been the place where he first kissed our mother. Mama said she saw stars that night even with her eyes closed. I wanted Zeb to kiss me that way, but he didn't — not right off. He just continued to hold my hand in his, which by then was feeling clammy and wet, not so much strong and warm.

"Isn't who pretty?" he asked.

"Matilda. Cliff's airplane. She's pretty, don't you think?"

"Ah, gee Grizzy, do you always have to talk about him? That plane doesn't even belong there. It's just blocking the view and . . . and besides, I think you're just the prettiest thing up here."

That was when he kissed me. I wanted to see stars. I tried to see stars, but I didn't.

I'm ashamed to admit this, but all I could think about at that moment was Cliff's airplane, and I'm pretty sure Zeb knew my mind was not exactly on him or the kiss.

"That was nice," he said. "I think. At least, it was for me."

"Oh, I'm sorry Zeb. I liked it well enough. Guess I'm a bit preoccupied."

"With what? Not Agnes, I'm sure. You don't have to go rushing home to her."

"No, not Agnes. Now come on, let's try it again, and this time I promise to keep my mind on you."

"Ah, nertz, Grizzy. You're thinking about that stupid plane. You're more interested in flying around with Cliff Cardwell than me."

"That's not true," I said, adjusting my rear end on the craggy rock. "I want to . . . fly with you. It's just that the plane is out there. I can see it. It must be very exciting to be up there." I looked into the sky. "It must be even more spectacular to be up there at night, among the stars, closer to them you know, Zeb, flying practically through them."

Zeb stood and wiped rock dust from his pants. "Come on, I'll take you home. Maybe someday you'll get all of this out of your system and stop having these . . . these flights of fancy."

We walked back to my house at a pretty

good clip.

"Good night, Grizzy. I . . . I just want you to know that I wish Cliff Cardwell never landed in Bright's Pond."

I supposed he was waiting for me to say something similar or to agree with him. But I couldn't.

Zeb reached around me and turned the doorknob. He pushed it open. "I'd kiss you goodnight, but I reckon your head is still dreaming about flying through the stars."

"I'm sorry, Zeb. I —"

"It's all right, Griselda. I guess I preferred it when you had your feet on the ground."

11

That was three days ago and in that time I will admit that my thoughts turned to Cliff Cardwell and his airplane more often than I would ever admit to Zeb or even Agnes. There was no getting around the truth — I wanted to fly. I heard he was still at the Kincaid's — something about needing something called a magneto for his airplane.

I probably should have gone straight to the library that Wednesday but I couldn't resist driving past Hector's Hill. The sun glinted off the plane's wings like rays of diamond light. More rain had been called for but so far I saw no signs of the weather changing that morning. It was butterscotch bright and cold. I saw Cliff walking around Matilda with a long silver wrench in his hand. I parked the truck.

"Cliff." I leaned out the passenger side window. "Cliff."

He waved with the wrench. "Griselda.

Come on over."

"Are you getting ready to leave?" I asked once I got within normal conversation range.

"I'm afraid not. I still haven't gotten that part I need. I was just checking on things. Tightened a couple of belts, tune up kind of stuff. I'm worried about the spark plugs. They might need to be changed, but they can be hard to get — probably near to impossible way out here in the boon-doggles."

I chuckled. "Boondoggles? We aren't that rural, Cliff. You want boondoggles you should check out the backwoods. Now there's some serious boonies."

"I didn't mean to be insulting. Some airplane parts can be hard to get no matter where you are, especially on an old plane like Matilda here."

"I've been meaning to ask you. Why did you name your airplane Matilda?"

He smiled and gave Matilda's wing an affectionate rub. "It was my sister's name."

"Oh, that's sweet," I said sensing a sad story. Cliff had a vibe that at times made me want to ask him who he was, really, and where he came from and why he started to fly.

"I was just heading over to the library

147

when I saw you," I said.

"I'm glad you did," Cliff said. "Are you in a rush or can you stay a while? I wouldn't mind a little company while I tighten a few more nuts."

Truth is I enjoyed hanging around the plane. I wanted to learn all about it and the best way I could think of was to watch the pilot. "I can stay a little longer. The library doesn't see much activity this time of the day."

He shook one of the struts and then bent down on one knee. "I've been meaning to ask you about your sister, Alice, is it?"

"Agnes."

"I'm sorry. Nate was telling me about her."

"Yeah, I bet he was."

"Ah, nothing bad. He told me stories about her performing miracles and stuff. Any truth to it?"

"She wouldn't say that was truth. She'd just tell you that God is in the miracle business. She just did the asking and if amazing things happened in Bright's Pond it was God's choosing, not her praying."

"So all that stuff really happened then, the healings and such."

I felt my eyebrows rise. "Yes. Except she doesn't pray like she used to. Leastways

148

people aren't lining up at the nursing home with their requests. She put the kibosh on that about a week after she checked herself into Greenbrier."

"But she does still pray." Cliff exchanged the long wrench for a smaller one from a candy apple red toolbox.

A sinking feeling struck me. "Now don't go telling me that this is a ruse about the plane and you came here because you heard about Agnes and need some kind of miracle. Because if it is, you can just take your plane and —"

He laughed. "No, no nothing like that. If I got any need I can go to God myself. I mean it's good to have folks praying for you, even nice to know someone is looking out for you in that way but no, I'm not here looking for a miracle. I don't need one."

"That's good to hear," I said. Cliff had at that moment become even more intriguing to me. "So in this case, God really is your copilot?"

"Copilot? No way. He's the pilot. I take orders from Him when I'm up there."

I figured Zeb might even be glad to hear what Cliff just said although like everything else in Bright's Pond it will take some time for folks to trust him. I watched Cliff move around the plane looking her over, making a few remarks to himself until he stopped and said, "I just have to ask, is Agnes really that . . . that, you know —"

"Fat?"

He looked at his boots. "I didn't want to say it quite like that."

"She is. But they got her on a diet over there and she's dropping pounds like crazy."

Cliff slapped the wrench in his palm. "Glad to hear it." He made an adjustment on a bolt and then looked away from me and asked, "Did Agnes pray for free or did she charge a fee?"

"Agnes never asked money from anyone. What a strange question."

"I'm sorry, Griselda. I was just thinking that an unscrupulous person would take advantage. You know, charge folks to see her and get prayed for. Seems the same as going to church and being asked to fork over money halfway through the service, you know what I mean?"

"That's different. Agnes has plenty of scruples." My annoyance level had just shot through the roof.

"I didn't mean to imply that she or you were unscrupulous. I just meant I could see how someone could come along and talk her into a few things."

I had to laugh. "Agnes? Agnes doesn't get

talked into anything."

"That's good to hear." The awkwardness of his comment still hovered in the air.

"Well, I better get back to work," he said. "I don't want to keep you from yours either."

"Don't feel bad," I said. "I had similar thoughts in the past. Maybe not about someone looking for a way to make money off her but I used to imagine all manner of crowds lining up with all manner of problems."

"I can see that too." He opened the plane door, the passenger side. "If you're not in a hurry would you like to take a look inside?"

"Me? Really?"

"Sure, Griselda. Come on."

Cliff opened the door and I took a step up and sat in the pilot's seat. A wall of lights and dials and levers spread out in front of me. "Do you need all these buttons and levers to fly this thing?"

"Yep. All of them. They wouldn't be there if they weren't necessary." He reached in near me and brushed my shoulder with his arm. "This here is the altimeter." He tapped a small round dial with numbers situated like a clock that went from zero through nine. "Tells me how high I'm flying and this over here is the attitude indicator, helps me keep Matilda level." The instrument, split in half by a line, was dark on the bottom and light blue on the top with a series of lines in between.

"Attitude indicator? Wouldn't it be nice if people had one of them on their foreheads? Then we'd know what we were getting into."

I couldn't help noticing his aftershave or cologne as he leaned close to me and chuckled at my feeble attempt at a joke. "I guess it works a little bit like a carpenter's level."

"Not really, but that's the general gist of the thing. The idea is to keep the middle line straight and true."

"That looks like the odometer on a car." I pointed to a round dial with numbers that went from zero to two hundred.

"That's pretty much it," Cliff said. "We call it the airspeed indicator."

I leaned back in the crinkly, vinyl seat and took a deep breath. "So many dials and things to remember. I don't know how you do it."

"Oh, it's like anything else, I suppose. How about if I take you up?"

"Now?"

"Well, no. After I get her fixed."

I felt embarrassed. "Oh that's right, for a second I forgot Matilda was broken."

"I should have her ready to fly in a day or two. Then what do you say? Want to go flying?"

My heart raced. "I have never been in an airplane. Not even a big, jumbo jet."

"Well, this is different, but I got to tell you, there is nothing like it. It's freedom up there in the clouds. Peaceful and quiet except for the engine noises. Looking out over the blue sky and seeing the patchwork quilt of a world below —" He shook his head. "It's like nothing you'll ever know."

"Let's do it." I said it fast like if I didn't I might not. "As soon as Matilda is ready to fly."

"It's a date."

When we made eye contact it nearly took my breath away.

Cliff helped me out of the seat and back onto ground. My legs wobbled and I wasn't even flying. "I'll let you know as soon as she's ready."

"Sounds good." I paused and touched the propeller. "It's amazing in a way. Kind of a miracle in its own right."

"Wait until you get up there."

"I'll look forward to it. But right now I've got to keep my feet on the ground and get over to the library before Boris notices and docks my pay."

Cliff scratched his right cheek. "Library, huh. I must say I have a lot of respect for libraries. I wouldn't necessarily let this get out among my pilot friends but I enjoy reading, mostly books about pilots — you know, Amelia Earhart, Charles Lindbergh, but a good romantic adventure is a welcome diversion sometimes."

I smiled. Cliff had a kind of innocent, little-boy quality that I appreciated. He had a sense of wonder that most adults have lost.

"Well, if you're going to be here much longer and you need something to read, come on by. I'll get you a library card. I can do that. I'm the librarian."

Cliff smiled. "And the prettiest librarian in Bright's Pond."

That was when I should have told him about Zeb. But I didn't.

I can't say if it was guilt or desire but I decided to swing by the café and see if I could speak with Zeb. I just needed to touch base or maybe touch him. Mildred's cruiser was parked out front and that was fortuitous. I needed to speak with her about the dance tickets.

She was sitting at the counter working on a baloney sandwich and reading through a small, red notebook.

"Hey, Mildred," I said. "I'm glad I ran into you. Whatcha working on there — a case?"

"I sure am. I'm calling it The Case of the Pumpkin Queen."

I took the stool next to her. "I keep telling you that Stella is not up to anything."

"Maybe. But I'm keeping my eyes peeled just the same. And my nose sharp. I'll sniff out the truth."

Dot Handy swung past me carrying a tray of breakfast plates. "Excuse me, Griselda."

"Where's Zeb?"

"Hold your horses a second, let me get these breakfasts delivered."

"I better get going, Griselda," Mildred said. She left money and change on the counter. "See that Dot gets that for me, OK, Griselda? I need to get out on patrol."

"Sure." That was when I saw Zeb's paper-hatted head in the kitchen. It looked like he was doing everything he could to avoid me. I waved twice and each time it went unanswered.

Dot plunked the now empty tray behind the counter and grabbed a yellow washcloth. She wiped the space in front of me. "He's been awfully surly lately. Won't tell me what's bothering him."

"He's mad at me," I said. "Even though I

155

didn't do anything that he should be upset about."

Dot glanced over her shoulder just as Zeb practically threw a plate of eggs and scrapple on the pickup counter. "Order up!" he called. "Get a move on, Dot. No time to be chitchatting with the regulars."

"Blow it out your socks, Zeb," Dot said. "I got it." Then she turned her attention back to me. "See what I mean."

"Zeb," I called, "you come out of that kitchen this minute. I want to talk to you."

He looked at me through the pick-up window. "I'm busy."

I leaned over the counter and tried to keep my voice quiet. "Look, you have nothing to be jealous about. Now stop this. My wanting to fly in an airplane is nothing to get upset about."

Finally the big lug was face-to-face with me. "Let's go outside," I said.

"I have scrapple frying."

"No problem," Dot called. "I'll handle the grill, you two go talk this out — please. I can't take it anymore."

Zeb wiped his paper hat off his head, crumpled it up, and tossed it in the trash.

We walked a couple yards away from the diner toward the town hall. "All I've done is sit in the plane and look at Cliff's . . . I mean the plane's dials and stuff. He said he'd take me for a ride when Matilda was ready. That's all."

"Dials and stuff, what stuff? I don't like it. You shouldn't be alone with him."

"Zeb Sewickey, you are acting like a jealous numbskull and you can't keep me from sitting in his plane or going for a ride with him."

"I still wish you wouldn't do it."

"Zeb. You can't tell me what to do."

He took a step back. "I can worry about you can't I? I am just looking out for you. And besides —" He kicked a stone. "People will start talking and rumors will start flying. I just don't want to see you put through that."

I looked off toward the mountains. They looked purple and brown and green and so far away yet so close. "You know what, Zeb? For the first time in my life I don't care. I don't care what people think of me. I might just like flying. You just have to trust me. I am not interested in Cliff in any kind of romantic way. And I don't really think people are going to talk or start rumors just because I went for an airplane ride."

"Geez, Grizzy, ever since Agnes moved into the nursing home you've been . . . been different."

"No I haven't. I'm still the same me. I think I just have more time now, you know, to do things I want to do. Don't have to rush home and take care of Agnes all the time. I'm more of my own person, taking care of me, and wouldn't you rather have a girlfriend who is happy than one who's not?"

"Is that what you are?"

"What?"

"My girlfriend?" His voice turned small and shy.

"I thought I was."

Dot appeared at the café door. "You better get back to the griddle, Zeb. I just burned the baloney. I can't do tables and cook all at the same time forever, not on what you pay me."

"You said you'd handle it, Dot," Zeb called.

"You better get back to your scrapple," I said.

"OK, I'll see you later, Grizzy."

12

No sooner had I set foot in the library than the phone started to ring. It sounded like a desperate ring to me. Not sure how I knew, I just did and ran to grab it.

It was Stella Kincaid. She sounded out of breath and frazzled.

"Slow down, Stella," I said. "What's wrong?"

"It's Nate. He just keeps getting himself all worked up over Bertha Ann. I can't wait until the weigh-off is over. And when he isn't tending to her he's with that pilot fella out in the barn. I heard them shooting guns last night. Probably shooting cans, but it could have been possums and coons."

"Well why do you sound all upset? I was just with Cliff and I got to say he is one of the nicest folks to drop by Bright's Pond."

"Ah, Griselda, I guess it's not just Nate. I just keep getting myself all worked up over this thing with my brother. I can't sleep, can't eat — well not like I'm used to — and Nate and me keep getting into spats about it."

I sat at my office desk and flipped on the small desk lamp. The sky had grown gray and overcast quickly. Clouds always made the already dim library even darker and mysterious. "You and Nate need to come to some sort of agreement about this."

"Well we did, only it's not the one he wanted."

"What are you saying?"

"Can you take me over there? To Greenbrier, I mean."

"Really? You mean you're going to visit Walter?"

"Let's just say I'm going over there whether Nate agrees or not and maybe I'll take a peek, Griselda. Just a peek."

"It's a start. I can come by after lunch, maybe around two. Is that OK?"

"Sure, that's fine, it will give me a chance to jump in the shower and do some housework. I was out tending to Bertha this morning. Fertilizer day and I smell to the high heavens."

I hung up the phone and set about with my usual library routine. There were some books to replace in the stacks and magazines to log in and put in the periodicals section.

It was quiet that morning, not even Mildred Blessing showed up looking for a supply of crime novels. But that was par for the course in Bright's Pond. Sometimes I didn't even think we needed a library what with the big one in Shoops being so close.

By one o'clock I was ready to head home and check on Arthur, maybe get a bite of lunch and then head over to get Stella. I was pleased that she was ready to take this first step. I turned off the lights, and just as I locked the door, the ominous clouds of earlier finally burst in an autumn deluge with thunder and cracks of lightning. I spotted Mickey Mantle under some bushes cowering, I thought, from the thunder.

"Come on Mickey," I said. "I'll take you home."

He wouldn't budge. He only looked at me, his head drooping and his eyebrows raised.

I grabbed his collar. "Come on. Let's go. It raining." I had to drag the poor beast to the truck, but once I opened the door he leaped in, glad to be out of the rain and safe from the thunder.

Ivy was standing on her porch calling his name when I pulled up. I pushed open the passenger door and out he romped straight for Ivy. I waved.

"Thanks, Griselda. Where'd you find him?"

"Library. I don't think he likes the thunder." But I doubted she heard me over the thunder that rolled overhead. So I waved goodbye and pulled the truck door closed and went home.

After feeding Arthur his second meal of the day, I changed into a dry sweater and made myself a tuna sandwich. I checked the mail and separated the junk from the bills and a magazine — *Family Circle.* I never knew why it kept coming to my house. I never subscribed to it.

I patted Arthur's head. "Okay, I need to run. Stella has agreed to see Walter." He purred and slinked off to find a comfy corner. Cats didn't seem to mind thunder the way dogs did.

Stella waited on her porch. I pulled up as close as I could so she wouldn't have to get soaked. She ran toward me with an umbrella shielding her from the now pummeling rain. Large heavy drops clattered the roof of my truck like bullets.

"You sure you don't mind?" she asked at the door. "It's raining something fierce."

"No, I don't mind, come on. It's just a shower. The clouds are rolling pretty fast so it'll probably blow over before we get to

Greenbrier."

"Okay," Stella said and she climbed in next to me. Shook her umbrella outside and then tossed it onto her lawn.

"Why'd you do that?"

"Ah, they're a pain in the neck."

We drove quietly for a few minutes down the Main Street of Bright's Pond. We passed the Full Moon and I couldn't help thinking of Zeb. Stella did also.

"So I guess you and Zeb are getting pretty serious," she said.

"Oh, I don't know. He's been acting weird. I think he's jealous of Cliff."

"Cliff? The pilot? Why?"

"He just doesn't like me talking to him. He's jealous."

"Well he is a big hunk of a man, Griselda. You gotta admit."

I swallowed. "He is. But Zeb is being silly. Silly and stupid. And he is none too thrilled about me going up in his plane."

"What? Are you going for a ride with him, really? When?"

"When he gets the plane fixed."

"No kidding. You're braver than me."

I looked ahead and then stopped at the sign just before we pulled out on the major road. The traffic picked up and the rain slowed down revealing some patches of blue sky. "There, see that," I said. "It's clearing already."

Stella stared out the window.

"You OK?" I asked. "Are you sure you're ready?"

"I guess I'm nervous. I was trying not to be. The whole way here I was trying to be brave but now that I'm here, I feel sort of wobbly inside. Do you think he's hooked up to stuff, machines and wires?"

"I don't know. But they must be feeding him somehow, and the only way to do that is through a tube, don't you think?"

She winced. "Hadn't thought of that. Boy if that don't give new meaning to drinking through a straw."

The rain stopped completely when we pulled into the Greenbrier parking lot. I was thankful for that, but we still had to dodge some mighty serious puddles on the way to the front doors. "Geez, you'd think they'd fix these potholes," I said.

Stella stopped dead in her tracks at the doors. "I can't do it, Griselda. I changed my mind."

"Oh, no, Stella. You're getting cold feet now. It's normal under the circumstances. Just a peek, right? You said you'd take a peek." I grabbed her hand. "Now come on. It can't be that bad."

Once again the smell hit me like a ton of bricks. The smell and the noise. I heard what I thought was someone crying — no, more like wailing — down the hall. Agnes had told me there's a woman who seems to cry and sob all day long. The thought made me sad.

The halls were empty except for passing nurses and aides. The man with no legs who flits around in his wheelchair passed us. "Va-room. Varoom," he said. An older gentleman stopped me. "Want to go on date," he asked looking me straight in the eye.

I shook my head and kept walking.

"What room is Walter in?" I asked.

Stella took a deep breath. "One sixty-eight."

"It's around the corner, just past Agnes's room.

"Should we stop in there first?"

"Do you want to? You can use all the encouragement I can find."

Agnes was in her bed. He eyes were closed so, thinking she might be asleep, I crept slowly toward her. Her eyes popped open. "Griselda, I wasn't expecting you. And Stella, hello."

She sounded hoarse. The way she did sometimes after an asthma attack. I kissed her cheek. "You OK?"

"Darn fool pickles. They gave them to me. So I ate them and, well, you know what pickles do to me."

"Why would they give you pickles? Don't they know they set off your asthma?"

"I think they know now. Had me on the nebulizer for a long time.

"Guess what, Agnes," I said. "Stella has come to see Walter."

"Well glory be, ain't that a knee-slapper? I'm so happy for you. And him."

"Don't get too excited, Agnes. I told Griselda I'd take a peek, that's all."

"A peek is good, Stella."

"We thought we should stop in to see you first," I said.

"I'm glad you did."

I watched her take a labored breath.

"Are the docs taking good enough care of you?"

"Not like Doc Flaherty used to. The docs around here seem to rush in, rush out. They listen to my heart and leave. No talking. No gossip. No news. No prayer requests."

"Well, you can pray for me," Stella said. "I'm scared nearly half to death about seeing Walter. I don't know what to expect."

"Don't expect anything, Stella," Agnes said. "Expectations cause the most trouble. The truth is you don't know what to really expect. You know what I'm saying? So it's best not to let your imagination run willynilly over your good sense. Imagination can be a powerful thing."

"I suppose," Stella said. "I guess maybe I'm scared."

"Course you are. If you were all excited about running in there like you can't wait to see a man in a coma I'd think you had problems — serious problems."

We talked a few minutes more until Agnes shooed us out the door. "Now go on. Go see your brother and then come back and see me if you want. I'll be praying." Then she closed her eyes and settled back into her pillow.

"I guess she's right," Stella said after we took a few steps down the hall. "Being scared is normal."

"Sure she is. You can do this. I know you can."

Stella and I found Walter's room. We stopped outside. The door was closed most of the way — opened just a crack.

"You go first, Griselda," Stella whispered.

I pushed on the door and it opened slightly more. Stella grabbed my arm. "What if she's in there?"

"Who? Gilda?"

Stella nodded her head. "I don't want to

see her, not yet. Not with Walter."

"I'll check."

I pushed the door until there was just enough space for me to get through. Walter lay in the bed flat on his back like a cadaver. He was covered in white blankets. I could see a tube protruding from his throat, it was thick and nearly white, more like pearl with a blue clamp. I followed it with my eyes to where it was attached to a machine with dials and buttons. The sound was of artificial breathing and it made me cringe to know that a machine was breathing for him.

Gilda was not in the room although there was a chair pulled close to the bed where I thought she probably sat when she visited. I pictured her sitting there, holding Walter's hand under the blanket, perhaps resting her head on his arm, hoping he'd awaken.

"She's not here," I said. "Come on in."

But when I turned around Stella had vanished.

13

"Oh gee, Stella," I said.

I bolted down the hall and found her standing near the exit surrounded by three female residents in housecoats.

"What gives?" I said.

"Agnes said if we saw this woman trying to walk outside we were to stop her," said a small, slight woman in a yellow robe. Her hair was mussed and flattened in the back like she had been sleeping. Her eyes were like two bright stars set against a desert landscape.

Good old Agnes.

"I can't do it," Stella said. "I can't face him. What if he wakes up? What if he never wakes up? What if he's drooling and breathing weird and has tubes stuck in him?"

"It's one tube, helping him breathe. I didn't notice any drooling but I didn't really look."

"Is she in there?"

"No, Gilda was not in the room."

Stella ran her fingers through her hair. She looked at me a little wild-eyed.

"You best be getting into that room," said the yellow-robed woman. "You need to face things in life or you get to be my age and have nothing but regrets, regrets and memories that have no good endings."

Stella looked at the woman. "How much did Agnes tell you all?"

"Enough to know you need to do this," she said.

"Oh, this is ridiculous," I said. "Come on." I grabbed her hand. "The man is in a coma for heaven's sake. He probably won't even know you're there."

"I wouldn't count on that," said the yellow-robe woman. "I was unconscious after one of my spells and I heard every word my good-for-nothing daughter was saying about me. So you better be careful what you say."

I pretty much dragged Stella into Walter's room. She stood there like a totem pole at the foot of Walter's bed, staring at him. Her bottom lip quivered.

He seemed an attractive man with a square jaw and probably a day's worth of whiskers. It was eerie and quiet save for the whoosh-pop sound of the ventilator.

"It's so, so weird," she said after a minute or so. "It's like he's asleep but different from sleep, deeper, he's farther away like he's standing on one side of a wide river and I'm on the other."

I watched her swipe a tear from her cheek. "He looks younger than I remember. He looks like he did when he was a teenager, seventeen or so."

A nurse in white walked into the room. "Oh," she said looking at Stella. "You're not that other woman, Gilda."

"No, no. I'm his sister, Stella."

"Nice to see you," the nurse moved closer to Walter and held his wrist. "She hasn't been here for a day or so. I thought —"

"Day or so," I said. "She says she's been here watching over Walter every day."

The nurse clicked her tongue. "I heard there was a sister. Glad you finally came by. I know seeing Walter like this must be hard."

Stella blew her nose into a tissue she pulled from a box on Walter's tray table.

"How long has he been here?"

"Only a couple of weeks." She adjusted something on his neck and tucked the blankets around him. Then she turned to the ventilator and twisted a small dial.

"When was the last time you saw Gilda?" I asked.

"I shouldn't say," the nurse said. "I just shouldn't say but that woman came by a few times, stayed all of three or four minutes unless she had a call to make and then left. She spent most of her time yakking on the phone."

Stella and I exchanged looks.

The nurse, a tall woman with curly blonde hair and a smile that added a much needed cheeriness to the darkened room touched Walter's cheek. "Glad somebody else will be coming by to visit him. Sometimes all the patients need is to know someone on the outside cares about them."

"But Gilda is his fiancée," Stella said. "You sure she doesn't stay longer?"

The nurse shook her head. "I better get back to the front desk, probably said too much as usual. But look if you need anything just ask for me, Sally Pinwhistle. I'm his nurse when I'm on duty. I got other patients, but Walter has a special place," — she touched above her left breast — "right here."

"I knew it," Stella whispered once Sally was gone. "I knew that woman was up to no good. Mildred Blessing knew it too, and she knows about these things."

172

"Now you don't know that. Maybe it's just too hard for Gilda to stay here. It isn't very pleasant you know."

"It's not that bad either. You'd think she'd stay longer than a few minutes. And who is she making calls to from her fiancé's sick room?"

"Don't go jumping to any conclusions. There could be any number of explanations."

"Well I don't like it. I don't want that woman doing anything to hurt my . . . my brother."

I smiled. "So, now everything is all right? Now you care about him?"

Stella looked at her brother. She moved closer and stood at his side. "He looks so quiet, safe. I wish I could say peaceful. But it's not. He's in there, Griselda. Walter is inside all that quiet, inside the distance, you know. I can see him standing way far away, on the other side of that river, jumping up and down saying I'm here. Come get me."

Tears welled in my eyes. I wrapped my arms around Stella. "I'm glad you came."

"Now that I'm here I can't still be angry. What good will it do? I reckon there are times in life when you have to get over your own foolishness and your own pride and put away those childish things you know."

"I'm glad to hear that." I put my hand on her shoulder. "I think he needs you Stella."

She patted Walter's hand. "It's warmer than I thought it would be."

"Well he ain't dead."

Stella and I both looked up and saw Gilda Saucer standing at the doorway.

"Why are you two here?" she asked. "I mean not that I mind so much. It's good for Walter to have visitors, but why?"

"Because he's m—"

I nudged Stella. "Because we were here visiting my sister, Agnes, and I remembered you told me about your fiancé so we just stopped in to see him. For company, you know."

She smacked gum against her teeth. "Yeah? Well, OK. That was pretty nice of you. Poor baby just lies there all day long. It's hard to watch but I come all the time and sit for hours sometime hoping and praying, asking the good Lord to wake him up."

That was when I nudged Stella again before she could say another word. "We better be going, Stella."

"Now don't go running out on my account," Gilda said. "We can all have a nice visit if you want. You can even have the chair, Stacy."

"Stella. My name is Stella."

"Oh, sorry, honey. I knew it was an S name, but I've been so distraught since Walter's unfortunate accident."

"I was thinking about that," I said.

"What?" Gilda said. "About me being distraught?"

"No, no about Walter's accident. What exactly happened?"

She clicked her tongue and shook her head. "Nobody knows for a fact. The cops said they found him lying there on the ground at the bottom of a pile of junk. He fell so hard it made his brain swell so much that he shut down like this. That's what's going on. Swelling and bleeding and, well, they're just hoping it will settle down and he'll wake up."

"Wonder what he was doing that made him take such a terrible fall?" Stella asked.

"Got me, sister. I think it must have something to do with that treasure. Maybe he thought it was up on top of that hill, buried under the rubble."

"Yes," Stella said. "But —"

"Well but nothing," Gilda said. "That treasure is mine — mine and my dear sweet Walter's. I'd go looking for it myself if I knew anything about looking for treasures. Walter had all kinds of fancy equipment that was stolen while he was lying there in a heap waiting for help to arrive — least that's what the cops think."

"Goodness gracious," I said. "This really is a case. Maybe Mildred is right. Maybe there's more to this than we can know."

"Mildred?" Gilda said. "You mean that woman cop in town? She's snooping around, huh?"

"She's just concerned," I said. "She takes good care of us in Bright's Pond."

"Is that right?" Gilda said. "That's good to know."

Stella grabbed my hand. "Come on, Griselda. We better get going. I need to get back to the farm."

"You do that," Gilda said. "I'm sure you got cows to rustle and chickens to tend to. I'll be here keeping my eye on things."

"I bet you will," Stella said.

This time I pulled Stella's hand. "You're right. We need to get back."

By the time we got to the parking lot Stella had steam coming out of her ears. "Do you believe that woman, letting on that she stays at Walter's bedside for hours and hours? And that whole treasure story. There is something fishy going on."

"Calm down, Stella. You can't go getting yourself all worked up like this. We really don't know much of anything. I think we should give her the benefit of the doubt and see how this plays out. Mildred will keep her eye out and, believe me, if she suspects anything she'll let you know."

I opened the truck door for Stella. "Are you gonna tell Nate about this?"

"No way. He'll just turn it into something worse than it already is and maybe even forbid me from coming back to see Walter."

I pulled out on the main road. "I got to say, you certainly changed your tune. I had to practically drag you to see him and now you're all protective like a mother bear."

"He's my brother, Griselda."

I shook my head and let go a nervous laugh. "That's what I told you. So let's just take it nice and easy."

Back at the Kincaid's farm I saw Cliff standing on their porch.

Stella saw him also. "Want to come in for coffee?" She winked at me.

"Um, sure. Coffee sounds good."

Now I knew that Stella had gotten it into her head that I was interested in Cliff Cardwell in a romantic way, and I knew I would have no luck trying to dissuade her.

"Griselda," Cliff called. "I was looking for you."

"Uh-huh," Stella said as she leaned close

to me. "I'll leave you two alone."

Stella walked on ahead into the house.

"How come you were looking for me?" I asked.

"I got Matilda running today. Still think I need plugs, but she'll fly. I plan to hang around Bright's Pond until they come. I had to order them from Wilkes-Barre."

"Nate could have driven you there," I said.

Cliff looked at his feet. "I know, but — well, to be honest, I like it here."

"Stella was putting coffee on," I said. "Want to join us?"

"Sounds good."

As I made my way to Stella's kitchen I realized for the first time since Agnes went to Greenbrier that I wasn't rushing to get home, to get back to Agnes. I sat at Stella's table and thought about how nice it was to sit with a friend and not worry if my sister needed anything.

"Thanks for taking me today," Stella said as she placed a cup in front of me. "I'm glad I went and I'm glad I know a thing or two now."

Cliff sat across from me.

"Mind if I ask what you gals are talking about?"

"My brother," Stella said. "I went to see him."

"Oh, oh, at the nursing home. The brother in the coma."

Stella nodded and then turned her back to get a pie off the counter. "It's Full Moon," she said.

"Fine," I said.

That was when Nate came in through the back door cussing up a storm. "Rain," was the first intelligible word out of his mouth. "I can't control the mildew with all this rain."

"You're doing the best you can," Stella said.

"Well the best isn't good enough. She's gonna collapse and die before the weigh-off if I can't keep her dry."

"How about a cup of coffee?" Stella asked. "Take a break."

"A break? A break? I still got thirty acres of corn to mow and that dang blame tractor is giving me trouble. And where on God's green earth have you been?"

"I'm sorry, Nate," Stella said, "I just thought —"

"You just thought. Maybe if you gave me some help around here. Now where were you?"

"I went to see Walter," Stella said. She ran her finger around her coffee cup.

"Walter? But I thought we agreed you'd

steer clear of him."

"You agreed, Nate. He's my brother. No matter what happened in the past. I couldn't just let him lie there with no family, no visitors. Well no visitors except that . . . that Gilda Saucer slinking around. I don't believe for one minute she really cares about him."

At that moment I saw Cliff's eyebrow's arch. "Course she does," he said. "They're getting married."

"Maybe," Stella said. "If he ever wakes up. Can't marry a man in a coma." Then she turned thoughtful. "Leastways I don't think you can."

Cliff pushed a large bite of pie into his mouth. "Don't know about that."

"I can't hang around here talking about your no-count brother anymore," Nate said. "I got a ton of work needs doing."

That was when my stomach started to roil. Fortunately Cliff eased the mood in the room. "Come on, Nate. I'll take a look at the tractor."

Nate took off his cap and rubbed his nearly bald head. "Much obliged, Cliff." Then he turned to Stella. "Thought you said you had coffee."

Stella grabbed a Thermos from a shelf and filled it with black coffee. "Here." She shoved it at him.

"Wow," I said. "How long have you guys been —"

"Nasty with each other?"

I picked at the piecrust. "Well yeah, I guess that's what I mean."

"Since right when Bertha Ann got bugs and mildew. It's like he's obsessed with that pumpkin and blames me for everything that goes wrong around here. And to tell the truth, Griselda, it seems like ever since Agnes moved to Greenbrier everything is going wrong."

I poured cream in my coffee debating whether to say anything about Agnes or not. When she admitted herself to the nursing home I vowed not to make her the center of every conversation I had and not to let the rest of the folks do the same. But I couldn't help myself.

"Agnes has nothing to do with Bertha Ann's bugs or mildew or for Nate's tractor breaking down."

"Just seems uncanny is all," Stella said.

"Don't you blame Agnes too. She's not magical. I thought we were over all that."

Stella took a deep breath and sighed it out. "Let's talk about something else. How's the dance plans coming? Studebaker asked Nate if he could build a saloon, a western saloon with swinging doors and all. He's got it nearly finished out in the barn."

"Yep. I'm surprised he's been able to do it considering all his troubles with the pumpkin."

"Nate loves two things," Stella said. "Growing pumpkins and building things."

"Are you coming to the dance, you and Nate?"

Stella didn't answer right off. But after she finished her pie she said, "Not sure. I didn't tell you but they moved the date of the weigh-off up a couple of weeks. Got a lot of people upset, but that's OK. They all have the same amount of time still, you know?"

"Oh, I hadn't heard that. Guess that would explain Nate's extra bad mood."

"Maybe. But anyhow, the weigh-off is now the same day as the dance. So I guess we'll see what kind of mood he's in afterward."

14

That weekend Bright's Pond enjoyed some of the best weather in weeks. Not a drop of rain, and I was happy for Nate. I imagined he was knee-deep in mildew control but probably relieved that the seeming monsoon season had passed. I spent Saturday cleaning, a well-needed cleaning in the kitchen and bathrooms. For years I had seen the kitchen as a place to make and keep food for Agnes.

I pulled pots and pans from the cabinet and noticed how stained and burned some of them were. I tossed them in the trash planning to purchase new pots, new pans. It was as though the sunny day had changed my disposition toward cooking. It was no longer a chore and something I only did to satisfy hunger.

"How in heaven's name did you manage this?" I said as I pulled a dead mouse out of the cabinet. I held it by its tail and showed it to Arthur who mewed and rubbed against my leg. I tossed it in the trash.

By the time I finished with the cabinets I had three cans full of trash, well, what I considered trash but thought someone else might find useful — an old toaster, two large slotted spoons, a few pots of varying sizes and a rolling pin that I had never ever used. I just didn't want it.

I pulled down the kitchen curtains and tossed them in the washer, then I scrubbed an inch of grime from the window sills. This had been the first time since Agnes moved out that I felt like taking care of the house. Oh, I kept it clean enough while I cared for her but now it was for me and me alone. Perhaps it was ego, perhaps Jesus might have frowned at my pride but I needed to enjoy what was beginning to feel like freedom.

When I opened the kitchen windows a breath of fresh, clean mountain air rushed in, air that smelled sanitized by all the recent rain, sanitized with a hint of juniper. Birds sang in the distance and I stood silent a moment when a red-tailed fox scampered into the yard. He stopped and turned and looked in my direction then disappeared.

At noon the doorbell rang and I realized I had not gotten out of my sweatpants all day.

I pulled the large, yellow rubber gloves from my hands and dropped them in the bucket of sudsy water.

It was Ruth.

"I came by to see if you noticed this bright, shiny day. Why it's like the good Lord is finally smiling on Bright's Pond again. Land o' Goshen, Griselda, I never thought the clouds would vanish. Every single day there were clouds somewhere on the horizon."

I welcomed her inside. "I suppose it couldn't stay cloudy and rainy forever, but I agree, Ruth, it does feel like a gift doesn't it, this day I mean?"

"Yes sirree Bob."

She followed me into the kitchen.

"You've been cleaning. Well I don't want to interrupt your work —"

"No, no it's fine. Sit at the table. I could use a break. Just let me finish wiping out this cabinet."

"Spring cleaning is good for the soul, you know. Even though it is fall and not spring."

"It is good for the soul," I said. "I don't think I've done this much cleaning in years."

"I swear by it, Griselda, but you know that. You know how every spring I bring out the rugs and mattresses and beat tar out of them. You've seen me hanging from the

185

windows cleaning the glass with vinegar and newspapers."

"Once maybe, I didn't pay it much mind. But vinegar and newspapers?"

"Best thing for glass. No streaks. I think that's why that crow slammed into my living room bay window last year. Fool thing thought he could fly straight through. I wrung his neck. Put him out of his misery."

I closed the cabinet door. "You're a good woman, Ruth." Then I dumped the bucket of dirty water down the drain.

"Might be better to dump that water in the basement," Ruth said.

"It's still a drain. All goes to the same place."

"Anyhoo," Ruth fidgeted with a twisty tie from a loaf of bread. "Speaking of misery, what is going on with Stella? I heard she went to see Walter. Is that true?"

"Sure is." I stretched my back. "I could use a cuppa."

"Me too."

"What time is it getting to be?" I asked as I filled the percolator.

"Going on two," Ruth said.

I shook my head. "I can't believe how fast this day is whizzing past."

"Gotta date? Word is that you are sweet on Cliff Cardwell, the pilot fella. How does

186

Zeb feel about that?"

"I am not sweet on him, Ruth. And Zeb is just being silly, acting all jealous."

"Well I don't see a ring on your finger, Griselda. You are free to play the field. It would do you some good. Do your heart good, course I'd go after him myself but I'm afraid my memories of my Bubba are just too fresh, and I might be a tad too old."

"I am not going after him."

She finished her coffee. "So how is Agnes and like I asked, what's the scoop with Stella?"

"Agnes is doing OK. She had an asthma attack the other day, but I think she is actually looking thinner, you know, especially in her face, her cheeks."

"That's good. Real good but I doubt she'll ever get skinny."

"Probably." I heard my stomach grumble. "I must be hungry. Didn't realize it."

"Wanna go down the café?"

"No, Zeb is picking me up for dinner and maybe a movie. He called a little earlier. I thought he was mad at me but I guess I'm wrong."

"Why would he be mad at you?"

"Because of Cliff. He thinks the same as you and probably everybody else in town that I'm sweet on Cliff."

"Oh, really? There see, it is kind of obvious."

"But it's not true."

Ruth poured herself a second cup of coffee. "I never told anyone this but when I first met Bubba I didn't like him even though my mother kept telling me he was the one. I kept denying it until Cupid's arrow finally found my rear end and I came to my senses, and we were happily married for twenty-six years."

"I don't need Cupid's arrow to find me. If I wanted to go out with Cliff I would, but I am going out with Zeb this evening, not Cliff."

"All right but denial is not just a river in Egypt. I read that in one of those self-help books that are becoming so popular. I think it was called *Embrace Your Inner Child* or something like that."

"Ruth. I am not in denial. And I have no inner child."

"OK, OK. Where's Zeb taking you?"

I chuckled. "Probably the café. He has never taken me anywhere else."

"Cheapskate. You should tell him you want to go some place special tonight."

I sipped my coffee and let it linger in my mouth a second or two while I considered what Ruth just said. "You know you're right.

I think I'll ask him to take me into Shoops. Maybe The Pink Lady. I could go for one of their burgers."

"Good for you. Sometimes you have to ask for what you want or you'll go through life wondering if you could have ever had it. I think folks assume too much. They assume that others know what they want when the whole time the other person didn't have a clue."

"You're confusing me and yourself. I already said I'll ask Zeb to take me some place besides the café."

Ruth brought the subject around to Walter. "That poor, poor man. I can't even begin to imagine what it must be like to be all locked up inside your brain, alive but not alive."

"Stella and I went to visit him," I said.

"You did? Why didn't you tell me? What was it like?"

"It was really sad, Ruth. I can't imagine what I would do under those circumstances, I mean if Agnes fell into a coma. Funny how they say that, a person falls into a coma like they fall asleep. Anyway, I don't think I could stand that."

Ruth nodded and wrapped the twisty tie around her little finger like a ring. "What's he look like?"

"Like he's asleep."

It took a few minutes but I was finally able to satisfy Ruth's curiosity about Walter. I was glad when the telephone rang. It was Zeb.

"Can I pick you up at six, or do you want to just meet me at The Full Moon?" he asked.

I took a breath and let it out through my nose. "Well, Zeb, I was hoping we might go on into Shoops, The Pink Lady is there. I'd like that for a change."

I waited a long uncomfortable minute before Zeb said, "Sh-sh-Sure Griselda, we can do that. Just seems silly when we can get the same food at the Full Moon and not have to pay for it, well not as much anyway."

"But I really want to get out of town a little. It's such a nice day, finally, probably going to be a nice evening. Maybe we can take a walk after around Shoops. They have some nice shops that stay open late. I need some new pots."

"Pots?"

"I threw mine away. I was thinking I'd like to buy new ones."

I could see Zeb shake his head in my mind. "You threw perfectly good pots away?"

"They aren't good or perfect. They belonged to my mother for heaven's sake. I want new ones. I don't do much cooking but I was thinking that I might like to start. I was thinking I might like to start cooking for guests, not just myself."

"I guess that makes sense, but old pots are still useful. Maybe you should give them to the Society ladies and let them give them to one of the backwoods families."

"That's a good idea. I think I'll do that, and you know what? I think I'll buy a couple of brand new pots for them to give away also."

Zeb didn't say anything to counter what I said but I knew he was thinking it.

"So what do you say?" I asked after a few seconds. "Let's drive into Shoops. I bet Stu would even lend you his Caddy for the evening." Zeb drove a beat up old pickup in worse shape than mine.

"Oh, all right. I'll talk to Stu and be by around six."

I hung up the phone feeling quite pleased with myself. There was something refreshing about taking a stand and refusing to move.

"Good for you," Ruth said. "Now look at the time. You'll want to be getting ready."

"It's not even two-thirty. I'm going on a date. It's not a coronation."

"Oh, I still think I'll get going. I thought I might visit Ivy and see how she's doing with Mickey Mantle."

"That's a good idea. I haven't seen much of her. I saw Mickey Mantle though, rooting around bushes and trash cans. He likes to come by the library on his way to the woods."

"I heard that, too, from Dot Handy. She says the dog is even more curious than Al Capone ever was. I just hope that nasty Eugene Shrapnel doesn't start trouble again."

"Tell Ivy hello for me and that we need to get together soon."

"I will. I'll be sure to tell her."

Zeb arrived at precisely six o'clock. I was standing on the porch waiting for him because if there was one thing Zeb and me had in common it was punctuality. Just as he opened the car door I heard a sound above me like an engine. It was Cliff, at least I figured it must have been Cliff zooming around in the sky in Matilda.

"Look," I said pointing. "That's Cliff. He got her running again."

"So what, Griselda? Maybe he's leaving town."

"Oh, I don't think so. He told me he likes it here." I looked up at the plane. Now I didn't know much about airplanes but I thought he might have been saying hello the way he tilted Matilda's wings over my house.

Zeb snorted like a bull and closed the car door.

"It was nice of Stu to lend us his Caddy. It's so . . . luxurious." I slinked across the seat, a little closer to Zeb. He slipped his arm around me.

"You know, you have nothing to be jealous about," I said. "I am not interested in Cliff Cardwell."

Zeb fell silent a moment and then removed his arm and adjusted the radio until he found a song he liked. "Ain't No Woman Like the One I Got" by The Four Tops. He seemed to relax and pull me closer. "I know, Grizzy. I'm sorry for the way I've been acting. I don't know what got into me."

"It was kind of silly, Zeb. But thank you for saying you're sorry. Now maybe we can have a nice evening."

Zeb pulled up outside The Pink Lady. I was just about to open the door when he grabbed my arm. "You know what? Let's get steak. It's such a gorgeous night. Let's go to the steak and seafood place, what's it called?"

"The Crabby Corral. But it's expensive, and we might need a reservation on a

Saturday night."

Zeb kissed my cheek. "I feel like splurging on my best girl."

"Best girl," I said. "You got others?"

He pushed my shoulder a little. "Come on. Let's go."

Zeb pulled the big, blue Cadillac into the Crabby Corral parking lot. He had to park a few hundred feet from the front door but that was OK. I kind of enjoyed walking the distance with him. As it turned out we didn't really need a reservation although one would have gotten us seated sooner than thirty-five minutes. But it was OK. We waited outside on the restaurant's porch. The place was nice, made up to look like a shack of sorts with lots of wood and shingles that seemed to be peeling, but I figured that was for effect. A life preserver, yellow with age, had the name Crabby Corral in bold, red letters all around. It advertised their name while a tall, cement seagull stood on a pylon that was connected to another pylon by a thick, strong rope. Zeb drank a cold draught beer while I sipped a cherry Coke with a long-stemmed maraschino cherry in it.

All in all it was shaping up to be a nice evening until I saw her. Gilda Saucer sitting at the bar. She held a red swizzle stick, which she used to stir a small golden drink and then wiped the stick across her lips much to amusement of the bartender.

"Let's get out of here," I said leaning across the table and nearly igniting my hair with the table candle.

"What? Why?" Zeb was still cutting his steak into one-inch pieces.

"She's here. Gilda. I don't want her to see us."

Zeb looked up. "Really? Where?"

"At the bar," I whispered through clenched teeth. "She's right over there. On the end. In the tight red skirt doing things with her swizzle stick."

Zeb's eyes grew wide. "Really? What kind of things?" He looked toward the bar. "Oh, I see her now. Maybe we should say hello."

"No, are you nuts. I don't want her to see us. Just finish your steak and then we should leave, quietly."

"Why? What's the big deal?"

"I don't know. I guess I don't want to think about her or Walter or Stella this evening."

But much to my embarrassment and chagrin, Zeb Sewickey decided he just had to speak with Gilda. He stood up and waved. "Gilda. Over here." He did this three times until Gilda finally saw him. She appeared shocked at first but then quickly settled down and walked — no, sashayed — toward us.

"Well, hi," she said still holding the swizzle stick. "Fancy meeting you here." She looked at me and I could feel definite tension rise between us.

"I thought you'd be at Greenbrier," I said.

That was when Zeb turned chivalrous and rescued the damsel. "Now, Grizzy," he said. "You can't expect the girl to spend all her time at the nursing home."

"Oh, but I was just there," she said, her big cow eyes with too much makeup dancing in the candlelight. "But a girl can only take so much misery."

I expected her to swoon.

"I only came in here to get a drink. Lord knows a girl needs a drink now and again, ain't that right, Griselda?"

"I wouldn't know." I sipped my Coke.

Zeb settled back in his seat. "Would you care to join us?"

I couldn't believe he had just asked her that. To which she replied. "Well if you don't mind, I am starved. That food they serve me over at the nursing home ain't fit for hogs. But that's not to say I don't like those baloney sandwiches you make, Zeb."

"Thank you," he said. "But a girl can only

handle so much baloney."

Ain't that the truth, I thought. *And I can only swallow so much of her baloney also.* As much as I tried to give her the benefit of the doubt I was really starting to have qualms about her. Big, giant, neon qualms that something was not quite right about Gilda Saucer and maybe even Walter.

There went the evening and my patience with Zeb Sewickey. Even though she had already told me, she went on and on about the buried treasure.

"Now I don't suppose either of the two of you know anything about that treasure."

"Not me," Zeb said. "This is the first I'm hearing about it. Have there been many people looking for it?"

Gilda sneaked a steak fry from Zeb's plate, dipped it in ketchup and munched it. "Now that I don't know. I mean I guess other folks have been looking. It's been missing for over eighty-some years now."

"And no one has found it in all those years." Even I heard how incredulous I was.

"That's right," Gilda said. "Walter said it was buried up there near that Sak . . . Sak-a-something Quarry."

"Sakolas," Zeb said.

"There you go," Gilda said. "Well, anyway, that's what he was doing when he got

197

bumped on the head. Darn fool climbed that heap of junk out there and probably lost his footing and came tumbling down just like Jack and Jill."

"And broke his crown," I said as I rolled my eyes.

Gilda chortled. "You are a funny one now, ain't you?"

Zeb chewed the last of his steak. "Do you think he was close to finding it?"

"Well see now," Gilda said as she swiped a third fry. "That we don't know. But the police officers that found him said they went back and looked around but they didn't see any signs of a treasure. They even asked some of the folks who live up near there if they saw it or knew anything. But they denied it."

"At least that's what they claim," Zeb said. "You might never know if someone found the treasure."

That was when Gilda turned on the water-works. Only a few drips at first. She blew her nose in the cloth napkin meant for Zeb. "I just don't care about it, the treasure I mean. I just want my Walter to wake up so we can get married and live happily ever after. He's my only treasure."

Then she looked at me and burst into tears. Big, giant crocodile tears that ran down her cheeks and splattered on the table. "I'm . . . I'm sorry. I just can't help it."

Even with the tears I still had a shaky feeling inside, butterflies with huge wings batted around in my stomach. I couldn't put my finger on it but something was not right and I found myself thinking that Mildred Blessing had Gilda pegged. Something stunk in Bright's Pond and it wasn't just Nate's pumpkin fertilizer.

15

The next morning I rushed over to the Kincaid farm fully intent on telling Stella that I saw Gilda at the Crabby Corral. I found her out back with Bertha Ann spraying for bugs. She looked like a visitor from outer space all dressed up in a vinyl suit and wearing a face mask with some kind of respirator attached to it. She was squirting some kind of liquid all around Bertha Ann's bottom.

"What in the world?" I said.

Stella stopped spraying slipped her face mask off. "Oh Griselda, I didn't know you were stopping by."

"What's with the getup?"

"Oh, I hate using pesticide, so I wear this protective gear. Nate doesn't care. He'd spray in his underwear if he could."

"It does smell bad, like it could give you cancer."

"The company swears up and down that

it's safe to humans."

She dropped the spray nozzle on the ground and pulled off her silver gloves. "Let's go on in the house."

"Good idea, I'm not too keen on pesticide either."

I waited until we were inside and seated at her kitchen table with tumblers of iced tea and Lorna Doone cookies before telling her about Gilda.

"At the Crabby Corral, really?" Stella said. "She was there? You sure it was her?"

"Yes. Zeb and I had dinner there and —"

"You don't say. You mean that cheapskate finally sprung for a nice dinner. That boy must be in love."

"Listen, Stella, she was dressed in a . . . a swanky outfit — tight skirt, red lipstick — and I tell you she was flirting with the bartender, the way she pulled that swizzle stick between her lips."

"Griselda, what are you saying?" Stella chewed a corner off a cookie.

"I don't know what I'm saying exactly except something doesn't feel right, Stella. I'm beginning to think Mildred is right about that woman."

That was when Nate came barreling in from outside. "Why'd you stop spraying?"

"Griselda came by. I'll finish up in a bit."
Nate glared daggers at me.

"Look," I said, "why don't you finish up with Bertha Ann and meet me later? Maybe we can go to the nursing home for a visit."

Stella glared back at Nate. "Fine, Griselda. Pick me up later."

"I'll be by around two this time," I said. "I got some errands and work and stuff."

I climbed back into my truck steaming like clams. I had about had it with the way Nate treated Stella. I wanted to tell her to stop letting him holler at her like that. The weigh-off was still three weeks away. And what's that compared to having a brother in a coma for crying out loud?

I dropped the gearshift into drive when I heard a quick rap on the passenger side window. It startled me and I turned quick expecting to see Nate or Stella. It was Cliff.

"Hey, you ready to go up. Get your head in the clouds?"

"Today? Now?"

"Sure, why not? It's beautiful day. The sun is warm. The birds are chirping, God is in his heaven, and all is right with the world."

"How can you be so cheery all the time?"

"Just wait until I get you flying. You'll see. I took Ruth yesterday."

"What? When?"

"Towards evening. We buzzed your house. Did you see us?"

"I saw you but I had no idea Ruth even wanted to fly in your plane."

"Come on, let's go. I'll tell you all about it."

"OK, I guess my day can wait. Jump in. I'll drive us."

Now that was weird. I could not believe that Ruth didn't come running to tell me, unless she thought I'd be jealous or some dumb thing. Or she was so traumatized that she is home in bed in the fetal position.

Cliff and I drove the short distance to Hector's Hill, and I will admit that the second I set eyes on Matilda I felt my heart go pitter-patter. There was something magnificent about her. Yet, I felt a twinge of trepidation as I stepped out of the truck.

"Ruth was a little frightened," Cliff said. "She made me take her down after just a few minutes. She kept covering her eyes and missed the whole thing."

"That sounds like Ruth. I am really surprised you got her to go."

We walked toward the plane.

"I saw her walking down the street near that woman's house — the one with the dog."

"Ivy."

"Yeah. I had just gotten Matilda ready to go and was on my way back from the café. I was itching to take her up when Ruth stopped me and asked me about the plane. I told her she was ready to fly and asked if she'd like to come."

"And she went. Just like that?"

"She said she thought her Bubba would be proud of her for taking the risk."

"Wow. That is not like Ruth Knickerbocker."

"Like I said. She was not too keen on it when we were up there."

Truthfully I didn't know if I'd do any better than her.

Matilda looked mighty pretty sitting there on Hector's Hill, strong, capable yet delicate in ways with thin cables and wings that on first glance appeared thin and breakable. I watched as Cliff made his way closer. He touched the wing with a gentle hand. Then turned toward me and with a flourish and a deep, chivalrous bow said, "Your chariot awaits, my lady."

"Why thank you, my good man," I said as I strode closer.

He led me around to the other side of the plane and opened the passenger door. He took my hand and helped me up on the footrest. "Go on, you've already sat in the driver's seat."

It wasn't the first time I sat in the plane. This time I expected the crinkly sound the vinyl made, but this being the first time I was going for a ride my stomach quivered a bit even though I had been dreaming of flying ever since Cliff had landed in Bright's Pond.

"Just don't touch anything," Cliff said.

"Don't worry. I wouldn't dream of it."

Cliff climbed into his side and then instructed me about the seatbelt, which he helped secure tightly across my lap. "That stick in front of you is called the yolk or stick. It's kind of the steering wheel. But for this ride I'll do the steering."

I smiled. "I still can't get over all the dials and gadgets."

"Well, yeah, I pointed most of them out to you the last time. Now those pedals on the floor are important. Don't touch them."

"Aye Aye, Captain."

With that, Cliff turned some dials and pushed a couple of buttons and then turned the key, just like in a car ignition, and then in an instant the propellers were spinning, the engine was growling, and we were rolling down Hector's Hill picking up speed as we went, faster and faster until suddenly and without a single hesitation the plane lifted off the ground. My stomach went wobbly and I grabbed the door handle but quickly pulled my hand away and sat with both hands in my lap, folded so tight my knuckles turned white.

I heard some squawks on the radio, but Cliff didn't seem to pay them any mind.

I looked out and down as the ground fell farther and farther away until it seemed a patchwork below. "How high are we flying?"

"Barely 2,000 feet. Just relax."

"Oh, I'm fine." And I was. I had never felt anything like it in my life. I was free and soaring over Bright's Pond. I could pick out the church and my house. The Kincaid's Pumpkin Patch looked pretty and green and brown and orange with a dot of purple near the middle that I knew was Bertha Ann in her tent.

"Look," I said. "That's Bertha Ann."

Cliff laughed. "You're enjoying this."

"I am, Cliff. I don't feel afraid at all."

"Ruth never opened her eyes. Sat there with her hands over her face the whole time."

"That's too bad because the world is so pretty from up here. It's smaller, you know."

"Look," he said. "The mountains ahead."

"I can see the trees, Cliff. From Hector's

Hill they just look green or brown in winter but up hear I can actually see trees, evergreens and maples."

"OK, I'm going to turn now. Head back. We'll fly over Paradise."

"The trailer park?"

From that high I could see all the multicolored trailers lined up like assorted crayons with trees and cars and a river of black asphalt snaking its way through the park. I took a deep breath and sighed it out as my head felt a little light.

"It's normal," he said reading my mind. "Lots of people can get a little light-headed. Just the altitude. You'll be fine."

"I'm not worried. I . . . I love this!"

Just a few short minutes later we were starting back down, and before I knew it Cliff had landed the plane and maneuvered it back to where she sat on the hill overlooking Bright's Pond with such a spectacular view. I barely moved in the seat the whole time but I needed to catch my breath.

"Thank you, Cliff. That was amazing."

Cliff touched my hand. "I bet you'd make a great student. Ever think about getting your pilot's license?"

My heart sped up as the propellers slowed down. "Me? Fly a plane? I don't know."

"Why not? Think about it. I might even

be able to teach you."

"I don't know. I might think about it, but, oh boy, me? Fly a plane? But I sure did have fun."

I pushed open the passenger door and Cliff took my hand and helped me down. My knees buckled under me. Cliff held me up. "It happens. Got to get your land legs again."

Land legs. I didn't want land legs anymore. I wanted to fly.

16

"You really seemed to like flying," Cliff said on the way back to the Kincaid farm.

"I did. I guess I'm kind of surprised. I thought it would scare me the way it scared Ruth, but it didn't. It was amazing."

In my periphery I could see a wide, toothy smile stretch across Cliff's face. "Well I am the world's best pilot," he said. And then he chuckled.

"I have no doubt about that. But then again I never flew in a plane before."

"Really? Never even in a jet, a commercial airliner?"

"I've never really been out of Bright's Pond, except an occasional trip to Wilkes-Barre or Scranton."

"Oh, dear, you need to see the world, Griselda. It's a beautiful place, especially from six thousand feet."

"Is that how high we flew? Six thousand feet?"

"Not this time. We were only at two thousand, which doesn't sound like much when you compare it to TWA or Delta. Commercial jets fly at thirty."

"Thousand?"

He laughed. "Yep."

I pulled up to the Kincaid house and glanced at my watch. It was now nearly noon. I hadn't realized I had been lollygagging that long.

"Can you come inside? I'm sure Stella would like to see you," Cliff said. "Nate is probably out in the fields."

"Oh, I can't. I already visited with Stella and I really need to get to the library before Boris Lender figures out that I kind of make up my own hours and fires me."

"Ah, never happen. Say, Griselda, I've been meaning to ask you, do you think there is any truth to Walter being in these parts to look for treasure, stolen loot from a train robbery?"

"How did you hear about that?"

He glanced at the house and wrinkled his mouth, which wrinkled his forehead, which furrowed his brow and made him look a wee bit sinister as a shadow draped across his face. "Nate told me. If there's one thing I learned about Bright's Pond it's not the place to come if you have a secret to hide."

"Yeah, I guess you got that right."

"So what do you think?"

"About the treasure? I have no idea. I do know that train robberies were pretty much a daily occurrence in these parts, or more out west a bit. And coal mines had pretty substantial payrolls and such, considering."

Cliff nodded his head. "So it could be true, then."

"Sure. I can try to do some research down at the library if you want? Thinking about looking for yourself?"

"Nah, not really. I was just curious is all. I'd hate it if that poor fella was out there and almost got killed over nothing, you know?"

"That would be adding insult to injury," I said.

Cliff looked past me for a second. "I guess you better be going and I promised Nate I'd lend him a hand today so —"

"Right. Thanks for the ride," I said.

"Think about those lessons," Cliff said. "You're a natural."

I waited until Cliff got to the front door just in case I caught a glimpse of Stella. But she wasn't there. Probably doing her housework or back to spraying Bertha Ann. I dropped the gearshift into drive and pulled away from the curb when I spotted Mickey Mantle loping across the street with a bird in his mouth. "Must be part retriever," I told no one but myself.

Three minutes later I saw Ivy running down the street with her arms spinning nearly like a whirligig and her huge breasts bobbing up and down. I stopped.

"Are you all right, Ivy?"

"Have you seen Mickey Mantle? He ran out of the yard again lickety split like he had something on his mind. I think that boy has a girlfriend."

"Didn't you get him fixed? Wasn't that the deal from the SPCA?"

"Yeah, yeah, but I just couldn't do it. I couldn't let them cut his —"

"All right, Ivy. I saw him not five minutes ago running that way with a bird — looked like a robin — in his mouth."

"That scoundrel. I told him no more birds."

"Maybe it's a gift for his girl. Want a lift?"

"No, I'm better on foot. I know his hiding places. I'll find him."

I waved good-bye and drove to the library. I parked in my usual spot and noticed Stella sitting on the library porch. *Now what is she doing here,* I thought. Stella was not a library regular.

"Hey Stella," I called. "Didn't I just leave you at your house?"

"That was an hour ago." she said. "Where've you been?"

"I got delayed after I left you. Cliff took me for a ride in Matilda."

She stood as I got closer.

"No kidding. Did you like it? He asked me if I wanted to go but Nate said no, like it's his decision. He said he doesn't want me alone in the cockpit with Cliff."

"What's he think you're gonna do?"

"He's just so jealous of everyone. But that's OK. I didn't really want to go flying."

"Oh I loved it, Stella! It was the most . . . exhilarating thing I have ever done, flying so high with my head in the clouds looking down on the earth, on Bright's Pond. I thought I could . . . could fly forever."

I unlocked the door and pushed it open letting Stella go inside first. Then I flipped on the lights. The rush of book smell hit my face the way it did every morning. Books and dust. The library was in need of a fall cleaning.

"I think I'll ask Sheila Spiney to make an announcement in the church bulletin that I need volunteers to help clean the library. We always have a good turnout."

"Long as there's lemon squares and pie

and coffee, folks will help."

I dropped my bag on the check-out counter. My bag was an olive drab canvas satchel I had been carrying for years. It belonged to my father and I could never part with it. Ruth had sewn patches of pretty colors here and there and replaced the snap a dozen times at least.

"So what brings you to the library?" I asked. "Does Nate know you left your post?"

"Ah phooey on him. He can spray the pumpkin all by himself. You know he's got me spraying her down with milk now?"

"Milk? You mean regular old milk?"

"Yep. He claims it's good for her and will help guard against cracks."

"That's just weird."

"Sure is. But, who knows, it might help."

Stella fidgeted with some papers on the counter, mostly government-issue pamphlets and tax return forms. "I've been thinking about what that Gilda Saucer said about Walter looking for buried treasure, and I don't know whether to be mad or glad or just chalk it up to being nothing more than Walter being Walter — always looking for one quick-rich scheme or another."

We talked as I made my rounds, replacing books on shelves, picking up trash, checking in new books.

"But that's his business. It doesn't matter to you that much. Let the man chase his windmills you know what I mean?"

"Yes, I do, and I believe that, but I was also letting myself think that maybe he was up here looking for me. That maybe he knew I was living nearby and was planning on dropping by, but no, he was up here trying to line his greedy pockets."

I hadn't thought about the situation like that. If it was true then maybe Stella was right about him. Maybe he's still just as big a rat fink as he ever was.

"I was thinking, Griselda, that maybe I could at least find out if there was any truth to her story, you know here, maybe a book or newspaper report about a robbery."

My eyebrows rose at the idea of delving into some research. "It's what they pay me for. We could do some checking. I do know train robberies were pretty frequent out near Harrisburg. They carried the miners' payroll usually."

"Really? So it could be true?"

"Sure. I just wish we had an exact date, something more to go on than 'around fifty years ago.' "

"We can't just look up train robberies in the Britannica?"

"No. I'm thinking old newspaper articles

would be the way to go."

"That sounds like a lot of work."

It was, but I felt determined to help Stella figure this out, and I loved digging for the truth. We started by researching train robberies and within an hour managed to find information about three in which the loot was never recovered.

That little discovery only solidified Stella's harsh feelings toward her brother.

"So, it could very well be that the creep was out looking for gold. Sounds about right."

I left Stella alone to read through the microfiche of newspaper articles that went back to 1914. The Bright's Pond Library had many rolls of microfiche but the collection was far from complete. After another hour I asked Stella if it was worth knowing the details.

"I don't know," she said stretching back in the chair. "I think I'm pretty curious now. I did find this article about a train robbery. But it wasn't for half-a-million dollars."

"Let me see."

"This is from an article written in 1924." Stella then read the account of a train robbery in which the owner of the mine, who was accompanying a safe filled with the cash, was stopped and robbed by three masked men. The owner, a man named Deaver, was shot and killed after being forced to give up the safe.

The safe was never recovered.

"You think Walter could have found out about the safe?" Stella asked.

I shrugged. "Maybe, but it's not really all that much money. I mean not really."

Stella pushed her chair away from the microfiche machine and stood. "If I know my brother, it's not just about the money. He likes the thrill. He likes getting his hands on what he considers found money, although that's open to interpretation."

"Truth of the matter is, Stella, that there is no crime in treasure hunting and if we're telling the truth you haven't exactly been breaking any records trying to find him either."

"I know. I know. Guess I'm just as guilty as him. Maybe I should have gone looking for him. Maybe I should have taken the high road as my mother would have said."

"Maybe. It's not too late. You can still take the high road and forgive him. God will help you with that. But you know all this don't you?"

"Golden rule kind of stuff, I suppose. I guess I'd want to be forgiven."

I looked into Stella's eyes. I could see both

pain and compassion. "Go on," I said. "Forgive him and mend the fences."

"He's in a coma. He might never come out of it. How would he know all is forgiven?"

I scratched my neck. "Now that's a good question, but maybe instead of asking 'what if he doesn't wake up?' you should be asking 'what if he does?' "

She shook her head. "So now what?"

"Make your peace with him. You should keep visiting your brother and pray that he wakes up."

I turned off the microfiche machine and looked at my watch. "Geez, you've been at this for a long time. It's nearly four o'clock."

"Oh, crud," Stella said. "I better get home. Nate is going to be madder than jumpin' blue heck. I never got his lunch and now dinner will be late."

"You worry about him too much. He's a big boy. He can take care of himself."

"I know, Griselda. I just want to keep the peace. At least until after the weigh-off."

"Well, blame it on me," I said as she scurried out the door.

Funny how quickly the library could grow so quiet when I was all alone. Even with all the hundreds of books, the many voices and characters moving about on the pages, the stories held between the bindings, the library could be such a solitary place at times. I waited a little while longer in case some of the students came by.

I set about turning off lights and getting ready to call it quits when the library door swung open. It was Mercy Lincoln.

"I brought you your book back," she said. "I liked it. Can I have another?"

Mercy was all of nine years old and just the cutest little thing ever. She wore her hair in pigtails and dressed about as well as any of the backwoods children. That is to say she wore blue jean overalls that looked about six sizes too big — probably an older sibling's or a neighbor's. Her sneakers were worn and filthy with no laces. I made a mental note to tell the SOAP ladies that Mercy needed shoes and socks.

"OK, let's look."

A few minutes later I sent Mercy home with *Treasure Island*.

"Thank you Miz Griselda. I'll be sure and get it back. I gotta run on home now."

Of all the children in Bright's Pond, Mercy was my favorite.

17

I headed for the Full Moon, excited to tell
Zeb about my plane ride. But, Cliff beat me
to it. He was already there sitting at the
counter yakking up a storm about how I
was the next Amelia Earhart. Zeb looked
like he was about to explode.

"Hey," I said taking the stool next to Cliff.

"There she is," he said. "The best flyer in
Bright's Pond."

Cliff excused himself and headed to the
bathroom.

"Really, Grizzy, you really went flying with
him?" Zeb asked once Cliff was in the men's
room. "All alone in a plane, just the two of
you."

My heart sank. "Yes, Zeb. What in heaven's name are you implying?" He must have
been talking to Nate Kincaid.

"Nothing." He quickly wiped the counter
and went back to the kitchen. "I'm not
implying anything. I'm just saying you have

to be concerned about appearances."

"Appearances?" I whispered loudly. "There are no appearances."

Zeb tossed the damp cloth into a bucket under the counter.

This was getting to be too much. But, when Cliff returned and casually touched my hand when he sat down I had to wonder if maybe there was a shred of truth to Zeb's concern because my heart skipped a beat.

"So when we going up again, Amelia?" Cliff asked.

I fiddled with the paper napkin Dot Handy had put down. She smiled at me and winked. "I don't know, but I would love to go flying again." I said it loud enough for Zeb to hear me.

Cliff smiled. "You might say that Amelia Earhart had her heart in the air and I say you do too. You took to it like a duck to water."

"Pick up," hollered Zeb. "Come on, Dot, get a move on."

Dot shook her head. "I'm coming. Simmer down." Then she leaned into me and whispered. "You two better get this worked out. He's driving me nuts. Mickey Mantle is not the only dog in love around here."

In love? I had never even thought about it. As a matter of fact the possibility of Zeb knowing *how* to fall in love escaped me. I looked up at him and his silly paper hat weaving up and down in the kitchen. He glanced at me through the pick-up window. I smiled. He cracked a small grin and went back to his griddle.

Cliff moved back an inch or two. "I didn't mean to start anything. Is Zeb your steady?"

I really didn't know how to answer that question. I mean Zeb and I have been what some folks in town would call an item since high school if you can believe that. But like Ruth was always making a point of — I didn't see a ring on my finger.

"So anyway," Cliff said obviously embarrassed and needing to change the subject. "I heard Stella tell Nate she was investigating about that buried treasure?"

Now I don't know why but something about the tone of Cliff's voice put me on edge. "She was up at the library earlier. We found some information. Not much."

"Yeah, I heard her tell Nate that you helped her find information about a train robbery. Now unless there is some rule about librarians discussing what their customers research, I'd like to hear more about it."

"Not much to say except there was a train robbery about fifty years ago and the money was never found. The article we read mentioned the Sakolas Quarry and that's where Walter had his accident."

I called over to Dot. "Make mine to go." I suddenly wanted to go home and stop talking about being in love and treasures.

Cliff backed off and tried to make nice. He even apologized. "I'm sorry, Griselda. I think living with 'The Bickersons' is getting to me. I'm not used to all that arguing. So I apologize if I said something to offend you."

"It's OK, Cliff. It's really not you."

I drove home with my dinner in a sack next to me and started to miss Agnes as I thought about how many meat loaf specials and slices of pie I had brought home to her over the years in sacks just like the one sitting next to me. At least when she was there I never ate dinner alone. I used to think that was a bad thing. So I veered off Filbert Street and headed for Ruth's.

She was home and just sitting down to her dinner — leftover tuna casserole. I was glad I brought my own. Ruth made the worst tuna casserole in the world, which was highly irregular because Ruth could make just about anything else really well — especially lemon squares. I hoped she had some for dessert. I didn't even think her tuna casserole could qualify as food but she seemed to like it. Maybe it was just me, although even Agnes turned her nose up at it.

"So Ruth," I said once we set the table and filled our glasses with iced tea. "I hear you went flying with Cliff."

She dropped her fork on her plate, which caused a tuna-filled noodle to jump and splatter on her shirt. She wiped it off with the cloth napkin she had on her lap. "Why do we put these on our laps? The food always ends up on the shirt."

After another bite she said, "Please don't remind me. I have never been so scared in all my born days, except of course when that nice doctor told me and Bubba about his brain tumor. I thought I was gonna die in that airplane — more like a sardine can with wings with nothing but . . . I don't know what holding it up. I was fixing to crash and die in a ball of flames, so I closed my eyes tight, made my peace with the good Lord above, and waited for sweet death. I think I even saw my Bubba waiting for me on the other side of the Jordan."

She took another bite. "He looked good, Griselda — Bubba I mean, better than he had in years."

"Oh, Ruth. I am so sorry it was so miserable for you. I absolutely loved it!"

"You went for a ride with Cliff?"

"Yep, although saying 'went for a ride' makes it sound silly like it's an amusement park ride. I flew, Ruth. I flew in a plane and I never felt freer or lighter in my life. It was like I left all my cares on the ground."

And that was the truth. The only other time I felt anything similar was when I was out on the pond fishing with my father. I could sit out there for hours holding my rod, waiting for that slight tug on the line, waiting until the exact moment to set the hook and reel in a trout as long as my arm. That was freedom to me also.

"Sounds like you should be flying planes." She laughed. But I took her words seriously.

"You know, that's what Cliff said." He offered to give me lessons."

"Oh, no you don't. I was only kidding. I am not ready to lose another friend around here, Griselda. Too many people died now as it is. I won't lose you in a plane wreck."

"Crash. Plane's crash. Trains wreck."

"Whatever. Dead is dead."

"I won't die."

Ruth took a few more quiet bites of her tuna. We sat silently until she mentioned Stella and Walter.

"Oh, it's all over town now," she said. "I heard from Dot Handy and Hazel Flatbush that Walter was a bank robber digging up money he stole years ago. They say he had to wait until the heat died down."

"That's not true. My goodness the way rumors fly around here. I think he was a treasure hunter, that's all. I don't think there was anything nefarious going on at all."

"Ne— what?"

"Nefarious. It means immoral or evil. Wicked."

"Wicked. That's what it sounds like. I can just imagine what Stella might be going through thinking her brother, who we all know already cheated his family, is . . . was out in the world doing . . . nefarious things."

"I don't believe it," I said. "He was not doing anything illegal."

The telephone rang. It was the nursing home.

"How'd they know you were here?" Ruth asked as she handed me the phone.

I waved her off and took the call.

"It was about Agnes," I said when I returned to the table. "They said she had another serious asthma attack and is asking for me."

"Oh, Griselda, I'm sorry. Want me to go

with you?"

"Do you mind?"

"Not at all. We'll leave the dishes. How did they know to find you here?" she asked as she pulled on her brown coat.

"I gave them a few numbers . . . just in case of an emergency. I hope you don't mind."

"Mind? No, of course not. I was only curious."

I pulled the truck out on the main road. "The nurse said Agnes was recovering but seemed agitated. She can get that way after an attack."

"It's good you're going," Ruth said. "I remember her having a few of those really bad attacks when she was still living with you."

"If they served her pickles again I'm going to start screaming at people."

"You? You never scream. You don't even know how to scream. Even that night we screamed under the trestle. It wasn't a real scream just a —"

"You're babbling Ruth. Agnes will be all right."

I parked by the front door considering this was an emergency and it was after hours. An orderly opened the door for us. "Good evening, Griselda," he said. "The doctor is with her now."

"Thanks, Claude."

Ruth and I rushed down the hall to Agnes's room. The doctor, a tall, young man with long hair in a ponytail was listening to her chest. Agnes spied me and waved us in.

"Is she OK?" I asked.

The doctor took the stethoscope from his ears. "She'll be fine now."

"What set it off this time? Do you know?"

The doctor shook his head and patted Agnes's hand. "It's hard to say. I think it might have something to do with the ragweed blowing around out there. All the rain made it grow and now all the sunshine is just making it blow in the wind."

"Maybe we should keep her window closed."

"Probably. I'll add some Benadryl to her chart."

Agnes removed the nebulizer from her mouth. "I hate it when people talk about me like I'm not here when I so obviously am here."

"Sorry, Agnes," I said.

"I'll be on call all night if you need me, Agnes," the doctor said before he left the room.

"I came as fast as I could," I said. "The

nurse said you were upset and asking for me."

"It scares me so much," Agnes said. "The attacks — oh, hey Ruth, I didn't see you there."

"Hey, Agnes."

Ruth sat in the visitor's chair while I struggled to keep my rear end on the edge of Agnes's bed. "I was missing you tonight. I might have had a feeling you needed me."

"I've been missing you too. I'm glad you're here. I feel better now."

That was when I decided the asthma had nothing to do with ragweed and everything to do with Agnes missing me, missing home. She could get herself all worked up with sadness sometimes and instead of just admitting it to herself or anyone else, her body seems to take the brunt of it. But then again, her body took the brunt of most of the bad stuff that happened to Agnes. This time I didn't mind that she needed me.

"Guess what, Agnes," Ruth said. "Griselda went flying in an airplane."

"What? The dickens you say. In a big one, a jumbo jet?"

Her breaths became labored again. I replaced the nebulizer. "You just breathe and I'll tell you the story."

Her eyes stayed wide as half dollars

through the tale. "I loved it, Agnes. I never had so much fun or felt so free and far away from my troubles."

"But Griselda, that worries me, the notion of you flying around up there. It's dangerous."

"No, it's safe. Cliff is a good pilot. And besides, Agnes, don't you always say God is not taking any of us home until our time?"

"That's true, Griselda, that's what I say. I just don't need something else to worry about." She readjusted herself with the aid of her trapeze bar. "Now tell me about Stella. My sources here tell me that Walter has had no change and that Gilda's been in a few times. But she never hangs around very long."

"No change is right. Except a change in Stella. She's finally made her peace with him and is ready to forgive those terrible things he did to hurt her so much."

"Now that's an answer to prayer. I was hoping for that, especially if he were to die. It would be hard living the rest of her life knowing she never made peace with her brother."

Ruth perked up. "She says Walter was up here looking for buried treasure."

Agnes laughed.

"Don't laugh too hard," I said. "You'll set

off another attack."

"Buried treasure? Really? I heard about loot from train robberies never being recovered but no one ever looks for it. Least not that I know of."

"It might be true," I said. "But even so, it shouldn't matter. It's not like he robbed the train."

"That's right," Agnes said. "I think it's kind of exciting. Imagine that, buried treasure near Bright's Pond. Funny that none of my sources knew this."

Ruth started to laugh. "That's all we need is for word to get out. Folks will be scrambling all over looking for it. Studebaker Kowalski and Boris Lender, all of them will be out looking for it."

The thought sent a chill down my spine. Ruth was right. "Oh, let's hope not."

We stayed with Agnes until nearly nine o'clock when she finally fell asleep. Ruth was looking a little sleepy herself. "Come on," I said. "Let's head home."

"OK," she said with a yawn. "But I was thinking, can we go by Walter's room? Take a peek inside."

"How come?"

"I've never seen a man in a coma."

"He's not a circus sideshow attraction."

"I know that. I'm not being mean. Just

curious."

The nursing home hallway was quiet except for the sound of televisions and nurses talking quietly to the residents. We tiptoed near. The lights were on but dim in Walter's room. I stopped at the door when I heard voices.

"Shh, someone's in there."

"Probably just a nurse," Ruth said.

I moved closer to the door and listened. I heard a woman's voice first, and thinking it was a nurse, I pushed open the door a sliver and peeked inside. Gilda was on the telephone. I knew I should have just turned around and left, that eavesdropping was not the right thing to do, but I couldn't help myself. I leaned closer. Her back was to me.

"It's too much money," she said. "Too much to just up and run away. I'm gonna stay a while longer. He could wake up — especially with that fat woman praying for him."

18

I backed away from the door. "Come on," I whispered. "Let's just go home."

"Why? What's the big deal?"

In that second my mind scrolled through a hundred possible explanations, and none of them were very good. Gilda was speaking to someone who had an interest in Walter and quite possibly the treasure.

I grabbed Ruth's hand. "I don't want to interrupt if he has visitors."

"So what? It's not like you'll interrupt him talking or anything. What can anyone say to an unconscious man?"

We made it to the exit. "Gilda was in his room," I said in a hushed tone. "She was talking to someone on the phone about the money."

"The treasure money?"

"That's what I'm thinking. I got the feeling whoever she was talking to was her partner or something."

"No kidding," Ruth said. "This is really getting exciting. Bright's Pond in the center of a crime syndicate."

"Now who said that? You have quite an imagination."

We started down the road toward home and were just about at Ruth's house before I said a word. "Maybe I should tell Mildred what I heard."

"Sure," Ruth said. "You could do that. She's on the prowl anyway so you might actually be helping her. Kind of like you're doing a little spying also."

"Not intentionally," I said. "I've been trying to steer as clear as possible from all this."

Ruth twisted her mouth and then smiled. "But you are knee-deep in it now."

"I know. If it wasn't for Stella I'd just forget all about it but now I'm starting to worry about her."

"You think they might rub her out?"

"Who?"

"The syndicate. That's what they do. They rub people out, people who get in the way. Oh, dear, Griselda, maybe you shouldn't tell Mildred anything. I'd just hate if you had to enter one of them protection programs, you know?"

"Oh Ruth, you are so silly. We are not

dealing with the mafia."

"I don't want anyone to get hurt."

"I know. But listen. It's not that big a deal. It's only a little treasure not even worth all that much money. I think we should relax and let Mildred handle it — if there is anything to handle."

"OK, Griselda, but do me a favor and lock your doors at night."

"I will. And you do me a favor, please."

"Anything."

"Make sure you're in church this Sunday. We have to start selling dance tickets, and could you remind Pastor Speedwell to announce it from the pulpit?"

"I hope Sylvia remembered to put it in the bulletin. That woman's got a brain like a sieve. But yes, I'll tell pastor."

"That's why the whole committee needs to be there. The dance is only two weeks away. And we want to sell out."

"Don't worry, Griselda. We do great every year. The SOAP ladies will get their money."

Ruth was referring to the fact that every year the SOAP women get the profits from the Harvest Dance to use in their missions. For a secret society they sure had a lot of visibility. But it was how they liked it.

I waited until Ruth was safely inside her house and not because I was afraid of any hit man, I just felt responsible for her. I toyed with stopping by the café. Zeb lived in an apartment above the restaurant. His living room always smelled like grease and french fries. But I changed my mind. I think I would have had a hard time not telling him what I heard Gilda saying, and for now I wanted to keep it under wraps.

For three days I kept my news to myself. But I finally got my nerve up to speak with Mildred Blessing. I asked her to meet me at the library to talk. This way we'd be out of earshot of the town. If I asked her to come by my house someone would surely notice and ask why Mildred was there.

She showed up right on time, at precisely two o'clock, dressed in her uniform with a holstered gun. It was the first time I had ever seen Mildred with her gun. She preferred not to carry it, usually. She wore the holster though, just not the weapon.

"Why the gun, Mildred? It's a little off-putting."

She patted it affectionately. "Just in case. You can never tell."

We sat at the periodicals table. The library was empty except for an occasional mouse flitting about.

"So what's the poop?" Mildred asked.

"No poop. I wanted to run something past you."

"Shoot."

I eyed her gun. "I hope not. Listen, I was over at Greenbrier the other day and —"

"What day?"

"Monday night."

"What time?"

I felt my eyebrows wrinkle. "Why is that important? Around nine o'clock."

"That's late to be visiting Agnes."

"Will you let me tell the story, Mildred, I didn't ask you here to interrogate me."

"Sorry."

"Anyway. I was there to see Agnes, of course. And Ruth and I decided to go peek in on Walter."

"Ruth was with you?"

"Didn't I just say that? Ruth and I went to visit Walter and I heard a voice inside the room. I peeked inside and saw Gilda Saucer on the phone."

"Gilda? Did you hear what she was saying?"

I nodded. "I did. She said something to the effect of it being too much money to leave town now. I figured she must be talking about the treasure."

She didn't appear surprised. But I thought that might be just some on-duty cop training discipline.

"I know," she said. "It's true. And it's not the first time."

I couldn't help taking a deep breath. "What?"

"I have spies at Greenbrier. They tell me everything. They've heard her five or six times and each time she seemed to be almost arguing with someone about the money, about the treasure. I'm thinking she believes Walter knows exactly where it is and is waiting for him to wake up to find out for sure."

My mind swirled with possibilities. "Or, maybe Walter already found it and hid it again before he got hurt."

"That's a possibility also. It could be many things. What I know for sure is that Gilda Saucer and maybe even that Cliff Cardwell are up to no good."

"Cliff? Really?" I had learned not to dismiss Mildred's instincts as quickly.

"It seems a little too coincidental that she would blow into town and then he would make an emergency landing so close together. It's too weird."

"I don't want to think that Cliff is in on anything."

"I know you don't. I know you two been flying around together and —"

"It's not like that."

"I didn't mean it the way it sounded. But brace yourself now. I sent out for information on the two of them — to Wilkes-Barre and Scranton and I should probably call someone in Philadelphia also."

"You'll tell me if you find anything out, right?"

"Oh, sure, sure. Now you got anything else to tell me? Don't hold anything back. You never know when the tiniest detail could crack a case wide open."

I told her about that evening at the Crabby Corral.

"Well, I can't blame a girl for needing a drink. But I'm glad you told me. I'm thinking maybe we need to get our hands on that treasure and then see what happens. Maybe Walter and Gilda are part of a crime ring. He could be, you know."

"Oh, Mildred, I hope for Stella's sake you're wrong. From what I can tell, they've done nothing illegal. Treasure hunting is not against the law. But Ruth is saying the same thing. She's convinced the mafia is in Bright's Pond."

"I doubt that they're anything more than two-bit hoodlums. And you're right, treasure hunting is not illegal, but I got my suspicions that they're looking for more than a

239

payroll safe, and I hope for Stella's sake I get to the bottom of this and right quick."

And knowing what Stella already told me about Walter I wouldn't doubt that he could very well be up to no good.

"Now I am glad you told me all this Griselda. Please keep it under your hat. I don't want Gilda and Cliff getting spooked before we can figure all this out."

"I understand. But do you think we should tell Stella?"

"No, let's keep this between us. She's liable to do something and ruin the whole investigation."

"I guess you know best."

Mildred put her cop hat on, hiked up her holster belt and said, "Don't you worry, we'll nab these perps in no time and I won't let anyone get hurt."

I stood on the library steps and watched Mildred drive off in her cruiser in the direction of the town hall. It made me sad to think that Cliff might be knotted up in a crime ring. I didn't want to believe it. He was one of the nicest people to come to town and I never felt one iota of ill will from him. Not a single bad vibration. It made me even sadder to think that Stella's brother might be part of it. I had hoped he and Stella would reunite and become a family.

I made a quick trip to the bathroom and when I returned to the desk I noticed the SOAP women were seated around the periodicals table with a map of the backwoods spread out.

"Tohilda," I said. "Good morning."

She looked up. Tohilda Best was not what you would call a woman concerned about her appearance. And she didn't seem to mind. In a way her aversion to pretty, womanly clothes made her even prettier. She wore a straight, baby-blue dress that reached near down to her ankles, yellowish boots with a thick sole, and her hair was pulled back in a tight fist of bun. Her eyes were like two nearly purple gems. When she smiled, the edges of her eyes crinkled.

"I wanted to tell you about Mercy Lincoln," I said.

"Lincoln. Charlamaine Lincoln's daughter?"

"Yes. She's been coming by the library a lot and checking out books. I couldn't help noticing she could use socks and shoes, sneakers if you can. She loves to run and climb trees."

Tohilda made a note on her yellow legal pad.

"I saw Charlamaine the other day," Ruth said. "She was hanging around the Piggly

Wiggly. I thought I saw her pull scraps from the dumpster. An entire tray of old donuts — glazed and jelly, I think. And a bag of hot dogs."

"I wouldn't doubt it," Tohilda said. "They are the poorest of the poor. Most of them never get a square meal. The parents do all they can to keep their little ones fed."

I reached into my pocket and found a ten dollar bill. I dropped it on the table. "Buy two meatloaf specials for them. Can you do that?"

Tohilda took the money. "Why certainly, Griselda. Maybe it's time you joined the Society."

I shook my head. "No. Not right now. I only wanted to tell you about Mercy."

After finishing up my chores around the library and the SOAP women made their ritualistic exit in silence, I locked up for the day.

The air had turned crisp and very cool as October air rustled the leaves on the ground. I could smell wood smoke and burning leaves and rubbish and for the first time that season I believed autumn had gotten a grip on Bright's Pond.

Still not thrilled with Zeb's jealousy over Cliff, I decided to head for the café — just to check on things. He was there and so was

Gilda. I hadn't seen her at the café much that week, but there she was in all her skinny, bosomy glory once again dragging a straw through her lips while Zeb watched.

"Hey," I said.

Zeb looked my way and smiled. "Grizzy, hey. Come on in. Sit here." He indicated the stool next to Gilda. I debated whether to sit or take a booth but decided to sit next to her. Maybe I could wheedle some information out of her.

"Gilda tells me the doctors are hopeful that Walter will wake up," Zeb said.

"Really?" I said turning in her direction. "That's good news. How do they know?"

"His eyes fluttered and he seemed to be coming out of it, but then he fell back into that stupid coma."

"Oh, that's frustrating," I said. "But maybe good news. Maybe he's . . . he's closer to the surface."

"We can only hope."

I turned back to Zeb. "Has Cliff been in today?"

"Why do you want to know that?"

"I was just wondering. I might want to take another spin in his plane."

"Now isn't that cozy? Just the two of you up in the air like that. It smacks of a little romance to me."

"It's not like that. I just like to fly. Have you ever been up in a plane, Gilda?"

She sputtered and said, "No. I mean not a small plane. Not like what that pilot's got parked out there."

"Oh, so you've seen it."

She smiled and dragged the straw through her lips. "Everyone has. It's a bit of a curiosity, now ain't it?"

"Maybe. But I got to say that being high in the sky with Cliff, flying over the town that day, was one of the greatest experiences of my life."

This time Zeb coughed, but I ignored it. I was, after all, trying my hand at being a junior detective.

But before I could do anymore investigating to see if Gilda had anything to do with Cliff, if they had a relationship of some kind, Gilda excused herself. "I better be going. Don't want to leave my dear sweet Walter alone too long."

Zeb came lickety split from the kitchen. "Here," he said handing Gilda something wrapped in white butcher paper. "An extra baloney sandwich in case you get hungry at the nursing home."

"Why thank you, Sweetie," she said. She stuffed it into her purse and then stood on tippy toes and kissed Zeb's cheek.

"Ah, that's no trouble," he said. She paid her bill and then sashayed out the door with Zeb watching the whole time.

"She's not that pretty," I said.

Zeb returned his attention to me. "Ah Grizzy, she doesn't mean nothing to me. I'm only being neighborly. You're my best girl. I thought we established that."

"Then why do you look at her the way you do? Why do your eyes follow her every time she walks out that door?"

Studebaker Kowalski who had been sitting in a booth chimed in, "Because he's a man, Griselda. He can't help it."

19

I frankly didn't know what I was supposed to do with my newfound suspicions about Cliff and Gilda. And by Saturday I found that I was imagining all sorts of things. I decided to tell Agnes. I could trust her.

So after closing up the library early I headed over to Greenbrier by way of Hector's Hill. I saw Cliff near Matilda. I stopped and pulled close to the curb debating if I should go talk to him or not. Maybe twist more information out of him. But before I could make up my mind he saw me and waved and then called, "Griselda, hey."

I waved back as he motioned me to join him. I did, even though every cell in my body was against it.

"Hi Cliff," I said. "I haven't seen you in a few days."

"Yeah, I've been busy working on Matilda and had some errands in Wilkes-Barre."

"Did you fly there?"

"Nah, Nate lent me his truck. Say listen, I was just about to take her up for a spin. Want to go?"

My heart sped as the excitement grew to fly again. I couldn't resist. "Sure. Right now?"

"Why not?"

"Well I was on my way to the nursing home and —"

"Ah, too bad I can't land anywhere nearby or I'd fly you there."

I laughed. "That would be a riot. I can just see the commotion that would cause at the home. Give those people quite a start."

"Ah, it'd be good for their hearts, get them pumping again."

"Well, we can't so —"

"OK, just a quick spin and then right back."

I climbed into the plane and it was like climbing into my own little cocoon. It was immediately comfortable as I locked the seatbelt and settled back in the seat. Within minutes we were airborne and that wonderful rush of freedom hit me again.

"Want to fly her?" Cliff asked over the noise.

"What?" I pointed to my ear.

"Fly." He raised his voice. "Want to fly her?"

I pointed to my chest. "Me?"

He nodded.

"I don't know. I don't know how. What do I do?"

Cliff gave me a couple of instructions and then said, "Now I'm going to let go of the stick. You just hold her steady and watch your attitude, keep her straight." I felt Cliff release control of the plane, and as I took the yolk, I felt Matilda's power, power that surged through me.

"Good job," Cliff said. "Now pull up on the stick, just a little."

For five minutes I flew Matilda. It was glorious. It was like I was made to fly and just didn't know it all these years. I remembered watching jets pass over occasionally as a child, and smaller planes, crop dusters mostly, making their journeys, and the thought always intrigued me but I never thought for one second that I would ever actually fly in the sky, two thousand feet above the ground like a bird.

"Bet this is the first time a sparrow ever flew this high," Cliff said.

I smiled. He was right and I had just settled back in a comfortable position when the mountains came up quickly and suddenly. "Oh, my goodness, Cliff! The mountains!"

"Don't worry, they're close but not too close."

"Maybe you should take her."

"Darned if you don't even sound like a pilot. Now release the stick."

The plane banked to the right and then straightened out as Cliff turned toward Hector's Hill. He landed Matilda smoothly.

"I don't know if I'll ever be able to do that," I said.

"What? Land? Sure you will. It's all in the feelings. Learning to fly is like developing a whole new set of senses."

The feelings that emerged at that moment were almost too much to bear. "I got to go, Cliff. I'm late." I jumped out of the plane and ran back to my truck, hopped inside, and cried. I was in love. Not with Cliff or Zeb but with freedom, and I wanted more, only Bright's Pond still held me in her grasp like a kite. Able to fly but only so far as the string would go.

I did eventually make it to the nursing home that day. Agnes was in her chair and looked much better than the last time I saw her. Her cheeks were pink, her eyes bright blue. She wore a muumuu the color of a sunflower and white slippers I had never seen before.

"Where'd you get those?" I asked.

"What?"

"The slippers."

Agnes tried to look down. "Oh, I don't know, probably issued by the home. They just put them on me this morning. I don't get much say in what I wear."

"What's wrong with your pink ones? If you want to wear your pink ones then you should wear your pink ones."

"It doesn't matter," Agnes said. "I don't care what color slippers I wear. Why's it so important to you?"

"I don't know. I've just been thinking about freedom lately. You should be able to wear whatever color you want."

Agnes looked at me like she didn't know what to say. She breathed and let it go through her nose.

"I don't know," I said. "It's just weird that someone else is making those kinds of decisions for you."

"I really don't mind unless . . . unless you're feeling jealous because you used to make those choices. You bought the pink slippers, remember?"

I did. I remembered it well. She rejected them at first and now someone else comes along and makes a new choice and she doesn't care. "Yes, maybe that's it. In which case I am being silly."

"Come on," Agnes said. "Sit down. Let's have a proper visit."

"Do you remember the other night when Ruth and I came to visit, after the asthma attack — how you feeling by the way?"

"Better. Much better. That nice young doctor is taking good care of me."

"That's nice. He does seem nice and caring. But anyway, about the other night, Ruth wanted to stop and see Walter."

"Walter?"

"Curiosity I guess. She never saw a man in a coma before."

Agnes nodded. "That sounds like Ruth."

"We went to his room and the door was opened a little bit like it usually is. The lights were dim so I didn't go in right away, thinking maybe it was too late when I heard a voice."

"A voice?"

"Yeah." I looked out her window and pondered my next words. Should I really say anything? What if Mildred found out? What if Agnes told someone?

"I heard Gilda talking on the phone about the money and stuff. I think she's some kind of crook, Agnes. Like she's after the treasure not Walter."

"No kidding? Geez, I hope you're wrong.

I know she's a little strange, but it's hard to imagine anyone not acting strange under the circumstances."

"But she does seem focused more on the treasure than her fiancé."

"Um, that's not good. A woman shouldn't care all that much about some silly buried treasure when her future husband is lying in a bed unconscious."

"That's why Mildred is investigating."

"Investigating? Goodness gracious, Griselda, you people are making a federal case out of what is most likely a — what does Mildred say? — a trip for biscuits, nothing."

"Probably, but it does seem suspicious, and Mildred never trusted Gilda from the beginning. Neither did other folks in town. And I'm afraid it's all starting to rub off on me."

Agnes refused to get on board with what I was saying. She continued to assert that Walter was guilty of no crimes and neither was Gilda. "Does Stella know about it?"

"No. Mildred said not to tell her in case she says something to Cliff and it spooks him, just in case he's involved somehow."

"Spooks him. What? And then he'll run away like a frightened bunny and the big bad crime will never happen?"

"It does seem silly now, doesn't it? But

still, I am not saying anything until Mildred says I can. Just my luck I'd foil the whole caper."

"Oh, for goodness sake, now you're starting to talk like some hard-boiled detective novel."

"It's kind of fun, as much as I hate to admit it."

"The best thing for you to do is forget about it. Go back to Zeb and the library, let Mildred handle whatever supposed crime there might be. Don't give it anymore thought. Remember what Daddy always used to say?"

We said it together, "Never trouble trouble until trouble troubles you."

"I feel better now, Agnes. I guess I was getting all worked up over nothing, and guess what."

Just then the door swung open wide and an aide came in with Agnes's lunch. She placed it on Agnes's tray table. "Here you go Agnes. Tuna salad today."

"Oh, that's good," I said. "You like tuna."

"They don't make it the way you did. And," she lifted the lid from the plate, "they plop it on lettuce. No bread. Lettuce. Rabbit food."

"But look, you get apple slices and pudding."

"Yeah, the pudding is good. Now what were you saying — guess what?"

"Oh, right. I flew. In Cliff's plane again and this time he let me take the yolk — that's like a steering wheel only it's a stick and you move it up and down."

"The dickens you say! You flew? Not really though, he just let you pretend."

I shook my head and then picked at her tuna. She was right. It wasn't as good as mine. "No, he released control from his side and transferred it to me. I was actually flying. Only a few minutes but still."

"That's pretty exciting."

"I want to fly more. He said he'd give me lessons."

"So what's stopping you?"

"You mean you wouldn't mind?"

"Me? Why should I mind?"

"Well back home you got scared if I went to the movies."

"Ah, that's only because you left me alone. I didn't like being alone. But here, well there is always somebody here." And so for the first time I believed Agnes had released a little more string.

Before I left Greenbrier I wandered to Walter's room. Once again I stopped at the door and listened. Then I peeked inside without opening the door any wider than it already was. Gilda stood at Walter's bedside with the phone in her hand.

"I can't keep doing this," I heard her say. "I can't keep coming here waiting for the big lug to wake up. He ain't never coming out of it. And we ain't never getting that money."

20

My heart stopped. I fought the urge to push open the door and confront her but Mildred's words to be careful filled my mind. In that moment I couldn't do anything. I wanted to stay and listen longer but I didn't. I rushed away, down the hall, out the doors, and to my truck.

Mildred would probably be in her little office. That's where I needed to go. Straight to the police. I never made it. Stella stopped me at the town hall steps.

"Griselda," she called.

I waited until she got closer.

"I can't talk now, Stella, I need to see Mildred about —" I couldn't tell her.

"What? Why you so nervous?"

"Oh, I'm not. I might be a little tired. Been running around all day. I need to get the dance tickets for Sunday. She never stopped by my house like she was supposed to."

"Well she ain't in there. I just saw her driving down the street toward your place."

I stepped back. "Oh, maybe she's bringing me the tickets."

"Listen," Stella said. "I wanted to ask you if you'd take me over to Greenbrier. I want to see Walter."

I wanted to see Mildred but I couldn't turn Stella down. It was hard enough getting her to go in the first place, and I didn't want to make her suspicious of anything.

"I just came from there. I went to visit with Agnes a little while. I poked my head in Walter's room before I left. Gilda is there."

"She is? Well, I guess I better get used to her. She is going to be my sister-in-law someday I reckon."

My heart ached to tell her what I knew. What I heard Gilda say, but I couldn't. Not yet. Not until Mildred had proof and we had a plan. The last thing I wanted to do was put Stella in any kind of danger.

"Did you want to go right now?"

"If that's OK. I need to get out of the house anyway."

"Is Nate still a bear?"

"When isn't he? When I left he was spraying her with milk again. I couldn't take it anymore so I left."

"OK, why don't we just go then?"

"You want to stop home first?" Stella asked. "See if Mildred brought the tickets?"

"No, that's OK. She'll leave them on the porch, and I probably left the door open anyway."

"OK, then let's go."

The ride to Greenbrier was quiet. My mind was so chock full of thoughts I could barely contain it.

"Are you OK?" Stella asked. "You seem awfully distracted."

"Oh, I'm sorry. I might be a little what with the dance and all."

"That's coming up isn't it?"

"Two weeks."

"Nate has the mock saloon all built. He made it so you just have to unfold it and attach some latches. He's a genius when it comes to this sort of stuff."

"I can't wait to see it. You are coming right?"

"Yeah, we'll be there. I even picked out what I'm wearing. I might look a little like Annie Oakley."

"Ha, that will be fun. I still need to find something to wear. I hate getting dressed up in costumes."

I could feel Stella staring at me until she finally said, "I think you should dress up like one of them old-timey western school marms. You know they were kind of plain Jane and quiet. Like one of them women straight out of a Jimmy Stewart western."

"You think I'm plain and quiet."

"Oh, I'm sorry. I didn't mean it as an insult. You're just so bookish, and being the librarian and all, I thought it would fit."

She was probably right. I was not overly fashion conscious or vivacious. And I did not like to talk about it so I changed the subject. "I flew with Cliff again today. This time he let me actually fly the plane."

"No fooling? You mean you actually took the controls and didn't crash or nothing?"

"I'm still here."

"That's true. Did you like it, I mean it's not like driving a truck is it?"

"No, it was very different. Weird and scary at first but then I started to love it. I actually loved it."

I could feel Stella looking at me.

"I don't think I could ever find the nerve to go up in that little plane. It doesn't even look all that safe. But then again, I never learned to drive for the same reason. Too scared and nervous."

"Have you ever asked Nate to teach you?"

"To drive? He tried. He thought I should know on account of the farm. Sometimes

259

he needed me to drive a truck or tractor but I don't know. There is just something too scary about having all that power, controlling all that weight."

I pulled into the driveway and parked as close to the doors as I could. We both noticed an ambulance out front and a small crowd of residents.

"I wonder what happened," Stella said.

"I don't know." My heart went a little wonky. I guessed that sight would always make me worry that it was Agnes.

We walked closer in time to see them carry someone out. She was old and covered with a blanket.

"She's alive," Stella said. "Otherwise they'd cover her up all the way."

"Heart attack," I overheard Claude tell someone else.

I moved closer to him.

"Oh, hey Griselda," Claude called. "Back already?"

"Hi, I brought Stella to visit Walter. Will that woman be all right?"

Claude shook his head. "Don't rightly know. She took a pretty big one. And she's old, older than old. She just had her ninety-seventh birthday a week or so ago."

"Wow," was all I could say. "I'll say a prayer."

"Maybe you should ask Agnes," Stella said.

"Oh, I'm sure she already knows," I said. "News travels like wildfire in here. And I already saw her today. We can go right to Walter's room."

As usual I stopped outside the door and listened. I always worried I'd be walking in on something. Now more than ever.

"Go on," Stella said. "It ain't like he's getting dressed."

"I know. You go first."

Stella pushed open the door. Walter was alone. The lights were dim and the only sound was the woosh pop of the breathing machine. He looked exactly the same as he had the last time I saw him. Nothing changed in spite of what Gilda had said earlier that week.

Stella stood near his head. "What do I do?"

I shrugged. "Guess you just talk to him."

She stood there, almost like she was in her own coma. Then she brushed his hair back in a gesture of love. "You creep. You stinking creep." Her voice rose a bit. "You no-good, stinking creep of a brother. You think you can come back into my life after all these years, after what you did to me and Mama. Well I don't think so. And you can't even come back in one piece; no you have to be off looking for buried treasure that probably doesn't even exist. Looking for money. It's all about money for you, Walter. And now what am I supposed to do? Feel sorry for you?"

I took Stella's arm. "Whoa, maybe this isn't the right time to speak your mind. And I thought you were ready to forgive him."

"I am. But he's not getting off scot-free, you know. I'm gonna tell him how I feel and hope he doesn't wake up while I'm saying it and then I'll tell him I forgive his sorry butt. I can say everything I need to say and he won't hear a word. Won't be able to do one thing about it."

"That is not necessarily true," came a voice from behind.

I turned. It was Gilda. My heart raced. This might not be too good.

"What are you saying?" Stella asked. "He can hear me?"

"They just aren't so sure. The nurses told me to keep talking to him. Something might be sinking in. He isn't deaf. His brain is still alive."

Stella backed away from the bed. "Oh, my goodness gracious. So he might have heard all that."

"He might not remember," Gilda said. "He might think he dreamed it. If he ever really wakes up again."

Gilda, always in a tight skirt, sat in the visitor's chair and crossed her legs. "Seems you got a pretty big bone to pick with him. Course I didn't hear all you had to say. But don't let me stop you. Go on, say your piece."

Stella moved away from the bed. "I . . . I'm done now. I don't need to say anything more."

"Suit yourself, sister. So how long you girls stayin', then? If you don't mind me asking."

"Not long," Stella said. "If fact we should be going."

I couldn't keep my eyes off Gilda. I wanted to tell her what I heard the other day. And maybe if I wasn't standing there with Stella I would have done just that.

Gilda pulled an emery board from her purse and started to saw it across her nails. "Go on. Say a proper good-bye to your brother. Sometimes —" and she turned on the crocodile tears, "sometimes I have to sit and find my confidence to look him in the eye — well, more like the eyelids — but you know what I'm sayin'." She snapped gum.

"It's OK," Stella said. "I already said my good-bye."

Stella didn't say a word until we reached the Bright's Pond limits. "I'm not sorry for one minute that I told him how I felt. I have more to say, too, and would have if that hussy hadn't walked in. I got stuff on my chest, Griselda. And it ain't fair that just 'cause he's . . . sick that I can't say it."

"But maybe you should wait. Put your feelings aside until a better time?"

"Like you did with Agnes? What good did it do you to wait?"

I drove down the road slowly and pulled up to Stella's house. "I guess it didn't really do me any good, but it wasn't about me — not always."

Stella looked at me. Tears glistened in her eyes. "But when does it become about you? When is it OK to take care of yourself?"

I headed straight for Mildred's office with a quick stop at home to go to the bathroom and check on Arthur. Poor guy's been alone a lot, especially since Agnes has been gone. Mildred had left a box on the porch, which I carried inside and placed on the kitchen table. I grabbed a steak knife and cut the tape.

I pulled a stack of tickets out and examined them. After what happened last year I wanted to make sure all the information was correct.

Bright's Pond Harvest Dance
"Git Along Little Dogies"
Saturday, October 13, 6:30 pm
The Town Hall
$3

"Three dollars? Boris must have raised the price. I hope."

But all the information was there and spelled correctly. The folks at church on Sunday would get first dibs and then Zeb would put a stack in his café and they'd be available at the bank and the Piggly Wiggly. Ruth would make sure that Vera gets a stack to sell in Shoops.

All in all, I would say it was shaping up to be a great dance. I refreshed Arthur's water, filled his dry food dish, patted his head, and said, "Sorry, boy. But I have to go see Mildred. Have I got news for her!"

Arthur purred loudly.

I decided to leave the truck parked and walk to the town hall. It gave me time to rehearse what I was going to tell her. I didn't want to say anything more than exactly what I heard in case it was just an innocent conversation Gilda was having. When I saw Mildred's police car my palms began to sweat. Maybe it was the western theme for the Harvest Dance rolling through my head but I pictured a gunfight, a shootout at the nursing home. The thought made me chuckle inside. It wasn't hard to imagine Mildred acting the part of Wyatt Earp.

I pulled open the town hall door, a big solid oak door painted bright crimson red with two large knockers in the shape of eagle's heads.

And speaking of large knockers, I was met by Ivy Slocum who was on her way out.

"Ivy," I said, "fancy meeting you here."

"Griselda. Geez o whiz, you startled me. I guess I got my mind on Mickey Mantle. He slipped his collar and I can't find it anywhere so I had to come down and get him new tags. The vet said they'd replace the rabies tag, but I got to find him before Mildred does."

"Ah, she won't do anything. She's all hepped up over Gilda Saucer and Cliff Cardwell."

"Well, I know all that but we had a deal she'd leave him alone as long as he had his collar and tags and nobody complained.

But, just this morning that nasty Eugene Shrapnel called and said Mickey Mantle was digging up his yard. I swear the way that man is so concerned about holes in his yard you'd think he buried his wife back there."

"Ivy!"

"Well, I bet he even swiped Mickey Mantle's collar just to get him in deep doo-doo with Mildred. Have you seen him?"

I shook my head. "Not today, but you know he likes to go into the backwoods."

"Yeah, he's got a girlfriend. I just know that dog is out there making pups."

"I wouldn't doubt it and say, if he does have a litter, maybe I'll take one."

"Really? That'd be nice."

Ivy looked away toward the woods. "Can you help me out? Maybe drive me up to the library?"

"No, sorry, I have some business I need to attend to."

"OK, I better get on the lookout before something happens. Thanks anyway."

I felt bad about saying no. She didn't drive. But I also knew Mickey Mantle would come home. He always did, and right then I needed to see Mildred.

Mildred was behind her little desk looking

through some papers when I knocked on the open door.

"Griselda," she said looking up. "Come in. I was going to find you later."

"You were?"

"Yes. I left you the tickets."

"Thanks. I found them."

"Are they to your satisfaction?"

"Yep. But when did Boris raise the price?"

"The price?"

"Yes, it's usually two dollars. Been two dollars for years, and those tickets say three dollars."

"Ah, nertz, Griselda, I can't keep track of everything around here."

"Don't worry. Maybe it's about time we raised the price. Folks won't mind. And, I do like the little picture of the lasso in the corner."

"Oh, good. I took a little license, well the printer did. He stuck it on there. Called it clip art. But that's not what I really wanted to say. I heard back from the other jurisdictions and guess what."

"They found something?"

"Nah, nothing. We got bupkes. Cliff's as clean as a whistle. And there is no record of any Gilda Saucer anywhere nearby."

"In Wilkes and Scranton?"

"Whole state of Pennsylvania."

"No kidding. Well maybe another state."

"I'm doing some digging now."

"Well, Mildred," I said taking a seat. "I have something to tell you. It's probably nothing but I thought it could be something. You might think it's something."

"Spill it."

"I was over at Greenbrier and was fixing to visit Walter after a visit with Agnes, you know, just to check on him. And I saw Gilda in his room again talking on the phone just like before. I'm thinking to the same person."

Mildred leaned closer across the desk. "Yeah?"

"And this time I made a point of remembering her words exactly."

"What did you hear? Now tell me verbatim if you can."

"I just said that, didn't I? I remembered them, exactly. Anyhoo, I heard her say that she didn't think the big lug — that's what she called Walter — would ever wake up and that we would never see that money. I left right after that. I was too nervous to hang around."

"Ah, geez, that's not much to go on. She said 'big lug'? You're certain? Not 'Walter'?"

"Nope. Big lug."

"Well, now, see the judge is just going to

269

say that she could have been referring to anyone. We need more."

"But you think it's something, don't you?"

"Well, sure. It's practically an admission of guilt to me same as before. Gilda Saucer is up to her ruby red lips in crime filth. I can smell it. But we need more information before I can call in the big guns. Right now all we got is suspicions. We need evidence. Cold, hard evidence."

"Well how in the world are we gonna get that?"

"I'm gonna stake out her residence, and you should keep an ear out at Greenbrier and around town — especially at The Full Moon. Report anything suspicious, no matter how trivial it might sound."

"Yes, ma'am. Gee, I feel kind of like a deputy."

Mildred let go a strange chuckle. "Now don't go letting it go to your head. I can't deputize you. This is just between you and me."

"Gotcha."

"And, oh, about that pilot fella. I hear you two have been hitting it off up in the big blue yonder."

"I've gone for a ride with him a couple of times."

"Good. Keep going and get him talking.

He'll slip pretty soon. He'll let the cat out of the bag."

"You sure?"

"They always do. Most criminals want to get caught. It's something deep in their subconscious minds that feels guilty, unless of course he's a sociopath, which means he doesn't have a conscience."

"Just keep your eyes and ears open. Now I need to get out on patrol. Eugene Shrapnel called about Ivy's dog."

"I heard. Why don't you just leave the dog alone and arrest Eugene for being such a nuisance?"

"Crime is crime, and that dog is as guilty as they come."

She patted her gun at her side. Placed her hat on her head and offered me a two-fingered salute, which I returned and immediately felt stupid.

"We'll nab the no-goodniks," she said. "It's all about patience and timing. And you could, of course, always ask Agnes to pray that Walter wakes up and spills the beans."

21

My feelings of urgency gone, I headed back home and saw Ivy running down the street. She held Mickey Mantle's collar and leash in her hand.

"Griselda! Griselda!"

"What happened? Are you OK?" I rushed to her side. "Did something happen to Mickey Mantle?"

Tears streamed down her cheeks.

She blubbered and nodded furiously. "Oh, dear me. It's . . . it's . . . awful. I found him. In the woods. He was just lying there all in a heap with his leg stuck in one of them old, rusty bear traps they got out there. I thought he might be dead. I saw so much blood."

"Where is he?"

"I could only carry him as far as the library, couldn't get the trap off his leg. The dern fool thing dragged behind us and got so heavy I couldn't —" She gasped for a breath. "And then I came running looking for you or Studebaker."

"Let's go."

We jumped into my truck and found Mickey Mantle. He was still breathing but barely. I winced when I saw the trap gripping his leg like the jaws of a shark. "Help me get him in the back. The vet in Shoops will take real good care of him."

The dog whimpered with a whimper that came from somewhere deep inside when we lifted him. I had never seen an animal that was in so much obvious pain. I thought he might have even been crying. He looked at Ivy with both hope and pain in his eyes.

"Why did this have to happen to Mickey Mantle?" Ivy cried. "He wasn't out there looking to hurt anyone."

"No reason, Ivy. Some of those traps have been there for years. Mickey Mantle just happened upon one, probably hidden under leaves. But don't worry. Dr. Fish will take care of him."

Ivy sat with him in the truck bed. He was sprawled out across her lap, the trap chains dangling onto the metal floor, his leg bleeding. She had wrapped her jacket around him trying to keep him warm but he shivered and writhed with pain. How could he ever understand what was happening?

I drove as fast as I could and thought how insignificant missing loot from a train robbery really was when your best friend was dying. I wheeled into the parking lot and ran to the back of the truck. Ivy continued to sob.

"You stay with Mickey Mantle. I'll get help."

I dashed into the clinic.

"Help. My dog, my friend's dog is stuck in a trap. A bear trap."

A man and woman behind the desk dropped what they were doing and ran outside with me. The man pulled a stethoscope out of his lab coat pocket and listened to the dog's chest.

"Come on," he said, "let's get him inside. What happened?"

"I don't know for sure," Ivy cried. "I found him. Like this. In the woods. Trapped."

They lifted Mickey Mantle onto a long, silver table. The assistant examined him closer. He put his finger inside Mickey Mantle's lip and pressed on the gum a little. "Three seconds," he said. "He hasn't lost too much blood."

"Oh, my goodness," Ivy said with a sniffle. "You can tell that just by pushing on his mouth? He sure looks to be bleeding a lot to me." She swiped tears away from her eyes. "I — I thought for sure he was bleedin' to death."

"I checked his CRT, Capillary Refill Time. It's like when you press on your hand and the spot turns white and then red when you take your finger off. If it takes less than five seconds for the dog's skin to return to red then that's good. Not too much blood loss."

"Imagine telling all that from his gums," Ivy said.

"Start him on an IV and get Dr. Fish in here. She'll need to operate immediately."

Dr. Fish, a small, petite woman with long blonde hair and glasses rushed into the exam room. "Oh dear," she said. "This is bad. It looks like he's been trapped for a while. I'll do everything I can but I'm afraid he'll lose that leg."

Ivy swallowed, hard. "His . . . his leg? But he needs it. Can't you just sew him up? Reattach all the cords and stuff?"

"It's in pretty bad shape," Dr. Fish said. She looked into Ivy's eyes and then patted her hand. "We need to get him to the operating room."

Ivy nodded and wiped tears from her now red face.

Dr. Fish stopped and turned back. Ivy's eyes grew hopeful. "Yes, Doctor?"

"I was just thinking that since he'll be under anesthesia I could go ahead and neuter him. Won't take much to —"

Ivy jumped to her feet. "Neuter him! You mean take off his leg and his —"

"I only thought —" Dr. Fish said.

"No. It's too much. The dog at least needs his manhood."

"OK," Dr. Fish said. "I understand. Try not to worry."

"I am so sorry, Ivy," I said. "I should have helped you find Mickey Mantle. Turns out my business could have waited."

She patted my knee. "Don't fret about it, Griselda." Tears poured down her cheeks. She blew into a pink handkerchief. "He'll be fine. He'll be f . . . fine." She sobbed.

About an hour and a half later Dr. Fish emerged from behind a door. She smiled. A good sign. "He'll be fine." Then she took Ivy's hands in hers and looked into her eyes. "I had to amputate his leg. It was badly mangled."

Ivy gasped and wretched. She grabbed the doctor's hands. "Really? There was no —"

"No," Dr. Fish said. "I had no choice."

"Well, he's alive," Ivy said. "And that's most important. Can I go see him?"

"Not just yet. He needs to recover. Soon

though."

"How soon?" I asked. "Can you come back this evening, after dinner? That would be a good time."

Ivy nodded. "OK. But, you'll call me if anything —"

"Certainly. But really. He's going to be OK."

About half way home Ivy finally spoke. "Don't know what it will be like having a three-legged dog."

"Just the same as a four-legged I would think."

"I don't know. I threw out a table once on account of it only had three legs. Darn thing wouldn't stand up unless I propped it against something, and even then it wasn't sturdy. I can't figure how I'll keep Mickey Mantle propped up."

"Mickey Mantle is not a table. He'll get used to it real fast. You'll see. He'll learn to balance on three legs as well as four."

"I hope you're right."

"So you think he was going to visit his girlfriend when he got caught in the trap?" I asked.

"I sure do. I expect to see puppies soon."

I dropped Ivy at her front door making certain first that she'd be OK. "Now you sure you're all right?"

"I am, Griselda. I need to get a load off for a bit. Make a cup of tea."

"I'll be back after supper. We'll go visit Mickey Mantle."

The Full Moon was packed when I arrived. There was even a waiting line for meatloaf. But Dot took my hand and led me through the small crowd to the counter. "Go on, Griselda, take a seat. You look worn out."

"I am. I just got back from Shoops. Took Ivy's dog there. He got caught in one those bear traps out in the backwoods."

Dot gasped along with half a dozen other people. "Is he all right? Geez, even old Al Capone knew better than to get stuck in a trap."

I nodded my head. "He will be OK, but the vet had to amputate his leg." Another round of gasps filled the café. And that was when nasty Eugene Shrapnel spoke up.

"Serves him right. Dog's supposed to be chained."

No one said a word but a gravy-filled biscuit flew from the back of the café and smacked Eugene on the shoulder. Eugene was a mean old curmudgeon who hated dogs and people. We were kind of used to him. I turned instinctively when I saw the airborne biscuit. Eugene wiped his shoulder with his napkin, tossed it in his plate, and left as applause filled the restaurant.

I saw Gilda Saucer sitting at the far end of the counter, closest to the bathrooms. She looked intent on eating her meatloaf, oblivious to the crowd or Eugene. But that figured, she hadn't been in Bright's Pond long enough to have an opinion about Eugene or the dog situation.

Dot filled my coffee cup, and I saw Zeb moving around in the kitchen filling plates with the specialty of the house. He spied me through the window and winked. "Extra mashed tonight, Grizzy?"

I nodded. I was about as hungry as the bear intended for Mickey Mantle's trap. "Sure thing, Zeb."

Dot placed my dinner in front of me and the aroma immediately lifted my gloom. It swirled around my head and into my nostrils and made me feel at home and at peace. I ate amid the clamor of the regulars and the clatter of dishes and utensils. Gilda finished her meal and walked down the skinny aisle much to the delight of the men, I was sure. She stopped near me.

"I was just wondering if you might be going back to Greenbrier tonight or tomorrow?"

"I don't know. Probably to see my sister.

How's Walter?"

"Same. I was just wondering is all." Then she finished her runway walk out the door. Dot wiped the place next to me as Jasper York sat down. "That woman is up to something," Dot said. "It's all over town. Mildred Blessing is even staking out Cora's house waiting to see what happens."

"Steak?" Jasper asked. "Since when you got steak on the menu? It's meatloaf night."

"Not that kind of steak, Jasper. Simmer down," Dot said. "I'll get your special."

"I think you're right," I whispered. "I just don't know what to do. Or what I should do. I certainly don't want to see Stella get hurt."

"Me neither. I think Mildred should call in the real police."

"She is the real police. And the truth is that no crime has been committed."

"Pick up," hollered Zeb. "Get a move on Dot."

"Where's Babette?" I asked looking around.

Dot shrugged. "Not sure. She was supposed to be here seeing how it's our busiest dinner rush."

"Pick-up, now," Zeb called. "Stop your yakking, Dot, and take care of the customers."

"I am," she hollered. "Sometimes customer service is about talking to them." But that was as far as her argument got her. She grabbed the full plates from the pick-up window.

After I enjoyed my meatloaf I said goodbye to Zeb and Dot, both of whom were too busy to notice or care. Outside, I met Babette running like Alice's rabbit toward the diner, "I'm late. I'm late." She breezed past me, and then I saw Cliff near my truck. He was wearing his leather aviator jacket. It was worn and faded in places and made me think of John Wayne.

"How's it going?" he asked.

"Fine. How's by you?"

"Can't complain. When are you going flying with me again?"

My heart sped out of a sudden sense of thrill and trepidation. "Don't know."

"How's tomorrow?"

"OK, I guess. As long as nothing pops up."

"Good." He started toward the café. Stopped and turned. "Say, you planning on going over to Greenbrier anytime soon?"

I felt my brow wrinkle. Strange he should ask the same question as Gilda on the very same night. "Not sure. Maybe."

He nodded. "Well, OK. Are you going today?"

"Probably not until later. I need to take Ivy back to Shoops and check on Mickey Mantle."

"The dog I keep hearing about?"

"Yeah. Poor guy caught his leg in a bear trap."

Cliff winced. "That's awful. Is he all right?"

"Well, yeah, but let's hope he doesn't get another leg caught in a trap. A dog with three legs is one thing, but two?"

"Man oh man, it hurts just to think about it."

"I guess I'll see you tomorrow," I said. "I need to get going."

I knew Ruth would want to hear about the dog so I stopped at her place and invited her to come to Shoops with us.

"Oh, poor Mickey Mantle," she said. "Poor Ivy. How's she taking it?"

"Pretty well. A little worried about Mickey Mantle only having three legs, though."

"I can well imagine."

Ivy waited on the porch. She squeezed into the cab next to Ruth. "I'm so worried," she said.

"Did you get some dinner?" I asked.

"I couldn't eat a thing."

Ruth patted her knee. "He'll be OK, Ivy. Don't fret. Maybe they can make him a false leg, you know, like they do for them poor fellas that come back from the war."

"You think?" Ivy said. "I never heard of such a thing, not for animals."

What she said next escaped me. My mind kept turning back to Cliff and Gilda, suspicious of their sudden interest in my visiting Greenbrier.

It was dark when we got to the veterinary hospital but the door was open and there was a nice young man behind the front desk.

"I'm here to check on my dog," Ivy said.

"OK, what's the name?"

"Mickey Mantle," Ivy said. "Mickey Mantle Slocum."

The young man, who was wearing a pale blue lab coat, looked through a list of names on a clipboard. "Oh, here he is. Come with me."

We followed him into a back portion of the hospital. It smelled of kibble and antiseptic.

"Oh, dear," Ivy said. "Look at him, lying there all bandaged up in a cage. I never seen anything more pitiful in all my born days."

Mickey Mantle opened his eyes. He recognized Ivy and attempted to get up. But we saw him grimace as pain shot through his body.

"Is he OK," Ivy asked.

The young man, who said his name was Bruce, opened the kennel door. "Sure. He might have some pain. But he'll be fine. He did well with the surgery and all."

"All?" Ivy said. "All what?"

"I just mean the whole ordeal," Bruce said.

Ivy stepped into the kennel and knelt near her dog. She patted his head and side. He lifted his head and licked her cheek. "It's OK, boy," Ivy said. "Mommy's here."

It was a happy, albeit tragic reunion as I saw Mickey Mantle's bandaged stump.

"Can they give him a false leg?" Ruth asked.

"False leg?" Bruce said almost with a chuckle. "Nah. But don't you worry. The dog will get along just fine on three legs. He'll be running and jumping in no time."

It was, at that moment, hard to believe.

After a while we said our good nights to Mickey Mantle and returned to Bright's Pond. I dropped Ruth off first and then headed back home. I sat out front staring at the place. It was big, big and spooky at night, and for a moment I could hear my mother calling me from the porch. I saw Agnes up at her window looking down on the children playing in the street. My heart swelled with nostalgia that quickly turned to sadness and then concern. I glanced at my watch. It was still early, not quite seven-thirty so I decided to head to Greenbrier just in case there was some reason behind Gilda's question, some ulterior motive for Cliff's sudden interest in when I was going to visit Agnes.

22

The nursing home appeared quiet and peaceful at night. The three flags out front waved and furled in the mountain breeze that carried a hint of wood smoke and burning leaves on it. Inside, the halls felt different in evening, dim lights, not as many professional looking people milling around. It was quieter. I took a moment to notice that the windows and walls were decorated with construction paper cutouts of sunflowers and pumpkins, scarecrows and autumn leaves. I touched one of the leaves thinking it strange that these people had grown older and were now making crafts proudly displayed like they were made by kindergartners.

"Hi Agnes," I said pushing open her door.

She was in bed with the TV on. "Hi, it's late to be here isn't it? But I'm glad you came."

"It is but I needed to come by. This stuff

with Cliff and Gilda is getting strange. The whole town is talking about it. Rumors are swirling and even Cliff and Gilda have been asking questions."

"Really, tell me." She perked up and grabbed the dangling triangle and lifted herself straighter. "Doing more of this myself," she said. "I think I move more easily than I ever did at home."

"That's great." I sat in the visitor's chair. Agnes turned off the TV. "The physical therapy is paying off."

Filled with a sudden sense of just how tired I was I told Agnes what was going on. "And so that's why I came tonight. I had this feeling that maybe Cliff and Gilda were planning on being here."

"Together?"

"Yes. I just don't know why. I mean if it was all innocent. If they were friends why would they be hiding that?"

"It does sound like something isn't right."

"Now look, don't worry, just keep your eyes and ears open."

"I got my spies," Agnes said. "I'll have a few of them linger around and catch what they can. They'll let me know."

"Good idea, but Agnes —" She looked up. "Be careful. I mean what if they are criminals?"

"We'll handle that. God is looking out for us. Don't you worry."

"I don't want to see Stella get hurt or even Walter if he's innocent."

"Go on," Agnes said. "See what you can find out."

I made my way slowly down the hall. I stopped several yards away from Walter's room and listened. But I couldn't tell anything from that distance. I needed to be closer. I crept closer and pushed open the door a sliver. I peeked inside and much to my surprise I saw Stella sitting next to Walter. I paused.

"And so you see, Walter," Stella said. "I hate your guts and all but I don't want you to die, and there's all this talk about that supposed fiancée of yours and that pilot fella Cliff. Are you involved in something weird, Walter?"

I coughed just so she'd know I was there. She looked in my direction. "Griselda, I . . . I didn't know you were coming out here."

"I just decided. I'm glad you're talking to your brother."

She moved her chair away from him. "Ah, who knows what he hears. Honest to Betsy, this is some terrible pickle."

I took some steps closer to her. "I know.

But we'll get it figured out. Have you seen Gilda?"

"Nope. Just me. I've been here a little while —" she glanced at the clock. "My goodness, I've been here for over two hours. Well I had a lot to say to him. Making my peace I imagine."

"Is it helping?"

"I don't know. Feels good to get some of it off my chest but not knowing if he can hear is kind of like talking to a grapefruit."

A nurse came in and checked Walter's vital signs.

"They come in a lot," Stella said. "Checking this, checking that. Did you know they are feeding him through a tube? A tube stuck inside his belly. The other nurse showed me when she cleaned it and stuff. Hard to believe a man as big as Walter could live on liquid. Man needs steak."

The nurse left but not before smiling at us both.

"Speaking of steak," I said. "Mildred has decided to stake out Cora's house, and Agnes says she has her spies keeping a lookout too."

"For what?"

"Whatever. Some sign that something illegal is happening."

Stella shook her head. "All I know is that

they're all looking for that treasure, and knowing Walter the way I do I would not put it past him to be involved in some criminal undertakings."

I let a sound escape my nose. It was hard to know anything. All we could do was wait until something actually happened.

Stella touched Walter's cheek. "I really don't want him to die, you know. I hate his guts —"

"I heard."

"Yeah, well, I guess I'm finally hoping we can make things right between us. Money don't matter anymore."

"Say," I said. "How did you get here? I just realized it. Did Nate drive you?"

She chuckled. "Nate? You serious? No. I took the bus. Did you know you can get practically everywhere by bus? They picked me up over near Personal's Pub and drove me all the way to Shoops where I got another bus that brought me here. Practically to the front door. I never knew you could get around town like that."

"Well, good for you, Stella. That gives you a little more freedom now."

"Kind of. I mean it's not like you flying in an airplane, but it is good to know that I can get around by myself."

"I'm here now so I'll take you home, unless you want to ride the bus."

"Oh, no, I'd love a ride home. The bus is great but it took me the better part of an hour to get here, and I am a little tired."

I looked at Walter. He seemed to me a kind man, but I suppose even John Derringer looked innocent when he was sleeping. I said a silent prayer that God would nudge Walter out of his coma. It would take a God-sized nudge I thought.

"So how come you're here?" Stella asked. "Agnes all right?"

"Yeah, yeah. I just . . . felt like coming by. And I'm glad I did."

"Why?"

"To see you. And I must say that I am so happy you're making things right between the two of you."

"It's up to him now," she said. "I said all I can say. I can only hope when he does wake up that he'll want to make it right with me."

"Oh, I think he will. It's been a long time and time does have a way of making hurts smaller. It's the distance. It's like being in the airplane and looking down at Bright's Pond with all that space between me and the town. Everything looked so small, even my troubles. From up there I had a sense that any problem could be solved. It's about perspective, I think."

■ ■ ■ ■

Stella was not surprised to see Nate standing on the porch when we drove up.

"He's probably been standing there for hours looking for me. He probably stood outside a while, then went inside, out to the pumpkin patch, back to the porch, pacing like a tiger in a zoo cage."

"You didn't tell him you were leaving?"

"Oh, I told him. I think I've been gone a little longer than he thinks I should."

"He'll understand."

"No. He won't. He'll holler and get mad at me, but as soon as I put a big hunk of pie or something else to eat in front of him, he'll simmer down."

I watched for a minute, and she was right. I could hear Nate hollering.

"Where in jumpin' blue heck were you, Stella? I expected you hours ago."

I pulled away from the curb and went home to rest.

The next morning we held the final Harvest Dance Committee Meeting at the Full Moon Café. It was mandatory that everyone attend. The dance was now six days away and it was imperative that all the details were in place. I heard we sold out of tickets at church and Mildred ordered more for Vera Krug to sell in Shoops.

"Good morning," I said. Studebaker and Boris were there eating breakfast, as was Ruth. Dot had taken off her apron and squeezed into the large booth next to Boris. "I'll do my best to be here and take care of customers," she said. "Babette doesn't come on until after school."

"That's OK, Dot," Boris said. "We understand. Just keep an ear turned our way if you need to go handle a customer."

Zeb came out from the kitchen. "Morning." He kissed my cheek much to the delight of the committee. I tried my best to suppress a blush but I should have known better. It's just the way I am.

"Where's Nate and Mildred?" Studebaker asked. "They knew this was the final meeting."

"Nate will be here," Zeb said. "He's always late."

"But what about Mildred?"

"Oh, she's probably slinking around town looking for a reason to arrest Cliff Cardwell," Stu said.

"And Gilda," Ruth chimed.

"Criminy," Boris said. "I would love to know what is really going on, but like I told

Mildred, she's got no evidence of any wrongdoing and she can't go following people without due cause."

"She's looking for it," Ruth said. "That woman's got a nose for crime like a hound dog has a nose for rabbit. She'll sniff something up."

"Well, this is America," Boris said. "People are innocent until proven guilty. Proven guilty, I said. We can't go arresting people on sniffs of reason."

"Hear, hear," I said. "I agree, Boris, but you got to admit there is something odd going on."

He dabbed toast into his egg. "Happens when strangers come to town, Griselda. I for one refuse to harbor suspicions until I have facts. Cold hard evidence, indisputable fact."

"Goodness gracious, Boris," Ruth said. "You sound like a lawyer. Like a real lawyer."

"I *am* a lawyer, dag nab it. I just don't get to practice it much." Boris pulled himself up and thrust out his barrel chest. He always wore the same three-piece gray suit to meetings with a white shirt and a fancy tie. That morning he wore a tie with a hula dancer on it. Her eyes lit up when he pushed a small button on the back of the fabric. We'd seen it about a million times but he still got a charge out it. "What will they think of next?" he always said.

Nate finally lumbered into the café like one of his bulls. "Did I miss anything important?"

"No, not really," Stu said.

Nate grabbed a chair and pulled in as close as he could to the table. "Hope breakfast is on Zeb today. I'm starved."

"We were just talking about Cliff and Gilda," Boris said.

Nate craned his neck. "Ah, why doesn't everyone leave them alone? They ain't doing nothing wrong. Cliff couldn't help it if he needed to land his plane up on Hector's."

"Then why is he still here?" Ruth asked.

"He likes it here. Who knows, maybe he'll move here. Besides he said he discovered another minor problem with his plane. Needs a part, forget which one, but it needs to come from Wilkes-Barre."

"Why don't you just drive him?" Boris asked.

"He'd rather wait. Like I said, he likes it here."

Dot stood. "Let me get your breakfast, Nate, and then maybe we can discuss the dance."

"The dance," I said. "Yes. So where do we

stand on the arrangements?"

Boris cleared his throat in an effort to remind me that he was the dance committee chairman.

"Sorry, Boris," I said.

"Now, now," Boris said. "Where do we stand on the arrangements?"

Nate glanced around the table. "Where's Mildred? I hope she isn't out there spying on Cliff and Gilda. That woman should be arrested herself for unlawful spying or whatever you'd call it. Shouldn't she be arrested Boris? Can't you stop that woman from making a public nuisance of herself?"

"Don't worry, she'll be here. I know she had to take tickets into Shoops," Stu said.

"That's right," I said. "I heard we completely sold out at church last Sunday."

"And no," Boris said. "I can't do anything to stop her from driving around town keeping watch over things. The minute something does go wrong all you people will be up in arms against her for not stopping it, so I'd just let her be."

The squeal of Mildred's siren sounded through the café's thin walls.

"That's got to be her," Boris said. "Only Mildred Blessing would arrive at a dance committee meeting with lights and siren blasting."

I looked out the window in time to see Mildred pull into her parking spot like she was pulling up to a crime scene. "Now why would she need to make all that racket?"

Mildred burst through the door. "I'm sorry I'm late. Got here lickety split from Shoops. I'm glad you're all still meetin' because I got news. Bad news."

23

A hush fell over the café as all eyes, even those of the customers turned toward Mildred. She took off her cop hat and hung it on the coatrack. "It took me a little while but I knew I'd find something. I knew I'd get the goods."

"Now what kind of news could be so important that resorted to lights and siren?" Boris said. "Unless of course you ran out of tickets again."

"No, no, now listen," Mildred said as she adjusted her utility belt. "I delivered the tickets to Vera. No problem with that but then I —" She huffed like she'd run all the way from Shoops.

"Wait a second Mildred," I said, "come on, sit down and tell us. Maybe have a glass of water first."

"Thank you, Griselda." She grabbed one of the small, vinyl chairs Zeb kept on hand for large parties and sat close to Nate. He seemed a touch annoyed and moved his chair toward Boris an inch or two.

Dot returned, coffeepot steaming. "Who wants more?"

"I'd love a cup," Mildred said, "and maybe some eggs and toast and some of the chipped beef if Zeb has any left."

"You're the only one who eats it," Stu said. "I hate that stuff. Reminds me of the army."

"Me too," Boris said. "You know what we used to call it?"

"All right now, let Mildred tell us this bad news," I said. "What can be so terrible to make you come blazing back from Shoops like you were chasing a bank robber?"

"I stopped in to see Dabs Lemon," she said. "You know the reporter from the paper down there. I asked him to do some snooping and see if he could dig anything up on that Cliff Cardwell character."

"Here we go again," Nate said. "You need to leave that man alone. He's not a criminal. His plane broke, that's all. End of story."

"Not so fast, Nate," Mildred said. "Dabs found some dirt. Dirty dirt. Seems I was right all along. That Cliff Cardwell is a thief. A thief and a rat and an all-around no-goodnik."

"What?" Nate said. He straightened his

back against the chair back. "Prove it."

"Dabs said he found records indicating that Cliff —"

Dot dropped off a full plate of food in front of Mildred. And then stood there with her arms folded across her chest listening.

"Hold on a second, Mildred," I said. I called Zeb from the kitchen. "You might want to hear this, Zeb."

Mildred cut her chipped beef on toast into bite-size chunks while we waited for Zeb and everyone else to get settled. Ruth excused herself to use the bathroom.

"Now don't go saying what you came to say until I get back," she said squeezing around Studebaker and me. "I don't think I can wait. Besides I'll hear better with an empty bladder. Don't you find that's true, Griselda, when you have to go to the bathroom so bad that your back teeth are floating it's almost impossible to pay attention?"

"Just go, Ruth," everyone said in unison.

Zeb joined us after a few minutes. "Looks like all the customers are satisfied so I can sit a while." He wiped his hands on his apron, grabbed a chair and sat next to Mildred.

"Maybe you should hang the CLOSED sign on the door," Dot said. "Until we finish our talk."

"Good idea," Zeb said. "Go on, Dot, hang the sign."

Dot clicked her tongue and hung the sign on the door. There were only six people in the café at the time and they looked like truck drivers only interested in filling their bellies.

Ruth returned and squeezed herself between us. Mildred finished her chipped beef, wiped the plate clean with a piece of raisin toast, and excused herself as a belch formed in her throat.

"How can you eat that stuff?" Zeb said. "I make it and I don't even like it."

"So here's the scoop," Mildred said wiping her mouth on a paper napkin. "Cliff Cardwell, aka Cliff the Griff, has been arrested five times on bunco charges in Florida, North Carolina, and once in New York."

"Bunco," Ruth said. "What's bunco? I knew a Bunco the Clown once, or maybe that was Bucky the Clown, he had these really long front teeth."

"He's a flim-flam artist," Mildred said. "A grifter."

Ruth fanned herself with the one-page menu. "Oh, he's a confidence man. Like that fella who tried to sell the Eiffel Tower. That scoundrel nearly got away with it."

All eyes turned toward Ruth. "Why are you looking at me like that?" she said. "I read it in a book once. This is exciting. Imagine it, a man trying to sell us —" She looked at Mildred. "What's he trying to sell us?"

"Nothing that I know of, leastways not yet," Mildred said.

"He's done nothing here that I can have him arrested for," Boris said.

Nate dropped his fork in his empty plate. "Where'd that Dabs Cucumber —"

"Lemon," Mildred corrected.

"OK, then, Lemon," Nate said. "Where'd he get his facts?"

"Newspapers and police reports," Mildred said.

"So what did he do — exactly?" I asked.

"He bilked little old ladies out of their life savings by pretending to be a contractor," Mildred said. She straightened herself to her full height as she made her report. "And he is known in North Carolina for pulling what they call the pedigree dog scam."

"Oh come on," Nate said. "Cliff's too smart for all that bait-and-switch nonsense."

"Can't be stupid to be a bamboozler," Studebaker said. "But I still don't get it. What's he doing in Bright's Pond? He hasn't tried to swindle anyone in town —"

leastways that I know about."

We continued to discuss Cliff Cardwell until the knocking on the café door got so loud Zeb couldn't ignore his lunch patrons anymore.

"So what are we supposed to do Mildred?" I asked. "Not talk to him?"

"Oh, no, no, that would be the worst thing you could do. It's important that he thinks he's luring us into his trap and then we'll be ready when he strikes."

I couldn't help smiling at how ridiculous it all sounded. Cliff came across as a perfectly reasonable, nice man and I hated all the suspicion that was mounting against him. But, if Mildred was correct, then it would follow that he was doing exactly what he was supposed to be doing — gaining our confidence.

"That tears it," Zeb said. "I will not let you go up in his plane anymore, Griselda."

"What?" I said. "You can't tell me what to do and besides he's been nothing but a perfect gentleman."

"But he could be planning something," Zeb said.

"No, no," Mildred said. "I think Griselda is right. Let her go. She might get some information out of him, and we don't want to make any sudden changes that might alert him that the jig is up or is about to be up."

"I still don't like it," Zeb said. "But you're right, Griselda, I can't tell you what to do."

"Well it's not up to you, now is it?" Ruth said.

In an effort to change the subject I said, "We should really be discussing the dance. Not Cliff Cardwell."

"Griselda is right," Ruth said. "We came here to discuss the dance."

"I agree with Griselda," Nate said. "I'm working steady on the scenery and props. I finished the saloon and if I say so myself it is pretty dang good. I'll get the props set up in plenty of time. You all take care of the food and music and we're good to go."

"Music," Studebaker said. He snapped his fingers. "I forgot to check with the Barley Boys."

"Barley Boys?" Ruth said.

"Yeah, they're a group of guys from Shoops who like to play country and call square dances. They're a little more blue grass, but they'll do."

"He got them for a good price," Boris said. "Just make sure they're at the town hall on time, Studebaker."

The committee members settled down and finished off cups of coffee or tea until

Boris excused us. "If no one else has any more business I say we adjourn until, well, until the dance."

"Yee haw," Nate said. But his heart was not in it.

By the time I reached my truck, my head swam. God bless Mildred. She knew she smelled a rat and was not going to give up until she caught him. Trouble was I didn't know what I was supposed to do with this information. I didn't think it was a good idea to tell Stella what with Cliff staying at their place. I knew her and I knew she'd get nervous and maybe even spill the beans. The real question remained though. What did Gilda Saucer have to do with all this?

I hadn't thought to ask Mildred if she did any digging on Gilda. But she probably did and came up empty.

Ruth caught up with me outside. "Can you drive me home? Studebaker already left."

"Sure. Come on."

Ruth climbed into the truck while I went around to the other side. I saw Cliff standing several hundred feet away. Just standing there, leaning against a lamppost looking in my direction. My stomach flip-flopped even after he waved. I waved also and climbed behind the steering wheel. It was hard not to feel a tad nervous under the circumstances, but I refused to find a man guilty until there was just cause in spite of what my stomach might have been telling me.

"Should I wait for him?" I asked.

"Who?"

"Cliff. He's standing right over there." I turned to point in the direction of the lamppost when he appeared at the window. I quickly lowered my finger.

Cliff smiled wide and indicated to me to roll down the window.

"Where you off to?" he asked.

"We just finished up our meeting, and I was taking Ruth home."

He leaned to the side and said hello to Ruth. "When you going flying again?"

Ruth's eyes grew wide as she shook her head. "Not me. Never again." Her whole body quaked. Cliff laughed, but it wasn't out of derision. It sounded sympathetic. "It's OK, Ruth," he said. "It can be scary up there."

I patted Ruth's arm. "I don't know, Cliff. I got the dance and my work and all."

"Ah, come on. I'll give you a lesson. You'll be flying over Bright's Pond solo in no time. Like I said, you are a natural flyer."

My insides quaked as much as Ruth's outsides. And not because I was afraid of flying but because I was suddenly afraid of Cliff. All the talk around town and from Mildred finally got to me.

"Oh, don't worry, Cliff, I'll go flying again. One of these days."

"So, what are you going to do?" Ruth asked when I stopped in front of her house.

"About what?"

"You know, Cliff and Gilda and Walter and all. It's becoming scary. To think we got criminals running lose in Bright's Pond. Thieves! Why it scares me to the bone. I mean why us?"

"Ah, don't worry, Ruth. This is all going to blow over, and nothing bad will happen. Gilda is more interested in Walter than us. And even though I am starting to feel a little nervous about Cliff, I think it's just the effect of the talk. Gossip, rumors are like a drug. It gets into your system." Of course my hands went sweaty as I said the words. I couldn't be sure what they were planning but I wanted Ruth to rest easy.

"Likely to bring my ulcer back," Ruth said as she opened the door. "Well I'll tell you this much. I am not opening my door to either one of them."

■ ■ ■ ■

I opened up the library before going to Stella's. I needed some time to consider how and what I would say to her. The SOAP ladies would probably show up also to discuss their annual shoe drive. Every year at the Harvest Dance they make a plea for money so they can purchase shoes for the needy backwoods families. But it is Boris Lender who makes the request on their behalf, and folks drop money into a bucket near the town hall door. They raise quite a bundle that way.

After completing my usual business of opening mail and such, I went about the library — an old Victorian house — with my duster and a can of Pledge. There were so many nooks and crannies in the old girl it could take the better part of the day to clean her properly. I asked Boris if I could have a cleaning service come in once or twice a year to do a proper job but he always shot me down.

"I have enough trouble keeping the doors open and the shelves stocked," he'd say every single time. "Budget constraints, you know? Course if you want to give part of your salary —"

So the job fell to me. And I will admit as I made my way through the stacks and tables I saw that the place needed a good stiff cleaning. Then right on time the front door opened and in walked Tohilda Best, Ruth, and the rest of the SOAP ladies.

"Morning," called Tohilda. "You want us to set up in the usual place?"

I nodded toward the periodicals table. "Yep."

Ruth waved. She was an odd bird. Outside the group she was talkative and flighty at times, but when she was with the SOAP she became very staid and quiet and barely acknowledged my presence. Must have had something to do with the secretive nature of the group. Ruth worked very hard to keep their plans under wraps, although she seldom succeeded.

But that day, even Tohilda spilled some of the beans when she assured me that Mercy Lincoln would be receiving new sneakers and socks.

"Thank you," I said. "There's something special about that child."

"They're all special," Tohilda said. "I wish we could do more."

After work I headed over to the Kincaid's farm and found Nate in the back tending to

309

Bertha Ann. He was snipping scraggly weeds from around her bottom and talking to her at the same time.

"Now you just keep growing, Bertha Ann. Don't you worry about these weeds. Daddy will take care of them. You just keep growing."

"She is really getting big," I said holding back a snicker. It was not often that I heard Nate sound so gentle.

Nate scratched under his Burpee Seed cap. "Oh, Griselda, how long have you been standing there?" He seemed a bit embarrassed. "I . . . I was just."

"It's OK. I read somewhere that talking to plants helps them grow."

He closed his shears and stood making a noise like he had a crick in his back. "I think I got this year's winner even considering all the trouble we went through with the gopher and the mildew. I heard some talk down at the feed store about a couple of pumpkins, but I think Bertha Ann's got them beat by at least a few pounds."

"I think you might be right. I have never seen a pumpkin this big."

Nate just shook his head and patted his pumpkin. "I hope you're right. Pumpkins have a way of looking smaller when you pick them from the vine."

"Is Stella around?" I asked.

"No, no she ain't here," he said. "Ever since she discovered the bus she's been going all over. Like she sprouted wings or something, and say, speaking of wings, I heard Cliff take off and fly overhead about an hour ago. He just up and left, too, without telling me a word. He was supposed to help me in the barn today."

"He probably had business."

"Yeah and if I listened to you people I'd say it was criminal business."

"Oh Nate, don't be like that. Mildred can't help herself, and you got to admit the information she discovered is pretty serious. But I'm not judging him or anybody until we see some kind of proof."

"Listen," Nate said, "men are like pumpkins. I can always tell a good one from a bad one and when a bad one cracks it ruins the whole gourd. Cliff has no cracks. I'm betting that he's changed and he's making an honest living now."

Nate knelt on the ground and pulled a long, skinny greenish yellow vine away from Bertha Ann. "I better get back to work."

"OK. Tell Stella I stopped by."

I started to walk away from Nate. He stopped me.

"Griselda. Are you going to tell her all this

nonsense about Cliff?"

"Are you?"

"There's nothing to tell."

Just then we heard the buzz of Cliff's plane and watched as it came into view.

"Looks like he's landing."

I jumped in the truck and headed toward Hector's Hill. I waited in the truck until Cliff secured Matilda.

"Hey Griselda," he called. He walked toward me carrying a small box.

"Looks like we keep running into each other. I was just in Wilkes-Barre. Got the spark plugs I needed."

"Oh. So now Matilda will be in tip-top shape."

"Sure will. I wanted to make sure she was all set before your lessons."

I would have gone with him that minute if he asked. But he didn't.

"Except that I promised Nate I'd help him today. Maybe in a day or two if that's all right with you."

"That's fine. We have the weigh-off and dance coming up."

He rested his arms on the truck's opened window. "Speaking of which, I guess you'll be going to the dance with Zeb."

"I will. Are you coming?"

"Now that depends, little lady," he said in

a John Wayne voice. "Do you think he'd mind if we had just one dance?"

"Nah. I think that will be just fine with him . . . and me."

Cliff smiled into my eyes and once again I noticed butterflies had taken up residence in my stomach. It was no wonder he made such a good con artist. His voice was so soft and inviting I could hang on every word.

24

Saturday arrived, and we could not have asked for a more tailor-made day for the weigh-off or the Harvest Dance. The sun shone bright, a slight mountain breeze carried hints of cayenne pepper as small, puffy clouds rolled overhead like tumbleweeds. Arthur mewed at the door until I finally let him out. I knew full well that he would bring me a mouse or a shrew later. I had come to accept his love offerings.

It was still early, only seven o'clock, but I knew the men would be at the town hall setting up for the dance and the women would be tucked away in their kitchens making final food preparations. I opened the kitchen window and could smell Hazel Flatbush's famous five-alarm chili in the air. I winced when I thought about Darcy Speedwell's cottage cheese–lime JELL-O delight. We tolerated it. I doubt anyone could or would ever tell Darcy that her

JELL-O delight was not all that delightful.

Frank Sturgis was sure to be in his kitchen that morning stirring a pot of fudge while Ruth baked pie and lemon squares. Charlotte Figg from Paradise was set to bring her pies. We all knew her pies would be in competition with Zeb's, but I think we all looked forward to a little good, wholesome pie fun.

"It'll do Zeb good," I said aloud as I rinsed my cereal bowl. No one had ever challenged Zeb's pie skills, not since his mother Mable died. She was the queen of pie and was well-known in the area for having baked, along with several other women and men, the largest blueberry pie ever made in these parts. I had a picture of it somewhere and was going to go find it to show Charlotte when I heard a knock on the door.

It was Zeb. He was standing on the porch in his blue jeans with his white apron tied around his waist. He was obviously already up and baking.

"Are you going into Shoops for the pumpkin weigh-off?" he asked.

"I told Stella I'd be there. Are you?"

"I can't leave the café today. There is so much to do to get ready for the dance. Wish they hadn't changed the pumpkin date. But

I'm glad you're going. I feel kind of awful that I can't be there. First one I've missed."

"I know, lots of folks will miss it because of the dance. But I think I'll go. Stella needs someone there."

Zeb stepped inside. "Listen, Grizzy, that ain't the only reason I came by so early in the morning."

He followed me into the old viewing room from the days when my house was a funeral home. "I needed to apologize."

I sat on the red velvet sofa that had sat in our house in the same exact spot for almost forty years. "Apologize? For what?"

"Yeah, apologize." He looked away. "I've been acting badly about that Cliff fella."

I sighed. "Yeah, you were. But now I don't know what to think after hearing what Mildred had to say about him being a con artist. And I like flying so much. It's like nothing I've ever experienced before, Zeb. It makes me feel happy, not that I'm not happy on earth but flying is different."

"I know you feel that way. Your eyes get bright when you talk about it. So I want you to know that if you really want to take flying lessons, you can. I'll even pay for them — just not from him. But you have to promise me you won't fly too far away." He patted my hand.

My heart sped as I tried to figure out what it was about Zeb's offer that disturbed me. "Wait a second," I said, finally figuring it out. "I don't need your permission, Zeb, and I can pay for lessons myself."

Zeb stood. "Ah, Grizzy, I didn't mean it like that. I know you don't need my permission. I was just saying that it's OK. Maybe more OK for me. I'll try not to worry while you're up there flying around."

"In that case, then. I'll accept your offer, and I'll even let you pay for my lessons."

He smiled and then took my hands in his and looked me in the eyes. "We're good then?"

"Uh huh. We're good."

Then he kissed me and my knees turned to jelly and I felt a blush warm my face.

"OK, then," Zeb said. "I better be getting back to the café. Tell Nate I said good luck."

"I will. But I'm hoping he doesn't need any."

I watched Zeb walk down the street. He had a little bit of a spring in his step and I will admit that I felt a little bit of a spring in my heart.

Stella said Nate had insisted they get into Shoops by eight even though the weigh-off didn't even start until nine o'clock. Believe it or not it takes a long time to weigh a bunch of pumpkins but I figured they'd make it back to Bright's Pond in plenty of time for the dance.

I wore jeans and a flannel shirt but grabbed my peacoat on the way out the door. The weather girl had called for the temps to rise into the fifties later in the day, but I had learned not to trust mountain weather. It had a way of changing pretty quickly, and you could almost always count on the breeze to kick up, especially in autumn.

I stopped at Ruth's first. She was busy making lemon squares.

"Where's your pies?" I asked.

She screwed up her face and flicked a crumb from the kitchen table. "I didn't make any. I hear that new woman up in Paradise is making about a dozen pies. Everyone says hers are the best. What's her name?"

"Charlotte."

"That's right. Charlotte Kumquat."

"Figg."

"Figg, kumquat, what's the difference? She's the new pie queen in town."

"Don't be jealous. God doesn't want you to be jealous. And he doesn't want Zeb to be jealous either. You still make Cora's lemon squares better than anyone."

"I added something a little different, this year," she said with bright eyes. "Make them more my own, you know, real lemon zest. Cora never did that. She just used the juice, but I added a bit of the peel."

"Good idea. I came by to see what you were up to. I promised Stella I'd go to the weigh-off."

I looked around Ruth's kitchen. I counted seven trays of lemon squares tucked under Saran wrap.

"Is that today?" Ruth asked.

"Yes, they changed the date."

"You know what," Ruth said taking off her watermelon decorated apron. "I am sick and tired of lemons. I say it's time for pumpkins. How 'bout if I come with you?"

"I was hoping you'd say that."

"Just let me freshen up, maybe a little lipstick, and I'll be right with you."

"OK. We have plenty of time. I think I'd like to stop in at Ivy's. Check on her and Mickey Mantle. She's been quiet lately."

"Oh, I saw her a few times here and there," Ruth called from her downstairs powder room. "She says Mickey Mantle is doing real good. But she doesn't like leaving him for long. And she doesn't like getting those pills down him."

"Pills?"

"The antibiotic the doctor gave her. At first Ivy was having a heck of a time getting Mickey Mantle to swallow them but the vet told her to hide it in some liverwurst. Worked like a charm. He laps it up in a second."

After Ruth checked her stove and locked the back door we headed over to Ivy's house. I knocked on her front door but got no answer.

"I wonder if she's out walking the dog," I said.

"She might be but —" Ruth pointed. "There she is, out back with Mickey Mantle."

Ivy had him on a short leash. His leg, or what was left of it was still bandaged, but he seemed to be standing on three legs like he didn't even miss or need the fourth.

"Don't suppose he lifts his leg to pee now, does he," I said.

Ruth couldn't suppress a chuckle.

Ivy shook her head. "Griselda you slay me. Everyone knows he'd fall down if he does. Poor fella has to squat like a girl dog and go. Kind of pitiful. He used to have quite a reach when he could aim it better."

Mickey Mantle looked at me. I gave him a good scratch behind the ears. "You are a good pup, aren't you?"

He barked.

"How are you doing with all this Ivy?" I asked. "You OK?"

"I'm doing just fine," Ivy said. "Mickey Mantle is getting used to things and so am I. The doc came out the other day and checked him over. She says he's doing good. She even said I can take the bandage off when I'm ready."

"What's stopping you?" Ruth asked.

"Just ain't ready to see it."

Ivy gave a slight tug on the leash and Mickey Mantle followed her inside. He went to his doggie bed, a large gray pillow near the fireplace and lay down.

"We're on our way to Shoops for the pumpkin weigh-off. Want to come?"

"And leave Mickey Mantle?"

"He'll be OK. Just a few hours. It'll do you good."

Ivy looked over at her dog who was now sound asleep and snoring. "OK. But we'll be back for the dance, right? Course then I'd have to leave him again. I just don't know."

"Come on, Ivy," Ruth said. "We can't let Stella be there without a fan club now can we? Mickey Mantle will be OK as long as he has food and water, and he just did his business and all."

Ivy appeared pensive a moment. "Well, OK. I would like to get out, and the Shoops Pumpkin Festival is always a nice time. They can pretty near make anything with pumpkin."

"Oh good," I said. "This is going to be fun."

By the time we made it into Shoops the streets were already lined with parked cars, clear out to the main road. We were forced to park at least two miles from the activities on a fallow cornfield. Fortunately two of the sponsors of the event, Piggly Wiggly and The Pink Lady, ran a shuttle bus from the parking to the center of town.

It was one of those short, yellow school buses with banners advertising many of the local shops and businesses. But the gimmick I liked best was the huge plastic pig on the roof. He had a sign around his neck that read, "This little piggy went to market — The Piggly Wiggly Market."

We boarded the standing-room-only bus and stood shoulder to shoulder with all manner of folks — farmers, business people, children. My toes touched the "Do Not Cross" line that separated the driver's cab section with the passenger section. The only good thing was that we were the first to get off. Ruth couldn't wait. She never liked tight spaces and would rather climb six flights than take an elevator. Ivy didn't seem to care, although she did remark that her extra-large breasts often made such situations uncomfortable.

The town was decked out in all its pumpkin puffery with tents shielding craftspeople hawking macramé and pottery, blown glass, and baked goods including pumpkin pies, of course. There were concession stands selling everything and anything that could be made from pumpkins from face wash to bunion cream to lamps.

"Oh boy," Ruth said. "I want to try some of that pumpkin beauty wash." She bought a jar, a pretty little fat jar with a quilted yellow and red fabric sticking out from under the lid. The label read, Patty Premont's Pumpkin Pie Beauty Cream.

Ivy purchased zucchini and pumpkin soup mixes that were hand mixed, according to the label, by Mrs. Casimir Puchta and an odd little carved gourd clock wrought by none other than the hands of Mr. Casimir Puchta himself who stood proudly behind his table.

"You like?" he asked Ivy. "I make many, many more for you. All shapes. All sizes."

"No, no," Ivy said. "I only need one gourd clock."

"It's gourd-geous," I said.

We walked a little farther through the crowded fairgrounds. I picked up a little set of pumpkin salt and pepper shakers. "These are cute," I said. And the little girl behind the cash drawer beamed. "I made 'em myself. Well, leastways I painted them and fired them at the craft store. Pretty ain't they? That there one with the green stem is the salt. The other one, with no stem is the pepper."

"Thank you very much," I said. "You did a very nice job."

Our next stop was a white tent with a multicolored sign next to it that read, "THE LORD'S GOURDS." The artist, Mazy Dalton, was proud of her many hand-painted gourds, some tall and skinny, others short and squat. "See there," she said. "That's Jesus walking on the water. And this one here," she held up an ecru-colored gourd, "is of Jesus feeding the five thousand. Took me a whole month to get it just right."

I had to swallow a chuckle, not very sure if I should be amused or horrified.

"Come on," Ivy said, also about to burst into laughter. "It's getting close to eight-thirty. We should find Stella."

Along the way we passed the *Shoops Sentinel* where Dabs Lemon worked. He happened to be standing outside the office smoking a cigarette. He recognized me.

"You're Griselda Sparrow," he said.

"Hi, Mr. Lemon. How are you?"

"Fine, fine." He flicked his cigarette butt into the street. "How's your sister? Still making miracles?"

Dabs Lemon interviewed me once for a story he did on Agnes. Not a very flattering story. "She's fine."

"Hear you got more trouble up there in Bright's Pond." He practically licked his chops.

"Trouble?" Ruth said. "What trouble?"

"Stuff that policewoman asked me to investigate. The pilot?"

I was not about to start discussing what was happening in Bright's Pond with Dabs Lemon. The last thing I wanted was my name in the paper again or to see him snooping around town.

"Mildred is handling it," I said. "Nothing to get excited about."

"I don't know about that," Dabs said. He looked away down the street. For effect, I suspected. "That is to say —" he stretched the word "say" out like it was a piece of gum stuck to the bottom of his shoe. "I wouldn't

325

worry too much about Cliff Cardwell. He's strictly two-bit. I'd put my money on that woman Gilda Saucer to be the trouble-maker."

"What makes you say that?" Ivy asked. "She seems OK."

Dabs grinned. "I'll let you know for sure soon. Got some feelers out." He lit another cigarette. "I got a nose for news."

I waved the smoke away and took Ruth's arm. "You'll have to excuse us. A friend is expecting us at the pumpkin weigh-off."

Dabs laughed and then coughed like the laughter got stuck in his throat. Served him right I figured. "That stupid contest? At least I don't have to report on it this year. Bunch of pumpkin freaks if you ask me."

"Well you don't have to be so mean about it," Ruth said.

At the end of the main drag we saw a sea of pumpkins spread out on wood pallets. They varied in size and shape and color from small to big to huge, from near white to greenish to bright orange, the kind of orange you'd expect for a pumpkin. Men in flannel shirts and caps milled around the sea scrawling numbers on the pumpkins in large, black letters. I looked for Bertha Ann. She was registered in the Gargantuan Division.

The three of us waded through the pump-kins and finally found Stella and Nate standing near Bertha Ann who all of a sudden didn't look so big. The funny thing about pumpkins is that when they grow so large they kind of flatten out in a kind of Salvador Dali–painting kind of way. Bertha Ann sat between two enormous gourds half again as big as the Kincaid entry. Bertha Ann, although bordering on flat sided was still quite round and pretty.

"How's it going?" I asked.

"Ah, Nate wants to go home. He says there's no way Bertha Ann will stack up against these giants."

"I can't figure where they got their seeds," Nate said. "I thought I had the biggest growers going."

Stella patted his shoulder. "They aren't that much bigger. They might be all mass. You got volume."

"That's right. You won't know for sure until she gets weighed," Ivy said.

"I hope they crack and collapse," Nate said.

"Now that's not very kind," Stella said. "How'd you like it if someone wished ill will upon Bertha Ann?"

"Where's Cliff?" I asked looking around. "I thought he'd be here."

"He said he had some business to tend to," Nate said. "Might come by in a bit."

"Oh. Well, I'm sure he'll get here in time for the big event. Do you know what time that will be?"

Nate looked at his watch. "Not for a couple of hours yet. They weigh off the kid's divisions first. The Four H-ers and then the smaller groups. The big guys are always the last to go."

"That's good," I said. "That will give Cliff time to get here. Maybe he'll fly in if he can find a place to land Matilda."

Just then the fellow standing near the larger of the two pumpkins close to Bertha Ann pulled out a tape measure. With the help of who I assumed was his son, they wrapped it around their pumpkin.

"See that?" the man said. "I told you she grew a little overnight. She's just over nine feet around."

"You're right, Dad," the boy said. "We're sure to win!"

"Ah, I'm takin' a walk," Nate said as he threw up his hands.

"Poor guy," Ivy said. "He really thought he was a shoo-in this year."

"Yeah and after coming so close last year," Stella said. "I hope he takes third or maybe even second."

I sighed. "OK. Well maybe we'll wander around for a little while and meet you back here."

"Yeah," Ivy said, "I'm hungry."

"Plenty to eat if you like pumpkin," Stella said.

"I smell ribs," Ivy said, "coming from that direction."

There was no way Stella would leave Bertha Ann. Whether she admitted it or not she was almost as emotionally invested in the pumpkin as Nate.

An hour later we made our way back to the judging stands. They started with the smaller pumpkins and awarded ribbons for first, second, and third places. Another hour and a half went by before they were finally ready for the largest gourds.

A forklift picked up the pallets and drove them to a large circle where they were lowered and wrapped with yellow straps.

"Like babies in a sling," Ruth said as we watched them lift each pumpkin and weigh it on a contraption that looked much like a giant fish scale.

Nate looked like he was about to bust all his buttons when it came time for Bertha Ann. He directed and hollered at the men as they secured her in the sling.

"Careful now. Careful. Don't drop her."

The men, apparently used to temperamental stage parents, simply did their jobs.

"One hundred twenty-nine pounds, seven ounces." The official declared Bertha Ann's weight.

"Wow, heaviest so far," I said. "He's got a chance."

But it wasn't to be. Bertha Ann lost to a monster named Goliath who weighed in at one hundred fifty-two pounds, five ounces. Bertha Ann took third place.

Nate said precious little. He made noises and harrumphed off toward his truck. Stella followed shouting words of encouragement, which Nate waved away.

"Sometimes I wish he'd keep on walking," Stella said. "It's like that dang stupid pumpkin is all he cares about."

"Ah, he loves you," Ruth said. "This is just hard after he invested so much time."

"Oh, I know," Stella said. "But I still would like to ride home with you if that's OK. He won't even notice I'm not in the truck."

25

Ivy graciously offered to sit in the back of Old Bessie since there was no way all four of us would fit in the cab. By the time we were on the road it was nearing two o'clock.

"The dance starts at six-thirty," I said.

Ruth, who had her arm out the window feeling the rushing air said, "What do you suppose that reporter fella meant?"

"Ah it's just his nature to be suspicious," I said. "He wouldn't be a good reporter otherwise. He's just looking for a story to get him to the big leagues."

"What are you two talking about?" Stella asked.

"I'm not entirely sure," I said. "We ran into that reporter fella at the *Sentinel* and he said he had some suspicions about Gilda."

"Gilda?" Stella said. "What kind of suspicions? I mean I should know, shouldn't I, seeing how she's fixing to marry my brother?

331

I turned my blinker on and passed a hay wagon that was going about five miles an hour in a thirty-five-mile zone.

"I bet it's nothing," I said. "She's new in town. I kind of think he'd investigate anyone new. I heard when Bob the pharmacist moved to Bright's Pond he investigated him and got all bothered when he discovered he scored pretty low on his pharmacy exams. Remember how upset everyone was when they thought we got an inferior pharmacist and everyone would be getting mixed-up pills?"

Ruth laughed. "Yeah. I remember. Turned out that young Bob just froze on tests. He's the best pharmacist there is."

"See that," I said. "We should just relax. Get ready for the dance and have a good time."

"I don't know," Stella said. "I never liked Gilda from the start. She's cagy if you ask me."

"And a hussy according to Dot Handy."

"Let's keep our eyes and ears open," I said.

"Agreed," said Stella.

I glanced in the rearview and saw the wind blowing Ivy's hair every which way. She seemed to be hanging on for dear life. Ivy Slocum was a good egg.

Ruth was first to be let off. "See you in a little while," she said. "Now don't forget I got bandanas for everyone down at the town hall."

I let Ivy out in front of her house. "I hope Mickey Mantle is OK," she said. "Thanks for taking me though. I had a good time."

"I'm glad you came, and I'm sure Mickey Mantle is just fine," I said.

Then I drove up to the Kincaid farm. "If I'm lucky," Stella said, "Nate's probably sitting in the dining room poring over his seed packets and agricultural pamphlets trying to figure out what he did wrong. He won't have much to say for a while."

"He'll still come to the dance, won't he?"

"Don't know. But I'll be there and I might just dance with Cliff Cardwell if Nate stays home."

Truth be known Dabs Lemon's words haunted me as I prepared refreshments for the dance. I wasn't much of a cook except that I could make really good iced tea. That was the limit of my expertise. Of course, Agnes always said I made the best tuna salad on the planet. But you don't get much tuna at a western-themed hoedown.

I couldn't help wondering if Dabs had anything on Gilda, as they say. She was a strange character. But she didn't look like a criminal.

Ruth had dropped off a pair of cowboy boots she thought would fit, one of her red and white paisley bandanas, and a set of chaps and spurs she thought would be "cute." I wasn't going to wear them. I did choose a blue and white flannel shirt and found a belt in my closet with a turquoise buckle.

I prepared three gallons of iced tea. It would be plenty. There would certainly be coffee and lemonade.

Not wanting to get there exactly on time I left the house at six-thirty, choosing to walk the short distance to the town hall pulling a wagon behind me carrying the jugs of tea I made. I moseyed past Ruth's house.

"Now don't you look so pretty?" Ruth said when she opened the door. "But where are your chaps and spurs?"

"I decided not to wear them. No offense, they just weren't that comfortable."

"That's OK."

Ruth looked like Annie Oakley in her cowgirl outfit. She had everything just right. She wore her hat hanging down her back with a string loosely tied around her neck. She wore a blue-and-white-checkered shirt with silver snaps, a suede vest with fringe, and a red skirt held at the waist with a leather belt with a large bronze buckle. And to complete the ensemble she wore calf-high, pointy-toed, white boots decorated with rhinestones.

"You really went all out," I said. "Your outfit is perfect."

"Thank you, Griselda. I wanted to be as authentic as I could."

"Where's your lemon squares?"

"Stu came by earlier, while we were at the pumpkin festival, and brought them to the town hall."

"That was a good idea. Let's go pick up Ivy."

As we walked to Ivy's house we saw other townsfolk making their way to the dance hall. Most of them were in western attire, especially the children.

"I've been thinking," Ruth said. "That Dabs Lemon fella might be right about Gilda. She is a little bit of an odd duck, and as far as I can tell, she still hasn't bought groceries or aired out the house. It's like she just sleeps there and then leaves every morning. I mean I'm wondering why she even bothered to rent the house unless of course she was hoping to bring Walter home to it — yeah that makes sense. I bet that's what she was thinking."

"Well she's spending her time at the nursing home, I reckon," Ivy said with a hitch in her giddyup. She decided to wear the spurs and a strange little bolo tie with a slide shaped like a steer head.

The crowd was lining up at the door. We could hear the Barley Boys from the street. They were whooping it up inside.

"They're having a rootin' tootin' good time already," Ruth said. "You got your tickets?"

Ivy pulled hers out of her pocket. "Right here. Three dollars this year. Price sure has gone up."

Ruth and I didn't need tickets since we were on the committee but I always bought one anyway, just to help out with the funding.

Babette Sturgis, in a pretty little corn-colored dress and cowboy boots and a cowboy hat, was taking tickets at the door. She sat on a stool next to a large barrel with the word "DYNAMITE" stenciled on it.

The line moved quickly and noisily into the hall.

I caught Zeb's eye almost immediately. He was all dooded up in his cowboy duds. Denim jeans, flannel shirt, and boots but no cowboy hat. He looked handsome standing near the lamppost obviously waiting for me. But then I saw Gilda sashay up to him swinging her hips like a pendulum. I stopped. She was about as country as she could get I supposed with a green skirt and plaid shirt. But, unfortunately, her hip-high, shiny white go-go boots did not exactly scream country.

"Howdy," I said when we got close enough to them.

"Howdy," Zeb said.

Gilda looked me up and down. "Girl," she said. "You have got to remind me to take you shopping some day. How do you expect to land this nice young man in clothes like that?" Then she patted Zeb's cheek. "He is just so cute."

Zeb blushed and pushed Gilda's hand away.

Ruth looked at Ivy. Ivy looked at Ruth.

"Come on, Zeb," I said. "Why don't we go check out the pies?"

"That's right," Ruth said. "Let's go have us a shindig."

Ivy and Ruth went in one direction while Zeb and I headed for the pie table. A medium-height woman with short brown hair, kind of wavy, wearing a paisley dress stood behind the counter.

"Is that Charlotte Figg?" I asked.

"Yep," Zeb said. "And they're her pies. She must have baked three dozen of them."

We stood off to the side a moment while people gathered around her table. Some were taste testing each variety and others were grabbing presliced pieces on red paper plates for thirty cents each.

"The cherry looks good," I said.

"I hate to admit it," Zeb said. "But her cherry pie is like nothing I ever ate before. It is so good, and she plops a little whipped cream on the top if you want."

"Go on, buy me a piece."

Zeb introduced me to Charlotte.

"This is Griselda Sparrow," Zeb said.

She shook my hand. "Oh, the librarian I heard about. It's nice to meet you."

"You too," I said. "Your pies are becoming legendary around here."

"Ah, that's so kind of you to say. Thank you. Can I get you a slice?"

Zeb and I walked away with a slice of cherry crumb each. I took my first bite a little out of earshot of Charlotte. At first it was tart but not too tart and then the tartness turned to sweetness that dribbled down the back of my throat. The crust was perfect — flaky and tasty.

"Ah, man," I said. "She should sell these."

The music grew louder and louder as folks took to the dance floor. I didn't know what the Barley Boys played but they sounded so sweet. I saw one guitar player, a fiddler who looked to be a hundred and two years old with long white hair and an even longer white beard, one banjo picker, and a tall stringy man plucking an upright bass. They all wore the same black suit with a white shirt and skinny black ties.

Nate's scenery transformed the town hall into a western style saloon. Bob the pharmacist stood behind a long counter made to look like a bar and served drinks — fruit punch, lemonade, and my iced tea. He played the part well wearing a striped button-down shirt with purple garters around each arm to keep his shirtsleeves from getting wet with drinks.

A long table covered with a red-and-white-checkered tablecloth displayed about an acre of other goodies from brownies and Ruth's lemon squares to cookies and even vegetables with dipping sauces homemade by Edie Tompkins.

"Your Full Moon pies — I mean Harvest Pies — look so inviting," I said. "They really do look like harvest moons."

"I was going to put them on the pie table with Charlotte Figg's but then I thought better of it. Let her have her own table."

"Have you tasted her apple?" said Edie Tompkins who sneaked up behind us. "It is just the best, the absolute best. She should open a store."

"She really should," Frank Sturgis said. He was standing near Edie's husband, Bill. "She does make the best pie."

Zeb grabbed my hand. "Come on," he said. "All this talk about pie." He started to pull me toward the center of the floor but Studebaker caught up with us.

"I've been giving it some thought," Studebaker said as he hitched up his pants. They were being pulled down by a pair of six-shooters holstered around his waist.

"Giving what some thought?" asked Zeb just as the four Speedwell boys whizzed past him carrying plates piled high with brownies and cookies. Their mother ran behind them.

"Matthew, Mark, Luke, and John," she hollered, "that's entirely too much food. It's gluttony. Pure and simple — gluttony. You put some of that ham back this minute or you're gonna catch it but good."

"That poor woman has got her hands full," I said. "She is always running after those boys. I mean where is her husband?"

"Over there." Zeb pointed. Pastor Speed-well was standing very close to Gilda near the bandstand. He looked about the same as he always did no matter what the occasion. Tall and skinny with his ubiquitous black suit and shiny black shoes. Except in honor of the western theme of the evening he wore a white cowboy hat, one of those ten-gallon hats.

"Wonder what he's telling her," I said.

"He's probably telling her that Jesus loves even sinful city women."

"I think you're right. Look at her. She is trying so hard to get away from him."

"Never mind them," Stu said. "I'm talking about the treasure everyone is so hepped up about. I want to go looking for it."

"What?" Zeb said.

"The treasure," Stu repeated. "Why don't we go looking for it? No one knows if that fella in the coma ever found it. Why not?"

"Ah, that's just silly," I said. "No one except Walter has a clue about where to dig. I mean that's a lot of ground up there."

"But we have that one clue," Zeb said starting to sound very interested in what Stu was saying. "Between the high road and the low road. All we need are shovels."

"I got shovels," Stu said. "What do you say?"

I half expected to see Stu and Zeb shout a Three Musketeer–type victory call but they didn't because that was when we all spotted Cliff walking across the dance floor. He wasn't wearing cowboy garb except for one of Ruth's bandanas tied around his neck. I must say though that with his leather flight jacket and blue jeans he didn't need a cowboy hat to help with his swagger.

"Howdy," Cliff said. "I saw you all standing over here and thought I'd mosey on over."

"Howdy," Stu said.

Zeb tipped his imaginary hat, and I just said, "Hi Cliff."

"We were just discussing the treasure," Stu said. "I was thinking maybe we should go looking for it."

"I was wondering when someone was going to suggest that," Cliff said.

"So you think we oughta?" Zeb said. "You think we oughta go rooting around the quarry for some buried treasure."

"Well if you don't I will," said Bill Tompkins. He had just meandered close to us. "I mean, what the heck? It's out there. All that money. Imagine that, a million dollars buried so close to Bright's Pond all these years."

Zeb appeared pensive a moment. "Don't you think it could be dangerous? That fella, Walter, got hurt out there. How can we be sure that won't happen to us?"

Bill's eyebrows arched. "No problem," he

straightened his shoulders, "we all grew up around the mines. We know how to handle slag heaps."

"I guess we could at that," Zeb said. "But that means we need to split the treasure."

"Fair enough," Studebaker said. "Even Steven. We'll split it —" Zeb counted the people involved in the present conversation. "One, two, three — how about you Cliff? You in?"

Cliff looked at his feet and shook his head. "Nah, I've had my share of treasure hunting, wheeling and dealing and all that. I'm through. Count me out."

"So it's just the three of us then," Stu said. He looked at me. "Unless you want to join in, Griselda, but seeing how you'd be with Zeb, that would be like you get two parts."

"Don't worry, Stu, I don't want any part of the treasure."

It didn't take more than a few minutes for talk of the treasure to spread through the crowd. By seven-thirty the joint was jumping with rumors and theories and guesses about where the treasure might be buried. Folks even stopped dancing to discuss the possibility of a treasure. But that didn't seem to bother the Barley Boys. They kept on picking and singing. Even Jasper York was telling Harriet Nurse his theory. I heard him confiding in her on my way to the bathroom with Ruth. "Of course you can't tell about treasures," Jasper said. "Bank robbers leave false clues all the time — just to throw folks off the scent."

Harriet agreed with him. "You might be right, Jasper. How can anybody trust a thief?"

Suddenly the fair distribution of the money had become a bit more complicated.

"I say it's every man for himself," I heard Bill Tompkins say when I returned. "Finders keepers, losers weepers."

"Me too," Zeb said. "Whoever finds it gets to do whatever he wants with it. Keep it all, split it up, give it away to charity."

That was when Gilda Saucer wiggled on up to the bar.

"Howdy, Gilda," Zeb said. "Where'd you get off to?"

"Nowhere in particular," she said. "I was just hanging around. And then I had a hard time getting away from that preacher fellow. He kept trying to tell me about Jesus, and I kept telling him that I didn't want or need to believe in a ghost. I told him I was good enough just the way I am." She grinned and sipped what looked like lemonade from a paper cup.

No one dared argue with her.

"So, whatcha all discussing?" she asked.

Alarmed glances flitted through the small group until Cliff said, "Treasure hunting."

She took a step back and nearly tripped over Bill Tompkins. "Oh dear, excuse me. I stepped on your toes."

Bill, who had to grab her around the waist to keep her from stumbling, didn't seem to mind. At least not until Edie glared daggers.

"The treasure?" she said. "My dear sweet Walter's treasure? Why, it's his. I'm sure he's fixing to go looking for it just as soon as he can, just as soon as he wakes up from that horrible comatose state he is presently in."

I was prepared for the crocodile tears to pour.

"We didn't mean to step on his toes," Bill said. "We just figured since he was . . . was, well —"

"Yeah," Stu said. "Since Walter is otherwise incapacitated we might as well —"

"Go hunting for what is rightfully his." Her voice took on an edge that cut the air.

"Now come on, Gilda," Cliff said. "Walter has no claim on that treasure until after he finds it. This is not really the old west. It isn't like he staked a claim."

"But . . . But." Gilda began to sob. "It was what we were depending on to get married and set up our home right here in Bright's Pond. That's why I rented that pretty little house."

Oh boy, she could not have poured it on any thicker.

Cliff did not appear moved by her display of emotion. "Not a whole lot you can do about it, Gilda. If they want to go treasure hunting, it's their right."

Zeb offered Gilda a slice of pie. "I wouldn't worry. I doubt these folks will ever find it. I mean most of them can't find their way around town without help."

She dabbed her eyes with a paper napkin, making sure not to smear her thick mascara very much. Although she did start to resemble a raccoon but that just seemed to endear her more to Zeb.

"Now you got your eyes all red and . . . black. Maybe you should go and pretty yourself up again. You'll feel better."

Ruth and I looked at each other. "Can you believe him?" I whispered.

Gilda put her slice of pie on the table. "Will you watch it for me, please, while I go and . . . and freshen up?"

We all watched her sashay across the dance floor.

"Now see here, Zeb," Studebaker said. "I am still planning on hunting for that trea-

346

sure. It's fair game."

"Of course," Bill added. "Just because that city woman gets all teary-eyed and misty over it is no reason to keep us from looking."

"That's right," Edie said. "Besides, that man might never wake up from his present state of unconsciousness. You know what I'm saying? And then what good is the treasure doing?"

That pretty much summed up what everyone else was thinking. But thankfully I surveyed the hall and realized that most of the townspeople were oblivious to what was being discussed at Zeb's pie table. "That's good," I told Ruth. "Maybe it'll just be the three of them out looking for that money. I don't think anyone else has a clue or even thought about taking on the quest."

Ruth laughed. "Quest. You make it sound sort of bookish, you know? It ain't the gall darn Crusades. It's money stashed in a hiding spot, and a pretty good one to boot. I don't think any of these fellas will find it. They'll be frustrated and bored and hungry in no time."

The clock struck eight and Studebaker climbed the three makeshift steps onto the bandstand. He looked very dapper in his cowboy duds complete with chaps, black hat, and skinny bolo tie clasped with a silver snake head with glowing emerald eyes. He tapped the microphone several times like he was Dean Martin hosting the Emmy awards. "Attention," he said. "I need everyone's attention. It is now time to kick this hootenanny up a notch." Unfortunately Studebaker's enthusiasm was left with the treasure hunting discussion. He sounded like he was directing mourners into the funeral home. "So you all grab your partner and we'll do-si-do."

This was not something I was about to do so I slinked off into a corner. Zeb scurried behind a table to serve food, but just about everyone else joined in the dance. One of the Barley Boys came down on the floor and helped people get into position forming six squares of four people. From where I was standing in the shadows I could see that just about everyone was confused and trying to figure out what they were supposed to be doing. Boris Lender, who had some square dancing experience, helped get things organized while the Boys played something that sounded like *Turkey in the Straw* to me.

After a few minutes they were set to go. I believe it was the Virginia Reel.

Everybody, forward and back,
Once more, forward and back.
Once around with the right elbow.
Two-hand swing and around you go.
Head couple sashay down,
And sashay back.
Head couple, the elbow reel.
A right to the middle and a left
on the side,
A right to the middle and a
reel on down.
Now meet in the middle and a
sashay back.
Cast off and down you go.
Now raise that arch and raise it high,
Duck through and away you fly.

Of course, it was a mess with people moving left and right and around in circles not really knowing which way to go. It was all pretty comical, but the Barley Boys kept right on playing and calling the dance while Ruth and Studebaker argued over who was the head couple and what it meant to sashay down.

Cliff joined in the dance for a few minutes, but he looked relieved when the next group of squares took the floor. He made eye contact with me and headed my way as Zeb watched his every move.

"Never was much of a square dancer, or dancer of any kind," Cliff said. "I'm much more comfortable standing on the sidelines."

"Me too," I said. I looked at Zeb. "And Zeb also. I think he'd rather have a cavity filled than dance."

"So you two are . . . what?" he asked. He put his hand against the wall above me and kind of leaned in close.

"We're friends," I said. "And I guess you can say we're . . . dating."

"But nothing serious. Nothing exclusive."

I looked over at Zeb who had taken up with Gilda once again. I was pretty sure it was his way of making a point, but I was sick of his points and his jealous fits.

"No," I said. "We're not . . . serious."

Cliff smiled wide. "Well dogies! How about a plane ride then? I'll take you to dinner in Wilkes-Barre."

My heart sped either from excitement or sheer nerves, I wasn't sure, but the offer of dinner in a town other than Bright's Pond or Shoops was pretty interesting and one I was sure going to consider.

"But only after a lesson," I said.

"How 'bout tomorrow then? after church?"

"Sounds OK to me. I don't have any

plans," I said even though Zeb and I had a kind of standing date on Sunday afternoons.

He tipped his bandana to me. "I reckon I better mosey on back to the farm and see how Nate is getting along. He was pretty upset over Bertha Ann's third-place showing."

"I know he is. Tell Stella I was asking about her."

It would have been a different story if he had a big, blue ribbon to display. I missed not seeing Stella but I also knew that she made the choice she had to make and stayed home to nurse Nate's wounded pride.

Cliff left through a side door and it took Zeb all of thirty seconds to appear at my side.

"Why you keep taking up with him?"

"Me? What's with you and Gilda? I saw you. You were practically swooning over her."

"Ah, Grizzy, she don't mean nothing. You know that."

I wished I could have said the same thing to him about Cliff.

26

By nine-thirty the adults in the crowd were yawning and the children were running amok as their tired parents chased after them. Most of the folks in Bright's Pond found it difficult to stay up much past ten o'clock so this was not unexpected. Zeb and Ruth and Ivy and me stayed until the end when the Barley Boys packed up. Charlotte Figg collected her pie tins, which she said were very important to her. I understood that. A woman who could make pie like that deserved to be particular about her tins.

Nothing remained of the food or the pies. Anything left over was spirited away in brown bags, except of course for Darcy Speedwell's, cottage cheese–lime JELL-O delight. It stood on a silver platter, a testament to perseverance, a green monument to Darcy's stick-to-it-tive-ness and unflappable faith that someday, at some church function, someone will eat her food. Nate's

spectacular saloon designs and western dé-
cor stood behind and gave the place a kind
of a ghost-town ambience. A few bits of
trash were scattered about but for the most
part folks used the cans set out. In fact, the
can near the front door had overflowed onto
the floor.

"We'll get the rest of this taken care of
tomorrow or Monday," Boris said.

We bleary-eyed dance goers agreed. Zeb
and I walked Ruth and Ivy home in spite of
the obvious tension between us.

"It sure was a nice dance," Ruth said at
the curb in front of her house. "And the
SOAP did pretty well, I think."

"I should think so at three dollars a head,"
Ivy said.

Zeb and I went back to my house where
we sat on the red sofa and talked quietly.
But every time I thought I was getting
through to him he'd say something else to
set me off.

"I told you I'd pay for lessons, just not
from him."

"But I like to fly and he is the only pilot
in town and I refuse to believe he's a crook.
Besides, Mildred suggested that I stay close
to him, find out what I can. As a matter of
fact, we're going up after church tomorrow.
He's giving me another lesson."

By eleven o'clock I was yawning pretty regularly and Zeb took the hint. I walked him to the porch and he kissed me good night.

"I'm not liking him in the way you think," I said even though I wasn't 100 percent convinced myself.

Zeb twisted his mouth. "I guess I know that, Grizzy. It's just hard to see you with another man."

Sunday came suddenly. I must have slept like a rock because I barely remember letting my head hit the pillow. Those who came to church straggled in still talking about the success of the Harvest Dance. It took a while, but Pastor Speedwell finally managed to get folks to quiet down and pay attention to him.

"Good morning," he said. "Now I know you're all tired from last night's festivities but this is the Lord's Day and we're here to celebrate that fact."

Sheila Spiney let go on the organ with "O for a Thousand Tongues to Sing" and we all joined in. I have to say that the singing still managed to swell to the roof and fill the room like it always did.

Edie and Bill Tompkins sat in front of me, and they sounded in good voice. Studebaker was his usual cheery self as he passed the offering plate later in the service although I did notice a bit of straw from the dance decorations still stuck in his hair and he was wearing his rhinestone studded boots.

"Poor guy probably rolled right out of bed straight to church without combing his hair or shaving," I said.

Zeb agreed. "Probably up the rest of the night going over a map trying to figure out where that supposed treasure is buried."

Bill turned around. "I bet I can find it."

Edie tapped Bill's shoulder and lifted her finger to her lips telling him to shhhh.

After the special music from Babette Sturgis who had a voice like an angel, Pastor Speedwell stood for the sermon.

"Today's text if you like to read along is taken from Matthew the sixth chapter, verses nineteen through twenty-one. 'Do not store up for yourselves treasures on earth, where moth and rust destroy, and where thieves break in and steal. But store up for yourselves treasures in heaven, where moth and rust do not destroy, and where thieves do not break in and steal. For where your treasure is, there your heart will be also.' "

A collective gasp filtered through the auditorium as folks looked at each other.

Some smiled. Edie's hand flew up to her mouth and she started to practically beat Bill's arm. I watched Studebaker's eyes grow wide, and Boris started to look around the room. Nearly everyone squirmed and wiggled, and hushed whispers swirled in the air.

Pastor Speedwell realized he had touched a nerve, trouble was he didn't know why. So as he spoke his voice rose to an almost fevered pitch, thinking perhaps that the Holy Spirit was moving among his flock. I could see impatience growing in the congregation the longer he talked. Bill looked at his watch about a dozen times.

"They can hardly wait," Zeb whispered.

"You don't suppose —"

"I do," Zeb said. "They're planning something. All of them."

Even as Pastor prayed folks wiggled and squirmed and spoke among themselves. I heard the woman behind me make arrangements with someone to watch her children after the service.

"I'm sure Harriet Nurse will look after my Maggie, Moe, and Harry," she said.

At least they waited until after the benediction. But only a second because I would say that nearly ninety percent of them leaped out their seats and took off for the doors like someone had just yelled FIRE!

"They're going after the treasure," Zeb said.

"I don't believe it."

Zeb grabbed my arm. "Come on."

"Where?"

"Treasure hunting."

I yanked my arm back. "No. I don't want to go. It's ridiculous. I have plans to go flying with Cliff."

Zeb averted his eyes a moment. "Fine. Go on. Be with your real boyfriend. But don't forget that even he said it was a good idea to go looking for it. And what if, Grizzy? What if I find it? No more troubles."

"I don't have troubles that money can fix, Zeb."

"Come on, I'll buy you an airplane. Heck, I'll buy you a whole entire airport."

"You go ahead."

I sat back down and watched a stunned Pastor Speedwell, who had not taken his usual place in the front of the church to shake hands, speak quietly to his wife, Darcy. Then he looked at me, one of the few left. Even Ruth and Ivy had gone.

"Do you know what just happened, Griselda?"

Sheila Spiney continued to play her version of "Amazing Grace."

"Treasure hunting," I said. "They all went after the treasure that's supposed to be buried out near the old Sakolas Quarry."

Pastor shook his head. "My sermon did not get through."

"Oh, it got through," I said. "They took it as a sign, a sign from God to go looking."

"Oh, dear," Darcy said.

"Sorry, Pastor. They'll be back," I said.

He hung his head. "I fear that I've failed. I failed my flock."

Darcy patted his arm. "Come on, dear. Let's go home."

I headed for the door and that was when I noticed Cliff sitting in the back. "You still here," I said. "Why aren't you going out treasure hunting?"

He laughed. "Like the Pastor said, I already got the most important treasure. Inside." He pointed to his heart and I immediately knew that no one had Cliff to fear.

"Besides," he said. "We're going flying."

After stopping at home to check on Arthur and change clothes I met Cliff at Hector's Hill. He was making the check of the plane. He walked around Matilda and examined her from top to bottom making certain the prop was secured, he moved the flaps up and down, looked at every nut and bolt on the outside of the plane then checked the oil and, last, he sumped the gas. He put a long glass tube into the fuel tank and then checked the color of the extracted gasoline.

"All set," he said.

He opened the door and in I went. I buckled my belt and looked at all the instruments. I wanted to know what every one meant. The thing about Cliff's airplane was that nothing was wasted. Every inch of space was used to its fullest. I liked that notion.

We took off and I felt the now familiar sensation of liftoff as the plane climbed until Cliff leveled her off at one thousand feet.

"Not quite a mile," he said. "But that will do fine. Now take the controls."

I took a deep breath and wrapped my hand around the yoke and felt Cliff release the plane to me. I checked the horizon indicator and kept Matilda steady.

"Great," he said. "You sure you don't have a license already?"

"Nope. But . . . but I got to say it sure feels right."

"I can't help thinking of that verse about soaring on eagles' wings," Cliff said. "Some of us get to do that in a real way."

I glanced over at him but not for long before my eyes went back to the instruments. Cliff made me smile.

"OK, now," he said, "let's take her a bit higher and head for the mountain."

"Mountain? I don't think I'm ready to fly over the mountain."

"No, no, we won't try that. Just head for it."

A few minutes later we were flying over the old abandoned mine near Sakolas Quarry. He knew all along exactly where we were headed, and I will admit that I felt a pang in my chest. I felt like a spy of sorts, even though I wanted to find Zeb.

"Look down," he said. "Do you see them?"

"The treasure hunters?" I could easily make out the folks of Bright's Pond scurrying around like groundhogs digging holes everywhere they could.

"They are really looking for the treasure," I said. "I can't believe it."

"Ah, let them have their fun. They won't find it. I did some checking and that treasure hasn't been found in over eighty years. Leastways no one admitted to it. It's probably been found and the money spent by now."

The plane jerked slightly and I felt a tug on the stick.

"It's OK, you're doing fine, but let me

take over."

I was relieved and frustrated. I wanted to keep flying. For the first time in my life I felt like I was doing something for me. Learning something new. Something that made sense. Flying made sense to me even though Zeb and Ruth thought it was silly.

"Griselda," Cliff said after a few minutes of silence. "I know you all don't trust me. I know Mildred learned about my past. But, you need to know something."

"What's that?" I said as the nerves began to build again.

"It's not me you should be worried about. I just needed a fuel line when I came here."

"Then who?"

Cliff adjusted some dials and tapped on the fuel indicator. "Oh crud," he said.

"What? What's wrong?" I said.

"We're losing fuel — fast. I better set her down."

Although I knew it would do me absolutely no good I grabbed onto the door. "I think I just saw baby pictures of myself whiz by."

Cliff laughed. "We won't crash. Don't worry."

27

Cliff landed the plane smoothly. "I better check this." He shut down the engine and jumped out right away.

I unbuckled my belt and followed him to the front of the plane. He had the hood, for lack of a better word, opened.

"Yep," he said. "It's the fuel line. I guess I should have seen that coming. It's an easy fix. Nate probably has something in his barn that will take care of it until I get back to Wilkes-Barre."

"Are you leaving?" I said, suddenly feeling a sense of loss wash over my body.

"Probably. I have to make a living."

"I thought you did plane stuff."

"I do. Deliveries and such. And that's the trouble. I haven't delivered anybody or anything in a while. I'm running out of dough."

I nodded my head and remembered what he said in the plane just before the trouble.

"What were you saying in the plane? About worrying about someone?"

He wiped his hands on a rag. "Ah, I'm just talking. It's probably nothing. I shouldn't have said anything. I don't know for sure. Not real sure."

"So tell me anyway."

"No. Look, it's getting to be dinnertime isn't it? Stella usually makes a good Sunday dinner. You got plans?"

"Oh, I'll catch up with Zeb if he's done playing pirates of Bright's Pond."

Cliff laughed. "They'll get it out of their system. Unless of course one of them actually finds it, but the likelihood of that happening is pretty close to nil."

We started to walk back to Old Bess. "I should probably go see Agnes later, too. She'll love to hear about them racing out of church to go treasure hunting."

I pulled up in front of the Kincaid's. "You know, maybe I'll stop in for a minute. Check on Nate and Stella."

"Yeah. He's taking it pretty hard. He thought for sure Bertha Ann would win. He's been in there ever since looking through his seeds and reading catalogs and articles."

"He's obsessed or something. Too bad

they didn't have any human babies, you know what I mean?"

"Yeah. He'd make a good dad."

"They're still young enough. Well Stella is. She's only forty-one."

"That's a little old isn't it?"

"Nah. It could happen. If we can get those two to stop arguing long enough."

I parked the truck and went inside with Cliff.

He was correct. Nate sat at the dining room table looking at pumpkin seeds under a bright light and a magnifying glass. He looked a little like a mad scientist. Cliff joined him while I joined Stella in the kitchen.

"Griselda," she said. "I'm glad you're here. How was the dance? Sorry I missed it but Nate said he needed me to stay home, said he couldn't show his or my face in town yesterday."

"The dance was good. I missed you. The square dance was a disaster though."

Stella laughed as she peeled potatoes. "I bet. I can't imagine the people square dancing."

"So how is Nate doing?"

"Ah, he'll be better now that it's over. A few days and he'll be back to farming. The cows still need milking."

"Hey Stella," I said. "You guys ever think about having a baby instead of pumpkins."

She tapped a spoon against a pot. "Me? A mother? Nah, well we thought about it but Nate wouldn't hear of it. Not sure why either. He could use a boy around the farm."

Stella put coffee on to percolate while I picked at a pumpkin pie. I pulled my finger out of my mouth and stopped. "This . . . isn't Bertha Ann is it?"

"No. No. Those big pumpkins don't make the best pie. She's out back. Just sitting there under her tarp. Nate will get rid of her soon. Feed her to the squirrels and gophers."

"The very things that he was trying to kill he's now feeding."

"Weird world we live in, Griselda. Very strange."

"So anyway," I said. "I guess you heard about the treasure hunting going on." I said it casually because I was trying my best not to make a big deal out of it.

I grabbed a brown paper bag full of peas and a yellow, clay bowl and started to open the casings and drop little green peas into it. "The whole town is out by the quarry digging holes. Cliff and I just flew over. It looks like the surface of the moon. You should have seen it, all these craters all over.

Empty, stupid craters and people running around with shovels and pickaxes. Even Ruth went."

"Are you kidding? But —" She looked out the kitchen window. "That's Walter's treasure."

Her reaction surprised me. "Stella, I thought you wouldn't care."

"I know. But, still. It is Walter's treasure and they have no right. Not really. Considering Walter's condition and all." She turned back to the window and then to me again. "Staying for dinner?"

"Sure. Are you really upset?"

"About you staying for dinner?"

"No, about the treasure."

She paused a moment and considered her words. "I think I am."

Forty-five minutes later we were gathered around the table. Stella had prepared a typical Sunday dinner. Roast beef, mashed potatoes, gravy, peas, and biscuits. Nate took a knife and fork and sliced the beef into quarter-inch slices. He sawed off four when Cliff stopped him.

"I feel the need to pray."

Cliff proceeded to pray in a way I never heard anyone pray, not even Agnes. He thanked God for the day, the beauty of the earth, his airplane, the town of Bright's Pond, the food, the hands that prepared the food, and just when I was getting bored he thanked God for his new friends and asked that the Lord's will be done between Zeb and me.

We ate and passed food silently at first as though we had entered into some kind of holy moment that mustn't be disturbed. But Cliff broke the tension and got into a conversation with Nate about fuel lines, gasoline, and pumpkin seeds.

"I was thinking about heading over to Greenbrier after supper," I said as I passed the gravy to Nate.

"Maybe I'll go with you," Stella said. "I should check on Walter. Tell him everyone knows about the treasure. Maybe that will pop him out of his coma."

"It just might," Cliff said. "They say they aren't certain what a person hears when they're unconscious, so who knows? Maybe he needs a good shock."

"So you really think we can build a better seed?" Nate asked drawing Cliff's attention away.

Stella and I continued to eat quietly. Stella looked a bit pensive. I was just about to ask her what was on her mind when the telephone rang. Stella excused herself and dashed to the kitchen. I saw her lift the yellow receiver from the wall phone.

"Hello?"

"Yes. This is Stella Hughes."

Then I watched her jaw drop. She seemed speechless and then said into the phone, "Should I come? I'll be right there!"

She hung up and looked straight at me. "It's Walter. He's awake!"

28

"It was that nurse, Sally," Stella said. "She wanted to tell me before Gilda. Since I'm really his next of kin."

"Should we go?" I asked. "Or you and Nate?"

Nate turned around to see Stella. "You go with Griselda. It will be better." There was softness in his voice I hadn't heard all season. "Go on. Don't worry about dinner. Unless of course, you want to finish."

Stella touched her stomach. "Nah, I'm all of a sudden filled with butterflies or cucumber beetles or something."

"Go on," Nate said. "Call if you need anything."

Stella grabbed an olive green jacket from the coatrack near the front door.

"This is a good thing," Cliff said. "Your brother is waking up."

Stella cracked a half smile. "I'll be back."

That was when Nate walked closer to her.

He placed his hands on her shoulders and I saw just how much taller he was than her. She looked up at him.

"It's going to be all right, honey. It really is. Just go and be with him."

I pulled into the nursing home parking lot. It was crowded. Sunday was always the busiest visiting day as families, free from work and other obligations were able to come. Not seeing a parking spot right away I said, "This is an emergency. I'm parking in front."

I slammed the truck in park. It lurched slightly. "Geez, Griselda," Stella said. "He's waking up, not dying."

"Sorry. I'm excited."

Claude stood at the door and pushed it open for us. "You here to see Walter?"

Stella nodded.

"He's the talk of the building. Go on now. They called Doc Silver in to see."

Stella grabbed my hand and we made our way down the hall, passing a small congregation of residents in pajamas and sweat suits in the large community room. The area had been made up to resemble a church with a cross in the front and a podium. I saw seven or eight wheelchairs with residents sitting in them lined up across the front of the room and a group sitting in regular chairs behind them. A man in a red suit with a purple tie stood near the cross strumming a guitar. They were singing "What a Friend We Have in Jesus." It made my heart lighter just to hear the words.

Another smaller group hovered outside Walter's door.

"There she is," one said. "Let her in."

I let Stella go first. She took a hurried step and then stopped short. I banged into her. "Go on," I said.

She stepped lightly into the dimly lit room. I could still hear the sound of the breathing machine. The doctor and two nurses leaned over Walter. Sally looked up at us. "Stella. I'm glad you came."

The doctor took his stethoscope from his ears. Are you the sister?" He looked at me. I nodded toward Stella who looked like a deer in headlights. "I thought you said he was awake. His eyes are closed."

"He'll be in and out for a bit. I sedated him because he was bucking the vent," the doctor said.

"Bucking the vent?" I said.

"Yes. He's trying to breathe on his own but the ventilator is still doing the job. Patients don't like the feeling, and he got a little upset."

"You mean he's moving and talking?"

"Oh, no," Doctor Silver said. "He can't talk with the ventilator, and his movements are still pretty sporadic."

"Then take the tube out," Stella said.

"Not yet. Soon though, I'll keep a close eye."

Stella moved closer to his side. She touched his hand. "Oh, Walter. You can do this. You can wake up — all the way."

Then Walter opened his eyes. He looked right at her and blinked two times.

"He sees you," Sally said. "He knows who you are."

I watched a teardrop fall from his eye. Stella wiped it away with her thumb as he slipped behind closed doors again.

The doctor took Sally aside. "Continue the IVs and —" was all I heard before they left the room.

"Should we try to find Gilda?" I asked.

Stella shook her head. "I don't know. For someone who said she's here day and night waiting for her dear sweet Wally to wake up, don't you think she'd be here? I bet that Dabs fella is right about her."

"I do too. But it still might be the right thing to do, to let her know."

"Well, I don't agree. Let her find out however way she does. I mean I wouldn't even know where to find her."

"We could call over to Cora's house."

"Suit yourself," Stella said. "If you want to go to that trouble to find a woman who could and most likely is up to no good."

"OK, I won't do anything. Maybe I'll go see Agnes. I'll be back in a little while. You just sit with your brother."

She looked first at Walter and then me and then back at Walter. "Would you mind if I went with you?"

"No, of course not. I just thought you might want some time alone."

"Not yet. Not now."

Agnes appeared to be waiting for us. "It's about time," she said. "I've been sitting here for hours, it seems, waiting for you two to come by. I heard about Walter. It's a good sign. A good sign."

"Thank you, Agnes," Stella said. She rushed to her side and grabbed both of Agnes's fat, little hands. As heavy as Agnes was, Stella's hands seemed to swallow Agnes's. "Thank you."

"Now hold on there, Stella. What in tarnation are you thanking me for?"

"Praying. You have been praying. I know that's why he's waking up. You've been praying since the first day I told you about him."

Agnes pulled her hands back. "Now of course I've been praying, but I thought we were over all that. We talked about how it's God's doing not mine."

"Oh, I know. I know that's what you said and I know it's true but still . . . I can't help but —"

Agnes shook her head. "Don't go any further. You best be thanking the Good Lord for this miracle, if it is a miracle. I mean Walter is not the first person to wake up from a coma."

That was when I decided to step in and try to avert the discussion.

"How are you Agnes?" I asked brushing hair out of her eyes.

"Fine, just fine. Hungry though. They gave me nothing but a meat patty swimming in some kind of gristly sauce and a tiny side dish of hard vegetables." She shaped her hands with the fingers touching into a circle about the size of a half-dollar.

Stella reached into her bag. I grabbed her hand. "I hope you aren't fixing to pull a Milky Way out of there."

"No, no," Stella said. "I got some walnuts. Can she have walnuts?"

"Sure can," Agnes said. And she ate the nuts like they were the best food ever in spite of my protests.

I wandered over to the door and peeked down the hall, keeping an eye out for Gilda.

"So what's next?" Agnes asked. "For Walter, that is. I don't know too much about comas but does a person just wake up like nothing was ever wrong and go about their business?"

"I'm not sure," Stella said. "I kind of think he'll be here a while. He still has that breathing tube and IVs and stuff. It might be more gradual."

Agnes closed her eyes a moment. "It's all about God's timing."

By then the sun was setting behind the mountains, Agnes was starting to look tired, and Stella seemed to be getting more and more anxious as we talked. "Maybe we should go back to Walter's room," I said. "We can ask the doctor all these questions."

"That's a good idea," Agnes said. "I am feeling a little run down today — probably on account of they don't feed me enough for a hamster to live."

Stella kissed Agnes's cheek. "I know you don't want the credit. But I will always be thankful that you pray. And . . . and I have one more request."

"What is it, Stella?" Agnes asked.

"Just please pray that . . . that he forgives me."

"You?" I said. "I thought he was the rat. He was the one that swindled you out of your money."

"He was and could very well still be a rat but, you know, it's just money. I don't need it. Family is more important than dollars. I know it sounds trite to say but it's true. I should have found a way to stay in touch with him even after he did what he did and said what he said."

Agnes reached for Stella's hand. "It's not easy to take the high road."

"High road," I said slapping my knee. "That reminds me. Did you hear about the big treasure hunt?"

"Well I heard something about something. Hazel Flatbush came in to see her cousin, you know Old Miss Millie, and she poked her head in my door and told me the congregation went nuts this Sunday. She said they all dashed out the doors after the sermon like rats from a sinking ship, those were her words, rats from a sinking ship. She said they were all fixing to go up to the quarry and look for that treasure."

"That's right, can you believe it? Half of Bright's Pond is up at the quarry digging for treasure. I got a bird's-eye view of them from Cliff's airplane. They were scattered like prairie dogs out digging holes. Even Zeb and Stu went carrying shovels and pickaxes. Ruth even went along."

"Fools," Agnes said. "Anyone find it?'"

"I don't know yet," I said. "But I'm sure you'll hear about it the minute it happens. Someone will be whooping it up but good."

"Maybe they should combine their efforts and share it," Agnes said. "A million bucks is a lot of money."

"They thought about doing that — well Studebaker did — but then Bill Tompkins said it should be finders keepers, losers weepers."

Agnes made a noise. "Bill Tomkins. He's a pip."

Stella was starting to look a little antsy.

"Maybe we should get back to Walter," Stella said.

"Probably," I said. "We'll see you later, Agnes." I patted her leg and moved her tray table closer to her. "Got enough water?"

"Uh-huh, I'm fine. But keep me posted as events unfold. I want to hear about the treasure too."

The doctor was leaning over Walter when we got back and that alarmed Stella.

"What's wrong?" she asked. "Is he OK?"

"Yes. He's responding to stimuli," the doctor said.

"That's good?" I asked.

"Yes," Sally said. "It means he's becoming more aware of what's going on around him."

"But he's still . . . asleep?"

The doctor nodded. "Yes but don't forget I sedated him."

"I know," Stella said. "I don't know whether to be nervous or excited and happy."

"A little of both," Doctor Silver said. "We'll know more when he is fully awake. You should probably prepare yourself that he might have some deficits."

"Deficits?" Stella looked at the doctor like a confused puppy.

"Brain damage, memory loss, loss of movement," said Doctor Silver matter-of-factly. "But we won't know anything until he is fully conscious."

"Oh, I hadn't thought about that." She practically fell into the visitor's chair as though she had been pushed. "What if he has brain damage? What will that mean?"

"Let's wait until we know some things for certain." The doctor's voice turned smooth and compassionate. "No sense in guessing."

"That's right," Sally said. "Let's just wait a few more hours and see. I'll call you if there are any changes."

Stella took a deep breath and let it out through her nose. She reached through the bed rail and squeezed her brother's hand. He seemed to smile slightly at her touch.

"All right," Stella said. "But please . . . promise to call."

29

Nate and Cliff were still sitting at the dining room table still sifting through piles of pumpkin seeds when we arrived back at the farm. I don't know what it is about dining room tables but they always seem to become work zones. Even in my house, the dining room table is used for pretty much everything from figuring my taxes to folding laundry — only occasionally is it used for a meal. The men had baby food jars with seeds inside lined up like little glass soldiers. Each jar lid was marked with a year and a number.

"Now these here," Nate said, "came from a grower in Nebraska. He swore six ways to Tuesday that I would grow a pumpkin at least five-hundred pounds."

"Wow," Cliff said.

"Duds." Nate said looking over his glasses — Stella told me he only wore them for close work because they made his eyes look

380

a little buggy. "Only grew two pumpkins and they were just average."

That was when Cliff finally noticed us standing there listening to their conversation.

"Hello, girls," he said. "Back so soon?"

"Soon?" I said. "We've been gone for hours. You fellas must have been really excited about those seeds not to notice the time."

Nate pulled his glasses off and looked into the kitchen where a clock, made to look like a pumpkin with vines for hands read nine fifteen or so, it was hard to tell.

"Geez, oh man! It is later than I thought," Nate said. "So how is he? Did he really wake up?"

Stella sat in the chair opposite Nate. She fiddled with one of the jars. "Kind of. He started to wake up but the doctor said he became agitated and tried to pull his tubes out so he put him back to sleep."

"What?" Nate said. "Don't they want him to wake up?"

"Well sure," Stella said. "But they can't have him pulling his tubes and stuff out. He's probably very confused."

"That's right," I said standing behind Cliff. "I guess now the doctor can control things and let him come back slowly."

"I guess it makes sense."

"I think he recognized me, though," Stella said. He blinked his eyes right at me but then he dozed off again."

"And," I said, "not only that but at one point he even smiled at Stella."

Stella looked at the jar of seeds she held. "I think he even cried a little. I wiped a tear from his eye."

"Oh, that's amazing," Cliff said. "I hear that a lot of times people in comas wake up with amnesia, without a clue about who they are or what happened to them."

I sat next to Cliff. "The doctor also said he's responding to stimuli. That means he's aware of what's going on around him."

"I reckon they'll need to evaluate him for other problems," Cliff said. "But it sure does sound like he's coming around. It's kind of a miracle don't you think? Maybe your sister is still in business."

"Oh, please don't say that," I said. "This has nothing to do with Agnes. It's not unusual for a person to recover from a coma. Especially a pretty short one like Walter's. A month is not long at all."

"More like five weeks," Stella said.

"Imagine that," I said. "Sleeping for five weeks, only deeper than sleep, unconscious."

"I knew a guy who got a bump on the head and died." Nate snapped his fingers. "Just like that. Seemed fine one minute and poof. Gone the next."

"Oh, Nate," Stella said. "Don't say those things."

"I'm sorry. But it's true. Just goes to show you that you can never tell about these things." Nate went back to his seeds. "This one is from a champion pumpkin in Nova Scotia. Weighed almost two-hundred pounds. I'm telling you the day is coming when we'll be growing pumpkins more than a thousand pounds."

"Yeah, right," Cliff said. "A thousand-pound pumpkin. Do you know how big that is? It would have to be ten feet around — at least."

"I know, I know," Nate said. "I mean the gourd would collapse and crack all over the place. It's hard enough keeping a one-hundred pounder healthy. But I'd sure like to try and raise one that big."

Stella picked up a large, white pumpkin seed. "This one," she said. "This is the one for next season."

Nate laughed. "That? It's only an Atlantic hybrid. Nothing special. It's not even from a prize winner."

"Still," Stella said. "You never know.

Sometimes the most unspecial looking things become something special. Remember that year you took first place. It was just an ordinary seed from an ordinary pumpkin. But you knew it had promise."

Nate dropped the seed into a small orange envelope and wrote "Stella" on it.

I went straight home that night. Tired but happy that Nate and Stella had at least for the time being stopped arguing, Cliff had turned out to be a good guy, and Walter was starting to regain consciousness after five weeks in a coma. Now we just needed the full poop on Gilda.

The nights had grown cold in Bright's Pond and I lit a small fire in the fireplace content to watch TV and eat pie left over from the dance. Not that there was much. But I did manage to confiscate a slice of Charlotte Figg's lattice-top cherry. The woman had true pie talent. Moreso, I hated to admit and would never say aloud, than Zeb. There was just something extra special about Charlotte's crust. Special. The thought brought me back to the conversation at Stella's. Charlotte had a knack for taking unspecial ingredients — flour, shortening, a tiny bit of water — and turning them into something spectacular — culinary alchemy.

At seven-thirty I heard a ruckus outside. Screeching brakes and slamming car doors. I practically leaped my way to the front porch and flipped on the light in time to see Studebaker Kowalski jump out of his Caddy.

"Come on, Zeb, just another hour. We'll use the headlights to see."

"No more," Zeb said. "There ain't no treasure. We practically dug up the entire area. I'm tired. The people who live up there were laughing at us. For goodness sake they set up lawn chairs and packed picnic lunches. No more digging."

I waved to them. "What in tarnation is going on out here?"

Stu followed him onto my porch where I stood in the doorway with my arms folded against my chest shivering from the cold.

"Then tomorrow," Stu said. "We'll go back tomorrow."

"Maybe," said Zeb.

"Are you gonna tell me what's going on or not?" I asked.

"Zeb wants to quit the treasure hunt," Studebaker said.

"Can you blame me, Grizzy? We dug up every inch of that place. There's no treasure.

I think the whole thing is some kind of fairy tale."

"It can't be," Stu said. "That Walter fella came up here for a reason and almost killed himself over it. You don't get killed over nothing."

"Come on in," I said. "It's cold out here. Did everyone else go home?"

"Yeah, they left hours ago. Just dunderhead here and me were stupid enough to stay behind and now I'm just cold and dirty and hungry," Zeb said.

"I am not a dunderhead," Stu said. "You'll see. I'm going back tomorrow. I'll get my cousin Asa up in Paradise to help me."

"Go ahead," Zeb said.

The two of them stood on my porch staring each other down. All I could do was wait until it was over.

"So what do you say, Zeb," Stu said. "Tomorrow?"

"I reckon so," Zeb said.

I just shook my head as we watched Stu get back into his car and take off down the street.

"Dunderhead," Zeb said.

Once I got Zeb inside and a cup of hot tea poured for him I asked him about the hunt.

"Did people really come and watch?"

"Yes. A whole slew of people. One woman was selling hotdogs out of a cooler filled with boiling hot water — they were pretty good too. Made her own mustard."

"Really? That's kind of funny. Did you find anything? Anything at all?"

"All we found were chicken bones, lots and lots of chicken bones — musta been a slaughterhouse up there at one time. We found some small shards of garnet and ruby not worth a plug nickel and a strong box filled with tobacco. Old, stinking tobacco."

I closed the kitchen window after a strong breeze knocked one of my African violets off the sill and into the sink. "So no sign of a safe filled with a million dollars."

"Not a one. Not a single sign that would even suggest it, and we dug some pretty deep holes."

"I know." I laughed. "I saw them. Looked like the surface of the moon up there with all those holes. Swiss cheese."

"How would you know? You didn't come up there, did you?"

"Nah, I flew over — in Cliff's plane."

"I thought that was Cliff's plane I heard buzzing around. I looked but I didn't see you."

"It was us. We only made one pass over

the quarry before heading back to Hector's Hill."

Zeb appeared pensive as he sipped his tea. "I wonder," he said. "If we could use Cliff's plane to help locate the spot."

"What are you suggesting?"

"Maybe you could take another trip over and this time try and pinpoint the place, you know? Maybe you'd see something from up there."

"Oh, Zeb, I doubt I'd even know what to look for. I don't think there's a giant X marking the spot."

Zeb picked at a couple of leftover lemon squares from the Harvest Dance. "I guess I'm just kidding you, Grizzy. It would be a heck of a lot easier if that Walter fella would wake up and tell us what he knows."

"Oh," I said. "I guess you don't know yet."

"Know what?" He swallowed a bit of tart lemon.

"He's awake." With that, Zeb's ears perked up perkier than a Chihuahua going for a car ride. "Then maybe he can tell us where to dig."

"Well, he's not exactly jumping up and down. But he is regaining consciousness. I guess it's a slow process. The doctor had to sedate him, put him back to sleep. Imagine that."

"Well that doesn't seem to make much sense now does it? The man's been asleep for all those weeks, wakes up, and they knock him out again. Talk about a rude awakening."

"The doctor said he had to, something about the way Walter was bucking the vent — the breathing tube. It must have been weird to be breathing on your own and have a machine do it for you too."

Zeb suddenly became aware of his own breathing. "Yeah, I can see that. But still if he's waking up maybe you or Stella can ask him a few questions."

"Give the man a chance. He might not even remember anything. He could have amnesia, least that's what the doctor said. It wouldn't be unusual."

I sat down next to Zeb and put my hand on his cheek. "Does that treasure really mean so much? It's only money."

Zeb caught my hand just as I pulled it away. "You're right, Grizzy. I am acting kind of stupid over the whole thing. It's only money, and I don't need money."

He kissed my cheek. "So tell me more about Walter. How's Stella taking it?"

"She's taking it all pretty well, considering. It's a lot to take in after all these years."

"What about Gilda? I bet she's jumping

for joy."

"Sally, the nurse over there, Walter's nurse, said they didn't call Gilda because she's not considered next of kin or any kind of kin for that matter. Not until they are legally married."

"What?" Zeb stretched the word out. "You mean if I got hurt and was put in the hospital they wouldn't tell you."

"Nope."

Zeb stayed another hour or so until I finally had to tell him he needed to get home and get some sleep. He kept bringing the conversation back around to the treasure and I was getting pretty sick of it. But I guess he had gotten caught up in the adventure and seemed like a little boy when he talked about how much fun it was to dig holes and chase down possible leads.

"You should have seen Ruth," he said. "She was so funny — running all over the place with that little tiny shovel of hers, one of those collapsible ones they used in WWII to dig latrines."

"I can't imagine Ruth digging holes. I'd think she'd worry about getting her dress dirty."

"Oh she had a lot to say about the dirt but by the end of the day she was just as filthy as the rest of us. She went home with Bill and Edie long before Stu and me."

"I bet she's plumb tuckered out."

"Probably, but she said she'd be back. Said she wanted to find the money and then split it among everyone in town — use it for a good cause — maybe buy that church steeple you all are always talking about."

"That sounds like Ruth. She'd give it all away. Not a person in the backwoods would be without shoes and socks or food."

"I hope she finds it." Zeb yawned and I took that as my cue to toss him out the front door. "Go on now. It's late and we're all tired. I suspect everyone will be at the café early to discuss all this."

He yawned again. "You're right about that."

He stood on the porch bouncing on his feet for a moment.

"Maybe you should make a treasure-hunting special," I said.

"Yeah, I can bury pork links in the hash browns."

Not only did nearly the entire congregation of Bright's Pond Church of Faith and Grace show up at the café for breakfast, but Gilda to my surprise was in her spot at the end of the counter. It was obvious to me that she had not heard about Walter. The way folks were looking at her you'd think she was the one just waking from a coma. It seemed everyone in town knew but her.

I wasn't sure if I should be the one to tell her. But I figured it was only a matter of minutes or seconds before someone would blurt something out, so I took the stool next to her.

"Morning, Gilda," I said practically shouting over the chatter in the café.

"Morning. Sure is crowded in here for a Monday. I can hardly hear my mind think. Did something happen?"

"Ah they're just jibber-jabbering about the treasure," said Dot Handy. She placed a cup in front of me. "Morning, Griselda."

"My Walter's treasure?" Gilda said. She looked at me first and then Dot. "That ain't right."

"Unfortunately," Dot said, "your Walter does not have an exclusive claim on it. Seems to me that it's a free-for-all and if you had been up at the quarry yesterday you woulda gotten quite an eyeful. Folks were running all over the place like . . . lemmings or something, digging holes right and left, hollering across to each other. It was quite a spectacle."

"I saw it from the air," I said. "They did

look kind of silly."

Dot poured my coffee. "From the air? Were you up in that man's air-o-plane again?"

"I was. We flew right over the quarry, which by the way, is not nearly as big from that high up, and it's filled with black water. It gave me the willies."

"Well you didn't see me, I'm sure," Dot said. "I am not one for going on wild goose chases. If God had intended me to be a rich woman — moneywise that is — he woulda had me marry a Rockefeller. You know what I'm talking about, Griselda?"

"I sure do, Dot. I like you just the way you are. You don't need lots of money to be happy —"

"Can't hurt," Gilda said. "I'd sure like to give it a try some day. I can be just as happy poor as rich, and I think I would prefer to be rich."

"Well, it looks like your Walter is out of the running for that treasure now," Dot said. "One these folks is bound to find it. The thing about people in Bright's Pond is that once they get their minds fixed on something they're like snapping turtles. Ever see a snapping turtle with his jaws around a trout? Woo man, he won't let go for nothing until somebody conks him on the head."

I winced remembering of course that Walter had conked himself on the head somehow. I hoped that Gilda didn't hear it. But she did and there went the waterworks again.

"Just like my Wally," she cried. "I am so sorry I said anything to begin with. I should have kept it a secret like Walter wanted me too."

"Oh, well now, I'm sorry," Dot said. "I didn't mean nothin' by that remark. It's just a true statement about snapping turtles, but I figure a city girl like yourself wouldn't know from turtles now, would you?"

Gilda clinked her spoon on her coffee cup.

"It's OK, I know you didn't mean to upset me. I'm just a raw nerve these days. A raw, exposed nerve."

Oh boy, a raw nerve and I hadn't even told her the news yet. She was bound to turn on the tears again when I told her that Walter had woken up. But I put it off as long as I could.

"You want your usual, Griselda?" Dot asked.

"Sure. I'm hungry this morning."

I poured cream in my coffee and watched it swirl as I tried to come up with something to say that might make it easier for Gilda to think about other people going after that safe full of money. But there wasn't. She let the cat out of the bag. There was bound to be repercussions.

"I don't think anyone meant to step all over Walter," I said. "But this is a small town and having a treasure hidden somewhere nearby is pretty exciting news."

She soaked the last of her egg yolk up with toast. "Did anyone find it?" She had composed herself. I must say that Walter's illness and the treasure did not seem to affect her appetite. That little girl could pack it away with any of the Teamsters that came by the Full Moon.

"Not yet," Studebaker called from his usual booth. "We'll find it today. Ain't that right, Zeb?"

Zeb peeked through the pick up window. "I don't know, Stu. I'm beginning to think the whole thing is a hoax, a giant April Fool's joke. And we're the fools."

"No, no," Gilda said. "The treasure is for real. Walter said he knew just where to look. But he never made it. Too bad he can't tell me where to look. I'd head out there myself, if of course one of you strapping men would take me."

I watched Dot's eyes roll around in their sockets.

"Sure thing, Gilda," Stu said. "I'd take

you up there in my baby blue Caddy. The color kind of matches your eyes."

Oh, brother. I think Gilda had the same effect on every male in Bright's Pond.

I sipped my coffee and swallowed hard. I either had to tell her now or let her go on over to Greenbrier and find out for herself but that didn't seem fair. So I spoke up. "Oh, Gilda," I said. "That's kind of why I sat next to you, I mean besides just wanting to be neighborly. There is something I need to tell you since the nursing home never got a hold of you."

She looked into my eyes for the first time since we first met. Gilda was one of those people that always aimed her attention in some other direction like making eye contact was too personal or honest. "What is it? Something happen to Walter?"

"Yes," I said. "In a way, nothing happened to him, exactly —"

"Well, what is it?" Gilda asked. "Don't beat around the bushes. Just tell me."

"He's awake."

Gilda sucked all the oxygen out of the room. "Well thump my gums and call me a cab. When did that happen?"

"Yesterday. They called Stella on account of her being —"

"Immediate family," Gilda said with a

modicum of sarcasm. "I figured that's what they'd up and do since I am only his fiancée." She wiggled in her seat. "They told me they wouldn't be able to tell me too much since we ain't married. But I kept hanging around and hanging around so I'd be there when he woke up. But don't you know he'd go and do it while I was otherwise indisposed."

For some reason I felt a twinge of sympathy for her and patted her hand. "I'm sorry, Gilda. I know this must be hard on you."

"I'm practically his wife," she said as she jabbed a home-fried potato. "We were fixing to get married right after he got back from his little expedition as he called it." She put the bite in her mouth and chewed. "Had the license and all and that's as good as married in my book. Especially when you consider that we already — well, you know what I'm saying, don't you, Griselda? — on more than one occasion I might add."

"Well, don't yell at Griselda," Dot said. "She's only telling you what the nurse said. Being loose and easy don't count for much. It's the band of gold that gets you the rights."

"I am not yelling at her. I am merely stating my case," Gilda said.

"It's OK, Dot. But where were you yesterday, Gilda? You never came by the nursing home. Stella and I kept looking out for you."

"Well I needed a break for heaven's sake. A woman can only sit in that hospital for so long watching her —" she sniffed and then blew into a napkin, "her dear, sweet intended for so long before she needs a day off. Now that's only right, don't you think?"

"Sure, sure," Zeb said coming out from the kitchen, wiping his hands on his apron. "That's perfectly understandable."

"That's right," Studebaker said. "A girl can only take so much misery."

Oh, for heaven's sake, I thought. *They are pouring it on thick. A pretty woman walks into town and they fawn all over her.*

"Maybe you should go see him today," I said. "The doctor had to sedate him —"

"Sedate him? You mean knock him out again? If that ain't adding insult to injury, I don't know what is."

"Hold on," I said. "They had to so he'd calm down. He was pretty agitated at first and tried to pull his tubes out."

She winced. "That ain't so good I suppose. In that case, I understand them putting him on ice again."

"I'm sure he'll be happy to see you," I said.

"I'm sure he will," she said. "Now if you'll excuse me. I have a wedding to plan. I still got the license and then we'll see who is next of kin."

She pulled some dollars out of her thin, beige purse and dropped them on the counter. "You boys have fun hunting that treasure."

"Bye Gilda," said Zeb and Stu together.

The second she disappeared out the door the discussion continued about buried treasure. Studebaker thought he had it figured out. "I'm thinking it's got to be in one of the mine shafts," he said.

"Well nobody is stupid enough to go looking inside an abandoned mine," said Boris, who had been sitting quietly at the booth with Ruth.

"But I used to be a miner," Stu said. "Remember, I know those shafts. I can do it."

Ruth shook her head. "Oh Studebaker. Don't do it. They're dangerous places. That's why they shut them down. Cave-ins and all."

"Nah," Zeb said. "It's not inside the mine. If it exists at all it has to be buried somewhere. That's the story. The thief buried it between the high road and the low road. Probably too chicken to go into the mine, besides it was operational back then. He couldn't have gone inside."

I finished my toast and coffee while the wannabe millionaires continued to surmise and speculate.

"I think I'll go check on Stella," I said. "She'll probably want to go see Walter."

"Oh boy," Dot said. "Stella and Gilda in the same room. That's gonna be something. I mean I don't care how much that woman sniffles and cries over her dear sweet Wally. She is no good."

30

Deciding that I should probably check on Ivy on my way to Stella's I drove down Filbert Street and saw her out walking Mickey Mantle. This, I will admit was quite a sight. He kind of walk-hopped if you can imagine that. But he looked happy enough. I think the leash bothered him more than the missing leg, which by the way was still bandaged. I pulled Bessie a little ahead of them and parked against the curb in front of Vidalia Whitaker's still empty house. It had been for sale for several months and I often wished her daughter would buy it and move back to town.

The thing about Victorian houses is that when they stand empty for a long time they start to look sad. And Vidalia's was no exception with its long, winding porch that in better days seemed to smile but now seemed to frown. Studebaker did a good job of keeping the lawn trimmed, but the house desperately needed a family.

I waited until Ivy caught up with me and then scooted to the passenger's side of the cab and rolled down the window. "You ever gonna take the gauze and tape off of him?"

"When I'm ready. When he's ready. I think it will be a shock to his system to see his leg like that."

"Maybe we can do it together later."

Ivy smiled and thought a moment. "It might be easier with two of us there. Can you come by around supper time?"

"I think I can. It might depend though. I'm on my way to get Stella and then we're heading over to Greenbrier. Did you hear about Walter?"

She tugged Mickey Mantle's leash. "No. Is he all right? He didn't die did he?"

"No, the news is good. He's waking up."

"The dickens you say, Griselda! You for real? That man is actually coming out of his coma. I didn't want to come right out and say it but I figured him a goner."

Mickey Mantle barked twice.

"Lookie there," Ivy said. "Even Mickey Mantle is happy."

"He woke up yesterday for a time. The doctor had to put him back to sleep until they can assess him. But yes, he's breathing and moving. Stella is pretty happy about it."

"Stella? I thought she hated his guts."

"Seems she's had a change of heart." I had been leaning out the passenger window to speak with Ivy. So I repositioned myself for more comfort. "She's definitely taking the high road on this one. Who knows what will happen when he's recovered more though."

"Well that's just amazing. I'm a little bit proud of Stella. She always seemed to have a troubled heart, you know, and maybe this whole Walter thing, I mean the stuff in the past of course, is what troubled it."

"You might be right. But she does seem to have made her peace with it now."

"That's good. I'm glad ta hear of it. So you say you're heading over there right now?"

"Yes. Want to come?"

"Nah, but say, you don't know if any of the guys are heading back to the Sakolas Quarry today —"

I clicked my tongue. "Not you too, Ivy."

She looked down, apparently ashamed, and kicked a small pebble into the street. "I wasn't going to go but then, when I heard no one found it yet, I got to thinking that it might be sort of fun to go hunting."

"I guess I'm the only doubting Thomas in town," I said. "I just don't think there is any treasure. Someone would have found it yesterday what with all those holes they dug. The place looked like Swiss cheese."

She shrugged. "I don't know. They didn't have much to go on. Just that one clue about the high road and the low road. Maybe today's my lucky day."

"You should probably take Mickey Mantle home and get down to the café if you want to get in on today's expedition then, because Zeb and Stu and Boris are down there getting ready."

"Oh, gee, thanks a lot," She yanked on the dog's leash. "Come on, boy. We got to get home."

There was no need to knock on her door or beep my horn, Stella was already standing on the porch in her orange coat and a knit hat pulled down over her ears. I could see tufts of brown hair sticking out. She looked a little ragged from where I was, like she hadn't slept all night.

She hurried to the truck and climbed in.

"Where were you?" she said. "It is cold this morning. Don't you have any heat in this thing?"

I cranked up the thermostat as much as it

would go in my old Ford, which was not very high. "You OK?"

"Yeah, yeah, I'm sorry. I've just been standing out there for a while."

"I'm sorry I made you wait. I ran into Ivy and we got to talking."

She took a breath. "I'm the one who needs to be sorry. I didn't mean to snap your head off like that. I'm a little bit of a snit pixie this morning. I had a hard time sleeping last night. I think I'm a little scared about what might happen today if they take that tube out of Walter and he starts talking. What if he hates me? What if he doesn't remember me? I don't know which would be worse."

"No chance. I saw him look at you yesterday, you know, when he blinked. They weren't angry eyes."

"He could have thought he was looking at someone else. He might not even know me."

"Let's not worry about that until it comes true. If it comes true."

I pulled away from the curb. "Besides, I have a feeling it's going to be OK."

Stella squirmed. "Oh gee, Griselda, maybe I shouldn't go. What if he gets upset? What if the shock of seeing me after all these years sends him back into his coma?"

"Stop asking impossible questions. All I

know for sure is you can't stay away from him. He needs you."

"Me? Why? No one ever really needed me. Not like you, Griselda. Agnes really needed you. People in town need you. I'm just along for the ride. Nate doesn't even really need me except to weed the pumpkin patch and cook him meals."

"Now look, Nate needs you for a whole lot more than for chores around the house. You two are going through a rough patch. But it'll get better. You'll see."

"I hope you're right. He has relaxed some since the weigh-off and I think Cliff has been good for him. They're like friends now."

"That's good, Stella. I think men need friends just like women sometimes."

"You're probably right. You're always right."

"Not always. I don't think I was right about Agnes."

"What do you mean?"

I turned onto the main road. "Agnes needed me in a way that wasn't very good. And I've been thinking lately, especially when I'm up in the sky with Cliff, that maybe I needed her also, in a way that wasn't very good. Maybe what we had wasn't that healthy; that's what one of those radio psychologists would say. Our relationship was not healthy."

"What? You're as healthy as they come."

"Not in that way. Maybe I was afraid to be myself. Ever since our parents died — you know I was only a teenager — I kind of shrank away. Inside books. Like Emily Dickinson said, 'my wars are laid away in books.' "

"Ah, now you're talking like an English professor again."

I swallowed my thoughts and changed the subject.

"I wonder when he'll eat real food," I said. "I wonder what it will be like to eat regular food after five weeks."

"Yeah, maybe we should have brought a pizza. Walter loves pizza. At least he used too."

"I doubt they'll let him eat that right away. You know hospitals, they always make you eat JELL-O first and soft stuff." I laughed. "Probably should have brought him Darcy Speedwell's cottage cheese–lime JELL-O delight from the dance. It wasn't touched."

It was good to hear Stella laugh.

We drove a couple of more miles keeping ourselves entertained with pleasant conversation until I got to thinking about Cliff and wondering where he had gotten off to. It occurred to me that I hadn't seen him since the dance.

"Where's Cliff this morning?" I asked.

"I don't know," Stella said. "He left early again, two days in a row. Said he had business in Shoops."

"Maybe he's arranging a delivery to make with his airplane. He told me he needed to get back to work."

Stella didn't seem to hear me. She looked out the window, probably I thought, at something far, far away.

The sky had turned cloudy again and I pretty much expected more rain, except in the mountains you could never be certain. It could cloud over and then a strong mountain wind could come by and whisk the clouds away like a frustrated mother snatching a child from danger. I said a silent prayer for a large gust of wind to sweep down from the mountains.

We stopped in on Agnes before going to Walter's room. As usual lately, Agnes was sitting in her oversize wheelchair looking out the window. This time she had a magazine on her lap — *Good Housekeeping*. But she wasn't looking at it.

"Morning, Agnes," I said.

She paddled the wheelchair with her left

foot and turned to face us.

"I'm glad you're here," she said. "My spies tell me that Gilda arrived a little while ago. They said she was all excited and talking about getting married. Imagine that, yakking about wedding plans to the nurses even before her fiancé is fully conscious."

"She does seem anxious to make it official," I said. "That's what she said when she left the Full Moon this morning. She said she had a wedding to plan."

"What's she in such a rush about?" Agnes asked. "That man needs time to recover from his accident."

"Well they can't get married in a nursing home," Stella said. "Can they?"

"Sure they can," Agnes said. "A judge will come here and do the deed. All he has to do is sign the license and pronounce them man and wife. Just like that. Only take a minute."

"Do they have a license?" Stella asked.

I nodded. "Yes. Gilda said she had it yesterday."

"My goodness," Agnes said. "She's probably been carrying it around with her all these weeks just waiting until she could get him to say I do."

"I wonder if it's still valid," I said as I adjusted the shades on Agnes's windows.

"Sure it is," Agnes said, "if she's running around trying to plan the ceremony. I'm sure she's checked. Don't you think?"

"Maybe that's the hurry," Stella said. "Maybe it's about to expire and she wants to get it settled before it does."

Stella and I looked at each other and high-tailed it out of Agnes's room.

Sure enough, Gilda was in there next to Walter's side. "And so you see," we heard her say. "We only got a couple of days before it expires so we got to get married right away otherwise we have to get a whole new license, and I don't know if we can get one in this county with us not being residents and all and we still don't know if you can even sign your name."

I couldn't tell if Walter was awake from where I stood. I gave Stella a slight nudge into the room.

"Morning," Stella said.

Gilda turned with a start. "Oh, you're here."

Stella and I moved closer to her brother. The tube was gone from his throat although the machine was still in the room. His neck was bandaged and he seemed to be breathing OK, but he was sound asleep.

"Has he been awake at all?" I asked.

"He comes and goes," Stella said. "The

doctor said it could take some time before he says anything. He might even have some amnesia, that means he can't —"

"I know what amnesia is," Gilda said.

Stella brushed Walter's hair back. "Hi Walt," she said. "It's me, Stella, your kid sister." She squeezed his hand.

Walter's eyes opened but this time they looked startled, frightened.

"It's OK, it's OK," Stella said. "You're in the hospital, well the nursing home, remember."

Gilda pretty much pushed Stella out of her way. "Wally, Sweetie. I want you to know that I am going to arrange for a justice of the peace to come by today. He can marry us on the spot. Stella here can be the witness, my matron of honor. That's what you want, isn't it dear." Then she gazed into his once again closed eyes. "I love ya so much, Wally."

Stella took me aside. "Do you think she really loves him?"

"She might," I said. "But even so, there are a lot of things that just don't add up." I looked into Stella's eyes. I saw worry and concern for her brother. "You know what. I'm gonna try and get to the bottom of all this." I turned back to Gilda, who was still pouring it on pretty thick.

"What's your rush to get married, Gilda?" I asked. "The man can't even say 'I do' yet."

"Doesn't need too. I checked. He only has to blink his eyes in accordance with what the judge says. It's all legal, and besides we just can't wait."

"Now why in the world would you go and check on something like that?" Stella asked. "I mean in accordance with you being so grief-stricken over Walter."

"I . . . I am heartbroken," Gilda said. "Heartbroken that you would even say such a thing or take such an attitude. But the truth of the matter is I'm gonna be Mrs. Walter Hughes by sundown. And you, Sweetie, will be my sister-in-law. Now doesn't that just ring your bell?"

"But . . . but —" Stella looked at me as though I could pull the right words out of her mouth. "But you need a wedding. A real wedding with a cake and a pretty dress. You don't want to get married in that simple little skirt now do you?"

She looked at her clothes. "What's wrong with this skirt? And Wally's in the gown. HA!" Then she smirked in a way that made me terribly uneasy.

Gilda went back to Walter's side. She kissed him. "I'll be back with that judge in two shakes of a lamb's tail."

"I got to speak with the nurse or the doctor," I said after she left. "It's like she's railroading him."

"But why?" Stella asked. "He isn't Nelson Rockefeller. The treasure has not been found and it might not even exist. What's she got up her sleeve?"

"That's what we have to find out before she makes this happen."

31

I took Stella's hand. "Come on. Let's go find that nurse. What's her name?"

"Sally."

"Yeah. Let's find her and see what we can do."

Stella and I marched through the halls and saw no sign of Sally until we got all the way to the solarium clear on the other side of the building. She was sitting at a card table with four other residents. They were having what looked like an important discussion. One of the residents held a clipboard.

"We are sick of them lousy fish sticks," the man said. "We want something different like spaghetti and meatballs."

"That's right," said another resident. "I can't remember the last time I had spaghetti and meatballs."

"They're having a meeting," I said. "We can't just go barging in on it."

Sally looked over at us. She put up her

index finger. "Just a minute," she said to the residents. "I'll be right back."

"Are you looking for me?" she asked us.

"We were," I said. "We didn't mean to interrupt your meeting."

"Oh, that's OK. These floor meetings can go on for hours sometimes. Is there a problem?"

"It's Walter and that woman," Stella said. "She's fixing to marry him today. She can't do that can she? With Walter in his present condition?"

"I don't know," Sally said. "I don't see how a person can marry another person without the other person being there — completely. We're not even sure who he knows and doesn't know. Although I'm pretty certain he said Gilda's name this morning when I was tending to him."

"But what if she wrangles some loophole and gets a judge in there?" I said.

"Just see that she doesn't. I'll do what I can, but for now I suggest you two hole up in there and keep an eye out for Gilda and a justice of the peace. And try not to let Walter see you worry."

We went back to the room. To our surprise Walter was up and sitting on the edge of the bed with his feet on the floor. He was such a tall man — I hadn't noticed that when he was lying down. Doctor Silver was with him.

"You want us to come back?" I asked. But Stella couldn't contain herself and went dashing over to Walter, who looked at her like she had just that second sprouted broccoli from the top of her head.

"Walter, it's me, Stella."

Walter tried to speak but nothing came out except a couple of gurgles and a raspy sound.

"What's wrong with him, Doc?" Stella asked.

"He's got the worse case of laryngitis imaginable," Doctor Silver said. "It's kind of like his vocal cords have been sandpapered. His voice will come back."

Walter continued to stare at Stella. His mouth opened two or three times and all I could make out was one word, "Who?" His lips were dry and wrinkled. And he was having trouble swallowing his own saliva.

"I don't think he remembers you," I said. "Or maybe he just doesn't recognize you — it's been a long time since he saw you."

"It's Stella, your sister." She spoke directly into his face hoping to make some kind of contact.

Walter moved back on the bed. He shook

his head.

"He'll need some time," Doctor Silver said. "Just stick with him. I think his memories will come back. I already told him all I know of the accident. He doesn't remember that at all but that's completely normal. He might never remember getting hit on the head. But memories of the important people in his life will come back most likely."

Stella and I looked at each other. I knew we both had the same thought at the same time. *If he doesn't remember Stella yet, maybe he won't remember Gilda.*

Walter tried to lie back on the bed. He looked frightened and confused with his eyes darting from one person to another.

"He needs to rest," the doctor said. "Rest and get his strength back."

"Can he eat?" Stella asked.

"Not yet. Just liquids."

"I want to bring him a big, juicy cheesesteak," Stella said.

"Oh, not yet a while."

The doctor held Walter's wrist and then patted his hand. "Good. Now you two can stay and talk to him if you like. Try and jar his memories. Talk about growing up together about —"

"About the day he cheated his entire family and ran off with all of our mother's life save—" Stella swallowed the rest of her sentence. It seemed she had not found total peace about things.

"Actually," the doctor said, "sometimes highly emotional things do tend to reawaken certain memories."

"Nah, I'm sorry," Stella said. "It's just that —"

Walter coughed, or at least his version of a cough that seemed to get stuck in his throat.

"Walter," Stella said, "do you remember me now?"

A tear about the size of an almond dripped down his cheek. Stella swiped it away. "You do, don't you?"

Walter blinked, and I'm pretty certain he smiled.

"I guess I changed a bit over the years. Got a little skinnier. Farm work will do that."

Walter pointed to his head. "Shhh-short."

Stella let a little chuckle escape her throat. "Oh, yeah, my hair. It used to be so long — down to here." She indicated a spot on the small of her back.

Walter closed his eyes and leaned into his pillow the way Agnes did when she was tired and didn't want to talk anymore. "Maybe we should let him rest," I said.

"But he's just starting to —"

Walter's eyes remained closed like he had fallen asleep.

"I want to ask him about Gilda."

With that Walter's eyes sprung open like two window shades.

"Gilda," he said.

Yes," Stella said. "She's here."

"Where?" Walter mouthed.

Stella shook her head. "Not sure. She's been in and out since you got here a few days ago. You really want to marry her?"

"I do," Walter said.

Stella held his hand. "Do you love her?"

He blinked. "Yeah."

Stella heaved a great sigh. "OK, Walter. If that's what you want."

Walter fell asleep with a smile on his face.

"Come on Stella let's go home. We got some work to do. We have to get the goods on Gilda, and we're gonna need help."

But before we got outside, the doctor stopped us. "Say, any truth to the rumors that everyone in Bright's Pond is looking for treasure?"

"Yes. And it's just ridiculous," I said.

"Oh, I don't know," the doctor said. "I know for a fact that there's truth to the story. My grandfather was one of the men who apprehended the thieves. He said the treasure is out there. Looked for it until the

419

day he died."

"No kidding," Stella said. "Your grand-father was a lawman?"

"Now I didn't say that. More like a vigilante. He was one of the miners who never got paid. But Grappy talked about the treasure every single day. Even took me and my sister out there to look for it."

"That's what Walter was doing," Stella said, "when he got smacked on the head."

"I know," Doctor Silver said. "But he doesn't remember even being up at the quarry. That whole day is gone. Still, it doesn't seem right that someone else might find it before him."

I suddenly felt shame for my town. The doctor was right, Gilda was right. It was Walter's treasure.

"Maybe they won't find it," I said. "Maybe Walter will get back to looking for it."

"It's going to be a long time before he's ready to go climbing around there, digging holes. Could be best if he never remembers."

I stopped in to see Agnes before we left.

"Don't fret. I'll keep my spies on the lookout," she said. "They'll try not to let anything happen until we get this straightened out. But do it soon, Griselda."

I grabbed Stella's hand. "Come on. I want to find Cliff. He might be able to help us figure this out."

The first thing Stella did when we got to the truck was break down and sob like a little girl with a stubbed toe. I put my arms around her and let her cry not sure of exactly what brought the tears.

"How come you're crying?" I asked as I pet the back of her head.

"I don't know," she said with a sniffle. "I don't know if I'm happy or sad. It's all so much to take in."

"I know, I know. I felt a little like that when Agnes checked into the nursing home — happy and sad at the same time."

"That's right. I feel like I'm walking a thin fence between two countries."

"I can understand that. I really can."

The first place we went was Hector's Hill. Matilda was there but not Cliff.

"You really fly this thing?" Stella asked with wide eyes.

"I do. It's easy, well with Cliff it is. Not sure if I could do it by myself — solo."

"Sure you can. You can do anything you set your sights on."

Excitement burbled in my stomach when I looked at the plane. Flying had become more than a passing fancy to me. It had become a desire, a need, something I had to do in order to feel entirely myself.

"Maybe I'll get my license — someday. Cliff says I'm a natural flyer but speaking of which we have to find Cliff. Maybe he's back at the farm."

Stella shook her head. "He could be, but Nate went into Shoops earlier this morning. He had some errands to run and bills to pay. That sort of stuff. I know he wasn't planning on much farm work today."

"Let's check anyway and then go over to the café. Maybe he'll stop in for lunch."

Cliff was not at the farm. Stella checked through the house while I looked out back.

"It's weird," I said. "Where could he be? He's been gone a lot lately."

Stella and I sat in wicker chairs on Stella's porch.

"Are you OK?" I asked.

"Yeah, I'm good," she said as she retied her sneaker lace. "I guess what I really want is what's best for Walter, and that could be Gilda. I might have to get used to the idea of having her as my sister-in-law." She shivered for effect. "The thought gives me the willies."

"Me too. So what do you say we get a move on and find Cliff and whoever else we can find to help us stop this if we have too? Someone has to know the truth about that woman."

"I don't know, she's slippery — like a greased pig."

Lunchtime at The Full Moon on a weekday was busy. A lot of truckers parked at the town limit and walked the short distance into town. They said it was worth the hike for a baloney sandwich and a slice of pie, not to mention coffee. Dot Handy made the coffee better than Cora ever did.

"Do you see him?" Stella asked when we stepped inside.

"Not yet. Let me talk to Zeb."

But Dot saw us first. "Griselda," she called. "There's two down there." She nodded toward the empty stools at the end of the counter. "Go on and take them. I'll be right with you."

"No, that's OK, we're not eating."

"Not eating? How can you say that? Go on and sit."

"We were looking for Cliff," I said. "Has he been in?"

"Haven't seen him," Dot said as she refreshed one of the trucker's coffee.

"Why are you looking for him?" called Zeb from the kitchen.

"I need to ask him something," I said.

Zeb stuck his head through the pick-up window. "Anything I can help with?"

"I can't keep hollering," I said. "Can you come out here?"

A few seconds later Zeb was at the counter wiping his hands on his apron. "What's up?"

"Gilda is fixing to marry Walter as soon as she can. She's out looking for a justice of the peace right now. At least I think that's what she's doing."

"But Walter —"

"I know, I know, but she's getting all prepared so the minute the man can say I do, she will."

"Well you know, Grizzy, it's none of your business. Not really anyway."

"But it is mine," Stella said. "He's my brother."

Zeb shook his head. "It's his life, and what in tarnation does Cliff have to do with all of this?"

I leaned over the counter and whispered even though I knew Dot Handy had Dumbo ears trained to hear the slightest gossip. "He told me he knew something — about Gilda."

"Ah, you're all just sore at her. She's OK."

"I'm telling the truth," I said. "He

sounded very sure that he had the goods on her."

"The goods? Now you sound like Mildred."

"But it's true, and I for one in all good conscience can't just stand by and let this happen without getting to the bottom of it. I don't want to see Stella get hurt . . . or Walter."

"Ah, you just don't like her, Grizzy. Now look I need to get back to my scrapple. If I see Cliff I'll tell him you were looking for him."

"Please," Stella said. "I think I want my family back but even if that don't happen for some reason, I still wouldn't want to see Walter get hurt."

"OK," Zeb said. "I'll keep an eye out for him and Gilda. If I see her I'll try to keep her here."

"Thanks," Stella said.

Zeb went back to his kitchen and Dot moved closer to us. "I told you," she said. "I told you that hussy was up to no good. I knew it in my bones and my bones never lie."

"We don't know anything yet," I said. "It's all just a lot of rumors and conjecture. We need facts."

"Well sit a while and have some lunch.

You can think on it just as easy, maybe better, over a baloney with pickles."

"Good idea," Stella said. "I'm hungry. Bring me a baloney with pickles and a Coke, OK, Dot?"

"Sure thing. How 'bout you Griselda."

"A shake. Chocolate."

"That it? No fries?"

"And fries," I said.

It was close to one o'clock when Stella and I finished our lunch. We ate quietly with one eye trained to the door looking for Cliff or Gilda.

"What do we do now?" Stella asked.

"We wait." I sipped my milkshake. "We wait until Cliff shows up and tells us what he knows."

Dot slid two slices of blueberry pie toward us. "Want whipped cream on that?"

"Blueberry? Since when does Zeb make blueberry pie?" I said. "Especially this late in the season."

"That's Charlotte Figg's blueberry," Dot said. "Zeb is testing her out."

"Oh, that's right, he did tell me he was going to start serving her pies. That's really weird. I didn't think he'd go through with it."

"I heard that," Zeb called. "I figured it would be good for business."

Stella bit into hers. "This is really good. How'd she get it to taste so good?"

With nowhere else to go except maybe back to Stella's farm we decided to wait things out at the café. Everyone always came to the café at some point. We were just so surprised when we saw Gilda.

She strolled in with her chest held high just as I ate the last bit of my blueberry pie. I tapped Stella's shoulder. "She's here."

Stella whipped around on the counter stool. "Oh my goodness and look who's she with."

Gilda was holding fast to Boris Lender's arm. He looked so proud he could have burst his suit coat buttons.

"Well lookie here," Gilda said. "The whole wedding party. Well except for the groom that is."

"Now hold on Gilda," Stella said. "What are you talking about?"

"Well now, I guess I just went ahead and got my little ol' heart set on you being my maid of honor, or, I guess that would be matron of honor."

Boris continued to beam. I needed to hold Stella back although I enjoyed my mental picture of her tackling Gilda right there in the café.

"I never agreed to be your . . . you — I

can't even say the words."

"No prob," Gilda said. "I thought you'd want to do it for Walter. But that's your ball of beeswax." She looked at me. "Griselda, will you stand up with us? We need a witness and —"

"No thank you."

"Go ahead," Zeb said. "You can be the maid of honor."

I think my eyebrows arched so high they resembled the spires of Notre Dame.

"I will not," I said. "I hardly know Gilda or Walter."

"Well it makes no mind," Gilda said. "I'll just grab someone at the nursing home. One of the patients will surely love to be in the wedding, especially if I buy her a nice corsage to wear on her pajamas, you know, Stella, honey?"

"Don't call me that," Stella said.

"Ah, now is that anyway to talk to your future sister-in-law?"

"OK, OK," Boris said. "We just came in here to get a quick bite and then it's off to the nursing home so I can get the lovebirds hitched."

"What?" Stella said. "You mean today? You saying you're getting married today?"

"That's right," Boris said, "long as Walter can say I do and sign the license. The place doesn't matter."

"The license," Gilda said. "It's only —
what did you call it, Boris sweetie?"

"Valid," he said with soupy eyes looking
right at Stella. "The license is only valid for
another forty-eight hours and then you'll
have to go get a new one. Remember? I
explained all that to you."

"But Gilda," I said. "If you truly love Walter another few days won't matter. And it's
not hard to get a license. I'm sure Boris will
be glad to help you do that — when Walter
is better."

"Oh, but it will matter," Gilda said. "I just
can't stand the thought of even one more
day going past when I am not Mrs. Walter
Hughes. It just breaks my heart to think
about waiting, and well, we got the license
and we got the justice of the peace and we
even got a whole nursing home full of
people to watch us. It's going to be so nice."

"But what about Walter?" Stella said.
"Maybe he wants a church wedding. I mean
he used to believe in God."

"Now, now," Boris said. "God will be at
the nursing home."

"He does get around," Gilda said. "God I
mean. Seems he's everywhere — isn't that
what you folks believe?"

"What about a ring?" Dot Handy said.

429

"You need a ring."

"No problem," Stella said. "I went into Shoops and bought me this pretty little gold band. Eighteen karat gold." She pulled it out of her skinny little purse and showed it to Stella.

"Gold plated," Stella said.

Gilda clicked her tongue. "Now Stella, you really need to get used to the idea. I am marrying your brother the instant I am able. We're going over there right now to see how he's doing."

"What if he's unconscious again?" I asked.

"He wasn't this morning," Stella said. "I stopped in there bright and early and he was looking really good. He even said a few words."

"A few words," Stella said. "A man needs to be able to say more than a few words to have a marriage."

"Oh, don't you worry your precious little heart, I made sure he could say 'I do.' "

I had to grab Stella's hand again because this time she was truly fixing to deck Gilda.

"Anyhoo," Gilda said. "Let me have one of them baloney sandwiches, Dot. I need my strength for the honeymoon."

I winced. "Gilda, how in the world —"

"Oh, now don't get your bowels in an uproar, Griselda. I won't do anything to

430

hurt my dear sweet Wally.

"I'm just saying I don't want to faint dead away from lack of nourishment before Boris pronounces us man and wife. We'll take care of the honeymoon when we can."

"Seems to me you already *had* the honeymoon," called Dot.

"Come on, Stella. I can't listen to this anymore." I turned my attention to Gilda. "I don't care how sweet you make things sound. You are up to no good. And I'm going to prove it."

Boris looked daggers at me. "Griselda Sparrow, I am ashamed of you. This sweet young lady has nothing but the purest love for Walter."

Dot coughed up a lung.

"Let's go, Stella, before she sinks her fangs into anyone else."

"She's making Gilda zombies," Dot whispered as we passed by. "You know, they fall under her ruby-lipped, big-breasted spell and they're gone to Neverland."

32

Just as we got to my truck I heard what I knew was Cliff's plane overhead. I squinted into the bright sky. "Look, that's Matilda. Where's he going?"

"Oh, crud," Stella said. "Looks like we were waiting at the wrong place."

"Now what," I said. Without him we can't do anything because we don't know what he knows."

"I want to go see Walter," Stella said. "If he's talking maybe he can shed some light on it."

"Good idea. I think the best place for us right now is at Walter's side."

Stella climbed into the truck and pulled the door shut. "Are you sure about this? I mean don't you need to be at the library or anything."

"Yeah, I should be, but this is important. If there's some book emergency I'll handle it later."

I pulled away down the street. "What about Mildred? Should we talk to her?"

"Come to think about it," I said. "Mildred has been conspicuously missing through all of this also. You don't suppose she and Cliff are tracking down a lead together?"

"That's a distinct possibility," Stella said. "Let's stop in and see if she's in her office."

I stopped out front of the town hall. "Her car is missing."

"But she leaves it parked at home sometimes and walks to work," Stella said.

"Yeah, that's true. Let's check inside."

I pulled open the large town hall door. A breath of cold air rushed out. "Why do they keep it so cold in here," I said. "It's like walking into the frozen tundra."

"Boris Lender," Stella said. "He is one cheap bas—"

"Her door is open," I said. But Mildred was not in her office.

"Her too?" Stella said. "You might be right. Bet she's with Cliff." She stepped over the threshold.

"Where are you going?"

"To look for a clue."

"You can't just go traipsing into her office like that," I said.

"This is a matter of Bright's Pond security," Stella said. "Let's poke around."

I looked behind me, to the left and then to the right. The hall was empty. "OK, let's go."

There were stacks of papers and *True Crime* magazines on Mildred's cluttered desk.

"What a nice mug," Stella said. "It's from the police academy."

"Of course it is. What'd you expect? Barnum and Bailey Circus?"

"Hey," Stella said. "Look at this." She picked up a yellow legal pad. "She scribbled something. Looks like 'Darn Leapin'.'"

"What?" I took the pad. "Dabs Lemon. It says Dabs Lemon."

"That reporter fella?"

"Yep. I talked to him when we were in Shoops for the pumpkin festival. He said we should look out for her but nothing else. I bet they went to see him."

"What should we do?" Stella asked. "Should we go to Shoops?"

I touched Dabs's name on the paper and considered our options. "Nah, I think we should go to Greenbrier and wait. Just our luck we'll drive down there and miss them. Nah, let's just wait it out with Walter."

That was when Eugene Shrapnel appeared from a side office. He was his usual gargoyle self in a dark suit leaning on his fancy, goose-head cane.

"Griselda Sparrow," he said. "At least someone else is in this building. The place is a ghost town."

"Eugene," I said ignoring his remark. "You didn't happen to see Mildred when you came in did you."

He glanced past me at her office door. "Why are you looking for her?"

"We just are," Stella said. "Have you seen her or not?"

"Whoa, back off. I just came in here to argue this here trash collection bill. But I can't find Boris. I waited a little while but —"

"Did you see her or not?" Stella said. This time her voice sounded even more demanding.

"She was leaving with that pilot fella when I got here."

Stella and I looked at each other. "But he just flew overhead."

"She's probably with him," Eugene said. "That would figure now, wouldn't it?"

"Looks like we were right," I said. "They're tracking down something."

"Like a couple of hound dogs," Stella said.

"Say," called Eugene. "How is Ivy's mutt?"

I turned around. "What? Since when do

you care?"

For a second I thought I heard a twinge of compassion in Eugene's voice. "I just do, OK? How's he doing?"

"Why Eugene," I said. "You might actually care."

He snorted and wiped his bulbous nose with the back of his hand. "I'm just asking, that's all."

"He's doing fine. Ivy said he took to having only three legs right off, like he doesn't even miss the fourth one."

Eugene's head bobbed up and down like he was having a small attack of some sort. "Good." Then he walked past us. "Glad to hear it."

"Did that just happen?" I asked when he was out the door.

Stella who still had her mouth open said, "Yeah. Eugene Shrapnel sounded concerned about another living creature — a dog no less. He hates dogs."

"It's getting weirder all the time around here."

Walter was nearly wide awake when we arrived. Sally was with him.

"Take small sips, Walter," I heard her say. "Your throat is going to be sore for a while."

Stella stopped short. I grabbed her wrist

and could feel her heart beating like a trip hammer. "It's OK," I whispered. "You made your peace."

We crept closer and Sally moved out of the way. "Hi. He's doing much better. Better than we expected."

Stella stood at the end of his bed. I watched them make eye contact like they were seeing each other for the first time.

"Walter," Stella said. "It's me, Stella."

"I know," he said with a painful swallow.

"It sounds like someone sandpapered your vocal cords." Stella smiled.

"Don't make him talk too much," Sally said. "Yes and no questions. He can nod his head, but his memory is a little fuzzy. He doesn't remember what happened the day of the accident. But that's normal. It might come back. It might not."

"Doctor Silver told us," I said.

"Good, so he must have filled you in on things."

"A little bit," I said. "What I know about comas you could fit on the head of a pin, but I'd say he looks pretty good."

"He looks great," Sally said. "Now you all have a nice visit." She patted Walter's hand. "I'll be back in a little while, honey. You just take it easy and push that button if you need anything."

I walked with Sally to the door and whispered, "Has Gilda been here?"

We walked into the hall. "Haven't seen her, and I am quite surprised. I thought she'd be here banging down the door to get hitched to that poor sweet man."

"That's exactly what she's doing. She's getting set to come out and marry him today."

Sally put her hand to her mouth. "You don't mean it. She is brazen."

"We think she's got something up her sleeve. A couple of people are looking for answers as we speak."

"I hope they find them," Sally said. "I have a bad feeling about this, had from the very beginning and let me tell you, you don't work in a nursing home as long as me and not learn a few things about families and human nature, and that Gilda woman, she has got some kind of nature — the worst kind."

"We need to prove it or Walter is going to be married to her and her nature by sundown."

"Well good luck, honey," Sally said as she was interrupted by a resident looking for a key. "I know that cranky Mr. Stanilovsky stole it," I heard the resident say. "He's always taking my stuff."

I went back into the room. Stella was sitting close to Walter and they seemed to be talking, getting along all right.

"I'm Griselda Sparrow," I said. "Stella's friend."

A confused glaze fell over his eyes. He looked first at Stella and then me.

"I'm sorry," I said. "I should have introduced myself sooner. I've been here so much with Stella that it's like we already know each other."

This time he smiled and tried to speak. I put my hand up. "It's OK, just talk with your sister."

"She's been a good friend, Walter. It was Griselda who convinced me that I should come see you. I was a little afraid at first — considering."

Walter looked away and then back at Stella. "I'm sorry."

I had no trouble understanding that Walter was apologizing for the deeds of his past.

"I've missed you," Stella said. "I got married." She held up her left hand and modeled her silver wedding band. "His name is Nate. He's a farmer."

Walter's eyes lit up. He pointed at his chest. "Me too. Getting married."

Stella twisted her mouth and then put on a happy, brave smile.

"Do you love her — Gilda?"

His eyes softened. He smiled. "Yes."

I watched Stella's already sunken countenance fall even further. Walter averted his eyes to me. I said nothing. I only shrugged even though I wanted to shout that Gilda was no good. I just couldn't. Walter loved her.

Sally returned to the room carrying a little white cup. "Time for your Milk of Magnesia."

Walter made a face.

"I know, I know," Sally said. "But it's important. Doctor wants to get all your parts moving again" — she turned to me — "if you catch my drift."

Walter swallowed the liquid. It looked like it was a hard swallow, not only because it tasted like rotten fish but also because his throat was still so raw from the breathing tube. But he got it all down and looked quite proud of himself when he handed the cup back to Sally.

"Good boy," Sally said.

Stella seemed to be getting a little misty-eyed eyed and although that was the first time I ever saw a laxative bring out the love in a person, I understood her feelings. It was a little like the times I watched Agnes recover from a major asthma attack. All I could do was cry and thank Jesus.

"Should I leave you two alone?" I asked. "I can go visit Agnes."

Walter's eyes grew wide as silver dollars at the mention of Agnes's name.

"He knows about her," Sally said. She was still attending to him. "The other residents would come in and tell him stories about her while he was still unconscious. We think he heard a lot of it."

"Then I guess you heard me the other day." Stella looked out the window.

He looked at me — confused.

"It's nothing," I said. "You two visit a while. I think I'll go on down the hall and visit Agnes."

"What if you-know-who comes in?" Stella asked.

I knew she was talking about Gilda. "Stall her," I said.

Agnes was still in her bed. She wore a flowered nightgown that had a small tear on the collar. My first instinct was to take it home and sew it, but it would only get torn again. Agnes had a way of getting her nightgowns stuck under her massive girth and then yank on the material so hard it ripped.

"Morning, Griselda," Agnes said. "Did

you hear the good news?"

"You mean about Walter?"

"Yep. He's doing well. Real well."

I sat in the visitor's chair. "I did hear. That's why I'm here. Stella is having some private time with him."

"That's sweet," Agnes said. "I hope she can convince him to not marry that woman. You think she can?"

"No. He says he loves her."

"Oh gee willikers, he's a goner then. If he loves that barracuda there ain't nothing we can do about it. He probably won't care a lick about what she did or when she did it."

"If she did anything at all. We still don't have any real facts."

"Something will turn up," Agnes said. "It always does. I hope it comes in time though and maybe, maybe it will be enough to stop the marriage."

"But, like you said, if he loves her then it might not matter."

I yawned and stretched my arms. "All this running around is getting the best of me."

"You do look a little piqued."

"I'll be fine. But hey, this is odd. Walter seems to know all about you."

"He does?"

"The nurse told me the other residents had been telling him about you."

Agnes sighed deeply. She pulled herself up on her triangle bar. "You don't think they told him I was responsible for him coming out of the coma do you?"

"I wouldn't doubt it."

"Do you think they'll ever stop?"

"Someday, maybe. But how are you doing?"

"Doctor was in yesterday. He said I sounded good. They still got me on that crazy diet and I am so hungry, Griselda. I just want one meal. One good meal. That will keep me going a while. I actually dreamed about a meatloaf special, well dreamed I was the meatloaf swimming in Zeb's gravy."

"That's weird, Agnes. And no, I won't bring you one. You need to do what the doctor says."

Agnes looked sad a moment. "I know, but sometimes I wish I could just get out of here. I miss . . . home."

"I know. But look, if you lose enough weight I'm sure they'll let me take you home for a visit. Wouldn't that be nice?"

"Sure. That'll be the day. I made my peace with never seeing home again."

"But that's not the case. You'll be back to town. Just keep doing what you're told and I'll come pick you up and drive you back to town. The folks will come out for that Agnes. I bet they give you a parade."

Agnes slapped her knee. "Oh for heaven's sake, I don't want a parade. They'll drive me through the center of town like I was a Rose Parade float — stick some flowers in my hair and dress me up in a Hawaiian hula outfit. I can just see it in my mind. No thank you."

I laughed. "You're probably right."

"Of course I am. Now tell me, what is else is happening. Anything with you and Zeb?"

"Oh, I don't know. One day he seems OK and the next he's all jealous again of Cliff. I don't think he likes the idea of me flying, even though he says he's OK about it."

"So you're still flying?"

"I've been up a couple of times, but ever since Walter woke up I've been running around trying to stop Gilda. I think Cliff knows something about her. I've been looking for him all day, but he flew off earlier. I think he had Mildred with him."

"Maybe he's just taking her for a ride."

"No, don't think so. He started to tell me something the other day and I'm fairly certain he was referring to Gilda."

"Yeah, you're right. Mildred is not the joy-ride type."

"I hope they find whatever they're looking

for soon and get back here with it. Gilda is fixing to marry Walter the second she can. She has the license and — get this, Agnes — she even finagled Boris into doing the ceremony. Here. At Greenbrier. Maybe even today if we can't stop it."

Agnes clicked her tongue.

"I don't want to see him get hurt. Him or Stella."

"I know what you mean. Stella has had a rough life. Lots of heartaches. I'd hate to see more get piled on."

In all the years I had known Stella she didn't tell me much about her past. I know she confided in Agnes but Agnes never told me much, if anything. All I knew was that her father ran out on them when she was nine years old and that Walter did something to cheat her and her mother out of a lot of money. She told Agnes and me that when they got word that their father had died there was a large insurance check that Walter somehow scammed away from them.

Agnes sipped her water. "What's going on with the treasure?"

"Don't know. Some of the folks were going back up there to hunt some more. But they won't find it."

"Fools. But I guess if they're having fun."

"Yeah, maybe one of them will actually

find it. I kind of hope Ruth does — if there even is a treasure. Walter's doctor, Doctor Silver, says it's real. Never been found."

I looked at the clock on Agnes's bureau. "I better get back to Walter's room. Gilda could be there by now."

"Let me know if you need me."

Stella stood with her back to me, looking out the window. Walter's eyes were closed. I hoped he was asleep. I guess it would be weird for a while, every time the man fell asleep we'd wonder if he slipped back into a coma.

"Everything OK," I asked.

Stella turned with a start. "As OK as it can be," she whispered. "He really wants to marry her. There's nothing I can do to convince him. I didn't have the heart to tell him what we know."

"We don't really know anything."

"That's the trouble. If Cliff would come back. He might save the day."

33

"Sally told me that he'll sleep a lot," Stella said.

"It hard to understand why a man who's been asleep for five weeks can be so tired," I said feeling a little stupid once the words left my mouth.

"She said that because one of the things about a coma is that the patient doesn't really sleep, not like we do. There's no sleep cycle, and that's tiring, I suppose."

"Geez. Who would have thought that it would be hard to be in a coma."

"I know. She said the next thing to do is to get him on his feet. They already got him sitting on the bed."

"You mean walking."

Stella nodded. "Oh, Griselda, I don't want him to marry that woman. I know it ain't right. And it doesn't matter what he did to me in the past. He's still my brother and I guess I . . . I love him."

"Well sure you do. I remember times when I was so angry with Agnes I wanted to run away. Just up and leave her for good. But I love her. She needed me."

"She still does, maybe not as much, not in the same way. But she needs you."

"Oh, I don't know. Maybe. But that's OK too. It's different now, and I kind of like being on my own."

"And learning to fly," Stella said. "I would never have the guts to go up in that little bitty plane."

"I don't think I would have had the courage when Agnes was still living at home. It would have been too scary I think."

"Scary? Really?"

"Well she never liked it when I was gone — even just to go to the movies with Zeb. I can only imagine how upset she'd be if I was going flying. She'd be so afraid I'd never come back."

"I've been meaning to ask you about him. What's the deal? Are you two an item or what?"

"Oh, he's part of the equation, but I want to take it slow."

"I don't blame you. But with all this talk about getting married. I was wondering if —"

"If he asked me to marry him?" I chuckled. "Nah. He hasn't asked me. I don't think he'd ever come right out and propose. If we do get married I think it will be something that just happens, like an understanding."

"Nate proposed to me in the pumpkin patch. 'Stella,' he said, 'whatdaya say you hitch yourself to my star and we raise prize-winning pumpkins together?' "

"That was it? That's what he said?"

"At the time I thought it was the prettiest sentence ever spoken. But now? I think he only married me for my weed-pulling skills."

We talked for a few more minutes before Sally came in. "I think he'll probably sleep for a while now. Maybe you girls should come back later."

"I think I'd like to wait here," Stella said. "Just in case Gilda comes."

"Okie dokie," Sally said. "I was hoping you ran her out of town by now."

"Nah, she is fixing to marry him the instant she can," Stella said. "Say, I don't suppose you could do something to stop it."

"Me?" Sally said. "Not if he doesn't want me too."

I looked at the clock on the wall. It was nearly two o'clock, and I was getting tired myself. I had not been at the library all day and we really had no clue if Gilda was coming or not.

"Look, Stella. Let's go home."

"No. I want to stay. I want to be here when she comes and sets her claws into him."

"Then I'll sit with you."

We pretty much watched Walter sleep for another forty minutes or so, not really talking about anything when we heard a commotion outside his door.

"What in tarnation is going on?" I said.

Walter's eyes opened obviously startled by the loud voices.

"Gilda," he said. "Gilda?"

Stella went to his side. "No, no it's me, Stella."

"Gilda," he said.

"She's coming," Stella said. "Probably on her way."

I left the room closing the door behind me. A small but rowdy group had gathered at the end of the hall. I mostly saw residents in their robes and sweat suits, canes and walkers.

"Let me through." I heard a woman's voice.

"This is unlawful." I heard Boris Lender's voice and my heart raced.

I waited and then saw Gilda, holding Boris's hand, weave through the crowd like she was some kind of celebrity with her bodyguard.

"You all need to get out of my way," she said. "I am here to see my fiancé."

"Booooooo," I heard from the crowd. Then a small woman making her way down the hall with a walker stopped just at Walter's door. "We're on to you, you sassy hussy," she said. Her voice crackled like cellophane, "Agnes told us not to let you inside."

"What?" Gilda said. "You can't do this!"

"That's right," Boris said. "Now back to your rooms. All of you. This woman has every right to see her intended." He threw out his barrel chest.

All I could do was stand there and shake my head until Boris caught my eye. "Do something," he said. "Agnes is your sister. She's incited this riot."

I didn't know who I was more annoyed with — Agnes for telling all these people to set up a blockade or Boris for being so stupid and gullible.

"Go on everybody, please," I said. "Go back to your rooms."

I caught up with Boris. "Agnes is only trying to help."

"Help? Help?" Gilda squawked like a crow. "She has sent a mob after me. That is not help, sister. That is . . . well, I don't know what it is but it is certainly something and she has no right."

"It's obstruction of matrimony," Boris said. "That's what this is. Now these fine citizens are not teenagers, Griselda. They have every legal right to get married."

The crowd dispersed and the next thing I knew Gilda, Stella, Boris, and me were standing at Walter's bedside.

"I'm ready to get hitched, my darling," Gilda said. She touched his face and his eyes opened. He smiled wide at her and soft lines appeared at the corners of his mouth. That was when I noticed one small dimple in his left cheek.

"Walter, my name is Boris Lender, esquire, attorney at law, justice of the peace, and first selectman of Bright's Pond." He took a breath and let it out. It smelled of mothballs as though he had not spoken those words in many years. "Gilda asked me to officiate your wedding. Do you understand the words that I have spoken?"

Walter nodded. His eyes twinkled. "I do."

"That's fine. Now remember those two words young fella."

Walter's gaze shifted to Gilda. She wore a tight, off-white dress with the tiniest orange polka dots and a ruffled collar. She wore thin white gloves with lace at the wrist and a little white hat with tiny mother-of-pearl sequins. "Oh, Wally." She folded her little hands in front of her and tilted her head to the right. "I love you, my darling. It's been five long weeks." She looked around the room at each of us. I was holding Stella back. "Five loooong weeks. But we're here now, and you're OK, and that's all that matters."

Her speech was nearly heartrending. Even Boris wiped a tear and blew his nose into a pink handkerchief he pulled from his pocket.

"True love," he said, "knows no bounds."

I had to yank on Stella's hand to keep her in place. "Let it go," I whispered through clenched teeth. "Cliff and Mildred will get here. I just know they will."

Walter nodded and whispered. "Love you too."

Stella pulled away from me and walked to the windows. I could feel how upset she felt.

"Come on over here, Stella," Gilda said. "I still want you to be our witness."

Stella turned back around. She stood at the foot of Walter's bed. "Are you sure?"

He nodded.

Stella looked at me.

"Go on," I said. "It's what he wants."

Defeat sank into my chest. It seemed there was no stopping the wedding now. Everything was in place.

Stella stood at Gilda's side. The room grew quiet as I noticed a small crowd gathered at the door and music drifted down the hall. It was "Pomp and Circumstance" played on what sounded like a scratchy old record player. It was as close to the wedding march as Greenbrier could get.

Boris pulled a small black book from his inside suit pocket. He moved to the foot of the bed and cleared his throat. Gilda held Walter's hand while Stella stood next to her holding her tongue, I was certain.

"OK," Boris said. "I guess we're all set then."

Gilda beamed at Walter. Walter beamed at her. The music grew louder and scratchier.

"Dearly beloved," Boris said in his best justice of the peace voice. "We are gathered here in the sight of God to —"

When all of a sudden an alarm sounded in the hallway. It drowned out the music as we heard people scrambling all over and voices shouting directions. Sally appeared at the door. "Everybody out," she called. "It's the fire alarm. We weren't scheduled for a drill but we still have to evacuate."

"Evacuate?" Gilda said. "But I'm getting

married."

"Not right now," Sally said. "Follow the residents outside. An orderly will be by to get Walter."

"It's OK," Boris said. "I can push his bed."

"Brakes are on the side. Just maneuver him down the hall and out the main doors."

"Dammit!" Gilda said. She dropped Walter's hand like it was a hot potato and was ushered out of the room with the rest of the wedding party by the woman with the cellophane voice. "Come on you rapscallions. Outside. Everybody outside until the fire marshall gives us the all clear." She winked at me.

"Agnes," I said, "what about Agnes?"

"I'll help," Stella said.

"OK," I said. I unlocked the left side of Walter's bed as Boris unlocked the right. Alarm was on Walter's face as he tried to talk but no words came out, only raspy syllables.

"It's OK," Boris told him. "We just have to move you down the hall and outside. It's only a drill."

Stella and I made our way in the opposite direction of the wave of residents moving toward the front doors.

"What do you think is going on?" Stella asked.

"I'm willing to bet the funeral home that Agnes is behind this."

Agnes was still in her room sitting in her wheelchair. "About time you two got here."

"Agnes," Stella said. "Hasn't anyone come to take you outside?"

"Me? I am not going out there. It's cold."

"But —" Stella stopped talking and started to laugh. "You're behind this."

"Oh, maybe a little. But it was really Mrs. Chadwick's idea."

"Mrs. Chadwick?" I said.

"The woman you met earlier. Her voice sounds like broken glass. Poor thing smoked herself into a mess of problems."

I sat on Agnes's bed and laughed. "This is great. It broke up the wedding, but I'm afraid it's just a stall. As soon as the all clear sounds, Boris will start up right where he left off — about to pronounce them husband and wife."

"Well hopefully," Agnes said. "We bought a little time. Any word from Cliff or Mildred?"

I shook my head. "No, but they better get here."

34

It took the better part of forty-five minutes to get all the Greenbrier residents counted and back inside and situated in their rooms, including Walter who had grown pale and disturbed.

Sally stayed at his side as Claude maneuvered him down the hall and back into his room.

Gilda rushed to Walter's side. "Oh, my darling. Are you OK?"

Sally put the stethoscope in her ears and listened to Walter's chest. "This was quite an ordeal for him."

"Goodness gracious," called Stella running into the room. "What was that all about? Whoever figured on a fire drill at the nursing home?"

"We have to keep our residents prepared and ready for any emergency," Sally said.

Gilda's eyes found Walter's. "Oh, Wally, my dear, sweet Wally. Are you OK?" She rushed to his side.

"OK," Walter said. But then he closed his eyes as if to sleep. A hush fell over the room.

"Is he all right?" Stella asked.

"Yes," Sally said. "But he's tired now. He needs to sleep."

Boris entered the room accompanied by two male residents in terry bathrobes. "We found him wandering around on the east side. He must have got himself separated from the pack," said the taller of the two gentlemen.

"Boris," Gilda said. "You can still marry us. Now." She glared at him.

"Oh, now, I don't know about that," Sally said. "The fire drill plum tuckered Walter out. He should rest to avoid any further complications."

"Complications?" Gilda said. "What kind of complications?"

"Well now anything can happen after a coma. And now with all the excitement of reuniting with his dear, sweet sister, getting married, not remembering the treasure, which by the way, he has been wracking his brains about. All that stress and pressure could create any number of ill-wanted side effects."

Stella opened her mouth. I grabbed her elbow. "Shh. Just let her go."

"Especially one that, well any wife would NOT want, especially when she is just newly married. You know what I'm talking about?" Sally looked directly at Gilda.

"No, no what are you talking about?" Gilda turned toward Boris. "What's she talking about?"

He shook his thick head.

"I am talking about," she lowered her voice and leaned into Gilda, "impotence."

Gilda stepped back. "Really? You mean he might not be able to —"

"Well, now, of course he isn't ready for that kind of activity yet, but he will be and I'm sure you'll want him in tip-top condition. Doctor Silver will check his heart again tomorrow."

It was all I could do to hold back laughter. Stella had finally caught on also and squeezed my hand.

"But I want to marry him, now!" Gilda said.

Every eye looked at Walter who was about as unconscious as he was a week previous.

"Now see here," Boris said. "You're acting awfully selfish, young lady. I won't marry a man who can't speak or nod or blink or sign his name. You will just have to wait even if it means getting another marriage license."

She batted her eyelashes him. "I'm sorry,

Boris. I'm just so anxious to marry my sweetheart. You see we had intended on tying the knot on this very day."

Stella grabbed my hand and squeezed. "Yeah, right. I believe that," she whispered.

"I just thought that the good Lord had taken a shine to us and . . ." Gilda let loose with the crocodile tears and buried her face in Boris's fat shoulder. He petted the back of her head. "Now, now, Gilda. It's OK. It's all OK. Let's go home and wait a little bit. We might be able to come back in a little while."

"That's a good idea," Sally said. "I think Walter is going to sleep for a few hours." She started to usher us out of the room like a mother hen with chicks.

A curious but much less rambunctious crowd had gathered in the hall.

"Did they do it?" said one ancient woman standing there, hunched over, leaning on a four-footed cane. "Did they git hitched, or did the fire drill mess things up?"

"I got rice just in case," called another woman. "I got rice. Is it time to throw the rice?"

"Come on, Gladys," said Sally the nurse. She put her arm around the woman's knobby shoulders. "Let's put the rice away."

"Where's the groom? I see the bride,"

called a man leaning against the wall. "I'll take her on the honeymoon if he can't. If you know what I mean." And then he made some kind of disgusting noise and a Three Stooges gesture.

Boris put both hands in the air trying to take control of what was about to get crazy. "Simmer down. Simmer down, people, or I will clear this hallway. No, the wedding has been postponed."

"Clear the hall?" Stella said.

"He thinks he's in court," I said.

"Postponed. That's a crying shame," said the woman with the cellophane voice, sounding just a bit sarcastic.

Boris stopped in front of me. "I'm going to take Gilda back to Bright's Pond," he said. "She can use a couple of Bufferin, I think."

Gilda, who was still shedding tears looked up at Boris. "You're a good man."

Stella rolled her eyes and we watched them walk down the hall like it was death row. "Yeah, she's sufferin'," Stella said once they were out of earshot.

Boris led the grieving "Almost Mrs. Walter Hughes" out the door.

The residents padded back to their rooms. Stella and I went to Walter's room. She

461

plopped into the visitor's chair. "I don't believe what just happened."

"God bless them," I said.

"Who?"

"The residents. They pulled off a . . . what-do-you-call-it? a coup."

"I'll say. And I bet Agnes was behind the whole thing."

"No doubt. Agnes and the strange little woman with the crinkly voice."

"Yeah. She was great."

Stella went to Walter's side. "He seems far away again. I hope he's all right."

"I'm sure he is. Sally knows what she's doing."

"Sally?"

"Isn't it obvious. I think she slipped him a Mickey."

"No. Really? She wouldn't just do that, not without a doctor's orders."

"We'll never really know," I said moving next to her. "She won't ever admit to it."

"That's fine by me. But what do we do now? They'll be back later."

"We have to find Cliff and Mildred."

Stella flopped back into the chair. "Oh, Griselda, I am plum tuckered out. I feel like I've been toting jumbo pumpkins all over the place.

"It's been a crazy few days. I'm hoping

the worst of it is over."

Stella reached through the rail and held her brother's hand. "We used to be much closer. When we were kids. He was ten. I was thirteen. We used to have these races, barefoot in the field behind our house, and even though I could always run faster, I let him win — every single time."

"I know how you're feeling. I was thinking that we're both in kind of the same boat. I'm looking out for Agnes and you're looking out for Walter."

Stella wiped tears with her shirt. I handed her a tissue. "But I think one of the things we have to remember is that they're grown-up now, and we're really not helping if we keep taking care of them."

"It seems like I just got him back and now I could lose him again."

"Let's wait and see. The woman with the crinkly voice might have pulled the alarm but God is coming to the rescue. They won't get married if He doesn't want them too."

"I hope you're right."

"You stay here with Walter. Call the café if Gilda and Boris come back before me."

"Thank you, Griselda." Stella stood and gave me a very uncharacteristic hug. "For everything."

"It's going to be OK. You'll get your family back."

I drove back to Bright's Pond by way of the Sakolas Quarry thinking that maybe Cliff decided to join the treasure hunt and maybe because there was a part of me that was still curious about it and wondered if anyone had found it. There was no one there. All I saw were a bunch of holes in the ground and a broken pickax, a boarded-up mine shaft, and a dilapidated coal breaker that looked like some kind of eerie, other-worldy monster against the now setting sun. It was a gigantic barn-like building with a hundred windows and a long, slanted shaft that once carried tons and tons of coal into the building where it would be broken and sorted into usable sizes. It wasn't nearly as ominous when I saw it from two thousand feet.

I sat in my truck a minute looking for someone, anyone, but it was deserted. I thought they had either found the treasure or given up for the day.

Next, I made my way to Hector's Hill. Still no Matilda. The place looked desolate without the plane sitting there. She gave Bright's Pond an air of regalness, importance, almost as if we had finally made it on the map.

The Full Moon was once again packed out, but not for the food. A sizable crowd had gathered.

"What's going on?" I asked Dot.

She was at the cash register ringing up one of the truck drivers. "That'll be three dollars and twelve cents, Rolly."

"Worth every penny, Dot. Thanks." Rolly stuffed his change in his pocket. "What's all the ruckus about?" he asked.

"Oh, they've all come because that fella over there," she pointed to Studebaker, "has news about the treasure."

Rolly didn't appear impressed or interested. "See ya again, Dot."

I waved to Dot. She smiled back. "Go on take a seat," she said. "The show is about to begin."

"Come on, Studebaker," Zeb who was trying to keep one eye on his grill and the other on Studebaker said. "Tell us. Did you find it?"

Studebaker, still in dirty jeans and a flannel shirt was sitting on the first stool at the counter looking like the cat that swallowed the canary. "Well now, that's hard to say. We found something. Or I should say, Bill Tompkins found something. Show them Bill."

Bill, who was sitting at a booth with Edie

and Ruth held up a small, brown strongbox.

"That don't look big enough to hold a million dollars," said Frank Sturgis.

"It don't look big enough to hold a million fleas," said Zeb.

"That's what we thought," Ruth said. "That's why we brought it back and decided to open it up here. So everyone can see together."

"How can you be sure it's the treasure?" I asked.

"Well we can't," Stu said. "But it sure was buried like treasure, between the high road and the low road. And it is kind of like a safe. Just smaller."

"So open it," called Frank Sturgis.

Everyone in the café grew quiet as though a large wool blanket had been dropped over them. Bill pulled a screwdriver out of his pocket and used it to pry open the flimsy lock. The lid popped open. A wisp of tan dust blew out. Bill laughed.

"It's just a note." He held it up high so all could see.

"What's it say? Maybe it's a clue to the real treasure," Studebaker said.

"It just might be," Bill said.

"Well, come on," Edie said. "Don't leave us in suspense. Open it up and read it."

He unfolded the weather-worn, fragile

page. "It's hard to make out, but . . . oh no, I think it says, 'I O U one million dollars.' And it's signed, W. T. Sakolas. And look, it's dated. April 1, 1893."

"What?" called Stu. "It doesn't say that! Does it really?"

Edie pulled the fragile paper out of her husband's hand. "The heck it don't. I O U. Right there in the middle of the page." She flicked the page.

I let a small chuckle escape my throat. Within seconds everyone was laughing either from relief or disappointment or because it was just so darn funny that they found a promise and not a treasure.

Studebaker raised his voice above the crowd. "Gall darn it," he said. "That explains why the quarry shut down so fast. Good old W. T. Sakolas ran off with all the money. He probably masterminded the whole robbery."

"And he never got caught," Bill said. "Died a rich man."

"And I bet his wife was pretty happy, too," Edie said. She gave Bill a punch in the arm.

"So that man sent people on a wild-goose chase for a buried treasure that never got buried. He was a genius," Zeb said. "Oops, I got to turn some baloney."

"And that's just what we've got here,"

Ruth said. "Baloney. After all that work. We got baloney."

"Well, the news isn't all bad," I said. "You guys solved the mystery, a fifty-year-old mystery. Maybe that Dabs Lemon will want to write the story in the *Shoops Sentinel*. You'll be famous."

It was at that moment I had a revelation. "Dabs," I said. I found Dot. "Dabs Lemon. He's the ticket."

"Go get him, Griselda," Dot said.

"What about him?" Zeb said. "What about him?"

"Nothing. I better go."

I ran outside and stood in the street remembering what Dabs Lemon said to me the day of the pumpkin weigh-off.

"I'd put my money on that woman Gilda Saucer to be the troublemaker," he had said.

I ran back into the café and called for Ruth. "Come on, I need to drive into Shoops. And I want you to go with me."

"How come?" she asked.

"Because. I don't want to go by myself. I'll explain on the way."

"What's going on?" called Stu. "Why are you so excited, Griselda."

"I can't talk now." I grabbed Ruth's hand, and we ran out of the café like two pinballs.

Ruth climbed into the truck cab and I dashed around the side.

"Remember that day at the pumpkin weigh-off?" I said as I turned the ignition. "Dabs Lemon stopped us. Remember what he said?"

Ruth's eyes grew large. "Oh, oh, wait a minute now, Griselda. It's coming back to me. I remember. He said something about Gilda. He said he was leery of her — not in those words exactly but the feeling is the same."

"That's right. He knows something about her. He's got the goods. Or at least he can find out. I just hope we can get to him in time."

"In time for what?"

"In time to keep Gilda Saucer from marrying Walter and hurting Stella."

I dropped the gearshift into reverse and started to back out of my spot when I stopped on account of what I saw in my rearview mirror.

35

"Maybe we won't have to go," I said.

"Now what? Griselda, you're confusing me. Are we driving to Shoops or not?"

"Look, it's Mildred, and she has Cliff with her. I've been looking for them all day. Last thing I heard was Cliff and Mildred took off together, probably in his plane."

"Oh, my." Ruth rubbed her forehead. "This is turning into something altogether unpleasant. I feel like I just want to go home. I'm tired from treasure hunting. That's enough mystery for me, and for heaven's sake, if Walter wants to marry Gilda then God bless them."

I looked at Ruth. She did seem a little worse for wear. "You can go home, Ruth, but I have to speak with Cliff."

"As long as you don't mind. Maybe I'll go on over to Ivy's and visit with her and Mickey Mantle for a little while."

"That's fine. You go on. Maybe Stu will

drive you."

"No, no. I think I'll walk. The cool air will do me good."

Mildred pulled her car into her spot. I pulled back into mine.

"I'll see you later, Ruth." I jumped out of the truck and ran to meet Cliff and Mildred.

"Griselda, I'm glad you're here. I got some big news," Mildred said.

"I hope so. I've been looking for you two all day. Gilda came this close to marrying Walter."

"She didn't, did she?" Mildred asked.

"No. I just said she came close."

"That's good. We have to stop her."

"I was just on my way to see Dabs Lemon," I said. "I hope you have the news we need."

Mildred hitched up her holster. "Let's all go inside the café."

Most of the treasure hunters were still inside laughing at what they now considered the best April Fool's joke of all time.

Mildred raised her hand. "Quiet, please. Everyone quiet down." I half-expected her to fire off a round when the group continued to talk and laugh.

"Please," she said raising her voice even more. "Stop talking. This is official police business."

"Police business," hollered Edie Tompkins. "My Bill found that treasure box fair and square."

"It's got nothing to do with that stupid old treasure," Mildred said.

"Then what gives?" called Bill Tompkins.

"If you will all just settle down, I'll tell you."

Cliff sat at the counter on the first stool — the one Gilda usually occupied. Zeb came out from the kitchen and stood near him. "What in tarnation is going on? This is a restaurant not a police station."

"We've got some pretty interesting information, Zeb," Cliff said.

"Hey," Studebaker said, "isn't this where the lights go off and the criminal escapes?"

He got a chuckle from the crowd and seemed pleased with himself.

"Now are you all going to take this seriously or not?" Mildred said. "It concerns Gilda Saucer."

"Probably not," Bill Tompkins said. "No crime has been committed. And that pretty young thing just wants to get married. Nothing illegal about that."

"Not yet," Mildred said. "But —"

Unfortunately, Mildred did not get to say what she was itching to say. The door swung open and in came Gilda and Boris Lender.

The café hushed as all eyes turned to them.

"Howdy," Gilda said. "Whatcha all looking at?"

Boris put his arm around Gilda's shoulders. "We don't have to eat here. We can go on over to Personal's or maybe even The Pink Lady down in Shoops."

"No, no," I heard her say. "We can stay here. I just can't imagine, though, why all these people are here."

"Bill Tompkins found the treasure," Stu said.

Gilda Saucer's eyes grew about as wide as, well, saucers. She stood there transfixed on Stu for about ten seconds and then seemed to regain consciousness. "Oh, that's nice. I . . . I. Was it . . ."

"Not what anyone expected," Bill called from his booth in the middle of the café.

Gilda pulled away from Boris and found Bill who was holding the little strongbox. "Is that it?" she said. "That thing you got in your hand? Is that it?"

Bill held it up so she could see. "Don't know why you're so upset over it, but yeah, I found nothing but this box and nothing but an IOU inside."

The crowd laughed again as Gilda seemed to twirl around in one place looking for something to say or somewhere to go. "But it was supposed to be a million dollars. Walter said he was hunting down a million-dollar treasure."

"Well, Walter was wrong," Bill said. "We all were. We were all tricked."

"Tricked?" That was when I saw Gilda notice Cliff Cardwell standing off to the side like he didn't want her to see him.

"Did you know about this, Mr. Cardwell? Did you know it was joke? A lie?"

All eyes turned to Cliff.

"I just made an emergency landing in town," he said. "I didn't know anything about a treasure."

"But that isn't what your reputation would suggest, Mr. Cardwell, or should I say Mr. Cliff the Griff," Gilda said.

A collective gasp filled the room.

"I know who you are and so does everyone else in this little old town. You're the one everyone should be talking about. Not me."

"I've mended my foolish ways and turned a new leaf," Cliff said. "Wish we could say the same for you."

Harriet Nurse who had been sitting with Jasper York stood. She tossed a napkin on the table. "Oh, I just can't stand all this tension. Come on Jasper let's go home. I don't care two licks about treasure, flim-flam artists, or Gilda Saucer. A hussy is a hussy, and we can't go arresting hussies just because we don't like them in our town."

"I am not a hussy," Gilda said. "I'm just . . . stylish and sophisticated."

"That's right," Boris said. "She can't help it if she has a shapely body and —" He stopped talking.

Harriet pushed her way through the crowd followed by Jasper York who was followed by several other folks until all that remained were a few of the curious — like Edie Tompkins and Frank Sturgis. Of course, Studebaker stayed behind, and Dot had tables to wait. But Mildred certainly found the extra breathing room to her liking.

"That's better," she said after the door closed for the last time. "Now, Miss Saucer, or should I call you Mrs. Stern? Mrs. Irene Stern."

A second gasp filtered through the café.

Gilda sucked a breath and then seemed to have swooned and fell into Boris's arms.

"Now look what you did," Boris said. "You made her faint."

"She didn't faint," Cliff said. "She's just a good actress." He applauded what he no doubt thought a performance.

"Now look here, Mr. Cardwell," Boris said, "you might be new in town but around here we take care of each other."

Mildred bent down near Gilda and fanned her face. "Ah, she's all right. Somebody get her a glass of water."

Zeb hurried to her side. She opened her eyes and sipped at the drink with her big blue eyes gazing at Boris. "I'll be all right now. I . . . I just don't know what came over me. All this excitement and accusatory words. I . . . I just couldn't take it I suppose."

Cliff coughed.

"But Gilda," Boris said. "Is what Mildred said true? Is your name Stern. Mrs. Irene Stern?"

Gilda started to cry.

"Ah come off it," Cliff said. "She is still acting. We know the whole story."

That was when Zeb decided to take the situation in hand. "OK, OK. I don't know what's going on around here but this is a family café, not a court of law or any other kind of court. You all have a problem take it down to the town hall. I have a business to run."

Gilda clambered to her feet but still hung on Boris Lender. "Thank you, Boris. You're my true friend."

"I think Zeb is right," Boris said. "This isn't the place to work things out, and as your attorney, I must advise you not to say another word."

"But I ain't been accused of anything. Have I been arrested?"

"No, no," Boris said. "I want to protect you, that's all. We need to discuss this privately."

"Privately," Mildred said. "You can do just that but I'm here to say that Gilda Saucer, aka Irene Stern, is what we call a black widow."

A third and louder gasp rose to the ceiling.

"Now see here, Mildred," Boris said. "If you have charges to level against this poor, defenseless woman I suggest you do it. Otherwise you can't hold her on anything." Mildred backed off. "No, sir, I have nothing to arrest her on. But —"

"But nothing," Boris said. "Come on, Gilda."

The café quieted once again as Boris helped Gilda outside.

"Can you believe that?" Mildred said. "She has Boris snowed. Completely snowed."

"And they thought I was a great con artist," Cliff said.

Everyone looked at him.

"Oh, come on, I know you all know about me. I am not an idiot. But you have to know that I have turned a new leaf. I'm not the same man I once was and my coming to Bright's Pond was quite accidental." Then he looked at me. "Well, maybe God had it planned, but I certainly didn't."

Bill Tompkins stood with his strongbox. "Well, I for one am exhausted. I'm taking my treasure and going home. I don't care enough about Gilda or Irene or whoever she is."

"What are you going to do with the IOU?" Stu asked.

Bill shrugged. "Oh, I don't know, I might frame it. Hang it over my workbench in the garage."

Others followed suit and headed out with Bill until only Mildred, Cliff, me, and Zeb, who was busy in the kitchen, were the only ones left.

"What just happened?" I said. "I thought you had something. Something big. What exactly is a black widow?"

Mildred sat at the first booth and called to Dot. "Could you bring me a cuppa coffee, please."

"Sure thing, Mildred," Dot said. "But I want to know what this black widow stuff means, too."

"I'll tell them if you want," Cliff said.

"Go on," Mildred said. "I'm bushed."

"Gilda . . . I mean Irene or Georgia or Fern," Cliff said, "whatever she's calling herself, is in the marrying business. She marries men for their money — or their treasure — and then they mysteriously die or she gets a divorce — and their money. She's been arrested six times in the last ten years but always got away, scot-free."

"Oh no," I said. "That's why she was so interested in the treasure. Is that what you were going to tell me in the plane . . . before the fuel line broke?" I asked.

"Yes. But I only had suspicions then. Nothing concrete. Sometimes it takes a thief to catch a thief. That's why I went to see that reporter in Shoops. Reporters have a way of finding stuff that ordinary people don't."

"Poor Walter," I said. "Now we really have to stop her."

"But she's also in the clear so far," Mildred said. "She's been exonerated each and every time and has not committed any crimes since coming to Bright's Pond."

"We at least have to tell Walter and Stella," I said.

"Maybe Walter already knows," Cliff said. "It's possible she told him everything and it doesn't matter. We'll just see if she goes through with the wedding now that the treasure has been found and there's no million dollars to marry."

"Where is Stella, anyway?" asked Mildred.

"I left her at Greenbrier."

"You might want to get back there," Cliff said. "Keep an eye out and maybe run all this by Stella."

"She'll kill her," I said. "Stella will kill Gilda."

36

It was nearing seven o'clock, and I figured Stella was probably good and tired. But I knew I had to tell her the truth about Gilda that night. It would be best coming from me. I rehearsed what I was going to say on my way to the nursing home. No matter how many ways I put it, there was no way to sugarcoat the fact that her brother had been taken in by a con artist, a black widow only after his money. The only positive thing was that the treasure was a hoax. Hopefully, she'll run the other way and start looking for a new patsy.

Walter's room was dark. Stella sat in the chair next to him. It looked like she hadn't moved.

"Oh, Griselda," she said. "I just got back. I was in the nurses' lounge for a while. They served me supper — nothing spectacular, roasted chicken I think, but still it was supper just the same. Then I went and sat with

Agnes. She prayed for Walter and for me, and she even said some kind words for Gilda."

"That's nice, Stella; I'm glad you got something to eat. How's Walter doing?"

"About the same. He's been sleeping the whole time."

I stood near Walter's side and watched him breathe — slow and steady. He certainly didn't appear sick or injured. I had to wonder why they were still keeping him in the nursing home.

"The doc was in once to check him and said he looked good. Sally was here, you know, in and out taking his blood pressure, looking in his eyes, listening to him breathe. All without him waking up."

She looked past me out the window into the night.

"I got kind of worried and asked if she was sure he was still alive. He looks so . . . so lifeless there."

"I came to take you home," I said putting my hand on her shoulder. "You must be tired."

"Oh geez, Griselda. I guess I better get home. Nate is probably fit to be tied. No one there to make his supper and all."

"He's a big boy. I'm sure he fixed something himself."

She laughed. "Nate? Cook? The man can barely boil water or spread butter on toast."

I knew I needed to tell her about Gilda but right then it wasn't time. I didn't want to tell her in Walter's room in case he woke up.

"Let's go home, Stella."

"You think I should leave him? What if that Gilda comes back and tries to marry him in the night? Like a thief?"

"I don't think she'll be back, and besides, he's still pretty out of it and Boris won't go through with it until he's awake. We'll ask Sally to call if she sees Gilda, OK?"

"OK, but I want to come back first thing in the morning. I just know something is wrong. I can feel it in my chest."

"You're right," I said. "Something is wrong."

"I knew it. Tell me, Griselda. Did you find Cliff and Mildred?"

"Let's talk on the way home, not in front of Walter."

Stella walked out of the room ahead of me. "You sound awfully serious," she said.

"Let's find Sally first."

"OK, but please, you're sort of scaring me."

"I don't mean to scare you. It's just been a long day."

Sally actually found us. "You two still here?"

"We're just leaving," I said. "We wanted to ask you if you would call me if Gilda shows up with Boris again."

"You know I will," Sally said. "But trust me, Walter will sleep through the night."

Stella and I walked to the truck, where I told her the news.

"A black widow? I don't understand," she said. "You mean Gilda Saucer, or whatever her name is, is a professional marrier and maybe even a murderer?"

"That part's never been proved, but yep, she marries guys and then dumps them for their money."

"The treasure," Stella said.

"Oh, you don't know about that either. Geez, a lot has happened today. Bill Tompkins found it."

Stella sucked all the air out of the truck cab. "He did. Wow! Was the money there? Was it really a million dollars? What'd it look like? Holy cow!"

"Hold on, I don't have great news about that either. Bill dug up an old strongbox, looked like something out of Dodge City. He opened it in front of everyone at the café and —"

"It overflowed with money?"

"No. There was nothing but a note inside. An IOU for one million dollars."

"I don't understand."

"They figure that the quarry owner, W. T. Sakolas, masterminded the whole thing — the train robbery, the story about the safe being buried out there — the whole thing and then ran off with the money."

"No kidding. Well that means —"

"Yep. It means Walter has no money and maybe Gilda will turn tail and run."

Stella raised her hands. "Thank you, Jesus."

"Let's hope so."

Rain started to fall when we turned on to the main road. "I cannot believe how rainy this year has been. Most of the summer and now the fall."

My windshield wipers needed replacing. Why is it that the driver's side wiper is always the first to go and it always leaves a streak right in your line of vision?

Stella's house was dark. A half moon hung behind it, giving the place a silvery glow, but the second I put the gear in park, the porch light snapped on and I saw Nate standing at the door.

"Oh, he's fit to be tied," Stella said. "Just like I knew he would be."

"Just tell him the truth. Tell him you were trying to stop the wedding."

"He won't give a lick about all that."

"But it's the truth. Just tell him the truth."

"I'll try, but he won't listen."

"Good luck," I said. "I'll come get you in the morning, and we'll go over to Greenbrier."

"Early. I want to get there bright and early, hopefully before Gilda. I want to talk to her — sister to sister." She said the last part of that sentence with a smirk.

Early came much too early. I heard someone banging on my front door at five o'clock. Even Arthur was startled. He was lying on my chest and looked at me like it was somehow all my fault that we had an early morning visitor.

"Get off," I said. "I'll see who it is."

Of course my first thought was that it was Stella and that something happened between her and Nate the night before or maybe Walter took a bad turn.

"I'm coming, I'm coming," I said pulling on my robe.

I opened the front door and there was Zeb, standing with his arms closed tight across his chest.

"It's about time. I've been out here for

nearly an hour."

"Well get inside where it's warm. What were you doing out there for an hour?"

He followed me into the kitchen. There was no way I was going to have a conversation with him or anyone without coffee.

"I was hoping you'd wake up. But I decided to knock. I'm sorry it's so early, Grizzy, but I had to talk to you."

"Is everything all right? Did something happen at the café?"

I filled the percolator and measured coffee while Zeb stood near the kitchen door looking like he was about to bust wide open.

"Maybe you should sit down," I said. "Are you hungry?"

"Oh, I couldn't eat a bite. Not now anyway. Maybe after I say what I got to say."

"Well now you're scaring me. Just spit it out."

I sat at the kitchen table. "Come on, sit down."

"Nah, it's better if I stand."

My mind started to flip through the possibilities as Zeb stood there like a pillar trying to muster up the courage to say what he came to say.

"OK, look, Grizzy, is there anything going on between you and that pilot?"

"Cliff? No. Just flying lessons. That's all.

But you should know that."

"I guess I sort of do. But I had to ask seeing how there's nothing . . . nothing, you know . . . official between us."

"Does there need to be?"

"Maybe. You see, that's why I'm here, Grizzy. We've known each other since high school and everyone always said we'd end up married some day so . . . well what do you say? Will you?"

I felt my eyebrows rise. "Will I what?"

"Oh, you're gonna make me say it?"

"Yes."

"Marry me, Griselda. Will you marry me?"

I swallowed and fussed with some crumbs on the table.

"Oh, the coffee is ready. Want a cup?"

"No, Grizzy." He grabbed my hand. "Please. Will you?"

My mind swirled and my stomach churned. A few months ago I might have jumped at the idea of marrying Zeb but ever since Cliff landed in town and I started to fly I found myself more and more considering the possibilities that existed outside of Bright's Pond. More than I ever used to. I always wondered and imagined what was on the other side of the mountains I saw every day, wondered if there was more to my life than Agnes and the library. But this was the first time I ever dared believe it was possible to find out what life or God had in store for me.

"Oh, Zeb," I said taking his hand. "You mean the world to me and . . . and I —"

"So it's no, then, Griselda. I can't believe you're turning me down. Why? If there is nothing going on with Cliff, then why? I thought we had an understanding or something. I thought we had at least that."

I looked into Zeb's sad eyes and thought about giving him the whole it's-not-you-it's-me speech, but I couldn't. He wouldn't have really heard or understood.

"Let's just take it a little more slowly and see where it leads."

Zeb took a step back. "No. It's not leading anywhere I want to go anymore."

"At least let me explain."

"Explain what? You don't want me; it's as simple as that."

"No, it's not. It's much more complicated. I like being free, by myself."

"Free. There's that word again. So it does have something to do with that Cliff fella."

"Kind of. But not him. It's about doing what I want, when I want. It's about flying."

"I said you could fly. I said I'd even buy your lessons."

"Not just flying an airplane but flying in a different way."

"I don't get it. I'd never hold you down when we got married."

I put my hand on his cheek. "Oh, Zeb, yes you would. And that's not wrong. But for now —"

"For now you don't want me."

"It sounds worse than it is."

"It can't get any worse, Grizzy. I thought we —" He stopped talking and kissed my nose. "I'll leave you alone. That's what you want. Go ahead, fly."

I stood at the sink and looked out the window at our now scraggly and wild forsythia bush that was nothing more than a mass of brown, skinny branches. The yellow was gone until March, and I was OK with that because I knew it would bloom again. It always did.

37

At six o'clock that morning I headed over to Stella's. She was up and ready to go.

"I hope we get there before Gilda," Stella said as she climbed into the truck.

"We will. I doubt Gilda even knows there is a six o'clock in the morning."

"Oh, Griselda, I like it when you get snarky and sarcastic. You should do it more often."

"Me? No. I meant that."

Stella rolled her window down about an inch and let the cold air into the truck. It was almost too cold, but I didn't say anything. I still felt a little rattled by Zeb's visit and maybe even numb. I thought about telling Stella about it but she already had one wedding to think about. I didn't want to throw my proposal, such as it was, into the mix.

"Nate was pretty mad at me last night," she said.

"Did you tell him why you were so late?"

"I sure did and he just said it was none of my business, that Walter was free to marry who he wanted and to make his own mistakes. Just like we were. I'm still not sure what he meant by that."

The parking lot was pretty much empty except for a few cars, which I assumed belonged to the employees.

"I hope they let us in," I said. "I've never come this early."

"Oh, I think they get up pretty early. Breakfast is at seven."

"That's true."

The door was open, and we were immediately met by a resident in a ratty old terry robe the color of a peach, or at least it used to be. "Cigarette," she said. "Got a cigarette?"

I shook my head and tried to push past her but she blocked my way. Stella was able to get around her, but for some reason, the woman continued to crowd me and beg for a cigarette.

"No," I said. "I don't have one."

"Liar," she said. And then all of sudden she started to wail and pointed a finger at me and accused me of stealing her smokes, as she called them. Fortunately Claude rushed down the hall and took her by the arm.

"Easy now, Grace; don't bother the visitors."

"Oh," Grace said. "Is she a visitor? I thought she was my daughter."

"No, no remember, she died."

My heart sank and I wished for all the world that I had a carton of cigarettes to give her.

"Next time," I told Stella.

Stella and I stood outside Walter's room and listened like we always do for sounds of activity that we didn't want to disturb. Claude found us again.

"Don't mind Grace," he said. "She's been forgetful like that, but you know, she's been hanging around Walter a lot when you aren't here. She visits with him and tells him all about her daughter, Darlene. You'd think they were best friends."

I pushed open the door. No one was with Walter. Stella went right to his side. His eyes opened and he smiled and looked straight at her.

"Stella," he said.

She squeezed his hand. "I'm glad you're awake."

He looked confused. "What," he cleared his throat, "happened?" His voice sounded smoother, less raspy.

"The fire drill, remember?" Stella said. "Right before the ceremony. Before Boris Lender could marry you and Gilda. Don't you remember?"

He took a huge breath that seemed to pain him. "Yes, so we didn't —"

"No. You fell asleep after the drill — dead to the world."

I gave her a slight shot to the spleen.

Stella's hand flew up to her mouth. "Oh, sorry. I didn't mean —"

"It's OK? Where's Gilda? She all right?"

"She's not here. And I don't know where she is," Stella said. "And frankly, I don't think I care."

Walter pulled himself up as far as he could on the pillow and then adjusted his bed to rise slightly in the back. "What are you saying, Stella? I thought we were good again, I thought we worked things out."

"We did — you and me — but Walter there's something you need to know about Gilda."

He looked at me.

"I have to tell you that she's not who she claims to be. Mildred Blessing, she's the cop in Bright's Pond, which is where I live, found out that she —"

Walter put his hand up. "I know."

He seemed to take a labored breath. "I know all about her past doings. She told me everything."

Stella sat in the chair. She rubbed her palms along the arms. "And you're OK with it."

He nodded. "Sure. That's not why she's marrying me. She really loves me. I really love her. It's different."

"So the treasure doesn't matter," I said.

He shook his head. "It's not about money. Never was."

"So you've remembered about how you got hurt and all," Stella said.

"I remember the treasure. Never found it. Don't remember how I got hurt."

"So you believe that Gilda is still going to come here today and marry you — without the treasure. With no money."

Walter twisted his mouth. "Uh-huh. You'll see. She's different now." He cleared his throat again. "You might even start to like her once you get to know her."

I started to feel a little uneasy about being there for such a family-oriented conversation. "Listen," I said. "I'm very happy for you, Walter, you and Stella, but I think I'm going to leave you two alone and go see Agnes."

Walter looked at me. "Agnes. I know

Agnes but never met her."

I touched Stella's shoulder. "Maybe you can explain Agnes and me to him," I said.

As I made my way slowly down the hall I saw Grace again. She was outside on one of the patios smoking a cigarette. She looked cold and shivery.

I slid open the sliding glass door. "Why don't you come inside where it's warm?" I said.

She shook her head. "No. I like the air, the wind," she said. Just then several maple seed helicopters blew from the gutter over-hang and twirled to the ground. "Makes me feel like I can fly." She flicked the butt into the grass and then held her arms out and twirled. "Wheeeee. I can fly."

I stood there for a minute or two and watched Grace enjoying the cool winds. She held her head back and spun. "Watch me, Darlene."

"I'm watching," I said worrying that she'd grow light-headed and dizzy. Claude came by and brought her inside. "Come on, Grace. You shouldn't be spinning like that. Time for your medicine."

Grace looked me in the eye as she walked past. "Goodnight, Darlene. I had a good spin."

I knew exactly how Grace felt. Sometimes you had to find time to stand in the wind and twirl.

Agnes was still in her bed.

"Morning," I said.

"Griselda, it's awfully early for you to be here. They haven't even gotten me up and dressed yet."

"Did you have your breakfast?"

"Not yet. They're a little late but that happens from time to time. They got so many people to feed it's a wonder we all get a meal every day."

"Yeah, it's amazing that none of you fall through the cracks."

"Well now, look at me, Griselda. That would have to be a pretty big crack."

I sat near her. "I brought Stella over to see Walter. He seems to be doing well."

"I hear that," she said. "He's kind of the talk of Greenbrier. They're calling it a miracle." She cringed. "Guess you know how that makes me feel."

"Yeah, I imagine some folks want to give you the credit."

"I did pray for him, Griselda, and as much as I hate to say it I am a little concerned that folks will start coming to me again. I just don't want that anymore."

"I know. I thought of that too but we'll just deal with it if it happens. Guess you'll have to turn people away."

She made a noise. "Can't ever tell folks I won't pray. It's a sticky wicket all right."

"It turns out that Walter knows all there is to know about Gilda. He knows all about her being a black widow and doesn't care. He loves her."

"Well there you go then, can't do anything about it if it's what the man wants."

"I know but it still makes me mad. Stella is fit to be tied."

"Nothing you or she can do." Agnes adjusted herself as an aide walked into the room carrying her breakfast tray.

"Oatmeal this morning, Agnes. With blueberries."

"Look at that bowl, would you. That's not enough food for a bird."

"Well it's enough for a sparrow," the aide said. "Now eat up."

"That's right," I said. "And you know, Agnes, you still get more than the others even though it looks like less to you."

The aide smiled at me. "You must be Griselda. Agnes speaks of you often."

"Hi. Yep that's me. Thanks for taking good care of her."

"My pleasure, and my name is Lizzie,

short for Elizabeth."

Agnes slathered jam on a piece of toast. Then she dumped some milk into her oatmeal. "At home you always served my oatmeal with cream."

"But I hardly ever gave you fresh blueberries."

"Not true. You always remembered the little touches."

A few minutes later, Lizzie returned with a cup of coffee for me. "Would you care for this? It's not the best but it's hot."

"Thank you," I said. I poured a small amount of Agnes's milk in the cup.

I took one sip and nearly dumped it down my shirt on account of the commotion in the hallway.

"What in the heck is that?" Agnes said.

I put the cup on her tray table and went to the door. I saw a group of residents.

"Let me through."

"That sounds like Gilda's voice," I said. "She's back. Well I'll be doggone, I thought she'd run lickety split now that there's no treasure."

"You better get down there and see what's going on. But if those two want to get married, you better step aside."

I rushed down the hall and turned the corner to find Stella Kincaid and Gilda

Saucer toe-to-toe outside of Walter's room. Boris Lender was trying to wedge himself between them.

"You can't stop me from marrying Walter," Gilda said.

"Then why can't you wait until he's better, until he can stand up in front of the church all proper like? There ain't no rush."

"Because I . . ." she turned on the faucet again. "I love him that's why. Because I can't wait to be his wife."

"Now see here, Stella," Boris said. "There is nothing you can do. I keep saying that. Let the two people get married." He took Gilda's hand. "We can do it right now if Walter is up for it."

Stella saw me. "Griselda. Help me, please. I don't care what Walter says. We can't let him do this."

"We have to let them," I said. "You heard what Walter says. He doesn't care about her past. He loves her."

Stella released her lion's grip from Gilda's wrist. "OK. You're right. It's what he wants."

Gilda yanked back her arm. "Thank you very much."

I followed them into Walter's room. Gilda rushed to his side. "Oh, my darling. I hope our silly arguing out there in the hallway didn't upset you, but your sister tried to keep me away."

Walter looked at Stella. "I thought we talked about this. It's OK."

"All right," Stella said. "I'm here for you, Walter. I want us to be a family again, and if it means Gilda too, then, well, it's OK with me."

"All right then," Walter said. "Let's get married."

Walter gazed into his intended's eyes. "Come on over here, Sugar. Help me sit up on the bed. It might be hard for me to stand but I can sit on the edge, just watch out for my catheter tube and my bag of — well, they're still collecting."

Gilda grimaced. In that one expression I could see that Gilda had no more desire to help her soon-to-be husband than she did to scrub toilets. "Sure, my sweet."

It took a few minutes but finally Walter was sitting on the edge of his bed in his thin blue hospital gown. His legs dangling out, his bare feet just above the floor.

Boris once again stood at the end of Walter's bed and opened his little black book.

"Dearly beloved," he said, "we are gathered here today in the sight of Almighty God to join this man and this woman in the bonds of holy matrimony. If anyone here should have any reason that these two should not be joined let him speak now or forever hold his peace."

Everyone in the room, which by then included not only the wedding party but also Lizzie and Claude, Grace, the woman with the cellophane voice, and another resident clutching what I figured were fists of rice. A small crowd of miscellaneous residents gathered in the hall. I assumed most of them were armed with rice also.

Stella didn't say a word or move a muscle. Gilda cracked a tiny smirk that went unnoticed by Walter who seemed to be working hard to keep focused on the ceremony.

"Well then," Boris said. "Gilda, do you —"

But that was when Mildred and Cliff burst into the room.

"Stop the wedding," Mildred hollered. "Stop in the name of the law."

38

"What? You can't do this," Gilda said.

"Yes," Boris said. "What is the meaning of this? It is most irregular. Most irregular."

"I have information that might change your mind, Walter," Mildred said.

Walter continued to look dazed and confused.

"What is it, Mildred?" I asked.

Cliff stood next to me. "It's a doozy," he whispered.

"After last night's debacle," Mildred said, "I decided to do more checking and this time I decided to check on our boy Walter here."

A collection of gasps filtered through the room and down the hallway as more residents tried to push their way into the room. The orderlies shooed most of them out. "This is none of your business," they said. "Just go back to your rooms."

"Walter," snapped Stella. "What have you

done now?"

Walter didn't say a word while Gilda continued to hold his hand.

"There's a little matter of two million dollars," Mildred said. "I wasn't sure if, given your present medical difficulties, you would remember."

"I remember," Walter said.

"Two million," Stella said. "I thought the treasure was worth one million."

"It's got nothing to do with that silly treasure," Mildred said. "But it seems our boy Walter here won a lottery a short while ago. He's a rich man. A very rich man."

"What?" asked Stella. "What are you saying? Walter, why didn't you tell me?"

"But . . . but I was going to tell you," Walter said. "But you don't understand. It's not —"

Gilda shooshed him. "It's all right, honey buns, you don't owe anyone an explanation. That money is none of their concern, and there ain't no crime in winning a lottery."

"That's right," Boris said. "Shall we continue now with no more interruptions? Can't you see these two people want to be married?"

"I guess so," Stella said. "Two million dollars is a lot of money. I'm sure Gilda can't wait —"

Walter raised his hand. "Wait. The money." He looked up at Gilda.

"What about the money, my sweet?"

"It's gone," Walter said.

Gilda swallowed. She dropped his hand and then picked it back up again. Her eyes darted around the room.

"Well that shouldn't matter, Walter," Stella said. "Not to Gilda. Not to a woman in love. Ain't that right, sister?"

Gilda dropped his hand again. "What . . . what happened to it?"

"Gambling," Walter said.

Gilda stepped three paces back. "Oh, Walter, how could you?"

He grinned.

"Well, under the circumstances," Gilda said. "I think maybe we should . . . postpone the wedding until —"

"What are you saying, Gilda? You don't want to marry Walter because he has no money?" I asked.

Gilda clicked her tongue. "Well, you can hardly expect a woman to put herself in a position of —"

"Needing to get a job," Cliff said. "To help support the family. Especially when the babies come. That's what women do nowadays, isn't it, Gilda? Work and a career?"

"Hold on," Mildred said. "Gilda, or Irene

or whatever your real name is, already has a career. It's called being a scam artist. And no matter what she says, I for one do not believe that she is still not scamming."

"Why you conniving little hussy." It was Grace still in her tattered robe although she had pinned an artificial rose to the lapel. She made her way to the bedside and shook a gnarled finger at Gilda. "You get out of here and never come back. How dare you want to take advantage of my dear, sweet boy here?"

"Gilda," Boris said. "Is this true? I am so utterly ashamed of you. You only wanted to marry this man for his money."

"Ah, buzz off, lard man."

Boris tried to speak but only sputtered. He closed his black book, stuffed it into his jacket pocket, and left the room.

The crowd burst into jeers as canes were raised in protest. "Go on," they said. "Get out! Get out!"

Gilda looked at Walter.

"I guess you better go," he said.

Mildred took her by the arm. "I'll see to it you get out of here safely."

Gilda yanked her arm away. "I don't need your help, Captain Killjoy." She glared at Stella. "And you. You can just go back to your pumpkin patch and sit on your gourds.

You're all a bunch of yokels."

Cliff and I held Stella back as Gilda made her way out of the room.

Fortunately Doctor Silver pushed his way through the crowd and into the room. "What the devil is going on?"

"The devil just left," Grace said.

Mildred took the doctor aside to explain while the orderlies dispersed the crowd.

I stayed with Cliff and Stella who was now standing at Walter's side. She held his hand. "I'm sorry, Walter."

"Sorry? Oh, I'll be all right. I knew about Gilda all along, but I really thought she had changed until I saw that you all were so upset over it, and well, five weeks is a long time to think."

Stella smiled. "I'm glad we were here to help and I am glad you didn't go through with it. But I'm sorry about the treasure and about the money — your lottery money."

"Oh, I still got the money — most of it anyway."

"What? But you said —"

"Testing," Walter said. "If she really loved me, the money wouldn't have mattered that much."

Stella kissed her brother's forehead. "You rascal. You planned this."

"Only since this morning. I guess that fire drill was a good thing."

Cliff took my hand. "This calls for a celebration of some sort."

I thought I should have taken my hand back. But for some reason I let him hold it.

"A celebration?" Walter put his hand up. "Not yet. I'm tired."

"That's right," the doctor said. "You've had quite an ordeal. It's not good for you, all this excitement. So I'm going to insist that your company leave. I still want to run a few tests before I let you go home.

"Home." Walter looked away. "I'm not sure where that is anymore."

"You'll come home with me. Nate's gonna love having you."

"Oh boy," whispered Cliff. "This will be interesting."

"OK," I said. "I guess we all better get going so Walter can get well enough to come home."

Walter nodded. "Please come back."

"We will," Stella said. "We will."

"Oh, by the way," Walter said. "Where's Darlene?"

"Darlene?" Stella said.

Walter looked at us funny. "Yeah, Grace's daughter. She was in here a few days ago. Kept telling me to wake up."

"Darlene?" I said.

"Yeah. Pretty young thing."

"You must be thinking about Grace," Stella said. "Darlene's mother. She's a resident here. Old. Wears a tattered robe?"

Walter pushed his head into his pillow and stared at the ceiling. "No. I know who Grace is. But Darlene was the one who kept coming to visit."

We all exchanged looks.

"We haven't seen her," I said. "But if we do, we'll tell her you were asking for her."

Nurse Sally met us just as we left Walter's room.

"Well that little tramp sure left in a hurry. Of course, Grace was chasing her with her cane. Never saw Grace move so fast. She was calling that woman every name in the book."

We laughed.

"I don't think we'll be seeing Gilda Saucer or whoever she is anymore," I said.

"She's probably halfway to Philly," Sally said, "from the way she was booking it."

Stella and I started down the hall toward Agnes's room when I saw Grace looking out of a window.

"Excuse me, Sally," I said. "Grace's daughter," I nodded toward the old, apparitional woman. "Darlene. She's dead, right?"

"Yeah, sad story. Grace gets confused about it sometimes."

Stella and I looked at each other. "Um, OK well, see you later, Sally."

"OK. I'll be here."

"Let's stop in and see Agnes before we go," I told Stella.

"Good idea. She's probably wondering what happened."

"You don't have to tell me the whole story," Agnes said. "My spies were just in and told me everything."

"Yep," Stella said. "Looks like Gilda is long gone."

"How's Walter," Agnes asked. "Is he OK?"

"Better than OK," Stella said.

"Oh, that's fine. That's real fine. I'm glad it all turned out for the best. God has a way of bringing things together. But I am sorry that Walter lost all his money — but gambling? Probably serves him right."

"Not so fast, Agnes," Stella said. "Turns out my brother is still a very rich man. He lied to Gilda to see what she'd do."

Agnes slapped her knee. "No foolin'. Well if that don't take all."

Stella caught herself smiling and then

turned it into a frown. "I just hope it is a good thing. I hope my brother really changed."

"Now, now, Stella," Agnes said. "I suspect he has. A man doesn't have a near-death experience and not get changed."

"Time will tell," Stella said.

Agnes adjusted herself. "Griselda, could you please pull that blanket out from under my leg. It's bunched."

"Sure." It took a couple of tugs but the blanket came free.

"Now tell the truth, Griselda," Agnes said. "What's wrong? You seem kind of . . . quiet, far away."

"Oh, I don't know." I flopped onto the chair.

"Yeah," Stella said. "You have been quiet. Even through that whole thing with Gilda just now."

"Well that was your business. But, if you want to know, Zeb and I . . . well I guess we're broken up."

"Again?" Agnes said. "That boy has been running out on you time and time again. What was it this time? Refuse to hold his popcorn at the movie?"

"No. I refused to marry him."

39

"Refused to marry him?" Agnes appeared positively incredulous. Her face grew pomegranate red. "He asked you?"

"Yes. But I told him — well, I didn't really tell him anything except I wanted to take it slow. And that I needed some time."

"Slow. Time?" Agnes said. "You two have been an item since high school. That was a lot of years ago. You two go any slower you'll be walking behind each other instead of alongside."

I peered out the window. The leaves on the trees had practically all fallen.

"So how come?" Stella said. "Don't you love him?"

"I don't know. Sometimes I think I do and sometimes I don't and I can't get married without being certain."

"Ha," Stella said. "People do it every day."

"But it's not for me. I want to be sure."

Agnes made a noise and reached for her

water cup. "Would you fill that for me, Stella? Use the water in the nurse's lounge."

"Oh, OK," Stella said.

She couldn't have made a more obvious ruse to get Stella out of the room.

"It's that Cliff fella, that pilot, isn't it," Agnes said. "You got a thing for him. He's turned your head."

I didn't know what to say.

"I guess your silence is answer enough."

"The truth is that I do like Cliff. He's turned out to be a real nice guy even considering his shady past. And I do like flying, Agnes. I really like being up there in the clouds in the blue sky soaring like an eagle."

"But that ain't no reason to break up with Zeb. I bet that poor man's heart is broken in a million pieces. Just absolutely heartbroken."

"Maybe. He was pretty sore when he left this morning."

"You mean he just asked you this morning and you been running around trying to save Walter from that gold-digging hussy when the whole time you had your own crisis going on?"

"I guess. But Zeb and I are not having a crisis. Leastways, I'm not. It's a decision I needed to make, and besides, I always imagined Zeb asking me in a more romantic way — like he really meant it. Not because he was afraid he'd lose me to Cliff."

"Is that why he asked?"

"I think so."

Stella returned with Agnes's water. "What's going on?" She looked first at me and then at Agnes with that look when someone knows their presence is kind of unexpected or unwanted.

"Nothing," I said. "Agnes was just wondering if there was anything going on between Cliff and me."

Stella placed the water cup on Agnes's tray table. "Well there is isn't there? I think he's sweet on you."

I felt my heart race and my toes curl. "Oh, please don't say that. I just like him for his airplane. Nothing more."

The two of them hushed like they thought I was lying. "It's true. He's teaching me to fly — that's all."

"OK, suit yourself, Griselda," Agnes said. "But you need to examine your feelings a while," Stella said. "I see the way you look at him."

"OK, no more talk about me or Cliff or Zeb. I think we should just head back home. I haven't been to the library much and I want to check on Ivy and Mickey Mantle."

My timing was perfect because Agnes's physical therapist walked into the room. "OK, Agnes," he said. "Let's get you up and walking."

It did my heart good when I saw professionals working with Agnes. The most I could do for her was take her to the bathroom and back. But here at Greenbrier they had her on a plan, and she was making significant progress even if she hated the routine.

"Oh, George, I ain't ready to go walking down the hall like a herded-up cow. Come back after lunch."

I patted her hand. "No, you go now. I need to get back to town. I haven't been to the library all week practically."

"Yeah, and I need to get home too," Stella said. "Wait 'til Nate hears that his long lost brother-in-law is a millionaire and coming to live with us."

We both enjoyed a long laugh. It might have been a laugh born from all the stress of the previous twenty-four hours. But it felt good. Kind of like when Ruth sits under the train trestle and tries to scream louder than the trains. It felt good.

"What do you think he'll say?" I asked as we headed home. I rolled my window down a crack and let the cool air rush in.

"It's getting colder," Stella said with a shiver.

"Oh, want me to roll it back up?"

"No, I like the air. I'll just lower my window a little and let the air circulate better."

I thought of Grace twirling on the patio.

It was hard not to discuss with Stella the events that had unfolded that day, but at the same time it was like we both needed to sit and be quiet and ruminate in our own way about things. When I pulled up to her house I said, "So, you never answered me. What do you think Nate will say when you tell him about Walter's millions?"

"Not sure. He'll find some way to blame me for not staying in touch with him all these years. He probably thinks that I should get some of that money."

"He does owe you some, from before."

"I know, but I reckon the Christian thing to do is pray about it and let God convict his heart, you know, Griselda. I don't want to go asking or try to make a court case out of it. For me, it really isn't about the money anymore."

"I'm proud of you," I said. "You were so upset a few weeks ago and now look at you. Walter says he's changed and so have you."

Stella looked into my eyes and for the first

516

time I noticed she had tiny crow's feet at the corners of her eyes. "You've changed too, you know. Your decision not to marry Zeb yet is a good one. You take your time. Learn to fly."

"I will. Thank you."

I thought maybe my biggest mistake that afternoon was going to the library by way of Hector's Hill. Cliff was there looking over Matilda. I stopped and watched him a minute or two and was just about to pull away when I heard him call to me. He waved me over.

"What do you say, want to take her up?"

"Me? Actually lift off?"

"You're ready."

"But I've only flown it twice."

"It's OK. You can do it."

For some reason I looked around me like I was expecting someone to see what I was doing and get angry. "Are you sure you're allowed to teach me? Don't you need some kind of license or something?"

"Oh sure," Cliff said. Then he grinned. "But up here, in the hills, small town. Who'd be the wiser? I can't write you out a license or anything but when you're ready, I'll take you into Wilkes-Barre where you can take the test and bing-bang-boom, you're a pilot. Griselda Sparrow, the pilot."

I liked the sound of that.

"Now come on, get in. It's about time the little sparrow spread her wings."

I followed Cliff's instructions to the letter and before I knew it, Matilda was lifting off the ground, a little choppy, but still she lifted into the sky. We climbed and climbed.

"OK, level her off. Eye on the horizon. Make it straight."

"It was so easy," I said.

"You were born to fly, Griselda. Born to it. Just like me."

We flew over Bright's Pond low enough that I could easily locate my house, the church, the library. "You know I should be at the library," I said.

"Nah, this is better. You weren't meant to sit behind a counter and catalog books."

I wasn't so sure. Books had always been important to me. It was in books that I found meaning and solace, romance and intrigue. But ever since Cliff came to town I had a sense that I was ready for more.

"When can I fly over the mountains?" I asked.

"Soon. Let's get used to these easy flights first."

"OK. The mountains can wait."

Cliff instructed me on how to let down

the landing gear and extend the flaps as I somehow managed to land Matilda with just a few false hits and jumps. She came to a stop kind of twisted but at least she stopped before running over the cliff.

"Not bad," he said. "For a first-timer. But you'll never pass the test if you can't land smoothly."

"OK, Coach. Guess I'll keep trying." I found myself looking straight into his eyes.

"I better go," I said without moving.

Cliff put his arm across the back of my seat and inched closer. He took my chin in his hand and kissed me. I tried to pull away but stopped myself as he pulled me even closer. I had never been kissed quite like that. I thought I should have felt something more than I did, something sweeter but instead my mind turned to Zeb standing on my porch waiting in the cold for me to wake up so he could ask me to marry him.

40

"I'm sorry, Cliff," I said. "But —"

"Zeb?"

"Yeah, Zeb."

"You gonna marry him?"

I pushed open the door. "He should be the first to know that."

Ivy was at the library with Mickey Mantle. He looked good. She had finally taken the bandage off. The stump resembled a trussed up chicken breast full of stuffing and ready for a roasting.

"He looks great," I said.

"Him? He's doing fine. Like he doesn't even miss the leg. But he's been a little off in other ways."

I unlocked the library door. "Come on inside. It's chilly."

Ivy and Mickey Mantle followed me to the main counter. I dropped my handbag. "I'll put the heat up."

"OK, thanks, Griselda. That's why I came

by today."

"For the heat?"

"No, for Mickey Mantle's other problem. Do you have any books on dog stuff, like what makes them tick?"

"Um, you mean for training? That I have."

"No. More like to help me figure out what's going on inside of his head."

"Oh, you mean dog psychology."

"That's right. Dog psychology."

My brow wrinkled. "I don't even know if there is such a thing. But we can look. Are you worried?"

"Kind of. I let him out and he stays in the yard. He doesn't want to leave, and I know he must be missing his girlfriend."

"Oh, Ivy, you don't need a book. He's a little afraid that's all. He's afraid of another trap. I bet if you take him for walks back there, near where his accident happened, he'll come around."

"You think so?"

"I do."

"Maybe I should do that now. Take him into the woods and see what happens."

"Yes, but keep him on his leash. In case he gets spooked and goes running."

"OK, but I swear, Griselda, I think something should be done about those traps back there. What if it had been a child that got caught?"

"You're right. Let's bring it up at the next town meeting."

I finished my business at the library that day and decided to go to the Full Moon. I doubted Zeb would speak to me, but I needed to find a way to make him understand that I only needed some time.

Babette Sturgis was in for Dot who was out with a cold.

"Yeah, Zeb made her go home," Babette said. "He didn't want her sneezing all over the food or the customers. So he called me in. Course Mama was mad on account I should be studying, but this is fine. I brought my book."

"That's good, Babette. You can always study some in between customers."

"That's right, now what can I get you, Miss Griselda?"

"Oh, maybe just a cup of tea. Where's Zeb?"

"Oh, he'll be right in. He went out to the storeroom for more cheese."

She slid a cup of hot water on a saucer with a tea bag toward me. "You take cream in that?"

I nodded. "And maybe a slice of pie. Do you have any of the Charlotte Figg pie?"

"Sure thing. Blueberry or cherry or, say, she just dropped off two peach pies. It is delicious. Zeb's been giving her some test runs. Sells out each and every time." She leaned over the counter and whispered, "He's only a little put out by it."

"That sounds good, maybe put a little bit of vanilla ice cream next to it."

I watched the kitchen until I saw Zeb.

"Hello," I called.

He looked but barely acknowledged me.

"You know we need to talk," I said.

"We got nothing to say."

"Don't be that way." Babette placed my pie in front of me.

"Please, Zeb. We need to talk. I don't think I explained myself very well."

"You said no. That was plain as it can get."

"No —"

"There, you said it again."

"That's not what I meant. Now please will you come to my house after you close up?"

Babette gave me a long look.

"You two on the outs?" she whispered.

"Sort of. But not really."

Ruth and Studebaker came into the diner.

"Hey, Griselda," Stu said. "Heard you had quite a time at Greenbrier with that Gilda and all."

I turned on the stool. "Yeah, but it all

worked out for the best."

"I knew that woman was up to no good," Ruth said. "I can tell these things. I knew she was just after his money."

Ruth and Stu took a booth near the front of the café.

"Too bad the treasure turned out to be hoax," Stu said. "He must be pretty upset. Imagine that, he could have died over nothing. Over nothing but an IOU, a great big joke."

"But he didn't," Ruth said. "God saw fit to spare him. Come on, Griselda, join us. Boris is on his way over."

"Boris? He might not want to see me," I said.

"Oh, he's OK. More embarrassed than anything."

"Ah, he was just smitten with that Gilda woman, that's all," Ruth said. "But true enough, he could have married them and then where would they be? Having no money is bad enough. But no money and no true love, well that something else."

Babette poured coffee and set straws on the table for water. She took their orders.

"Coming right up."

It didn't seem my place to tell them that Walter was actually a rich man so I kept quiet and let them suppose what they wanted to suppose and ate my pie. Babette was right. The peaches were tender, cooked to peachy perfection. A kind of sweet perfume was released with each bite and lingered a second in my mouth before I swallowed the bite. The crust was flaky and melted like butter.

That evening, Zeb came by the house as promised. He changed out of his greasy short-order-cook clothing and put on a clean flannel shirt. He even shaved and dabbed a few drops of aftershave on that smelled nice, like winter.

We stood in the kitchen and talked. He stood near the back door. I stood by the sink. I thought he was going to explode when I told him that Cliff kissed me. But he simmered down when I said it didn't mean anything.

"He's more interested in being romantic with me. I just like his airplane."

Zeb smiled. "You mean it, Grizzy? You're mine? All mine?"

I nodded and let him kiss me and this time my toes curled in my Keds and my stomach felt funny, kind of wobbly but in a good way. And then my left leg lifted slightly just like my mother's did when she kissed my father.

"So, what do you say," Zeb asked. "Will you?"

"What?"

"Come on, you know. Will you marry me?"

"Oh, Zeb, no I won't marry you."

He backed away from me. "But I don't get it. You just said — we kissed. It was —"

I put a finger to his lips. "Nice. It was very nice. I'd like you to kiss me again. But I'm just not ready to get married. I feel like I've just been let out of a kind of prison, not in a bad way, but you know with taking care of Agnes and the flying, Zeb. I need to fly some more."

"You can be married and still fly."

"No I can't. I need to do this for me. And I think, in a way, for us. Two people can't have a marriage with a whole blue sky between them."

A week went by and Walter continued to improve. So much so he was released a couple of days before Thanksgiving and went home to Stella's. Stella invited Zeb and me for Thanksgiving dinner — turkey, roasted to golden brown poultry perfection, mashed potatoes, peas, homemade cranberry sauce, biscuits, gravy, and of course, pies. One of Charlotte Figg's peach pies, a pumpkin that was not made from Bertha

Ann, and two lattice-top cherry pies. At first Zeb was jealous that Stella didn't serve a Full Moon pie, but he got over it.

"I've decided that I'm gonna carry Charlotte Figg's pies in the café full-time," he said.

Walter and Nate were getting along fine, like two brothers should. Walter actually knew quite a lot about pumpkins and now that the cat was out of the bag and Nate knew his brother-in-law was rich there was talk of building a laboratory in the backyard dedicated to the study of jumbo pumpkins.

Cliff was there and enjoyed himself even asking Zeb if it was OK if he continued to teach me to fly.

"Just don't fly her over those mountains," Zeb said. "She needs to do that herself."

I squeezed Zeb's hand. "I'll fly back. I promise."

DISCUSSION QUESTIONS

1. Nate Kincaid blamed Agnes for his marital and pumpkin problems. He says she stopped praying and he and Stella started bickering and trouble came to the pumpkin patch. What do you think was the real root of their struggles?
2. Stella and her brother had not spoken for many years. When she learned he was in the nursing home she had to make a decision: see him or not? Have you ever had to make similar decision with a family member?
3. Griselda was finally able to confront Agnes about some issues. How did that make you feel? Did you cheer her on or question her?
4. Griselda decided to take flying lessons. Why do you think she jumped at the opportunity?
5. Sometimes a person really does need to lose the life they thought they wanted to

find the life God meant for them. Is this what Stella was finally able to do?

6. Stella never learned to drive a car or the tractor on the farm. She thought it was too difficult. But did Stella learn to fly in her own way? How does this differ with Griselda?

7. Griselda seemed attracted to the pilot, Cliff Cardwell. Was it him she liked or what he represented?

8. At one point, Griselda said that when she was flying all her troubles seemed smaller, further away. Talk about what it means to gain a new perspective on a problem. How do you do that?

9. Why do you suppose Griselda turned down Zeb's marriage proposal? What was she really looking for? In the end she said she'll fly back to him. Do you think she will?

The employees of Thorndike Press hope you have enjoyed this Large Print book. All our Thorndike, Wheeler, and Kennebec Large Print titles are designed for easy reading, and all our books are made to last. Other Thorndike Press Large Print books are available at your library, through selected bookstores, or directly from us.

For information about titles, please call:
   (800) 223-1244

or visit our Web site at:
   http://gale.cengage.com/thorndike

To share your comments, please write:
   Publisher
   Thorndike Press
   10 Water St., Suite 310
   Waterville, ME 04901